THE SCORCHED EARTH

Book Two of
CHAOS BORN

DREW
KARPYSHYN

DEL REY

1 3 5 7 9 10 8 6 4 2

First published in the US in 2014 by Del Rey, an imprint of The Random House
Publishing Group, a division of Random House, Inc., New York.

Published in the UK in 2014 by Del Rey, an imprint of Ebury Publishing
A Random House Group Company

The Random House Group Limited Reg. No. 954009

Addresses for companies within the Random House Group can be found at:
www.randomhouse.co.uk

A CIP catalogue record for this book is
available from the British Library

The Random House Group Limited supports The Forest Stewardship
Council® (FSC®), the leading international forest-certification organisation.
Our books carrying the FSC label are printed on FSC® -certified paper.
FSC is the only forest-certification scheme supported by the leading
environmental organisations, including Greenpeace.
Our paper procurement policy can be found at:
www.randomhouse.co.uk/environment

Printed and bound by Clays Ltd, St Ives PLC

ISBN 9780091952853

To buy books by your favourite authors and register for offers visit:
www.randomhouse.co.uk
www.delreyuk.com

To my mom, Vivian—strength comes in many

forms, and your courage is an inspiration

The Scorched Earth

Prologue

HE PEERS OUT from atop the battlements of his castle across the small, squat buildings of the city. The empty streets are cramped and twisted, lined with single-story hovels built from brown mud and gray stone. Dwarfed by the magnificent castle, they huddle against the high walls, stunted and misshapen. There are no other structures on the bleak horizon.

After seven hundred years in exile the number of his followers has grown tenfold, but the city has not. The land of their banishment is a nether realm—an empty shell of a world. Resources, even simple stone to build with, are scarce. Most of his subjects now live in the subterranean caves and warrens that dot the landscape like pockmarked scars.

There are no animal herds wandering the ashen plains, no flocks of birds in the sky. His followers subsist on a barely edible sludge concentrated around a few scattered underground pools of dank, stagnant water. Storms are frequent, the gray sky turning black in an instant to unleash a torrential downpour. But the rain is as foul and polluted as everything else in this forsaken land.

None of his subjects remembers the glorious wonders of the world left behind. Unlike their God-King, the mortals are countless generations removed from those who originally followed him: descendants of descendants many times over. Stories passed down tell of rivers and oceans, of hills and fields and forests brimming with life. But to his followers these tales are little more than myth and legend; the beauty of what was lost has faded over centuries in exile.

As has Daemron's own power. Trapped for centuries in this nether realm of his own creation, the divine spark of Chaos that sustains him has slowly petered out. Now only a flicker of his past glory remains.

Even an Immortal can die.

But he is not dead yet. And once the Legacy falls and he reclaims the Talismans—if he reclaims them—he will be reborn. The power of the Old Gods still burns strong within the artifacts: he can feel them in the distant land he once ruled. First came the Crown, a beacon calling to him across the Flaming Sea, guiding the spell that sent Orath and his other Minions into the mortal world.

The Ring has also been found. Only days ago he felt its fury unleashed, a storm of magic so terrible it summoned dark clouds and scathing rains that fell over Daemron's kingdom.

His subjects felt it, too. They know the time of their possible return draws near. And he knows some of them doubt whether their God-King will live long enough to see it.

They might not be wrong. Eventually, he will run out of time, and there are many questions still unanswered. Why and how has the Ring awakened? Was it the actions of one of the Children of Fire? Have the seeds from the ritual so many years ago finally borne fruit? Or was it the work of Orath and his ilk?

He has not heard from his Minions since he sent them into the mortal world. The ordeal of that ritual drained much of what was left of his power. Trying to reach across the Burning Sea to communicate with Orath again might be too much for him now. He must be patient. Bide his time. Conserve his strength.

He slowly turns away from the battlement, his serpentine tail swishing softly as he extends his massive, batlike wings and rolls his shoulders, frustrated with what he has become.

Once he was fearless. Champion of the Mortal World. Bold. Brave. Even reckless. He dared to challenge the Old Gods themselves . . . only to be cast into exile when he fled the final battle like a coward.

But he survived, and they did not. Now he is the last of his kind, the only true Immortal left. His life is too precious to risk in a fool's gambit.

He walks slowly toward the heavy wooden door leading back into the depths of his castle, his cloven hooves scraping over the rough stone wall. He reaches out a clawed hand but pauses before opening the portal.

Someone is lurking on the other side.

He can sense the dim spark of Chaos that exists within all living things. Like the Talismans, it calls to him. Narrowing his focus, he concentrates on the space beyond the closed door. Three of his subjects but none he immediately recognizes.

Trespassers. Assassins.

As rage rises within him, he steps back from the door and lifts his hands to the sky. Tilting back his horned head, he whispers words of dark power. A second later he throws his arms down to unleash the spell and the door explodes inward.

The force of the detonation sends a deadly shower of sharp wooden splinters into the stairwell beyond, ripping, slicing, and impaling the flesh of the assassin standing closest to the door, ending his life before he can even scream.

The other two hesitate only a second before rushing forward, weapons drawn. They carry short blades marked with arcane runes: relics forged in the mortal world, passed down from generation to generation in exile. The magic daggers have enough power to wound or even kill him, but the same cannot be said of those who wield them.

They are more canine than human: wolves with prehensile paws clutching their weapons. Brother and sister, united in their desire to slay the despot who rules them. Brave enough to strike against a God. Bold enough to die.

Growling and snarling, they attack with reckless desperation: a savage blur of fur and fangs and enchanted daggers. But he is their God, and they are nothing before him.

He meets their charge head-on. One clawed hand slaps aside the sister's blade, the other wraps around her throat. The brother is impaled by the barbed tip of Daemron's tail, lashing out to puncture his heart.

The brother falls to the ground, blood pouring from the gaping wound in his chest. The sister struggles in his grasp, feebly stabbing at his arm with her dagger as he slowly tightens his grip.

Ignoring the cuts and slashes to his arm, he carries her to the edge of the battlement, supporting her weight effortlessly in one hand. At the edge he flaps his wings several times, struggling with the extra burden of his would-be assassin. He only manages to rise a few feet into the air, but it is enough.

With a flick of his wrist he casts the sister over the edge. Her scream sounds like a howl as she falls, until the sound cuts off with a distant, wet thud when she strikes the ground below.

His arm is bleeding from several deep wounds, but none is serious enough to give him concern. Instead, he returns to the brother's still-breathing corpse. He doesn't speak but pauses to look into the dying eyes, and he sees sheer terror as the full understanding of what they have done dawns.

The rebels dared to strike against him. They tried to kill a God and failed. Now it is not just their own lives that are forfeit. Their allies; their friends; their families—all will suffer for what has happened here.

Satisfied the failed assassin realizes the terrible retribution that will fall upon all those he cares about, Daemron raises a heavy hoof and brings it crashing down on his skull.

Chapter 1

FERLHAME WAS IN ruins. Hundreds, perhaps thousands, of Danaan were dead; burned by fire, or crushed beneath the crumbling debris of the great wooden towers that had once lined the streets. But there was only one casualty that interested Orath.

He'd entered Ferlhame alone, ordering Gort and Draco to wait in the forests outside the city. In the gloom of the night, Orath could pass for one of the Danaan—the men and women running through the streets were too shocked by the carnage to notice the batlike features beneath the shadow of his hooded cloak. The same could not be said for his companions.

The dragon's corpse had been obliterated by the power of the Ring, the beast blown into a thousand pieces. Gruesome chunks of gore-covered flesh were scattered among the corpses and debris, and everything within a hundred yards of where the dragon had fallen was covered in a warm black ichor.

The remains of the Chaos Spawn still trembled with magic. He could feel it as he wandered the dark streets. It lingered, like the acrid clouds of smoke that choked the night air. Even dead and ripped apart, Orath could sense that the dragon had been magnificent.

And what did that say about the mortal who had defeated it? Orath had assumed that once he and the other Minions located the Talismans they could simply take them by force. But the grue-some aftermath of Ferlhame forced him to reevaluate his plan.

Their victory over the Pontiff and the others at the Monastery had given them a false sense of superiority. The Chaos had still flowed in their blood then; they had been strong. But in the weeks since that slaughter, Orath had felt his power fading.

Here, on the other side of the Legacy, it was much harder to unleash Chaos. The barrier that kept his master trapped in exile also thwarted his efforts to draw on the magical fires from the Burning Sea. The longer he and the other Minions stayed here, the weaker they would become.

After so many centuries cut off from the power of Chaos, is it any wonder the Pontiff and his followers were so weak and helpless?

Yet not all among the mortals were weak and helpless, he re-minded himself. A handful had been marked by Daemron's spell: the Children of Fire. Touched by Chaos, they could unleash the true power of the Talismans . . . power enough to destroy a dragon. Or a Minion.

Did Raven learn this lesson at the cost of her life? Is that why she hasn't returned with the Crown? Have our numbers dwindled even fur-ther?

Had his powers still been at their peak, he could have cast a spell to contact her, even across the entire distance of the mortal world. It might even still be possible. But Orath wasn't willing to try. Every incantation, every spell that he unleashed whittled away some of his strength. He had to conserve his energy; he needed to hoard the lingering remnants of Chaos in his blood for as long as possible.

Are the others aware of this? Have they sensed the slow, subtle ebbing of their power?

If not, there was no need to warn them. Not yet. Not when he could still make use of them.

In the wake of Raven's disappearance, he'd sent the Crawling Twins after the Crown. Individually they couldn't match her strength, but as a pair they were more than her equal. And what they lacked in intelligence, they made up for in savage instincts and unwavering loyalty.

But what if Raven had been destroyed by the mortal bearing the Crown? If that was the case, would the Crawling Twins fare any better? More importantly, would he?

He still might be strong enough to take the Ring by force. But strength alone wasn't why Daemron had anointed him as the leader of those he sent into the mortal world. Orath was cautious and cunning. Even though he could sense the Ring's presence moving steadily eastward, he had no intention of rushing off in pursuit and suffering a fate similar to that of the dragon.

Turning down a side street, he spotted a man in uniform, barking out orders to half a dozen others as they ran about the carnage to and fro.

These mortals have their uses, he thought, using the tiniest bit of Chaos to wrap himself in an aura of power and authority.

"You, there!" he called out. "I must speak with your ruler!"

"I beg you to reconsider, my Queen," Andar pleaded, his voice a low whisper, as if he was afraid the one waiting in her private council chamber might somehow overhear them.

"If you didn't want me to meet with this Orath, then why did you tell me of his request?" Rianna demanded, not bothering to turn her head as she marched purposefully through the castle halls. "Why bring him into the castle?"

"I was afraid to leave him wandering the streets unchecked," the High Sorcerer admitted. "And you have a right to know what is happening in your kingdom," he added as an afterthought.

"I also have the right to decide what is best for my kingdom," she countered. "We are in crisis. Our capital is devastated; our people are in mourning. We have need of allies. Powerful allies."

"Orath is an abomination," Andar warned. "A creature twisted by Chaos."

"The Order would say the same thing about us," the Queen reminded him.

As they rounded the final corner on their journey, Rianna pulled up short. The heavy oaken door of the council chamber was closed. Along the walls on either side stood a half dozen of the Royal Guard, faces grim and weapons drawn.

"Is Orath a guest or a prisoner?" she asked.

"He is dangerous, my Queen," Andar insisted. "Even with the Royal Guard in the room, I cannot guarantee your safety."

"Then the Royal Guard shall wait outside," Rianna insisted, raising a hand to stifle Andar's inevitable objection.

"Open the door," she ordered.

The guard nearest the door obeyed her command, hesitating just long enough to cast a brief glance at Andar before he did so.

Have I already been brought so low? Rianna wondered, though she understood his reaction. She had failed to protect her people from the dragon and the Destroyer of Worlds. Thousands of her subjects lay dead in the streets, and her own son had become a traitor to his people.

I was weak with Vaaler. I foresaw the danger in my dreams, but instead of ordering his execution, I chose to banish him. I acted like a mother instead of a Queen. I put my son's life ahead of my people.

It was a mistake she wouldn't make again. Her heart was hard now, her resolve steeled.

Even so, she balked when she saw what was waiting for her beyond the portal. Andar had warned her that Orath was neither Danaan nor human: he called himself a Minion. But that name had done nothing to prepare her for his unsettling appearance.

He was tall and thin, his frame bordering on skeletal. His clothes were black, as was the long cape draped behind him—a stark contrast to his alabaster skin. His face was long and narrow, his head hairless. His features were vaguely batlike: his pointed ears were too small and pressed close against his skull. His nose was sunken, his nostrils two diagonal slits in the center of his face. His eyes were yellow, the pupils narrow and dark, and his lipless mouth was lined with too many sharp, pointed teeth.

But even more disturbing than his malformed visage was the aura of magic she could feel emanating from him. Chaos enveloped him, surrounded him like a cocoon. The same power that had wrought destruction on her city.

What good is the gift of prophecy if I lack the conviction to act on it?

Taking a deep breath, Rianna entered the room. A second later, Andar followed. The Queen waved her hand without looking back, and behind her one of the guards closed the door, sealing the three of them in together.

"I am Rianna Avareen, Queen of the Danaan," the woman declared.

Her voice was strong and confident, but Orath could sense her revulsion, just as he had sensed it in the High Sorcerer when he first presented himself. He could have cast a spell to hide his appearance, a simple illusion to make him appear to be one of the Danaan. But it would tax his power unnecessarily. And he wanted the mortals to know he was not one of them. He wanted them to understand he could offer them things no other could.

"I am Orath," he said. "I have come here to propose an alliance."

"Come from where?" the High Sorcerer demanded.

He was afraid. Suspicious. So was the Queen. But Orath sensed something else in her as well. A hunger he knew how to feed.

At his unspoken command, the aura surrounding him grew stronger—a small sacrifice of his power to project an image of even greater authority, a subtle push that could help his arguments win these mortals to his side.

"I come from the depths of the Great Forest," he explained.

"Our patrols know every inch of the forest," the Queen declared. "We have never had any reports of a creature like you."

Orath laughed softly. "A creature like me," he muttered. "Once I was like you. Have I now become so hideous?"

"You're Danaan?" Andar asked, incredulous.

"Not Danaan. I walked these woods long ago, when the humans and Danaan were still one people. Before the Cataclysm."

"That would make you over seven hundred years old," Andar mocked.

"I have not seen seven centuries," Orath admitted. "For most of this time I have been … sleeping. Locked away in stasis by the Legacy."

"You fought with Daemron against the Old Gods," Rianna said, quickly assembling the bits and pieces of Orath's lie, just as he'd hoped.

"Not all of the Slayer's followers were banished with him when he fell," Orath explained. "After the Cataclysm, some of us turned our back on the carnage of the war.

"But we were still beings touched by Chaos, and when the Old Gods created the Legacy, we fell into hibernation with the Chaos Spawn."

"The Ring woke you," the Queen whispered. "Like it woke the dragon."

Orath nodded but didn't speak, knowing the less he said the better. His lies would carry more weight if the Queen believed she was figuring things out for herself.

"You spoke of an alliance," she added, urging him to continue.

"I can help you reclaim what is rightfully yours. I can help you get the Ring back."

"Why do you want to help us?" Andar demanded. "What do you get out of this alliance?"

This one doesn't trust me, Orath thought. The aura worked better on some than others. But he didn't need to win him over. The High Sorcerer's loyalty to his monarch would compel him to follow her orders despite his personal doubts.

"For centuries you and your line kept the Ring safe," Orath said, ignoring Andar and addressing the Queen. "You kept its power in check. Now it is in the hands of one who has no idea of how to properly control Chaos.

"What happened to your city was only the beginning," he continued. "If used again, the Ring's power will awaken armies of sleeping Chaos Spawn. They will unleash death and devastation across the world on a scale you cannot even fathom.

"I witnessed one Cataclysm. I know another will destroy the world, and me along with it."

"How do we know you don't want the Ring for yourself?" Andar asked.

"It would destroy me if I tried to use it," Orath admitted, countering the question with a half-truth. Using any of Daemron's three Talismans by itself was dangerous and unpredictable. Their powers were meant to be used in concert, with each artifact balancing out the other two. He would only dare to unleash their power once he possessed the Ring, the Sword, and the Crown.

"If I could take the Ring myself, I would," the Minion said. "To keep it safe," he quickly added. "But I'm not strong enough to stand against one who wields its power on my own. And neither is your kingdom."

He sensed her uncertainty, her confusion, her fear. His spell wasn't strong enough to compel someone to obey, but it could push them in a direction they were already leaning. She was lost, and she was looking for someone to tell her what to do.

"Do you believe we can get it back if we work together?" the Queen wanted to know.

"That depends on you, my Queen," Orath said with a bow. "How far are you willing to go to protect your people? What are you willing to do to reclaim the Ring?"

"Anything," Rianna promised. "Anything."

Chapter 2

Keegan couldn't move. He lay paralyzed on the battlefield that had once been a beach, surrounded by the bodies of the dead. Not all the bodies were human. Above him stood a towering figure bathed in Chaos fire, the blue flames so intense they burned Keegan's eyes. A deafening roar drowned out all other noise—the sound of the Legacy crumbling.

Terrified and helpless, the young wizard couldn't look away—an unwilling witness to the fury of the Talismans' full power finally unleashed.

He woke with a start, his heart pounding and beads of sweat trickling down his forehead. The stump of his left arm throbbed with heat and pain, and he could feel the phantom fingers of his missing left hand clenching and unclenching involuntarily in response to the nightmare.

In the flickering light of the campfire's dying embers, he could just make out Vaaler's form crouched beside him.

"What's wrong?" his friend asked. "Are you okay?"

Taking a deep breath to calm himself, Keegan muttered, "It's nothing. Just a bad dream."

"Your dreams are more than nothing," the exiled Danaan prince reminded him.

"I'm tired," Keegan protested, cradling his stump in his other arm and rolling over to turn his back to Vaaler. "I need to rest."

After a few moments, Vaaler got up and walked to the other

side of the camp, leaving him alone. Sleep came again quickly, and mercifully the dream did not return.

Scythe tossed and turned, her mind churning. When she heard Keegan thrashing and moaning in his sleep, she almost got up to check on him. But Vaaler beat her to it, so she decided to stay where she was.

Having Norr sound asleep beside her only made things worse. Normally the deep, rhythmic rumbles of his breathing helped her drift off, but tonight they had the opposite effect.

It's not his fault, she chided herself. *It's this whole damn situation.*

Unlike her barbarian lover, who could have snored his way through the Cataclysm, her nights had been spent in restless worry since the five of them had fled the destruction of Ferlhame.

It had taken them two days to reach the edge of the Danaan forest, their route angling northeast to give the Free Cities a wide berth. The trees hadn't thinned gradually as one might expect; instead, the border was sharp and unnatural. Within a few steps they passed from a forest so lush and thick its canopy blocked out most of the sun and onto the plains of the Frozen East.

The temperature was noticeably cooler than the moist, heavy air of the forest, and a thin veil of fog had blanketed the land their entire journey. The tundra stretched out to the horizon, flat and featureless save for scattered pockets of scrub vegetation and a few scattered hills barely visible in the distance.

Keegan's strength was returning, and Jerrod had tried to push their pace once they cleared the forest. But the horses struggled on the permafrost, their hooves sinking into the soft, half-frozen mud with every step. Their progress was further slowed by a chill headwind that had refused to let up for the past three days. To make up the lost time, they rode each day from just after dawn until well after the sun had disappeared.

Too many days of endless riding were taking their toll. Yet even though her body was exhausted after each day's ride, Scythe couldn't shut her mind off when they bedded down. She couldn't stop thinking about what she and Norr had gotten themselves mixed up in. Jerrod had the others convinced that Keegan was destined to be the savior of the world, but she still hadn't fully bought into the monk's madness.

The young wizard had destroyed a dragon and demolished the Danaan capital, but using the ring Vaaler had stolen from the Danaan Queen had nearly killed him. As far as Scythe was concerned, if Keegan tried to use it again, he'd basically be committing suicide.

Maybe that's part of the destiny Jerrod's pitching, she thought. *Maybe for Keegan to be the savior, he needs to be a martyr, too. Wouldn't be surprised if Jerrod kept something like that from him.*

She didn't trust the monk. He was using Keegan. But none of the others—not even Norr—could see it. Which meant she'd be the one who'd have to watch out for him.

But maybe you don't have to do it alone.

Vaaler had been even quicker than she to check on Keegan a few minutes ago. And he'd given up everything—his people, his family, his kingdom—to join their quest. If she could get him to see Jerrod the way she saw him, maybe the two of them could stop Keegan from doing something stupid down the road.

The night air was cold; autumn was upon them, and it wouldn't be long before the first snowfall covered this region. Bracing herself against the chill, Scythe rolled out from the bedroll and made her way over to where Vaaler was tending the smoldering fire.

When they had made camp the first night after leaving the forest, Norr had shown them how to dig a shallow pit in the permafrost to reveal the black, loamy peat beneath. The peat burned slowly—with too much smoke, an odd smell, and not enough heat—but the lack of vegetation on the tundra left few other options for fuel.

The Danaan looked up as she approached, his eyes haunted and hollow in the sickly flames.

Maybe Keegan isn't the only one who needs someone to look out for him.

"Heard you get up," she noted, coming over and crouching down beside him to capture the faint wisps of heat curling up from the fire pit. "Is Keegan all right?"

"Nightmare," Vaaler answered softly. "He won't talk about it."

"Can you blame him? After everything he went through, he probably just wants to forget about it for a while."

Vaaler shook his head. "I don't think these are memories. Keegan has the Sight. He's not just a wizard; he's a prophet, too. I think he saw a vision. It scared him."

"Maybe he's just overwhelmed by all this talk of being the savior of the world."

"He is the savior of the world," Vaaler insisted.

"You sound like Jerrod," Scythe muttered, casting a quick glance to check if the monk was around. She couldn't see him— most nights he took up a sentry position a short distance from the camp, using his mystical second sight to keep vigil in the darkness.

Satisfied she and Vaaler could talk in private, she asked in a low voice, "Did you ever think that maybe Jerrod's wrong?"

"I've seen what Keegan can do," Vaaler reminded her. "We studied together under Rexol—the most powerful wizard in the Southlands."

"So why isn't he helping us on this quest?"

"He's dead," Vaaler explained. "He tried to use one of the Talismans, and it killed him. Jerrod told me about it."

"You're not worried the same thing might happen to Keegan?"

Vaaler didn't answer, his eyes dropping down to the fire.

"I'm not doubting your friend," Scythe assured him. "But I just think Jerrod might be holding something back. He's devoted to his cause, not Keegan."

"Why this sudden interest in Keegan's well-being?" Vaaler asked, his gaze coming back up to challenge her. "From what I heard, you were trying to kill him yourself not too long ago."

"Things change," was her initial explanation. But she knew Vaaler would need more if she ever hoped to win him over.

"I'm pretty good at judging people," she added after a brief pause. "I can tell he's basically a good kid at heart."

Vaaler laughed. "Kid? He's the same age as you and me."

"But he seems younger. More naïve. More sheltered from the real world."

"I can't disagree with you there," Vaaler conceded.

"I've seen the way you look out for him," she pressed. "Like he's your little brother. You just want to keep him safe. And whether you believe it or not, so do I."

The prince pondered her words for a few seconds before asking, "But you don't think Jerrod feels the same way?"

"I think he's desperate to find his so-called savior, and he'll do anything to make it happen."

"You're right," Jerrod said, his voice coming from only a few feet behind them.

Both Scythe and Vaaler sprang to their feet and whirled to face the interloper. Neither had noticed his soundless approach.

Silence hung in the air for several seconds, awkward and oppressive. Scythe could feel her face burning with guilt and embarrassment, her mind fumbling with excuses and explanations. And then Jerrod turned away.

"Get the others up," he ordered as he left. "It's time to move. We're being hunted."

Chapter 3

JERROD COULD SENSE their pursuers gaining on them, but there was little he could do about it. The night was dark, the moon nothing more than a thin sliver barely able to penetrate the fog that had followed them since leaving the forest. It wasn't safe for the horses to move at anything faster than a slow trot over the soft, uneven turf.

It was doubtful the animals could have run much faster anyway. Grass was scarce on the tundra; the horses had been slowly starving ever since they left the Danaan forest. With only four mounts among the five riders, Scythe and Keegan had been doubling up for the journey, though even together they were less of a burden than Norr. Jerrod had been careful to rotate the riders so that no one animal was overtaxed, but without food to replenish their strength it was a losing battle.

The monk focused his mental energies, casting out with his second sight to try to get an image of the hunters, but it was difficult to form a clear picture. In the Danaan forest the lingering aura of Old Magic clouded his vision. Here his vision was also limited, but in a very different way.

Though the Order tried to keep it secret, the monks drew on Chaos as much as any witch or wizard. But instead of unleashing it upon the world, they internalized it, using it to heighten their perception and awareness of their surroundings, drawing on it to give them fantastic speed, strength, and endurance, even calling on it in battle to anticipate and counter the moves of an opponent before they happened.

Chaos on the plains of the Frozen East was weak and thin—like the air atop a mountain peak that left the lungs gasping and straining for breath. He'd heard many theories as to why Chaos was weak here, but none had ever made much sense. But the why mattered little to him now: all he cared about was how it was affecting him.

Everything was harder than it should have been. His body was slower and grew tired too quickly. He was unable to regulate his body's temperature properly, causing him to shiver with the growing chill of the night. His all-encompassing Sight was restricted to a radius of only a few hundred yards, and instead of being instinctual he had to concentrate to keep the world around him from dissolving into gray emptiness.

That was why he hadn't noticed the hunters before. He'd only become aware of them after slipping into a state of deep meditation when they stopped for the night: a half dozen Inquisitors traveling on foot, picking their way across the tundra as they followed the trail left by the horses' hooves in the soft ground.

Like Jerrod, they would be limited by the lack of Chaos. But though the Inquisitors were lessened, the monks would still be more than a match for him and his companions . . . especially with Keegan still weakened from his battle with the dragon.

With a flick of his heels, he urged his horse forward, moving from the back of the line past Keegan and Scythe, past the Danaan prince, and up beside Norr. Jerrod had hoped his familiarity with the land might give them an advantage over their pursuers, but it was clear that even with their barbarian guide it wouldn't be long before the hunt came to an end.

"They're getting closer," Norr said, as Jerrod's mount came level with his own. His words were more statement than question.

"Our pursuers travel faster on foot than we can on horseback," Jerrod answered.

"The same can be said of my people," Norr agreed. "Horses are ill suited for this land."

"Good—I'm tired of running," Scythe called out.

The horse carrying her and Keegan had fallen a few lengths behind the others, but in the still night their words had carried far enough for her to hear their conversation. She was sitting in front of the young wizard, her hands on the reins while he rode behind, his arms wrapped loosely around her waist to keep his balance.

"Let's send these Dweller bastards running back to the Forest," she continued. "No offense," she added, with a nod toward Vaaler as she drew up beside him.

"It's not the Danaan chasing us," Jerrod corrected. "It's the Order. Inquisitors."

"How many?" Keegan asked, poking his head over Scythe's shoulder to be heard.

"Six."

Norr laughed. "Six? Is that all? That's barely enough for us to work up a sweat!"

"These aren't simple mercenaries," Jerrod cautioned. "Your people are not born with Chaos in their blood, so the Order has never had reason to venture into your land. You have no idea what the Inquisitors are capable of."

"I've heard the stories," Scythe interjected. "Their reputation always seemed a little overblown to me."

"It's not," Vaaler chimed in, lending his support to Jerrod.

"How would you know?" she chided.

"The Order wants to eradicate my people. We'd be fools not to study them so we can separate fact from fiction. And the martial prowess of the Inquisitors is very real."

"Remember how easily I defeated you in the tavern," Jerrod reminded Norr. "The Inquisitors have similar training."

"You just caught me off guard," Norr protested, though his words lacked conviction.

"Do we have any chance of beating them?" Vaaler asked.

"Their power will be blunted here," Jerrod offered. "Something about this land is ... off. It will make them less formidable than usual."

"So we are going to fight!" Scythe exclaimed with a savage grin.

"Instead of fighting, we should try to hide," Vaaler suggested. "Is there a cave or hollow nearby?"

Jerrod shook his head. "We can't hide from the Inquisitors. Their awareness is limited in this land, but now that they have our trail it is still strong enough to track us wherever we go."

"We need somewhere to make a stand," Scythe noted. "Somewhere they can't sneak up on us or flank us."

"You wouldn't be so eager if you knew what we're about to face," Jerrod warned. "It's likely none of us will see the morning."

"We can't hide and we can't outrun them," Scythe explained with a shrug. "If battle's the only option, we might as well get up for the fight.

"Besides," she added, pointing her thumb back over her shoulder at the young wizard. "We've got him on our side."

"No!" Jerrod snapped before Keegan could reply. "He still hasn't recovered. If he tries to summon Chaos, it will destroy him!"

"I'm not strong enough to use the Ring yet," Keegan protested, "but I could draw on the power of Rexol's staff."

"Won't do you much good without any witchroot in your system," Vaaler countered. "And I agree with Jerrod. You're still too weak to use any kind of magic right now."

"So you're saying I should sit by and do nothing while the rest of you fight for our lives?"

"You cannot put yourself at risk," Jerrod told him. "You are the savior of the world. Your life is more important than all the rest of us put together."

"Speak for yourself," Scythe muttered.

"The longer we argue, the closer our enemies get," Vaaler interjected before Jerrod could say anything more.

"Scythe is right," Norr added. "If we have to fight, we need to find somewhere that gives us a tactical advantage."

"How well do you know this area?" Vaaler asked. "Any place like that nearby?"

The barbarian reached up and stroked his bushy beard with one mighty paw.

"I think we're close to the Gruun River. On the other side is a small plateau where the ancient clan leaders used to meet. The *Gerscheld*—it means "High Place" in our language. There's only one path to the top."

"How far?" Jerrod asked.

"Two, maybe three hours from here."

"Make it two," the monk told him.

Keegan clutched his arms tightly around Scythe's waist as their horse galloped through the night. The beast was nearing the point of total exhaustion: its legs were unsteady, its gait uneven. Combined with the unfamiliar terrain, the burden of two riders, and the night's gloom, it was a small miracle their mount hadn't already broken a leg and sent them both tumbling to the ground.

As it was, Keegan was holding on for dear life, his grip tenuous because of his missing hand. To compensate, he pressed his head and chest up tight against Scythe's back. He could feel her lean, taut muscles beneath her shirt, flexing in rhythm with the horse's gait.

Riding with her is the one good thing about being a crippled invalid, he thought bitterly.

He knew Scythe and Norr were together, but he was still drawn to the young woman. She was undeniably attractive—her body was fit and athletic, and her Islander features were exotic and mysterious. But his infatuation went beyond her appearance. There was a fire inside her, a wild passion that came out in even the simplest tasks. Her every movement was quick and precise, her every action and word decisive and confident.

It's no wonder she's attracted to Norr.

The redheaded giant possessed a similar, though more subdued, self-assurance.

Someone his size probably isn't afraid of anything.

Strong, confident, brave—Norr was all the things Keegan clearly wasn't.

If I can't even summon Chaos, then what good am I?

"I'm not going to just sit by while the rest of you fight to protect me," Keegan suddenly declared, speaking only loud enough for Scythe to hear him.

"Don't do anything stupid," Scythe answered without turning her head, her eyes focused on the dim outline of the charging horse ahead of them. "The monk's soft in the head about a lot of things, but on this one he might be right. Just let us handle it and try to stay out of the way."

"I won't let you sacrifice your lives to save me," Keegan countered. "No matter what Jerrod says."

"It's not all about you, you know," Scythe shot back, irritated. "The Inquisitors are out for blood. We're all mixed up in this now.

"Now shut up and let me concentrate."

Face flushing with embarrassment, Keegan held his tongue for the rest of the ride.

Scythe wasn't stupid. She recognized Keegan's clumsy declarations for what they were. Plenty of men—and women—had developed crushes on her before. She wasn't against using it to her advantage in the right situation, but this was neither the time nor the place for romantic games.

She felt a bit guilty about how she'd shamed the young wizard into silence. He was just a foolish kid who didn't know any better, and he'd already suffered through plenty of pain and loss. But the dynamics of their little group were already strained, and she didn't want to further complicate matters.

She wasn't worried about Norr. Her lover wasn't the jealous type, and he knew Scythe well enough to step back and let her deal with these kinds of problems in her own way. He'd just smile and let out a deep, rumbling chuckle if she told him about Keegan's feelings for her.

Vaaler probably wouldn't care, either. The Danaan prince had plenty of other things on his mind, given his banishment and the horrors he'd seen unleashed on his former people.

Jerrod, however, might see this as more than just a harmless crush. He'd probably accuse her of being a distraction, a temptation to lure his chosen savior away from the righteous path or some similar fanatical nonsense.

Not that she cared what some self-important monk thought about her. But Keegan listened to Jerrod. If the monk decided she was a danger to the young man's destiny, he might try to turn him against her.

Or do something even more drastic.

The monk had made it clear that he valued Keegan's life above anyone else's. She didn't think he'd do something as rash as attack her right in front of everyone; he was too smart for that. But Jerrod never seemed to sleep. If Keegan and Vaaler woke up one morning to find that she and Norr were gone, it wouldn't be hard for the mad monk to convince the others that they'd simply left.

She wasn't completely convinced he'd try something like that, but she wouldn't put it past him, either.

Do you really think Keegan's feelings are going to disappear just because you told him to shut up? This isn't over.

Scythe grinned, baring her teeth against the chill of the night air as her horse continued its stumbling gait.

Maybe I'll get lucky and the Inquisitors will kill us all so I don't have to deal with this.

She laughed quietly at her own joke, though she knew nobody else would find it funny. Even Norr couldn't appreciate her gallows humor.

As desperate as their situation was, however, she didn't feel afraid. She didn't want to die, of course. But for some reason she was convinced they were going to come out of this relatively unscathed. Instead of dreading the confrontation, she was looking forward to it. Eagerly.

Methodis had taught her about adrenaline; she knew it was natural to feel a rush of excitement in times of danger or stress. But this was different. She'd felt it ever since they left the North Forest, a feeling that grew stronger the farther east they traveled. Something about this harsh land spoke to her; it made her feel energized. Alive.

She imagined Norr felt it, too, even though he hadn't said anything about it to her. This was the land of his people, his home.

Or maybe his return is bittersweet.

Norr had never spoken about why he'd left the Frozen East and journeyed into the Southlands. Scythe suspected there were old wounds, and she wasn't about to start picking at the scabs . . . not when she had so many of her own.

And then all her thoughts were wiped away in an instant as the horses went down.

The focus of Jerrod's Sight was split between their immediate surroundings and the enemies pursuing them. Yet he was still aware enough to react to the sharp crack of bone as the fetlock of Norr's mount snapped beneath the barbarian's weight.

The animal screamed as it went down, taking the rider with it. Vaaler, following too close behind in their mad rush to reach the *Gerscheld,* couldn't change course in time and was caught up in the crash.

Third in line, Jerrod tried to wheel his mount to the side. But the animal didn't share the monk's supernatural reactions. Already pushed to the edge of its physical limits, the horse planted one hoof awkwardly as it tried to respond to its rider's urgent command. The ankle didn't give way, but the beast stumbled off balance and went tumbling forward.

Jerrod threw himself from the saddle to avoid being crushed by his own mount. He hit the ground hard, the wind knocked from his lungs even though he was able to tuck and roll to absorb some of the impact.

Behind him, Scythe and Keegan were swept up in the carnage as well: carrying two people, there was nothing the horse could do to stop its momentum from sending it headlong into the fallen riders ahead of them.

One second Keegan was riding behind Scythe, silently cursing himself for all the stupid things he'd said. The next he was hurtling through the air. His body did a half somersault before he slammed into the frozen turf, his neck and shoulders taking the brunt of the impact.

Disoriented and dazed, he lay motionless on his back, his eyes staring up at the dark night sky above. A burning, tingling pain radiated out from his spine and down through his limbs, and for an instant he feared he'd broken his neck. But after a few moments he managed to roll over and lift himself up to his knees, his arms and the fingers of his surviving hand numb but functional.

The high-pitched, bloodcurdling neighs of the horses drew his attention, and he turned to see a mass of twisted, writhing chaos. He couldn't tell how many horses were down; in the darkness, their thrashing bodies and flailing hooves made it impossible to tell one from another. But he could pick out other forms in the mayhem—the riders who fell with their mounts.

Still too woozy to stand, he started to crawl forward to help his friends. And then Jerrod was there beside him, holding him back.

"It's too dangerous!" he shouted. "One kick could stave in your skull!"

Keegan knew the monk was right, and he didn't have the physical strength to resist him anyway. Helpless, he was forced to watch as the mess of limbs and flesh slowly untangled itself. One of the horses sprang to its feet. Uninjured but panicked, it raced off into the night.

A massive figure—clearly Norr—crawled from the scrum on his hands and knees. He paused to grab hold of a shadowy form lying motionless, dragging the unconscious victim clear of the chaos before collapsing a few yards away.

Another horse managed to find its feet. Like the first, it bolted, heading in the opposite direction. Keegan could see that it was limping badly.

The remaining horses were screaming in agony; too injured to rise. But Keegan ignored their gruesome suffering; his attention focused on the two shadowy figures nearby.

Norr pulled someone out. Was it Vaaler or Scythe?

In the gloom the other person looked small and delicate beside Norr, but the barbarian dwarfed everyone. In the darkness, it was impossible to be sure from a distance.

Shaking free of Jerrod's restraining hand, Keegan rose to his feet and rushed over to his fallen friends. The monk followed close behind. As he drew closer he realized the figure beside Norr was Vaaler.

Both men were conscious now, sitting up gingerly and check-ing themselves for broken bones or other serious injuries. Keegan's relief at seeing his closest friend still alive was quickly washed away by his concern over the missing fifth member of their group.

"Where's Scythe?" he demanded.

Vaaler was still too shaken to answer, but Norr managed to shake his head.

"I didn't see her. She must have been thrown clear."

Before Keegan could even suggest looking for her, Jerrod tapped him on the shoulder.

"There," he said, pointing back toward the suffering horses.

Keegan could just make out Scythe's silhouette circling the wounded animals. She was crouched low to the ground, like a predator ready to strike. Driven mad by the pain, the horses still kicked and struggled, their shattered limbs flopping about at un-natural, sickening angles.

Scythe suddenly darted forward then jumped back. One of the horses shuddered, then a few seconds later it went still. By that time Scythe had already slit the throat of the second tortured creature, and it, too, became still as its life slipped away. Turning away from the animals she'd been forced to put down, the young woman made her way over to the others.

"How bad is it?" she asked.

"I'm fine," Norr assured her, grunting as he levered his bulk into a standing position.

"You know you're a terrible liar," Scythe warned him.

"Cracked ribs, maybe," her lover admitted. "A twisted knee. Nothing serious."

"What about you, Vaaler?" Keegan asked. "You weren't moving when Norr pulled you clear."

"I was wondering how I ended up here," the prince replied, slurring his words slightly. "Thank you," he added with an appre-ciative nod in the barbarian's direction.

"You didn't answer my question," Keegan pressed. "Are you hurt?"

"Took a nasty bump to the head. Everything else seems to be okay."

"Let me see," Scythe said, stepping forward to make a quick inspection. "You're cut. Bleeding quite a bit. Head wounds are always messy. But it looks worse than it is. You'll be fine."

Satisfied with Scythe's prognosis, Keegan extended his good hand and helped pull Vaaler to his feet.

"Now what?" the Danaan asked. "The Inquisitors are still after us."

"We're only a mile away from the *Gerscheld*," Norr offered.

"Maybe they'll split up to follow the horses that ran off," Scythe suggested. "Help even our odds."

"They won't," Jerrod replied. "They're close enough to sense us now, just as I can sense them."

"Grab what we can from the horses," the monk ordered. "We'll continue on foot."

Chapter 4

THEY WEREN'T ABLE to salvage much from the two fallen mounts. Most of the food had been on the animals that had panicked and fled off into the night, and the bedrolls and other camp gear would only slow them down as they continued on foot.

As far as Keegan was concerned, the only thing of real value was Rexol's staff. Somehow it had survived unharmed; even the horned gorgon's skull was undamaged. Whether this was a stroke of luck or an indication of the power trapped within, Keegan couldn't say. But he was grateful to have the Talisman with him as they marched on through the night.

Scythe quickly cut several strips of cloth from the bedrolls and wrapped them tightly around Norr's injured knee, then they set off again. The walked single file, the barbarian leading the way. Even with the support of the wrap, the big man was limping slightly, but his long stride still enabled him to set a pace the others had to work to keep up with. It wasn't long before they could see the outline of the *Gerscheld* looming ahead of them, a black shape rising fifty feet, set against a twilight sky that heralded the approaching dawn.

In addition to being significantly larger, the *Gerscheld* was also shaped differently than the other small, rolling hills that dotted the tundra. The *Gerscheld* was wider and flatter. Three of its sides were sheer cliffs, though the face they were approaching didn't shoot straight up. Instead, it was sloped like a steep ramp leading to the summit.

By the time they reached the base of the plateau it was light enough for Keegan to make out the uneven path winding through the jagged rocks that covered the sharp incline. An irregular, twisting trail had been carved into the rock face; in places it couldn't have been more than a few feet wide.

The path was clearly man-made, and Keegan suspected the *Gerscheld* itself wasn't a natural formation. To his eyes it appeared the earth had been wrenched apart, then folded back on itself.

This place probably dates back to the Cataclysm.

But if magic had created the *Gerscheld,* there was no lingering trace of its presence. The charge in the air Keegan had felt in the North Forest was absent; like the rest of the Frozen East, this was a place where Chaos was thin.

Still in single file, they trudged up the path to the top of the plateau. The ground was uneven and the going hard; Keegan had to lean heavily on Rexol's staff for support during the ascent. Even Jerrod seemed to struggle with the steep incline.

At least it won't be easy for the Inquisitors to get to us.

Reaching the top, he was surprised to find several dozen large, rectangular stones arranged in a wide circle near the center of the plateau. The stones were all the same size and shape—roughly six feet across, ten feet high, and four feet deep. They stood on end, evenly spaced from each other as if someone had set them there. They were fashioned from a smooth blue mineral unlike anything Keegan had ever seen.

"What is this place?" Vaaler gasped.

"I told you," Norr said. "It was a meeting place for the ancient clan chieftains. During times of conflict, they could come here to parley without fear of an ambush."

Keegan saw it was true; from their vantage point they'd have a clear view for miles in every direction once the sun came up.

"This was once hallowed ground," the barbarian added. "It was forbidden to spill blood here. But Pertor the Defiler violated the sanctity of the *Gerscheld* when he butchered his rivals during a parley."

"The Inquisitors," Scythe said, interrupting his tale and pointing back the way they had come.

Squinting in the gray light of the early morn, Keegan could just make out six figures on foot coming toward them. Their motions seemed purposeful, but controlled—as if they were walking briskly. But even at this distance he could tell they were moving with unnatural speed.

"Pertor's betrayal cursed the once-hallowed ground," Norr whispered. "Legend holds that any who come here now will know only suffering and death."

"Good thing I'm not the superstitious type," Scythe noted, breaking the awkward silence that followed her lover's proclamation. "Otherwise I might take that as a bad omen."

Jerrod knew they didn't have much time to ready their defenses: the Inquisitors were only minutes from reaching the *Gerscheld*. The plateau was wide and open, with plenty of room for a battle— if they had an advantage in numbers, it would make sense to try to draw their enemy up and attack them from all sides.

But there were six Inquisitors and only five of them.

And the real odds are even worse than that.

With only one hand, and unable to summon Chaos, Keegan wouldn't be much help. Vaaler still carried his rapier, but the Danaan's movements were sluggish and groggy, as if he was still trying to shake off the effects of the blow that had rendered him unconscious only a few hours ago. In his current state, Jerrod doubted he'd be able to stand for long against even a single Inquisitor.

Norr's size made him a formidable opponent, but the barbarian wasn't armed—he hadn't bothered to keep the heavy branch he'd used as a makeshift cudgel against the Danaan soldiers back in the North Forest. And Jerrod could tell his injuries from when the horses went down were hurting him more than he wanted to admit. His jaw had been clenched against the pain during their journey, his body was drenched with sweat, and his complexion was even paler than usual.

The twin blades Scythe used against her enemies were surprisingly effective; even Jerrod had been impressed with the savage fury she'd unleashed to dispatch the Danaan soldiers that had attacked them. But the Inquisitors were unlike any opponent she had ever faced. Her speed and quickness would be negated by their martial training and mystical Sight; they'd anticipate and counter her moves before she even made them.

Taking on all six at once is suicide.

There was another option. The winding path up the steep, treacherous slope narrowed sharply as it neared the top of the plateau. Jagged rock formations walling it on either side would effectively funnel their attackers into the tight quarters of the trail's mouth. If they made a stand there, the Inquisitors wouldn't be able to come at them all at once. At most they'd have to face two at a time.

But there won't be room for all of us, either.

"Norr and I will hold the Inquisitors here at the top of the path," Jerrod declared. "The rest of you fall back inside the stone circle."

"Nice try," Scythe snarled. "But I'm not sitting this one out."

"No, he's right," Vaaler chimed in. "This is the only way up—if we hold them here, they can only come at us in pairs.

"I wish I had my bow," he added bitterly. "I could pick them off while they were climbing up to the top."

"It wouldn't help," Jerrod assured him. "They'd pluck your arrows right out of the air."

"I always thought that was a myth," Scythe muttered.

"Myths about the Inquisitors are usually less terrifying than the truth."

"We'll hold them as long as we can, but eventually they will take us down," Jerrod continued. "When they do, you and Vaaler move forward to try to hold them."

"Norr's hurt," Scythe protested. "It makes more sense to put me on the front line and have him in the back."

"There's no room in here for you to move," Jerrod countered. "We need brute strength to hold this spot."

"We don't have time to argue, Scythe," Norr said softly.

"Here," Vaaler said, offering his weapon to the barbarian. "Take my sword."

Norr shook his head. "I have not earned the right."

"He never carries a weapon," Scythe explained.

"I wouldn't know how to use it, anyway," Norr added. "I will fare better with my bare hands."

"Here they come," Keegan said, pointing with Rexol's staff to the base of the hill.

The Inquisitors were already starting up the path, moving with alarming speed. They had pulled back the hoods of their heavy brown cloaks to reveal their shaved heads, and each was armed with a black, six-foot quarterstaff. With their gray, pupil-less eyes and hairless skulls, it was hard to visually distinguish between male and female, but Jerrod's second sight told him there were four men and two women in the group.

"Get ready, Norr," Jerrod said. "The rest of you fall back."

Keegan and Vaaler did as ordered. Scythe hesitated a moment, then followed the others as they retreated to a safe distance.

Jerrod focused his mind and prepared for battle. He called on his internal reservoir of Chaos to bolster his strength, speed, and stamina. But instead of the surge of power he normally felt, he was rewarded with only a faint trickle of energy.

The Inquisitors continued their ascent, silent and menacing. They paused about fifteen feet from the top of the plateau, just before the path narrowed. One of the men stepped forward to address them.

"Jerrod: Yasmin the Unbowed has declared you and your companions as heretics of the Order. You have been condemned to death. We are here to carry out your sentence."

The renegade monk didn't recognize the speaker: he was young, a fresh face who must have risen to his position during the years Jerrod was in hiding.

"How are we condemned with no trial?" he countered, hoping to sow the seeds of doubt in his enemies. "Now that Yasmin is the Pontiff, has she abandoned the ancient laws of the Monastery?"

"The old ways have failed." the monk replied. "The Monastery is in ruins. Now is the time for righteous action!"

Why are the young always so much more zealous in their fanaticism? Jerrod wondered. And then the Inquisitors fell on them.

As he'd hoped, only two of the Inquisitors were able to press forward while the rest were forced to hang back. Jerrod and Norr stepped forward to meet them, and everything became a blur.

The staves of the Inquisitors whirled and spun, lashing out with quick, hard strikes. Jerrod countered by dodging or redirecting each attack with a hand or forearm and trying to get in close to unleash a volley of kicks, elbows, and knees. His opponent countered by twisting away, jabbing out with the butt of his quarterstaff to throw Jerrod off balance and forcing him to stumble back. The extra space allowed the Inquisitor to reset and make another pass with the spinning staff, and once again Jerrod responded with a series of parries and blocks that flowed into another series of counterattacks.

The Inquisitor staggered back, and for a brief instant there was an opening for Jerrod to deal a crippling blow. But he was a fraction of a second too slow to seize the opportunity, and instead of driving his foot through the knee of his enemy and dislocating it, he only managed to deal a painful kick to the shin.

Jerrod was fighting in a fugue. He felt slow and sluggish. His attacks lacked precision, and his defense seemed haphazard and careless. Even his awareness of what was going on around him felt muddled and cloudy.

Fortunately, the Inquisitors were as slow and sluggish as Jerrod. It blunted their fury and prolonged what should have been a quick victory.

Beside him, Jerrod was dimly aware of Norr struggling but somehow holding his own against an overwhelming foe. Too big and too slow to avoid the monk's quarterstaff, Norr absorbed the full force of the punishing strikes with his meaty arms and shoulders, grunting in pain with each hit. But he refused to give ground, grasping and clawing with his massive paws to try to grab either his opponent or the weapon that slammed into him over and over.

Realizing the giant had the strength to crush the life from him with his bare hands, the monk facing Norr was being overly cautious. Instead of darting in to deal an incapacitating blow to the head or face, he was staying on the fringes of the battle and out of the barbarian's reach. Eventually Norr would succumb to the steady stream of crushing blows, but it would be a long, slow, brutal defeat.

Jerrod's focus snapped back to his own predicament just in time to react to an unexpected ploy from his opponent. Thrusting forward with the quarterstaff, the Inquisitor suddenly let go of his weapon and leapt at Jerrod, knowing that if he tackled him to the ground, the others would be able to rush up and join the fray. His fingers closed around the collar of Jerrod's shirt, clutching tightly as the Inquisitor snapped his head and shoulders back in an effort to yank Jerrod off balance.

Instead of fighting against it, Jerrod threw himself forward, using the momentum of his foe to transition into a forward flip.

At the same time he twisted in the air and brought his fist up into the throat of his enemy. The glancing blow didn't crush the Inquisitor's trachea as Jerrod had intended, but it had enough force to make him loosen his grip.

Jerrod landed on his feet, his enemy prone between his legs, coughing and sputtering for air. But before Jerrod could finish him off, one of the other Inquisitors leapt forward to defend her fallen companion. The quarterstaff whistled as it sliced the air in a series of short, savage arcs aimed at Jerrod's head. He ducked out of the way and fell into a backward roll, scooping up the abandoned quarterstaff of his first opponent.

He came up on his knees, the quarterstaff clutched in both hands as he parried a blow meant to cave in his skull. A quick sweep of his leg forced his opponent to spring back, and Jerrod scrambled to his feet.

The monk came at him again, the quarterstaves clacking and cracking as Jerrod repelled her assault and counterattacked. But even though he was now armed, Jerrod knew the battle was slipping away. Fatigue was already taking its toll on his limbs, and he was facing a fresh opponent. The Inquisitor he'd struck in the throat was back on his feet, coughing and gasping for breath but otherwise unharmed. In another minute he'd be fully recovered and ready to step in again whenever one of his compatriots began to tire.

They don't need to break through to the plateau, Jerrod realized. *They just need to wear us down.*

In the instant of his grim realization, Norr's balky leg gave out, and the big man went down. The Inquisitor sprang forward to finish him, only to have the killing blow knocked aside by Vaaler's blade as the Danaan leapt into the fray. A second later Scythe was there, too.

Her slim form darted in close, the early-morning sun glittering off the thin blade in each hand. Her knives flickered and danced and the Inquisitor screamed as Scythe slashed open deep gashes in his face and hands.

One of the blades sliced across a milky eye; a devastating blow to a normal opponent, but barely more than a superficial wound against one that used the Sight to perceive the world. But the ferocity of her attack drove the Inquisitor back, and Norr was able to regain his feet with Vaaler's help.

As Scythe pressed her advantage, Norr and Vaaler fell back, simultaneously giving her room to operate and giving themselves a chance to catch their breath.

Jerrod and his opponent had fallen into the familiar rhythm of battle—an ebb and flow as she attacked, he parried and countered, only to have her reverse the momentum and attack again. He was fighting on instinct now, falling into patterns ingrained into his muscles by years of training at the Monastery.

He knew he needed to focus and do something to break the pattern. But it was hard to concentrate with Scythe fighting beside him. In the mind's eye of his mystical Sight, she was little more than a savage blur. She seemed to flicker and flash from place to place in unexpected and unpredictable ways, disorienting and overwhelming her enemy.

The Inquisitor staggered back, bleeding from a dozen deep cuts. Scythe lunged forward, and he dropped his staff and threw his hands up to protect his throat from her deadly knives. At the last instant Scythe turned her wrist and changed the angle of her blade. Instead of carving across the flesh as she'd been doing, she drove the tip into the chest of her foe. Her aim was perfect. The blade slipped between the ribs and bit deep into the Inquisitor's heart, snuffing out his life.

Jerrod expected another to leap forward and take his place, but instead, the Inquisitor he was fighting disengaged and fell back.

They weren't expecting this kind of resistance. They're retreating.

Unwilling to let them get away, Scythe started forward in pursuit.

Before Jerrod could call out a warning, Norr's voice rose up in a deafening cry.

"Don't, Scythe! It's a trap!"

She pulled up short at his words and shook her head, dispelling the bloodlust that had almost betrayed her.

Never taking their eyes off the enemies atop the plateau, the Inquisitors slowly backed down the path until they reached the bottom.

Scythe watched them go, then turned and spat on the corpse of the man she'd killed.

"Told you we could take them," she hissed, a feral grin on her face.

"Their retreat is an empty victory," Jerrod muttered.

"Why do you say that?" Keegan asked, wandering over from the stone circle where he'd watched the battle unfold.

"Now they'll just wait us out," Vaaler explained glumly, recognizing their plight. "That path is the only way down. We have no food. No water. And no way to escape."

Chapter 5

Above Cassandra the dark clouds gathered, and she heard the rumble of thunder. She quickened her pace, knowing there was nowhere on the empty plain to seek shelter from the coming storm. The sky above was a mantle of darkness, too thick even for her Sight to pierce. Yet inside she could sense her enemy lurking, waiting to plunge down and rip the Crown from her grasp.

A hard rain began to fall, pelting her with cold water and stinging hail. A jagged bolt of blue lightning split the sky and arced toward the ground. Just beside Cassandra, the earth exploded, and the shock of the impact knocked her from her feet.

Confused and disoriented, she somehow managed to keep hold of the Crown. Rising to her knees, she saw a dark figure swoop down from the clouds—the Minion that had hunted her across the Frozen East. The creature had the body of a naked woman, but its skin was black and featureless—like a shadow come to life. It had the wings and head of a bird of prey; its fingers were long, sharp talons; its eyes burned red.

When it touched the ground, however, it transformed. The wings melted away and the body began to shift and shimmer, taking on the form of a woman Cassandra knew well.

"Give me the Crown," Yasmin said.

The tall woman towered over Cassandra, standing straight against the driving rain, seemingly oblivious as the hail struck her on the face and the scarred skin of her naked scalp.

"The Pontiff gave the Crown to me," Cassandra protested, pulling the Talisman close against her chest.

"Nazir is dead," Yasmin reminded her. "The Monastery is fallen. Because of your actions, I am the Pontiff now."

She stretched out her hand, palm up.

"Give me the Crown."

Cassandra shook her head.

"You are a traitor to our cause," Yasmin whispered. "A heretic. For that you must be punished."

Yasmin stepped back and lifted her arms to the sky. A ring of fire burst forth from the ground, encircling Cassandra. The flames hissed as the rain struck them, but instead of being extinguished, they grew higher.

Cassandra felt the heat as the fire slowly closed in. There was only one escape, one way out. With trembling hands she placed the Crown atop her head . . . and the world exploded.

Cassandra woke with a start, heart pounding so hard she thought it would burst through the bones of her chest. Her body was soaked in sweat, and even though it was blessedly warm in the Guardian's cave, she shivered.

"There is nothing to fear here," the deep voice of the Guardian reassured her. "It was only a nightmare."

Cassandra nodded. She was a prophet of the Order; she knew the difference between a nightmare and a vision.

This was no prophecy. But it was more than an ordinary dream.

"Are you hungry?" the Guardian asked.

In response to his words, or possibly the scent of stew cooking over the fire near the rear of the cave, Cassandra's stomach grumbled. She crawled out of her bedroll and crossed the cave in silence, her mind still trying to make sense of her dream.

The Guardian was hunched over the fire near the entrance of the cave, his back to the swirling snows of the blizzard outside.

The orange glow emanating from the flames cast a strange light across the blue skin of his naked, heavily muscled chest. Despite the howling wind just beyond the open mouth of his lair, no draft dared enter to disturb the warmth inside.

As she approached him, the Guardian stood and stretched, rising to his full fifteen feet and reaching up so that his massive hands nearly scraped the uneven rock ceiling. Though one of the Chaos Spawn, he appeared human save for his blue skin and massive size, though Cassandra had never seen any mortal man so exquisite.

His features were sharp and defined—the hard line of his square jaw framed by a short black beard, his eyes piercing and dark. He was naked except for a black fur loincloth and hard black boots that came halfway up his massive calves. As he stretched his arms up to the ceiling, the muscles of his perfectly proportioned limbs rippled and flexed, and Cassandra had to stop herself from letting out an awestruck gasp.

She knew there was more to the Guardian's unearthly beauty than mere physical perfection. There was an ancient wisdom in his eyes and a calm yet unyielding strength in his words when he spoke. He radiated an aura that made her feel safe and secure, and she knew that as long as she stayed under his protection nothing could harm her.

But I can't stay here forever.

The Guardian shrugged his shoulders, working out a knot in his muscular neck before sitting down once more. Cassandra took a seat next to him, her heart involuntarily speeding up as her host leaned in and handed her a bowl of steaming stew.

The bowl was enormous, and Cassandra had to use both hands to support its weight. Her grip was awkward; she'd lost the ring and pinky fingers of her left hand to frostbite traveling across the mountains to reach the Guardian's lair. But she managed to raise the bowl to her lips, tipping it back so the delicious broth spilled down her throat.

"You're getting stronger," the Guardian said approvingly.

But you're getting weaker.

It was subtle but undeniable. Though his features and frame were still inhumanly perfect, his appearance had changed. When she'd first arrived, the Guardian's blue skin had almost seemed to glow, as if he were illuminated from within by the spark of immortality. Since her arrival, that luster had begun to fade.

Cassandra glanced over to the back corner of the cave. A stone pedestal stood in a recessed alcove. At its base rested the Crown she had come so far and suffered so much to deliver into the Guardian's care.

Embedded in the top of the pedestal, blade pointed down and hilt toward the ceiling, was a magnificent sword. The handle was black, and carved with a subtle pattern that seemed to shift and flow as if it were alive. The silver blade radiated power, and when Cassandra glanced at it from the corner of her eye it seemed to take on a reddish hue—a lingering reflection of all the blood it had spilled.

Daemron's sword, given to him by the True Gods before he rose up against them. A weapon infused with the power of Old Magic, entrusted by the True Gods to the Guardian after the Cataclysm.

It was far too small for the Guardian to wield—in his enormous hand it would be little more than a dagger. When he left the cave to hunt for food, he armed himself with a heavy spear, the shaft as thick around as Cassandra's thigh.

Yet even if the Sword had been properly proportioned for the Guardian to use, Cassandra knew he wouldn't have dared. For him the blade was a holy relic; his entire existence focused on the single task of protecting the Talisman bequeathed to him by the True Gods.

In return for his unwavering devotion, the Guardian had become immortal. For centuries he had dwelt alone in the cave, sustained by the power of the Talisman. Until Cassandra's arrival.

Like all who served in the Order, she knew the history of the Talismans well. The Crown and the Sword, along with a magical Ring, had all been forged from the fires of Chaos by the True Gods. Yet each was imbued with a unique type of power. The Sword had sustained the Guardian for seven hundred years, but the mere presence of the Crown was slowly killing him.

Such are the ways of Chaos. Opposition and conflict are inherent in its nature. Even the True Gods couldn't change that.

"The one who hunted you is gone," the Guardian said. "She has fled back over the mountains though to what purpose I cannot say."

Cassandra nodded, remembering the dark avian figure that still stalked her dreams.

"She may return," the Guardian warned. "Or others may come. I will try to protect you, but my power ebbs."

This was as close as he would ever get to admitting the truth. The Crown was anathema to him, slowly poisoning him. Yet he would never cast her out. The Guardian would sacrifice his own life without a second thought to keep her safe.

But eventually he would succumb. And once he was gone, Cassandra would be defenseless.

You are not defenseless! You have the Crown and the Sword! Use them to destroy your enemies!

Cassandra shook her head. The words were not her own; they seemed to materialize from some unknown source. But just for an instant, she considered them.

The Talismans will destroy you! she reminded herself. *Rexol was the most powerful mage in the Southlands, and the Crown devoured him when he tried to use it.*

And even if she were strong enough to survive, unleashing the power of Old Magic could bring down the Legacy, unleashing Daemron the Slayer and his hordes of Chaos Spawn upon the mortal world.

"I can't stay here forever," Cassandra told him. "My fate lies outside the safety of your cave."

"Where will you go?"

The obvious question, but one which Cassandra couldn't answer.

"Rest awhile longer," the Guardian urged, taking advantage of her uncertain silence. "A few more days to recover your strength."

Surrounded by the warmth of the cave and with her belly full, Cassandra could find no reason to argue.

Setting down her empty bowl, she watched the Guardian in silence as he filled his own dish. He was Chaos Spawn, but he was no twisted monster. And it wasn't just his physical perfection; there seemed to be a spark of the divine inside him.

"Did you know the True Gods?" Cassandra asked him.

He nodded, then set his meal down on the ground beside him.

"The Old Gods created me," he whispered. "Back when the world was young. They called me forth from the ice and stone of the mountains and breathed life into my form.

"Back then," he added after a momentary pause, "even the Gods did not understand the dangers of creation."

"What do you mean?"

"The spell that gave me life sent ripples through the Chaos Sea. In the slime and filth far below the burning waves, a vile brute was born. My dark twin. The ogre."

Cassandra nodded, remembering her lessons in the Monastery. *Chaos rebels against order.*

"The Gods gave life to this world, but in doing so they unwittingly called forth creatures like the ogre. Monsters that crawled from the Burning Sea to wreak destruction on these mortal shores.

"Once they understood the terrible consequences of their actions, the Gods realized they could no longer dwell in this realm. Their very presence caused ripples in the Chaos Sea that would bring harm to those they sought to protect. Yet they could not abandon the people, either. They needed a hero to defend this realm."

"But why did they choose Daemron?" Cassandra asked. "Why didn't they choose you?"

"He was a mortal naturally born into this world. I am a creature formed from Chaos." The Guardian spoke slowly, choosing his words with great care, clearly uncomfortable with the question. "The Talismans they gave to Daemron would have affected me in dangerous and unpredictable ways."

Like how the Sword has sustained you for all these centuries, she thought, *yet the Crown is now slowly killing you.*

"In the beginning, I fought by Daemron's side," the blue-skinned titan continued. "Together we drove the Chaos Spawn into hiding."

"What was he like?"

"A great warrior," the Guardian replied. "A powerful wizard. A brilliant prophet. A mighty king."

As he spoke, he looked away from her and reached down to pick up the bowl from the ground beside him, his gaze focused intently on his meal.

"Were you friends?" Cassandra asked, sensing he was holding something back. "Before he betrayed the True Gods?"

The boldness of the question surprised her, but if the Guardian was offended, he gave no sign.

"We were allies," he answered, turning his head to look at her once more. "But there was always something dark within him."

"A true hero fights for something greater than themselves. He or she is willing to sacrifice everything to protect those who cannot protect themselves."

Like you, Cassandra thought.

"But Daemron was different. His courage was selfish. He risked his life for glory and praise. He was fearless, but only because he was so proud he did not believe he could die.

"It wasn't enough that the Gods had chosen him as their Champion. It wasn't enough that they had gifted him with the Talismans. He believed he was their equal; he believed he deserved to be immortal. And he used the very gifts the Gods had given him to take what he thought he deserved."

Is that so wrong? To seize what you want?

Once again Cassandra was momentarily caught off guard by the words that sprang unbidden into her head. The concept went against everything she had been taught, everything she believed in.

"Didn't the True Gods sense Daemron's corruption?" Cassandra asked, ignoring the stray—and unwelcome—thought.

"All mortals are corrupt and flawed next to the perfection of the divine," the Guardian countered. "Perhaps they felt Daemron was the best they could find."

"But you knew he was dangerous," Cassandra pressed. "Didn't you try to warn them?"

"Who was I to question the judgment of the Gods?" he countered. "I thought my doubts about him were evidence of my own failings: manifestations of my jealousy and resentment that they had elevated him over me. It was only after his betrayal that the truth became evident to all.

"The Talismans were imbued with the essence of the Gods themselves," he continued. "They possessed the power of raw Chaos: the power of life and creation. Daemron discovered a ritual to unleash that power; he used it to transform himself from a man into an Immortal. But the backlash of his spell changed him in other ways, too."

"How so?"

"The darkness inside him grew stronger; it consumed his mind and spirit. And his physical appearance was forever altered. The

Chaos changed him from human into something demonic and twisted. His exterior form became a reflection of the evil inside. He became as monstrous as the Chaos Spawn he once fought against—a being that fed on violence, suffering, and death."

Cassandra knew the rest of the story: Daemron the Slayer, former hero and protector of the mortal world, rallied the Chaos Spawn to his banner . . . along with thousands of mortal men and women who chose to follow him instead of the Gods that had given them life. But in the end, his rebellion failed.

"Were you there when Daemron fell?" Cassandra asked.

"He never fell," the Guardian corrected her. "He fled.

"I fought on the side of the Gods in the final battle. I was locked in mortal combat with the ogre, my dark twin, when Daemron realized all was lost. In a last, desperate act he cast a powerful spell, ripping open the fabric of existence to create a portal to another realm."

"The Cataclysm," Cassandra whispered, suppressing a shiver.

The Guardian nodded. "The fury of the Chaos he summoned split the mortal world in two, unleashing earthquakes, floods, and fires across all the lands.

"Daemron and many of his followers fled through the portal, abandoning the mortal world. In the confusion, the ogre escaped me though I cannot say for sure if the beast made it through the portal before it snapped shut.

"Many of the Chaos Spawn did not; they were trapped here. But with their leader gone, they scattered, disappearing in the turmoil of the Cataclysm. Acting quickly, the Gods combined their power to heal the rift in the mortal world before everything was completely destroyed. But the ritual crippled them; in saving us all, they themselves were mortally wounded."

The Guardian paused in his tale, as if gathering his thoughts. When he spoke again, his voice was thick and choked, as if holding back tears.

"The Gods knew they were dying, so they had to act quickly. With the last of their strength they created the Legacy, a barrier between this world and the Burning Sea that trapped Daemron and his followers in their banishment.

"No longer able to draw freely on the power that had created them, the Chaos Spawn that were left behind quickly became weak. To survive, they went into hibernation deep beneath the earth: a sleep from which we hoped they would never wake.

"And then the Gods just ... slipped away." The Guardian's voice had dropped to a low whisper, and his eyes' gaze was distant and unfocused.

"The True Gods gave of themselves to bring peace to the mortal world," Cassandra added, reciting the familiar words from her earliest lessons in the Monastery. "They sacrificed themselves that we could live on, bequeathing the Legacy to us that we may preserve it for all time."

The Guardian bowed his head and closed his eyes, and Cassandra realized that she could never fully comprehend the depth of his grief. She had spent most of her life worshipping the True Gods: revering them and seeking to honor them by protecting the Legacy. But the great titan had actually known them. He had spoken with them and walked at their side. He had felt the love and glory of the True Gods firsthand, only to have it taken away as he watched them die with his own eyes.

He's been alone in this cave for hundreds of years—trapped with nothing but the memories of what he has lost. And I just forced him to confront those memories head-on.

She wanted to say something to comfort him, but she knew any words she spoke could do little to ease his suffering. And so she watched him in silence. After a few minutes he seemed to regain his composure, and he stood up to his full height, his right hand clutching his massive spear.

"The storm is waning," he told her, his voice rough and catching slightly in his throat. "It's time to hunt, or tomorrow we will run out of food."

Cassandra nodded, though she sensed this was just an excuse to end their conversation. Clearly she had touched a nerve in her otherwise stoic host.

He disappeared into the swirling snow beyond the entrance, leaving her alone in the warmth of the cave. Doing her best to ignore the Sword in the far corner of the cave, she curled up near the fire and closed her eyes, hoping her sleep would not be plagued by more nightmares of Yasmin or the dark-winged hunter.

Chapter 6

ROGGEN WAS THE first to see the unusual tracks—a single set of footprints in the thin layer of snow, partially obscured by the hooves of the elk herd they'd been following since dawn. He held up his right hand in a fist, and the other five members of the Sun Blade hunting party immediately came to a halt.

Crouching, he took a closer look. They were fresh, and clearly human—medium-sized boots; but judging by the depth and the gait of the stride he guessed they were made by a woman rather than a man.

The footsteps headed off in the opposite direction of the herd. The clan was running low on stores; they couldn't abandon the hunt. But Roggen couldn't ignore the tracks, either—trespassers couldn't be allowed to cross through clan territory unchallenged.

Odd to find solitary tracks. Is she some kind of outcast from one of the neighboring clans?

Exile was a rare punishment, reserved only for the most heinous of crimes: treason, cold-blooded murder, or cowardice.

"Berlen," he called out to the largest of the hunters. "Follow these tracks. Find out who this woman is and why she's here."

Berlen hefted his spear and nodded. Just before he broke away from the rest of the group, Roggen grabbed his forearm.

"Be careful," the leader warned, seized by an urgent but vague premonition of danger. "She might be armed."

The big man scowled. "If you don't think I can handle it," he snarled, "then send someone else!"

Roggen released his grip, realizing he'd overstepped.

Berlen knows how to look out for himself. That's why you chose him.

"I just meant don't kill her unless you have to," Roggen back-pedaled, releasing his grip on his friend's arm. "You know how you get."

A lie, but one necessary to avoid giving offense. Mocking Berlen's infamous temper was far more acceptable than casting doubt on his martial prowess.

"I'll bring her back in one piece," Berlen promised, his bearded face breaking into a grin.

Feet crunching over the crystal carpet of snow blanketing the ground, Raven walked with a smooth, steady pace. Another storm was rolling in, but she ignored the icy wind clawing at the exposed flesh on the face and hands of her new human form, just as she ignored the rumbling of her empty stomach.

In her youth, she had spent many nights shivering on the desolate, ashen plains of Daemron's blighted kingdom. Before rising through the ranks of the Slayer's followers, she had fought and clawed with others of her kind to claim a share of the foul-tasting sludge that was the realm's only source of sustenance. But with power and position came privilege, and it had been decades since she'd felt the pains of cold or hunger.

Yet Raven understood that these physical torments were ephemeral, an illusion brought about by her transformation into a flesh-and-blood woman. Born and bred in a realm where the power of Chaos was not blunted by the Legacy, she was stronger and more resilient than the weak and physically vulnerable denizens of this world. And though she had cloaked herself in the essence of a mere mortal—a tall, dark-haired woman dressed in the style of the local clans—beneath the surface Chaos still sustained her true form.

It would have been possible to alter her appearance with a simple glamour, a superficial veneer that would blind the eyes of any ordinary men and women she encountered. But those touched by the power of Chaos wouldn't be fooled by such artifice. The mortal she had hunted, the one carrying the Crown, would still sense her presence, as would the Guardian who now gave her prey sanctuary. Like calling to like.

It wasn't these two she most feared, however. She had failed in her mission, and Orath did not forgive failure. By now, the leader of the Minions had probably sent others after her: most likely the Crawling Twins. Those who had come to power under Daemron's rule had not done so by being merciful, and any excuse to eliminate a potential rival would be eagerly seized. If they sensed Raven's presence nearby, they would be quick to turn on her.

Yet there was more to Raven's plan than simply hiding from the wrath of her fellow Minions. The Crown alone wouldn't be enough to bring down the Legacy and usher in Daemron's return. Orath was searching for the rest of the Talismans, and eventually he would learn what Raven already knew—the Sword was with the Guardian. She had felt its power just before she had abandoned her hunt and fled beyond the Guardian's reach, muted and faint but unmistakable. Merely returning to Orath with news of the Sword's location wouldn't be enough to atone for her failure. She would need to do much more if she wanted to redeem herself.

Soon the Crawling Twins would arrive. Unlike Raven, Erus and Cerus would not hesitate to challenge the Guardian. Together, they might defeat him though she suspected the battle would destroy them as well. She was not so willing to throw her life away. But if she could find some way to defeat the Guardian and claim both the Sword and the Crown for Daemron, she wouldn't just be returned to favor—she might even usurp Orath's position at the Slayer's right hand.

Until then, she would bide her time, dwelling among the locals and waiting for her chance to strike.

Berlen caught his first glimpse of the lone figure as the snow began to fall. From a distance, she seemed attractive: tall and broad-shouldered, with long, unbraided black hair fanning out behind her in the wind.

Seeing she wasn't armed, he broke into a run and closed the distance between them. Fifteen feet away he stopped, but the challenge he was about to call out died on his lips as the woman suddenly whirled around to face him.

Up close, he could see that his first impression was right: She was attractive. Beautiful, even. But there was something in the sharp features of her face that chilled him to the bone. Her eyes were cold and empty, and her expression was one of hateful contempt.

The warrior shook his head to dispel the irrational fear: the woman was half his size and wasn't carrying any kind of weapon.

"Who dares enter the land of the Sun Blade clan without permission?" he demanded.

The woman tilted her head to the side and her eyes narrowed, as if she was trying to understand the meaning of his words.

"Who are you?" Berlen repeated, gripping his spear tightly with both hands and holding the tip out toward her, waist high. "What clan are you from?"

Slowly, the woman began to walk toward him, her head tilting slowly from side to side like a hungry hawk contemplating its next meal.

Resisting the urge to take a step back, Berlen held his ground.

"Stop right there!" he shouted, raising the spear a few inches. "No closer!"

Either she didn't understand him, or she was ignoring him. Whatever the explanation, the tall woman continued to walk toward him.

Letting loose a battle roar, Berlen stepped forward and thrust the spear into the woman's midsection. The tip dove through her fur vest and plunged into her stomach, burying itself several inches deep.

The woman stopped her advance but didn't scream or cry out. She didn't fall to the ground, but instead wrapped her hands around the shaft of the spear protruding from her gut and slowly began to pull it out.

Berlen was still gripping the other end of the weapon, and he tried to resist by shoving the spear deeper into his adversary. But the woman barely noticed his attempt as she effortlessly slid the tip free. With a quick flick of her wrist she wrenched the shaft from Berlen's grasp and casually tossed the weapon aside.

The barbarian staggered back, his eyes transfixed by the gaping hole in her stomach. Ragged bits of flesh dangled down from the fist-sized puncture, but instead of blood gushing out, there was only a slow trickle of black ooze.

Following his gaze, the woman looked down at her wound. Then she grasped it by the dangling flaps of skin on either side and slowly began to pull it apart. There was a sick, wet sound as the tissue ripped, and she tilted her head back and screamed— a hideous, inhuman screech.

Berlen dropped to his knees and pressed his hands over his ears as blood began to drip from his nose. The woman continued to tear at her own flesh, peeling it off in great, dripping chunks. In seconds everything human had been stripped away, revealing a living shadow nightmare beneath: a naked, muscular woman with perfectly smooth, black skin and the head and great unfurling wings of a bird.

Scrambling on his hands and knees, Berlen tried to flee. But the shadow fell on him, ripping and tearing with vicious claws instead of fingers. Seizing his shoulder, it flipped him over so that he was facing the sky. Then a hooked talon sliced horizontally across Berlen's belly, carving a long, wide gash. The other hand plunged inside, seized his innards, and ripped them free, sending Berlen into shock.

Still alive, he lay paralyzed and helpless on the ground as the horror gorged itself on his stomach and intestines. The stench of his own eviscerated bowels wafted up into Berlen's nostrils, causing him to gag and retch. The mutilated remnants of his stomach reflexively clenched and a wave of agonizing pain sent his body into spastic convulsions.

After a few seconds the shadow broke off its gruesome feast and crouched beside him, tiny red eyes peering out over its cruelly curved beak as his seizures slowly passed.

Closing his eyes, Berlen silently prayed for death as his body finally went still. Before the merciful darkness could take him, a clawed hand seized him by the top of the head, two talons plunging deep into his skull.

Berlen's eyes snapped open and his jaw stretched in a silent scream as the monster began to feed on his memories. Ravenous, it took everything: his language, his culture, his clan, his friends, his family, and even his own identity were all stripped away.

When the creature finally finished and stepped away, all that was left of Berlen was a quivering lump of mindless flesh. Still technically alive, he saw but didn't register as the creature crouched low to the ground, its arms wrapped around its knees, a huddled lump of blackness on the white snow.

Gurgling and choking on the blood crawling up into his throat as the last of his life spilled out of his mangled stomach, his eyes blinked instinctively as the shadow was enveloped in an intense green light. When the light vanished seconds later, his stripped and ravaged mind couldn't even recognize that the monster had transformed into a perfect replica of himself.

His doppelgänger picked up the fallen spear and came to stand over him.

"Good-bye, Berlen," it said in the big man's own voice, though he no longer recognized the language of his own people.

And then it plunged the spear into his heart, ending his suffering.

The hunt was over and Berlen had still not returned. Roggen was on the verge of taking two of the others and setting off to look for him when the big man finally appeared, his unmistakable silhouette walking slowly through the falling snow toward them.

"What happened?" Roggen asked, setting aside the knife he'd been using to skin the elk at his feet.

Berlen didn't answer right away. Instead, his eyes flickered down to the bloody carcass on the snow.

"Where's the woman?" Roggen demanded, trying to snap him out of his stupor. "Did you find her?"

The big man turned his head away from the kill, and for an instant Roggen half imagined his eyes weren't their normal blue, but rather a bright, fiery red.

"She attacked me," Berlen said, speaking slowly. "She was . . . mad. I had to kill her. I had no choice."

"Did she say anything?" Roggen asked. "Anything that might tell us who she was?"

Berlen shook his head. "She was a Southlander," he said. "A young blond woman."

Something about the whole situation felt very wrong to Roggen, but he wasn't sure why. It almost felt like Berlen was lying, but he couldn't come up with any reason for his friend to do so.

"Maybe we should go examine the body," he wondered aloud. "Maybe there's some clue as to who she was or why she was here."

"The storm won't hold off much longer," Berlen countered. "We should finish dressing the kill and get the meat back to the camp."

"You're right," Roggen agreed after a moment's consideration. "We have more important things to worry about.

"Give me a hand," he added, dropping to one knee, his suspicions swept away by his desire to finish skinning his kill before the storm hit.

Chapter 7

FROM ATOP THE plateau, Scythe watched the rays of the early-evening sun crawling away from them toward the distant horizon. The temperature was already beginning to drop as the sun retreated, and dark storm clouds were rolling in. Remembering the frigid chill of the previous nights, she pressed herself close against Norr. The barbarian responded by wrapping his massive arms around her, swallowing her up.

She reveled in the heat of his fleshy embrace, knowing he would soon have to abandon her to take a turn on watch in case the Inquisitors camped below tried to sneak up on them under the cover of night.

Not very damn likely. Not when they can just wait us out.

They'd been trapped on the *Gerscheld* for three days now. They passed their time in silence. They had no food and no water, and there was nothing important enough to say that was worth wasting the spit required to speak. The only sound was the rumbling of their empty stomachs—a pointless objection by their bodies. They all knew they'd die of dehydration long before starvation took them. It was hard to imagine a worse way to go.

On the second day the fog that had surrounded them since leaving the Danaan forest had lifted, swept away by a harsh eastern front bringing the year's first real taste of winter. That night they huddled against the stones for shelter, shivering as the icy wind whipped across the plateau, bringing with it a burst of half-frozen rain. Pelted by the stinging drops, Scythe decided dying of thirst might be preferable to succumbing to exposure and hypothermia.

Perched high above the surrounding terrain, the temperature atop the *Gerscheld* had to feel twenty degrees colder than what the Inquisitors were dealing with down below. The conditions made sleep almost impossible, and by morning the hours of uncontrollable shivering had left her feeling utterly exhausted.

Today had been spent much like the first two—grim and silent as they waited for the inevitable: hungry, thirsty, and very, very cold. Every few hours another storm would roll through, bringing more rain and sleet. With another night rapidly approaching and more dark clouds looming in the distance, Scythe knew they couldn't hold out much longer.

She cast her gaze over the others, taking in the hopelessness and defeat etched on their features. Then her eyes fell on Keegan. The frail wizard lay on his side, huddled in a tight ball pressed up against the edge of one of the standing stones. He hadn't moved since the morning. His eyes were closed, his breathing shallow. Every few minutes his body would jerk or twitch and a soft, pitiful moan would escape his lips. Otherwise he was still and silent as the dead.

He might not make it to morning, Scythe realized. *And in another couple of days, we'll all be in the same state.*

Summoning the last of her reserves, Scythe shook off the dead-weight of Norr's arms and struggled to her feet.

"I'm not going out like this," she declared. "Not while I've still got strength enough left to take one or two of those Inquisitors down with me."

The men stared at her in silence. Then Norr slowly stood up beside her.

"We will die like warriors," he vowed, gently placing a heavy hand on her shoulder.

Scythe patted his hand, grateful to know they would face their end together. Then she turned to Vaaler. He met her eye and gave her a slight nod, then rose to his feet as well. To her surprise, Jerrod joined them a moment later.

"I thought you'd try to talk me out of it," she told him.

"When all hope is lost, it doesn't matter if we walk the path of a fool," he answered, and Scythe couldn't help but smile.

"What's our best strategy?" Vaaler asked. "Wait until nightfall and try to surprise them in the dark?"

"The Inquisitors are disciples of the Order," Jerrod reminded him. "Once the sun goes down you will struggle to see, but our Sight will be unhindered."

"I say we just charge down the path and try to catch them off guard," Scythe suggested. "Hit 'em hard and fast."

"Nobody's going anywhere," Keegan croaked.

His voice caused all of them to jump in surprise; Scythe had thought he'd slipped away into unconsciousness.

The young man didn't rise to his feet. He barely had the strength to sit up. His face was pale, his eyes glassy. But his voice was stronger when he spoke again.

"We need to wait."

"If we wait, we die," Scythe explained, speaking slowly as if to a confused child. "A slow, agonizing death. At least if we fight, the end will come quickly."

"Help is coming," Keegan countered. "I can see them."

Scythe tipped her head back to stare out at the vast emptiness of the tundra surrounding them. From the vantage point of the plateau they could see miles in every direction. Her eyes were sharp; she studied the landscape closely, turning slowly in a full circle, watching for signs of movement.

"I've been watching all day," Vaaler whispered, quiet enough that Keegan couldn't overhear. "There's nobody out there."

Scythe stepped away from the others and came over to crouch down beside the young mage.

"Nobody's coming to help us," she told him. "We're alone."

"I've seen them," Keegan insisted. "Wolves."

"Wolves?" Scythe asked.

"Wolves," he insisted. "A pack of wolves, coming to save us. I've seen them in my dreams. The pack leaders walk on two legs."

"Wolves that walk on two legs?" Scythe said, shaking her head in confusion.

"He's probably hallucinating," Vaaler offered.

"Maybe not," Norr chimed in. "Some of the clans use dogs to hunt game. The Pack Masters run with their animals. We call them the wolves with two legs."

"Is that what you saw, Keegan?" Jerrod asked, coming over to join Scythe. "Are Norr's people coming to help us?"

Scythe rolled her eyes in exasperation.

"Is this how your prophets see the future?" she demanded. "A few mumbled words, and you feed them a story you hope is true?"

"They're coming," Keegan repeated. Then his eyes flickered and closed, and he slumped forward.

Jerrod caught him and lowered him gently to lie flat on the cold ground. Keegan gave no indication he was aware of what was happening.

"Is this possible?" Vaaler asked after a few seconds of uncomfortable silence, directing his question at Norr. "Are your people coming to help us?"

"This is not the territory of my people," the big man explained. "But none of the clans like outsiders. The Pack Masters patrol this region; they protect it. They will see the Inquisitors as a threat that must be dealt with."

"If they even know we're here," Scythe objected. "You're all jumping to conclusions."

"Keegan is a True Prophet," Jerrod declared, turning away from the unconscious young man. "What he sees will come to pass."

"So we just sit around and wait?" Scythe asked, her voice betraying her frustration. "And if nobody shows up, then what? We die?"

"If we challenge the Inquisitors without help, we're dead anyway," Vaaler reminded her.

"But at least we'll go out fighting! At least we're not giving up!"

As usual, it was Norr's calm, deep voice that made her see past the red veil of anger that so often blinded her.

"We're not giving up, Scythe," he promised her. "We're holding on for our one chance to get out of this alive."

Scythe chewed her lip, trying to find a hole in his logic to rip apart his argument. But in the end she had to admit he was right—they were better off waiting.

She dropped to the ground beside Keegan, pulling her knees to her chest and wrapping her arms tight around them.

"You better be right about this," she warned him. Of course, he made no reply.

The storm hit them an hour after dusk. The thick clouds completely blotted out the moon, but the near-absolute darkness didn't bother Jerrod as he peered out into the distance with his second sight, desperately searching for some sign of their prophesied rescue.

He stood apart from the others, away from the meager shelter of the stone circle. Hailstones struck him with enough force to leave welts and bruises on his exposed skin, but he ignored the pain.

If Keegan is wrong—if no one is coming—then we are all doomed.

Jerrod knew all too well that prophets could be wrong. He had once been a Seer of the Order; he understood that his visions were only glimpses of possible futures. What he foresaw was never inevitable. Sometimes his dreams were warnings, showing him what would happen if he didn't take action to prevent it. Other times he dreamed of things that could only come to pass if he worked to make them real. Usually, though, his dreams were open to interpretation: symbols and portents with numerous meanings.

It was the same for the other Seers. A prophet's dreams were spawned by Chaos; by their very nature they lacked clarity. It was easy to misinterpret or be misled by a vision; it was possible to walk down the wrong path for the right reasons.

But with Keegan it was different. He was one of the Children of Fire. He wasn't just touched by the flames of Chaos; the divine spark of the Old Gods burned inside him. Or so Jerrod believed.

But what if I'm wrong? What if Keegan isn't special? What if he isn't the savior? Or worse, what if he is and I've led him down the wrong path?

"See anything yet?"

Jerrod barely managed to conceal his startled reaction. He'd been so focused on scouring the surrounding plains that he hadn't noticed Scythe's approach.

"Not yet," he admitted. "But I know they're coming."

"How long do you plan on waiting?" Scythe wanted to know. She stood with her shoulders hunched against the storm, her head down and her arms crossed tightly against her chest.

"If they don't come tonight, then what?" she pressed. "Do we wait another day? Two? Three? Or at some point do we finally decide to fight?"

"Are you really so eager to meet your death?" Jerrod asked.

Scythe shrugged. "If death is coming, I want it to be on my own terms.

"Besides," she added, "I've been in impossible situations before and fought my way out."

"I could have guessed that," the monk replied. "You have an irrational confidence in your own abilities."

"You put your faith in prophecies," she countered. "I like to put my faith in myself."

"Admirable. But surely there are times when you must doubt yourself."

"Sometimes," Scythe admitted. "But I usually get over it."

In spite of himself, Jerrod smiled.

"What about you?" Scythe wanted to know. "You ever have any doubts about your faith?"

Jerrod didn't answer for a long time. When he finally broke the silence all he said was, "They're coming."

"You can't ever admit you're wrong, can you?" Scythe sighed.

"No," Jerrod clarified. "I can see them now. A few miles off. They're coming."

On the very edges of his Sight's awareness, he could just make out a score of canines and three humans, crouched low to the ground as they ran and somehow keeping pace with their four-legged companions. The pack closed in quickly, covering the last few miles to the *Gerscheld* at a full run.

The animals were massive; far larger than the domesticated dogs in the south. Most were covered with thick black fur though a handful were pure white. Their sharp white teeth gleamed brightly against their black mouths and gums, and their lupine eyes glowed yellow in the night.

The humans—two women and one man, he realized as they drew closer—were clad in heavy pelts from head to toe to shield them against the cold. Jerrod had expected them to be armed, but they carried no weapons, though their bare hands sported half-inch-long fingernails filed to sharp points.

As the pack neared, he could hear the humans communicating through a mix of whistles and long, high-pitched howls that pierced the wind and rain. In response, the dogs fanned out, with several circling around to cut off any chance for the Inquisitors to escape.

Jerrod knew the Inquisitors had no intention of trying to run. They were young and passionate: too eager to prove themselves to the new Pontiff to even consider retreat. However, despite their enthusiasm, they had no chance of victory.

Outnumbered four to one, their supernatural speed and strength wouldn't be enough to overcome the unfavorable odds. Not against this kind of enemy. The Order trained its warriors to fight human foes, not animals. The attacks and counters that proved so devastating against an armed opponent would be far less effective against a swarming pack of savage beasts.

More importantly, the mystical ability of the monks to peer into an enemy's mind to anticipate and counter every move wouldn't work. The dogs weren't rational and calculating; they didn't rely on strategy and technique. Their attacks would be driven by raw and brutal instincts, making their actions impossible to predict.

Sort of like Scythe.

"When the fighting starts, we can hit them from behind," the young woman suggested eagerly, almost as if she sensed that Jerrod was thinking about her. "They won't stand a chance with enemies on all sides."

"That wouldn't be wise," Norr warned.

The barbarian had braved the storm to come to stand with Scythe and Jerrod once the howls began to pierce the night, leaving Vaaler to watch over Keegan in the shelter of the stone circle.

"The dogs will attack anyone who isn't part of the pack," Norr explained. "They could just as easily turn on us as the Inquisitors."

"But if the Inquisitors win the battle, we're not any better off than we were before," Scythe objected.

"They won't," Jerrod assured her.

When the attack came it was quick, violent, and decisive. Even through the storm and the night's gloom, Jerrod's awareness allowed him to witness the slaughter in all its graphic detail.

The pack rolled over the Inquisitors like a wave of fur, teeth, and claws. Spinning their staves, the Inquisitors flipped, spun, and twirled with terrifying speed. But the dogs never faltered, never hesitated. The sharp crack of bone as a hound's ribs were broken with a precise strike was drowned out by the wet rip of an Achilles tendon being torn out by sharp teeth. The yelp of pain as the butt of a staff was driven into a wolflike eye was offset by the snarling snap of jaws clamping down on a wrist and refusing to let go. Soon, even the screams of pain as flesh was shredded and torn into bloody chunks by savage fangs couldn't rise above the barking, baying cacophony of the hunt.

The Pack Masters never even entered the fray, content to merely watch as their pets dragged the Inquisitors down and literally ripped them apart.

That's why they don't carry weapons, Jerrod realized. *They don't need them.*

The battle was over in less than ten minutes. Once the last Inquisitor had fallen, the shrill whistles of the Pack Masters called the dogs to heel though four of the animals were too injured from the fight to answer.

With his Sight, Jerrod watched as the humans tended to the fallen hounds. Two were put down, their wounds too serious to treat. The other pair were bandaged with a care and tenderness that contrasted sharply with the brutality of the recent massacre.

As the Pack Masters tended to their injured animals, the fury of the storm passed and the night fell into a grim silence. Jerrod and the others waited without speaking, each hoping the deadly pack would simply move on. Of course, that didn't happen.

"They know we're up here," Norr finally acknowledged. "The dogs can smell us."

"Great," Scythe muttered. "They saved us from the Inquisitors. Now who saves us from them?"

"Let me go talk to them," Norr offered.

"No!" Scythe snapped. "Those beasts will rip you to shreds!"

"The Inquisitors were Outlanders," Norr explained. "They

were not worthy of anything but death. But the *Gerscheld* is a sacred place among all the clans; it's a place of parley. Even though I'm not one of their own, the Pack Masters might be willing to strike a bargain with me."

"Because you're an Easterner?" Scythe asked.

"That's my hope," Norr said, but Jerrod sensed he was hiding something.

"I'm coming with you," Scythe declared.

"No—they see you and they'll set the dogs loose," Norr warned. "Any of you. Stay here until I come back."

Scythe opened her mouth like she wanted to say something else, then closed it when she realized there were no other arguments to be made.

Jerrod stepped forward and clasped the other man's meaty wrist in a firm grasp.

"May the Old Gods watch over you," he said.

"They don't hold much sway among my people," Norr reminded him.

The big man turned and marched slowly away, limping slightly as he made his way down the *Gerscheld's* twisting path to the waiting pack below.

Watching Norr disappear into the gloom of the night, Scythe felt like throwing up. She knew he was right—he had to go down alone. But she didn't have to like it.

Despite his outward calm, she could tell he was nervous. Anxious. There was something he wasn't telling them.

Maybe he doesn't really believe they'll parley with him.

It had been too dark for Scythe to see the battle at the base of the *Gerscheld,* but it wasn't hard to imagine what had happened from the sounds rising from below. She felt no sympathy for the Inquisitors, but getting ripped apart by dogs was a bad way to go.

What if I hear those sounds again?

She tried not to imagine her lover suffering such a gruesome fate, but the possibility of it lingered in her mind.

From the night, she heard Norr call out a greeting as he neared the bottom of the path. A low growl rolled up from the pack, and Scythe's heart began to pound. A sharp whistle from one of the Pack Masters cut the growling short.

The silence that followed was almost unbearable, but it was better than the sickening sounds of the pack taking another target down. Wet and cold, Scythe shivered as the minutes passed.

After a while, she began to pace, trying to burn off her anxiety and helpless frustration with quick, angry strides.

What's taking so long? What's going on down there?

She stopped when she heard the sound of someone coming up the path, freezing in place.

"They've agreed to help us," Norr said, speaking just as his enormous silhouette materialized from the gloom.

Relief hit Scythe so hard she gasped and struggled to catch her breath. Ignoring the others, she raced over and threw herself at Norr. He caught her easily, lifting her up and drawing her into his chest. She wrapped her arms around his massive neck, burying her face in his shoulder so that she could feel his beard softly tickling the back of her neck. In the embrace neither of them spoke, content simply to hold each other close.

"Do they have any supplies they can spare?" Jerrod asked after several seconds, intruding on their private moment.

"We're going with them," Norr explained, loosening his grip and letting Scythe gently slide back down so that her feet could touch the ground. "They'll escort us to their camp."

"Keegan isn't strong enough to walk," Jerrod pointed out.

"I'll carry him," Norr offered. "It's only a few miles."

"They have supplies there?"

Norr nodded. "They found our horses after they fled. That's

why they were patrolling this area. They knew that Outlanders had entered their territory."

"Maybe it would be better for Keegan if we brought one of the horses back for him to ride," Scythe suggested.

"The horses are gone," Norr said. "Winter is coming. The herds are migrating to the Southlands. Food is scarce, and the pack needs to feed."

Scythe's stomach churned, but she didn't say anything else as Norr walked over to where Vaaler was watching over the fallen wizard.

"How is he?"

The exiled prince shook his head. "Not good. He needs food. Water. Warm clothes."

Norr nodded. Then, ignoring his bad leg, he bent over and scooped Keegan up, cradling him in his arms like a child. The smaller man groaned, but otherwise didn't stir.

"Follow me and stay close," Norr said. "No sudden movements."

He led them single file down the path, limping slightly. Jerrod quickly fell into step behind him, staying as close to Keegan as possible. Scythe went next, with Vaaler trailing a few steps behind.

With the passing of the storm, the moon gave enough light for them to pick their way carefully down the path. When they reached the bottom, one of the Pack Masters was waiting for them—a tall woman clad in a heavy cloak stitched from animal pelts. She was flanked on either side by one of her pets. To the left was a large, black hound, its dark fur making it blend into the gloom so that it almost seemed to be a creature of shadow. The animal to her right was white as snow though its muzzle and chest were flecked with dark maroon stains from the recent battle.

The Pack Master whistled twice, and the rest of the dogs came over, moving slowly. They began to circle the newcomers, sniffing curiously.

Scythe tried to stay completely still as she felt the hot breath of the beasts snuffling up against her leg but couldn't contain a small shudder. She didn't like dogs; in her experience they were either hungry, vicious strays wandering the streets of Callastan, or trained killers guarding the estates of the wealthy.

None of those mutts would stand a chance against these brutes. They're more like wolves than dogs.

The inspection lasted several seconds before the Pack Master called them off with another whistle.

She said something to Norr, speaking in the Eastern tongue, then turned away and started off.

"It's time to go," Norr explained.

"What about those two?" Scythe asked, nodding over to where the other Pack Masters were still milling about in the darkness.

"They're harvesting what's left of the Inquisitors."

"Harvesting?" Scythe mumbled, her stomach turning once again.

"Meat and bones," Norr confirmed in a grim whisper. "The pack has to feed."

Chapter 8

THE BLACK LAKE needed no other name. Located deep within the Danaan forest, its waters were the color of ink, even beneath the midday sun.

There were no settlements along the shore—the murky liquid was too foul and toxic to drink. No fish swam beneath the surface, and even the trees seemed to keep a distance, resulting in a wide band of barren soil that ringed the shoreline.

Andar didn't like this place. There was something sinister about the lake beyond the poisonous waters—a malevolent power hidden below the surface. In ancient times, Danaan sorcerers had tried to study the Black Lake, but expeditions to plumb its mysterious depths had always ended with tragedy and death. The lake became anathema—a cursed location that the Danaan simply avoided. Until now.

At Orath's urging, Rianna was preparing her people for war. The armies of the North Forest were massing; soon they would venture forth into the Frozen East on a crusade to reclaim the stolen Ring, crushing any who dared oppose them.

Andar had argued against such a course. He had tried to make his Queen understand that they needed to focus on rebuilding Ferlhame and securing their borders. But Rianna was deaf to his counsel, and she'd brushed his words aside.

"It's time," a thin, reedy voice whispered at Andar's side, causing him to jump.

Orath had crept up silently behind him, flanked on either side by Draco and Gort, the companions he had mentioned upon first meeting the Queen. The High Sorcerer nodded in reply, doing his best to keep his expression from revealing the revulsion he felt every time the Minions were near.

As disconcerting as Orath's unnatural appearance was, the other two were far more monstrous. The one called Gort was a bestial abomination—eight feet tall and covered in fur the color of dry blood. Its head was somewhere between human and simian though it was topped by a pair of stocky horns. Its body was thick with muscle and fat. Its long arms hung low, so that its savage four-inch claws reached almost to its knees, and a long, thin tail trailed behind, twitching and writhing.

The second—Draco—was a reptilian horror: the head of an alligator atop a humanoid body buried beneath heavy green scales. A pair of massive leather wings were folded close against its back. Unfurled, Andar imagined, they would evoke memories of the flying wyrm that had razed Ferlhame.

"Begin the preparations," Orath instructed.

Neither Gort nor Draco ever spoke—whatever twisted mutations Chaos had wrought upon them had rendered them mute. But even after revealing his hideous allies, Orath still had the Queen's ear. After listening to the Minion's offer, Rianna had granted him authority second only to her own. Unwilling to betray his monarch, Andar had no choice but to obey.

He turned to address the assemblage of Danaan mages who had joined him on the shores of the Black Lake, subtlety calling on the power of Chaos to augment his voice.

"We are about to undertake a powerful and dangerous ritual," he began. "We must be vigilant in our preparations; every detail must be precise and perfect. If we are careless or lax, we will unleash a terrible evil upon this land."

There was no need to give further warning; the destruction of Ferlhame was still fresh in their minds. They understood the consequences if the ritual failed.

But, Andar silently wondered, *what will the consequences be if we succeed?*

Orath and the other Minions moved slowly among the Danaan mages as they painted arcane symbols of power on the dark, lifeless soil that encircled the lake, watching over their work with a highly critical eye.

He no longer projected the magical aura of authority and influence; after several days of meetings with the Queen and her council his subtle spell had wormed itself deep into her psyche. She trusted him above all others now, and though the aura had been only a minor drain on his reserves, there was no point in wasting his power any more than he had to.

The Danaan did their best to ignore him and his two monstrous companions though he could sense their unease. Crouched on their hands and knees, they kept their eyes focused on their task, carefully transcribing the intricate runes into the earth. Occasionally they would stop to check for accuracy against the symbols on the parchments Orath had drawn for them, but otherwise they worked without pause.

Despite their apparent diligence, Orath was determined to personally inspect every rune. Spells of summoning were complicated; a single mistake could disrupt the ritual, allowing the beast that slumbered at the bottom of the Black Lake to break free from his control and turn against him.

It wasn't that he feared betrayal; these mortals were like sheep— docile and mindlessly loyal to their Queen. But the Danaan weren't well versed in rituals and spells. Chaos clung to the ancient trees of the North Forest, allowing the mages to call upon its power with relative ease. Those with the Gift didn't need talismans, symbols, and words of power to perform magic; it came to them naturally and instinctively.

The coming ritual would be different. Waking the ogre required the power of Old Magic; without the proper safeguards the Chaos Orath needed to bind the monster to his will would surge out of control.

Though not as powerful as the dragon that had ravaged Ferlhame, the ogre was still a formidable foe—a mindless brute driven by insatiable hunger and unquenchable bloodlust. Unfettered, it would rip the Danaan limb from limb, devouring their quivering, still-warm flesh before turning its attention to Orath and the other Minions.

Together, he, Draco, and Gort might have the strength to defeat it, but even a victory would drain Orath's slowly dwindling power. Cut off from the Sea of Fire by the Legacy, he would be weak and vulnerable, and he had no intention of putting himself in such a position. And they needed the ogre if they had any hope of reclaiming the Ring.

Each of the Talismans was unique; each called upon Chaos in precise and specific ways. Unlike the dragon, the ogre was a beast of the earth. Born of sludge and stone, it was more resistant to the arcane magic of the Ring. Back when Daemron still served the Old Gods, he had defeated the ogre with the power of the Sword—Chaos shaped into a tangible, physical tool. But the Ring unleashed Chaos in the form of pure energy; the storm that had felled the dragon would barely slow the ogre.

Even if the mortal uses the Ring to obliterate the entire Danaan force, the ogre will simply walk up and rip his arm off, then deliver the Talisman to my waiting hand.

Assuming, of course, the ritual went as planned.

— — — — —

"Lei. Sharl. Terress. Ko. Lei. Sharl. Terress. Ko."

The voices of the Danaan mages rose up in a steady, rhythmic chant, reciting the mantra Orath had taught them. Andar joined in, a reluctant participant in the Minion's ritual. But while the words fell from his lips, his mind wandered.

"Lei. Sharl. Terress. Ko. Lei. Sharl. Terress. Ko."

It had taken several hours before Orath had been satisfied with the preparations for the ritual, examining and reexamining the runes to ensure they were without flaw. By the time the ritual began, night had fallen. The full moon shining down gave enough illumination to see even though the dark waters of the lake reflected none of its light.

"Lei. Sharl. Terress. Ko. Lei. Sharl. Terress. Ko."

The words were strange and unfamiliar. Andar didn't know their meaning, but he knew their purpose. This was magic in the style of the humans to the south; many of the specifics were foreign to him, but the Danaan High Sorcerer still understood the underlying theory.

The symbols and words helped to call upon the power of Chaos, drawing it out from the ancient trees of the forest, concentrating and focusing it. Yet even though the Danaan mages were an essential element of the ritual, Andar had no illusions about who was in control of the spell.

The chant was too short and too simple to have any significant effect on the shaping of the Chaos. It was only to unite the will of the Danaan in a common purpose—Orath's purpose. They were conduits: Whatever power they gathered would be bent and shaped by the leader of the Minions.

"Lei. Sharl. Terress. Ko. Lei. Sharl. Terress. Ko."

Andar could sense the strength of the spell building. The still air became hot and heavy until sweat was running down his brow. In his ears he felt a growing pressure, causing them to pop again and again. A tingling in the back of his skull ran through his jaw and into his teeth, uncomfortable and unnerving.

A fierce wind sprang up out of nowhere, swirling around them, tearing at Andar's hair and clothes. The Black Lake began to bubble, like a simmering pot. The wind intensified, knocking several of the Danaan mages off balance. But even as their bodies stumbled, their words did not, and the chant continued unabated.

"*Lei. Sharl. Terress. Ko. Lei. Sharl. Terress. Ko.*"

There was a deep, heavy crash, like a clap of thunder from far beneath the earth. Andar didn't hear it so much as feel it in his feet. A second later, a geyser erupted from the center of the lake, spewing fetid water fifty feet into the air.

Something roared, an inhuman sound of anger and pain so loud it caused Andar to reflexively cover his ears. More geysers shot up from the lake, showering the Danaan with the foul liquid and releasing the sickening odor of noxious gases trapped for centuries beneath the surface.

Struggling against his rising gorge as the stench rolled over them, Andar continued the chant. The geysers suddenly stopped and the wind fell still. The air around them grew instantly cold, causing Andar to shiver uncontrollably. And then the ogre breached the surface of the lake and crawled out onto the shore.

The creature was massive: a squat, powerful mound of muscle. Even though it was hunched forward—the knuckles of its enormous three-fingered hands braced on the ground to help its thick, stubby legs support its girth—it dwarfed the Danaan.

The beast was naked, its bloated, graying flesh covered with sores and slime dredged up from the bottom of the lake. It had four oversized teeth protruding from its lips like tusks, two on top and two beneath. Long, uneven strands of filthy black hair hung from its disproportionately large head, which tilted side to side at unnatural angles to fix its tiny yellow eyes on the circle of chanting wizards.

"Lei. Sharl. Terress. Ko. Lei. Sharl. Terress. Ko."

Its gaze settled on Orath and the other Minions standing off to one side, and the ogre reared up to its full fifteen-foot height. Thrusting its heavy fists high into the air, it slammed them onto the earth and bellowed its defiance.

Orath nearly gasped aloud when the ogre first appeared, awed by its magnificence. A physical monstrosity, it was both repulsive and compelling. It radiated power—the raw, untamed power of Old Magic not seen in the mortal realms since the Cataclysm.

Drawing on the strength of the Danaan wizards, Orath reached out with an invisible hand and touched the ogre's mind. It was bestial, primal—driven by simple instinct and base emotion: hunger and hate.

Sensing the intrusion, the ogre turned to face him, its massive, tooth-filled maw unleashing a deafening roar.

Steeling himself, Orath began a chant of his own. Not the simple, rhythmic mantra of the Danaan but the intricate words of power that would dominate and bind the Chaos Spawn to him, enslaving it to Orath's will.

The ogre staggered back as if physically struck, its grotesque features twisting into a mask of horror and fear. It tried to turn, to flee back into the depths of the Black Lake, but Orath refused to let it go.

Speaking so quickly his words were an indecipherable buzz, the Minion raised his left hand, palm up and his long, thin fingers spread wide. Slowly, he clenched it into a fist.

Thrashing and wailing, the ogre realized escape was impossible. In an instant, it switched from flight to fight. Beneath its bloated flesh muscles rippled and tensed as it prepared to charge its enemy.

Orath brought up his right hand, arm extended and palm out, to keep the beast at bay. The ogre hesitated, its momentum temporarily halted. Orath held it there, frozen in its tracks, as his words shifted to a deeper pitch. Once again, he reached out to the ogre's mind, seeking to bind it to his own.

It snarled in response and hunched low to the ground, using its hands to gain leverage in the soil. Slowly, it began to crawl toward Orath.

Realizing the ogre's will was stronger than he'd anticipated, the Minion switched his chant. The words took on a higher, keening pitch as he reached out to the circle of Danaan wizards. Instead of just uniting their latent power, he began to siphon it off, rapidly and violently draining every last drop of Chaos from their blood in a desperate attempt to bring the ogre to heel.

Andar sensed the change in the spell immediately; he had a deep and instinctive connection with Chaos. But it took him a few moments to recognize what was happening. By the time he realized that Orath wasn't just calling on the Danaans' power, but their very life essence, several of the weaker mages had already collapsed into unconsciousness.

The High Sorcerer tried to pull away, but he was caught up in the power of Orath's spell. Unbidden, his lips continued the rhythmic chanting, unable to break free. Inside, he felt as if he was being ripped apart: bits and pieces torn off to feed the Minion's hunger as he battled the Chaos Spawn. He was being drained; sucked dry—soon all that remained would be a withered, lifeless husk.

But it wasn't just his own death he felt. United by their chant, Andar felt the suffering of all the Danaan—just as they felt his. A shared torment; an unbearable torture multiplied dozens of times over.

That's it. That's the key.

Alone, he wasn't strong enough to break free from Orath's spell.

But he wasn't alone. He and the other Danaan mages were as one, their minds and their power united through the ceaseless chant. Together, they might be able to resist the Minion.

But should we?

Breaking free would end the ritual prematurely, leaving the ogre unfettered. Without the constraints of Orath's spell, the Chaos Spawn would wreak further destruction on the Danaan kingdom. And without the ogre, the Queen would never be able to reclaim the Ring.

He—like all the other Danaan—had sworn an oath of allegiance to his monarch. They'd all vowed to give their lives in the service of their liege. To end the spell now would be treason.

No! To abandon Rianna now, when she is weak and vulnerable, is the real treason! We cannot leave her under the influence and control of Orath! We must fight for our kingdom and our Queen!

There wasn't time to reach out to the others and explain his plan; by then Orath would have already taken too much. His only hope was to try to call upon the will of his fellow Danaan and hope they followed him, immediately and without question. If they hesitated out of confusion, fear, or misguided loyalty to the Queen, or if they were too overwhelmed by their own suffering and agony to join him, then all was lost.

There's no other choice. We have to do this now.

As the ogre continued its slow but inevitable advance, Orath continued to feed on the Danaan wizards, drinking deep of the Chaos in their blood. The Queen might be angered over their deaths, but Orath was confident he could explain it away as an unforeseeable accident. And without Andar to oppose him, it would be even easier to manipulate and control her.

The power flowing into him had gone from a steady stream to a raging river. Orath continued to take it in, gathering it for a final burst that would break the ogre's will once and for all. And then suddenly it was gone.

Entirely focused on the ogre, he didn't sense the gathering will of his victims until it was too late. Somehow, they found the strength to wrench themselves free of the spell at the last possible second; the chanting circle fell instantly silent as all the Danaan simultaneously collapsed, exhausted but alive.

The ogre sensed it, too. The power holding him back dissolved away, and the beast reacted by springing forward in a mad charge.

Fortunately, Gort and Draco were there, stepping forward to take the place of the Danaan once they saw them fall. Unable to form the words of the ritualistic chant with their malformed mouths, they gave support to Orath by opening themselves up fully to their leader so he could draw upon their power to tame the beast.

They don't understand what really happened, Orath realized. *They just think the Danaan faltered because they were weak.*

The power of the other Minions washed over Orath in a massive wave, and he swallowed it all in a single gulp. In an instant the ogre's rush was halted, the beast frozen in place. But the creature's will still refused to yield.

As he had done with the Danaan, Orath began to draw on the Chaos trapped deep within the other Minions, sucking it from their blood and the marrow of their bones. Like the mortals, Gort and Draco recognized what he was doing and tried to pull away. But the Danaan had caught Orath off guard. This time he was prepared, and he would not allow the ritual to end prematurely.

Gort howled and barked, Draco hissed and screamed as Orath bled them dry. His companions were strong, but Orath was stronger. It was over in seconds, their bodies transformed into desiccated, mummified husks that fell lifeless to the earth.

The sudden influx of power allowed Orath to lash out with one last, desperate attempt to crush the ogre's will. The beast roared and thrashed its head from side to side, then collapsed onto the ground. Whimpering, it curled up into a ball and lay still.

Orath tried to approach, but his body was completely spent from the ritual. Staggering in the soft earth, he fell face forward where he lay motionless and only semiconscious.

When he heard the ogre begin to move once more he struggled to rise but could only manage to roll over onto his back. He saw the beast was crawling toward him again, and this time Orath was powerless to stop it.

The creature slowly rose to its feet as it reached his side, a foul-smelling mountain of swollen gray flesh looming above him. Orath braced for the killing blow, knowing a single swing of one massive fist could pulverize him into nothing. Instead, the ogre dropped to one knee and bowed its head.

"Master," it croaked out in a thick, wet voice.

Chapter 9

KEEGAN COULDN'T REMEMBER much about the journey to the barbarian camp. He vaguely remembered the arrival of the Pack Masters, and he could recall Norr carrying him as they trudged through the wind and rain. Everything else was a hazy blur of fever dreams and hallucinations.

At one point he'd imagined Norr as some kind of monster—an ogre that had crawled up from the bottom of a dark and sinister lake, coming to kill him. Another time, he imagined himself to be an elk, racing across the tundra with an army of barking, slavering dogs in pursuit. Most of the time, however, he'd just slept.

But he was feeling better now. Two days had passed, or maybe three. It was hard to track the passage of time inside the small deerskin tent. Apart from Vaaler's checking up on him numerous times, he'd had no contact whatsoever with the outside world.

Keegan welcomed the visits from his friend, though he was disappointed none of the others had come to see him. Especially Scythe. At first, he'd been too weak to wonder about their absence; just staying awake and eating the warm soup Vaaler fed him was all the effort he could manage. This morning, however, he had woken up feeling refreshed and strong. And he couldn't help but think something strange was going on.

Maybe she's avoiding you because you made a fool of yourself last time you talked to her.

Even if that were true, what about Jerrod and Norr? He couldn't think of any good reason why they wouldn't have at least come to check on him.

Knowing he wouldn't find any answers trapped inside the tent, he kicked away the heavy hides he'd been sleeping under. Someone had removed his boots; in the darkness of the tent he fumbled around until he found them tucked away in the corner.

Before he could pull them on, a stream of light poured in, followed by a cold blast of air as Vaaler squeezed through the tent's small slit of an entrance.

"You're awake," the Danaan noted with surprise.

The tent was too small to stand up in, so Vaaler had to crawl forward on his hands and knees. Once fully inside, he turned and closed the entrance behind him, quickly lashing the thin sinew strips dangling from the hide-flap door to the tent's bone frame.

"Are you hungry?"

With the flap closed it was once again dark inside, turning both men into dim silhouettes. But Keegan was able to see that his friend was holding something out toward him.

"Jerky. Figured you'd be sick of soup by now."

Keegan took the strip of dried meat and tore into it, his stomach rumbling. It was so tough to chew, it made his jaw ache, and so salty, it made him wince. But Vaaler was right—he'd had his fill of soup.

"How come you're the only one who's come by to see me?" Keegan asked between bites.

"Sorry if I'm boring you," Vaaler said, taking mock offense.

"I'm serious," Keegan pressed. "Jerrod and the others—are they okay?"

"We're all alive and well," Vaaler assured him. "But everyone's been acting a little strange since we got here."

"How so?"

"Jerrod told me he doesn't want to put you in danger. The Pack

Masters don't trust him; they're watching him pretty close. He probably figures it's best to keep his distance. Avoid drawing any extra attention your way."

"Normally he won't let me out of his sight," Keegan muttered. "Why the sudden change of heart?"

"I think seeing the pack take down the Inquisitors rattled him," Vaaler explained. "He's afraid the Ice Fangs will set their dogs on him if he so much as breathes funny."

"Ice Fangs?"

"That's the name of this clan. I think the literal translation is actually "snow tooth," but Ice Fang sounds more impressive."

"Did Norr tell you that?"

"No. I've studied Verlsung enough to pick up a few phrases here and there."

Keegan recognized the formal name of the Eastern language from his studies under Rexol, though most people in the Southlands simply called it Clan-speak.

Keegan wasn't surprised by the admission, and he suspected Vaaler's command of the foreign tongue was far greater than he made it seem. He spoke Allrish, the language of the Southlands, without any accent whatsoever—it was almost easy to forget that Danaan was his native tongue.

He's probably just as proficient in Clan-speak.

Vaaler had expected to rule the Danaan kingdom one day; it only made sense for him to try to learn the culture, customs, and tongues of neighboring peoples. And during their time together under Rexol, Vaaler had shown a fluent mastery over the strange words and arcane chants they'd had to memorize for their spells.

He always learned stuff quicker than I did. Probably still remembers every word of it, too. He would have been the perfect apprentice—or the perfect King—if Chaos hadn't played such a cruel trick and left him blind to the Gift and the Sight.

"Norr hasn't been talking to anyone lately," Vaaler continued, oblivious to Keegan's train of thought. "It's like he's gone into some kind of deep depression. Even Scythe can't snap him out of it."

"That's why she hasn't come to see me," Keegan realized. "She's worried about Norr."

"He's keeping secrets," Vaaler added. "Big ones. There's more to his past than he lets on."

"What makes you so sure?"

"The Ice Fangs don't know I can understand them. I've heard some things."

Keegan understood his friend's hesitation. Norr had kept his secrets from the group for a reason; exposing them might seem like a type of betrayal in the loyal Danaan's eyes. But keeping the truth hidden could put all of them at risk.

"If you know something important, you can't keep it to yourself," Keegan told him.

"Okay," Vaaler relented, clearly relieved to finally be able to share his news with someone else. "But you can't tell Jerrod or Scythe. They tend to overreact. That could make things worse."

"Worse? You mean they're already bad?"

"The Ice Fangs didn't exactly rescue us," Vaaler confessed. "We're not guests of the clan; we're prisoners."

"What do they plan to do with us?" Keegan asked.

"I think they're planning to turn us over to another clan in exchange for supplies and weapons. Ransom us off, basically. They've sent envoys to the Rock Spirit clan. Or maybe Stone Heart is more accurate. Names are difficult to translate properly."

"Let's go with Stone Spirit," Keegan suggested.

"Fair enough," Vaaler conceded. "But whatever we call them, I think they're Norr's former people."

"I can understand why he wouldn't want to tell us," Keegan admitted. "Jerrod wouldn't like the idea of our being prisoners."

"There's more," Vaaler said after a brief pause. "Most of the

Eastern clans are nomadic. They don't normally take prisoners—they just use up food and resources the clan has been storing up for the winter. If they don't kill you in battle, they'll usually just strip your weapons and supplies and set you off to fend for yourself."

"Sounds like a death sentence to me," Keegan muttered.

"Depends on the weather and how close the rest of your own clan is," Vaaler countered with a shrug. "It's just the way things are done out here. But if they capture someone special, they might make an exception."

"What do you mean by special?"

"Somebody important. Somebody so valuable that another clan would be willing to pay a heavy ransom to get them back. Maybe a famous warrior or champion. Or, more likely, someone closely related to the clan leader's family."

"You think Norr is some kind of barbarian royalty?"

"The clans only take prisoners if the payoff is going to be worth the cost of keeping someone around until the exchange can be made," Vaaler noted. "The Ice Fangs figured Norr was valuable enough to keep all five of us around."

"So this is a good thing," Keegan said. "If Norr's that important, then the Stone Spirits will make the exchange. Then he can get them to help us."

"Just because you're royalty doesn't mean your people want you back," Vaaler cautioned bitterly. "We don't know why Norr left in the first place. Maybe he was sent into exile. Maybe he fled because he lost some kind of power struggle.

"The Stone Spirits might not want him back. If they refuse to pay the ransom, the best case is that we get set loose on the tundra with no food or weapons."

Keegan didn't want to ask about the worst case. *I bet the dogs are always hungry.*

"And even if they pay the ransom," Vaaler continued, "it might be because Norr fled some kind of clan justice. They could want him back just to finish him off."

"No wonder Norr is upset," Keegan muttered. "Any more good news?"

Vaaler shook his head.

"So what do you think we should do?"

"We don't have a lot of options. We can't fight our way out of here, and if we try to run, the dogs will hunt us down."

"So we just sit and wait to find out if the Stone Spirits will pay the ransom?"

"The Ice Fangs are expecting an answer in the next day or so," Vaaler told him.

Instead of replying, Keegan popped the last bit of jerky into his mouth, grimly chewing the leathery meat until he could force it down his throat.

"I'm going to wander around the camp and see if I can learn anything else," Vaaler said to break the silence.

Keegan watched his friend go, his thoughts bleak. Once the Danaan was gone, he shoved his boots in the corner and crawled back under the hides. For some reason, he no longer felt up to leaving the tent.

It actually took three more days for the Ice Fangs to get their reply. During that time, Vaaler could feel the bitter, hateful gazes from the Pack Masters and the other threescore members of the clan following him wherever he went.

Outlander. Interloper. You eat our food and take the heat from our fires; you sleep in our tents, and you give us nothing in return. You have no place here, you do not belong.

Vaaler shrugged their hatred off; he was used to being an outsider. But he knew their smoldering resentment would explode into violent anger if they didn't get the answer they wanted from the Stone Spirits.

Fortunately, it didn't come to that. When the envoys finally returned they came bearing good news for the Ice Fang clan—their ransom terms had been met.

Of course, that wasn't how Norr explained it to the others.

"The scouts have tracked down my people," he told them in a brief gathering. "My family. My clan. The Pack Masters will escort us to them tomorrow morning."

The big man was clearly relieved as he delivered the news; obviously, he hadn't been sure the Stone Spirits would want him back.

But we still don't know why they want you back, Vaaler thought. *And it might not end well.*

Scythe reacted to the announcement with uncharacteristic reserve. She simply squeezed Norr's hand, and in a subdued voice muttered, "I imagine it will be good to see them again."

Norr nodded and gave a noncommittal grunt.

She knows he's still keeping something from her, Vaaler recognized, *but she can't bring herself to ask him about it. Maybe she's afraid of what he'll tell her.*

Jerrod's response was stoic silence, betraying no hint of his emotional state.

He's used to being in control. Taking charge. He doesn't like being forced to sit around and rely on others.

Keegan and Vaaler both played along with the ruse, smiling and congratulating Norr on the pending reunion. They gave no indication that they knew more than they were letting on save for a single, shared glance of concern.

The next morning they set out on foot, leaving the Ice Fang camp behind. The weather had warmed slightly; the wind was light and the sun was shining. The Pack Masters led the way, accompanied by a half dozen other members of the clan.

The dogs came with them, too, swarming around the humans with seemingly boundless energy. Some ran excitedly up ahead, others dropped behind to investigate something that caught their eye, only to quickly return to the rest of the pack. Their ears perked up and their tails wagged, and it was hard for Vaaler to see them as the same monsters that had torn apart the Inquisitors at the *Gerscheld*.

The Pack Masters were unarmed, but the regular Ice Fang warriors carried heavy wooden spears, giant battle-axes or massive, crudely crafted swords. Vaaler couldn't help but think the weapons were almost primitive in their quality. Combined with the motley assortment of ragtag, ill-fitting fur garments they wore, it was easy to understand where the stereotype of the Eastern savage originated.

As they set out, the Ice Fangs had a casual, almost carefree air about them. It really did seem like they were being escorted by allies rather than marched off as prisoners to a ransom meeting.

Is that because Norr asked them not to alarm us, or is it because they know they have nothing to fear from us?

They set an easy pace, but Vaaler could tell that Keegan was laboring to keep up as he leaned on Rexol's staff for support. Jerrod noticed it, too. Despite his worry of drawing unwanted attention, the monk had fallen into place only a few steps behind the young wizard.

It's strange they didn't take the staff away from him, Vaaler thought, before remembering that magic was all but unheard of in the Frozen East. It was possible they thought it was some kind of exotic Southern weapon. They hadn't bothered to take Vaaler's rapier or Scythe's razors away, either, so maybe it wasn't that odd for them to let Keegan keep his staff.

The barbarians clearly favored brute force over precision. With skill and proper training, a sharp, light blade could be devastating.

But to someone unfamiliar with their usage, Scythe's small knives and Vaaler's thin rapier blade looked dainty and fragile.

They don't think our weapons are even worth confiscating. Either that, or Norr somehow convinced them to let us keep them as part of the ransom negotiations.

The Danaan let his eyes drift over to the big man, wondering just how high a price he'd promised the Stone Spirits would pay.

Norr was walking with his head down, his limping gait uneven. The big man's brow was tense and furrowed, his jaw clenched— possibly due to pain from his injuries, though Vaaler suspected he was more bothered by the coming reunion with his clan.

Scythe walked beside him, her own features reflecting the anxious stress of her lover. In the short time Vaaler had known her, he had seen Scythe's temper flare up several times. She wasn't one to keep her feelings hidden. It was odd to see her now, struggling— and failing—to hide her growing frustration with Norr's secretive behavior.

They continued marching for several hours, none of them speaking. Vaaler was on the verge of telling them they needed to stop to let Keegan and Norr rest when one of the Pack Masters held up her hand, bringing the entire party to a halt.

"We're here," Norr informed his friends.

There weren't any landmarks Vaaler could make out—they had stopped at a place on the flat, featureless tundra that looked like every other location to his eye.

"Where's your clan?" Scythe asked.

"They will come soon," Norr promised, gingerly lowering himself to the cold ground and settling in to wait.

He put an end to further discussion by digging into the jerky rations they'd each been given at the start of the journey. Vaaler thought Scythe might push him for more information, but instead, she settled in beside him and they ate in silence.

Vaaler and the others did the same. He noticed the Ice Fangs weren't eating, however. They seemed more alert; more on edge than before. Keegan shot him a look that indicated he'd noticed it as well, but with Jerrod hovering close by, the two weren't able to discuss what it might mean.

They waited almost an hour before the Stone Spirit envoys arrived. There were fifteen of them, traveling on foot: twelve men and three women. They were all armed—like the regular warriors of the Ice Fangs, they favored spears, axes, and heavy swords. But the craftsmanship of the Stone Spirit weapons was clearly superior, even at a distance.

The Ice Fangs aren't a wealthy clan, Vaaler realized. *They have to make do with whatever they can scrounge.*

As the new arrivals drew closer Vaaler could see that their clothes, though similar in style to the Ice Fang garb, were also better made. Instead of an ill-fitting assortment of crudely stitched animal skins draped haphazardly on the wearer, the Stone Spirits sported heavy fur vests that left their arms bare and short, hide-sewn skirts that reached almost down to their knee-high, cured-leather boots.

Outnumbered and sporting inferior weaponry, the Ice Fangs would have to rely on their dogs to even the odds if things turned ugly. Seeing the hard expressions of the Stone Spirit warriors, Vaaler wasn't sure that would be enough.

Hopefully it doesn't come to that.

The Stone Spirit delegation stopped their approach about fifty yards from where the Ice Fangs had made their camp. Three of them—two men armed with swords and carrying large burlap sacks slung over their shoulders and a tall woman wielding a heavy spear—advanced alone.

The Pack Masters went out as a trio to meet them halfway, ordering the dogs to stay in place with a series of short, sharp whistles.

"These are the prisoners?" the tall woman asked to begin the parley. She was speaking Verlsung, her voice loud and clear enough that Vaaler could easily make out every word. She was addressing the Pack Masters, but she seemed to be looking past them directly at Norr.

Even if she hadn't been the one to speak, it wouldn't have been hard to identify her as the leader of the group. She carried herself with the confident bearing of someone in charge, her head held high and her shoulders thrown back. She looked to be about Norr's age—maybe ten years older than him, Keegan, and Scythe.

There was something striking in her hard, pale features: a cold and dangerous beauty that reflected the land of her birth. Her auburn hair was twisted into a long, thick braid that hung down her back, the bangs held out of her ice-blue eyes by a simple silver circlet. Her shoulders were broad, her alabaster arms lean and muscular. Each forearm was covered with a metal bracer running from wrist to elbow, polished so that they glinted in the sun.

Unlike the simple weapons of the Ice Fangs, the shaft of her spear was painted with symbols Vaaler couldn't quite make out. A pair of feathers—one white, one black—and several small charms dangled from where the metal tip had been lashed on with thick sinew cords.

"On behalf of the Stone Spirit clan," the woman said, her voice taking on the tone of a formal, ritualized performance, "I ask what is to be the fate of these prisoners?"

"The penalty for trespassing on our land is death," one of the Pack Masters responded. "But out of respect for the mighty Stone Spirit clan, we will show mercy."

"And out of respect for the mighty Ice Fang clan, we will give you these gifts," the woman responded.

The Stone Spirit envoys stepped forward and dropped their sacks at the feet of the Pack Masters. The two Ice Fangs who hadn't spoken quickly rummaged through, then nodded to the third.

"We accept these gifts from the mighty Stone Spirit clan."

They turned to go, but stopped when the auburn-haired woman spoke again, this time in a less stiff, more normal tone.

"Hadawas has called for a Conclave."

"The Ice Fangs do not pay tribute to the Chief of the Sun Blades," the Pack Master answered.

"Neither do the Stone Spirits," the woman noted. "But many of us are gathering to hear his wisdom."

"We will not answer his summons," the Pack Master insisted. "If Hadawas wants to share his wisdom with the Ice Fangs, let him come to us."

"I will give him your answer," the woman replied, and Vaaler couldn't quite tell if her words were meant to be a threat.

With the conversation at an end, the Pack Masters were eager to return to the rest of their clan. A few quick commands and sharp whistles, and the entire troupe was up and moving off, headed back the way they'd come.

As they retreated, the rest of the Stone Spirit delegation moved forward. Their weapons were still held at their sides, but they were tense and ready to spring into action.

"Welcome back, Norr," the woman said, still speaking in Verl-sung. "I never thought to see the day you would return."

He didn't say anything in reply.

"Take their weapons," the woman ordered her followers.

Several of them stepped forward, only to stop abruptly when Norr held up his massive hand. Vaaler couldn't help but notice the tall woman scowling at their reaction.

"Don't be alarmed," Norr said, speaking in the Southland tongue to his friends. "But we have to turn over our weapons."

"Why?" Scythe demanded, suddenly suspicious. "I thought these were your people. Your family."

"They will not harm us," Norr reassured her. "Shalana is an honorable woman. We can trust her."

"You didn't answer my question," Scythe countered. "And I'm not giving up my blades until you do. What's going on?"

To Vaaler's surprise, it was the tall woman who answered them in Allrish.

"Give over your weapons," she warned, her accent even thicker than Norr's, "or we cut you down and leave you for the dogs to find."

"Don't speak to her like that!" Norr snapped in his native tongue.

In response to the big man's anger, the Stone Spirit warriors all took an instinctive half step back. All except Shalana.

"You want my weapons, come and take them!" Scythe snarled, dropping into a fighting crouch as her knives materialized in her hands.

The Stone Spirit warriors had recovered their composure. Seeing Scythe's knives, they raised their own weapons and stepped forward. This time it was Shalana who stopped them with a gesture.

"Keep your weapons for now," she said told Scythe, her voice calm. "It's foolish to kill prisoners we paid so much for."

"Prisoners?" Scythe exclaimed, her focus shifting from Shalana to Norr as she relaxed her posture and slipped her twin blades back out of sight. "Did you know about this?"

The big man opened his mouth to explain, then closed it and hung his head in silent shame, unable to meet Scythe's accusing gaze.

"You must be dangerous," Shalana noted while arching one eyebrow in Scythe's direction. "Not many can scare my husband into silence."

Chapter 10

IT WAS HARD for Cassandra to track the passage of time inside the Guardian's cave. The fire always burned warm and bright inside, while outside there seemed to be an endless storm of icy wind and swirling snow that obscured the rising and setting of the sun behind dark clouds.

But it was more than that. Time seemed to move differently in the cave, as if they were sheltered from the world outside. Warm. Safe. Yet Cassandra knew the safety was an illusion.

I'm becoming too comfortable here.

Nazir had often warned his students that the greatest threat to the Order was complacency; the subtle slide into comfort and contentment could be as deadly as any army. The longer she waited, the more powerful the forces gathering against her would become. She'd already seen proof of that in her dreams.

The avian huntress who had stalked her during her initial flight from the Monastery was gone, slinking away in defeat rather than challenge the might of the Guardian. But a new threat had emerged to take her place. Cassandra had seen them in a recurring vision over the past three nights: two deformed, naked figures— one red, one blue, but otherwise identical—coming for her. Though humanoid, they scuttled across the icy tundra of the plains on all fours, their limbs long and spiderlike. They moved more slowly than the flying woman, keeping their snouts pressed close to the ground as they tracked her trail through the South-lands and into the Frozen East. She knew they wouldn't be fooled by the false paths she'd conjured to confuse and mislead her previous pursuer. And they wouldn't be afraid to challenge the Guardian.

The blue-skinned titan was sitting with his back against the wall near the entrance of the cave, peering out into the snowstorm.

As far away as he can get from the Crown, Cassandra noticed.

Ever since she realized the toll the Crown was taking on her host, she'd studied him carefully, searching for more telltale signs he was growing weaker. But it was like trying to watch someone age: the changes were imperceptible yet nonetheless relentless. Though still a magnificent physical specimen, his once-flawless immortal beauty was now marred by scattered gray strands in his dark hair and beard and faint creases around his eyes. The aura of invincibility, the glow of enduring, eternal power that had once radiated from him, was gone.

He will die before he casts me out.

"I have to leave," Cassandra told her protector, rising to her feet and coming over to stand beside him.

"The storm will pass in a day or two," he assured her. "Rest until then."

A familiar refrain, but one it was hard to argue against. Her journey would be hard enough without having to battle the elements.

Does he believe he can keep me safe if I stay here? Or after so many centuries alone, does he just like having someone else around?

She knew the storm wouldn't slow the creatures she had seen in her vision. And in his weakened state, she wasn't certain the Guardian could defeat them. She had to leave. Soon.

Tomorrow, then. Even if the storm doesn't break.

Why wait? the voice in her head that was not her own insisted.

The storm is nothing compared to the power of the Talismans! The Guardian is tired; he is ready to pass on his burden. Ask for the Sword, and he will give it to you! Take it and the Crown and leave now!

Cassandra shook her head, knowing she couldn't do that. The Crown was already too much for her to bear. If she dared lay claim to a second Talisman, she feared the temptation of such power would be too much to resist.

Would that be a bad thing? the voice demanded. *Daemron used the Talismans to turn himself into a God! Why can't you do the same?*

With a sudden start, she realized why the unwelcome voice sounded so familiar. The ruthless ambition and arrogance reminded her of Rexol. She knew her former master was dead—consumed by the power of the Crown when he tried to use it. But he had marked her before his death; he'd cast some kind of spell over her that had made her betray the Pontiff and help him escape his prison in the Monastery.

His spell must have awakened something inside me. Conjured up buried memories of him from deep within my subconscious. Or maybe it unlocked something selfish inside me that seeks to undermine all I learned during my time in the Order.

Recognizing the source of the voice did nothing to quell it, however.

If you won't take the Sword, at least ask the Guardian about it. You need to learn more about the Talismans. You need to understand their power. You need to unravel their mysteries if you hope to stop the Slayer's return!

The words still didn't seem like her own, but in this case she found it harder simply to dismiss them. Huddled in the cave so close to both the Crown and the Sword, it was hard not to obsess over them. There were many questions Cassandra wanted to ask about the Talismans, but she had held her tongue for fear of upsetting her host as she'd done when she'd asked him about Daemron and the True Gods. But balanced against the fate of the entire mortal world, her fears seemed foolish.

He is the last surviving link to a forgotten age, she admitted, conceding the argument to the other voice. *I cannot stay here forever, and there may come a time when I have need of his knowledge and insight.*

Gathering her courage, she dared to break the silence of the cave.

"May I ask you something?"

The Guardian stiffened; she could see the thick muscles running from his neck to his shoulders tensing ever so slightly. But he nodded his approval.

"The Sword. The Crown. How did they get here? In the mortal world, I mean? When Slayer fled the final battle, didn't he take the Talismans with him?"

The Guardian's posture relaxed, and a sly smile slowly crossed his features as he chuckled softly.

"Daemron was not as clever as he thought. The Gods had created the Talismans to protect the mortal world; the physical artifacts were bound to it. They could not pass through the portal into the Slayer's nether realm, and when he fled they were left behind.

"In their weakened state, the Gods did not have the strength to destroy the Talismans, and they knew the combined power of all three would be too great a temptation for any one individual.

"So before they passed, three of us were chosen, each tasked to guard and protect one of the Talismans. The ring was given to a powerful wizard named Lassander Avareen; he and his followers hid it deep in the forests of the North."

Cassandra recognized the name. According to Danaan legend Lassander Avareen was the founder of their kingdom, the first in an unbroken line of monarchs that continued to rule the Dwellers even to this day.

"The Crown was given to the prophet Salidarr; the founder of your Order. As you well know, he took it deep into the deserts of the South. And the Sword was given to me."

"The Order revered the history of the Old Gods," Cassandra said, confused. "Why have I never heard this before?"

"The Gods feared another mortal might try to possess all three Talismans, as Daemron had done. They didn't tell Lassander or Salidarr about each other; only I knew the full story."

Because they knew you couldn't use the other Talismans even if you wanted to, Cassandra realized. *Just being near the Crown is poisoning you.*

"And even what they knew could have been lost over the centuries," the Guardian added. "The presence of the Talismans would have been a closely guarded secret. Even if they passed the tale down from generation to generation through their successors, mortal memories are not perfect. Details would be lost or confused."

Or someone might have died before sharing everything he or she knew, Cassandra thought, recalling the Pontiff's violent end. How much of the truth had he known? How much, if any, had he passed on to Yasmin before his death?

"The Sword protected me from the effects of the Legacy," the titan continued. "It gave me strength to endure while the other Chaos Spawn went into hibernation."

"But the Crown is doing the opposite," Cassandra noted.

His lips tightened, but he didn't deny her accusation.

"Each of the Talismans is different," he said. "Surely you've felt that during the time here in my cave?"

Cassandra nodded. While carrying the Crown, she'd felt its power enveloping her. It was difficult to describe with mere words, but it had wrapped her in an aura that was complex and layered, subtle and amorphous.

In contrast, the Sword felt more physical, more direct. She

could still sense the divine spark of the True Gods inside the blade, but instead of reaching out to surround her it seemed to draw her in, as if trying to absorb the Chaos that flowed in her own blood.

"The Sword gave Daemron strength and prowess in battle, but it also protected him from the spells and magic conjured by the enemies he faced," the Guardian explained. "The Ring, on the other hand, was designed to allow him to reach into the Burning Sea and draw on its power without the necessity of complex rituals."

"And the Crown?"

"The Crown balanced the other two, bridging the gap between the body and spirit. It also gave him foresight and allowed him to peer into the minds of others, so that he could guide his followers down the proper path."

Cassandra nodded, but in her mind she was mulling over the implications of what she had just learned.

Lassander took the Ring into the North Forest and founded the Danaan kingdom. Salidarr took the Crown into the desert and founded the Order. The Guardian took the Sword to the Frozen East and founded . . .

"The clans," she gasped aloud as understanding came crashing down on her.

The Guardian gave her a quizzical look.

"That's why there are no prophets or mages here in the Frozen East," she explained, speaking quickly with the rush of realization. "The Sword's presence made them evolve a warrior culture. And that's why Chaos feels so faint here—the Sword absorbs the power from the land and its people!"

Her head was spinning. She had known the Talismans were powerful, but the idea that the entire history of the Frozen East had been shaped and guided by the mere presence of the Sword was mind-boggling.

"It's the same for the Danaan," she continued excitedly as her theory began to crystallize. "You said the Ring allowed Daemron to call on the power of the Burning Sea at will. The history and culture of Lassander's kingdom were shaped by the Talisman he was given! They evolved into a nation of wizards!"

She looked to the Guardian for confirmation, but he only shrugged and shook his head.

"I remember what used to be," he told her, "but the world has changed, and I know little of what is beyond these mountains."

"It has to be," Cassandra stated with a confidence that surprised even herself. "It all makes sense."

"If that is true," the Guardian asked, "then what of the Crown?"

Cassandra paused. She couldn't define the Southlands as easily as she'd labeled the Danaan and the clans. Was that because the Crown's power was more subtle or because she had grown up there and it was harder to see the truth about her own people?

"You said the Crown balanced the other Talismans. In the Southlands, children are born with Chaos in their blood, though it is more rare than in the Danaan kingdom."

And the Crown helped Daemron rule and control his followers, Rexol's voice chimed in. *Just like the Order manipulated and controlled the nobles of the Southlands.*

Cassandra didn't like the implication, but she saw no point in arguing with the contrarian part of her own mind, so she let the comment slip by unacknowledged.

"If the Talismans are strong enough to guide the evolution of an entire people," she said slowly as another realization hit her, "then they are surely strong enough to cause changes in the weather."

"The storm?" the Guardian asked.

"It hasn't let up since I arrived," Cassandra reminded him. "Even here in the mountains of the Frozen East, that must be unusual."

"It is," the titan admitted.

"It's because of the Crown," she declared. "It's in conflict with the Sword. It's poisoning you, and it's causing this blizzard."

"You don't know that's true."

She had no physical evidence, no way to prove her theory. But Cassandra knew she was right.

"This storm won't pass," she told him. "And there are other enemies coming. I've seen them in my dreams. They won't be slowed by the blizzard."

"I can protect you against them," the titan vowed, though she saw in his eyes that even he didn't believe the words.

"You've done so much for me already," she assured him. "You gave me shelter and protection while I recovered my strength. But now it is time for me to return to the world beyond this cave."

When he didn't object, Cassandra knew he was suffering even more than she suspected.

"Where will you go?" he asked instead.

Cassandra had wondered the same thing herself. Staying in the Frozen East, hiding from the barbarian clans while trying to survive the brutal winter, wasn't an option. She might be able to reach the Danaan forests, but the Tree Folk killed any who entered their kingdom without permission. And in the Southlands, Yasmin would have the Order searching for her. She could avoid capture for a time, but if she remained there, they would inevitably find her.

"Callastan," she said. "I'll find a ship and head for the Western Isles."

"Your enemies will follow you," the Guardian warned. "The Crown will call to them, even across the ocean."

"There is no other choice," she explained. To her dismay, he didn't contradict her.

"Take whatever you need before you go," he said. "Anything I have is yours if you wish it."

She knew what he was offering, but despite the desperate pleas from Rexol's voice inside her head, she wouldn't ask him for the Sword. She knew better than to overreach her own capabilities.

The Sword is not meant for me. The Crown is burden enough.

"I wish I could stay here with you," she told him, "but that is not my fate."

The Guardian nodded but didn't speak, though he did reach out his arm to gently caress Cassandra's cheek with the back of his massive hand. Even now, she felt a sudden thrill at his simple touch.

The moment passed and his hand fell back to his side. Reluctantly, Cassandra turned away and headed to the back of the cave. She took the Crown from where it lay on the ground at the base of the Sword's pedestal and placed it back inside the plain leather sack she had used to transport it during her previous flight.

Closing her eyes, she slipped into a light meditative trance. Focusing her will, she prepared her body and spirit for the journey ahead. As she readied herself, she could once again sense the Crown on the edge of her awareness, shining like a beacon. Ignoring it, she called upon the restored reserves of her own inner strength, steeling her flesh so it could survive the fury of the storm. She would still suffer from the cold—and fatigue, and hunger—but at least she would be able to sustain herself during the journey.

Once she was done, she rose to her feet, slung the leather sack over one shoulder, and crossed back to the front of the cave where the Guardian stood waiting. In his eyes she could see a sorrow so deep it made her heart ache.

A wave of pity washed over her. The Guardian's entire existence was focused on a single purpose: protect the Sword; defend it against the enemies of the True Gods. For centuries he had lived a solitary existence, sustained only by the knowledge that he was invincible, unassailable. But her arrival had taken that from him.

The Crown had left him vulnerable, and in her hour of need he was forced to admit that he was too weak to protect her.

"The creatures hunting me want the Crown, but they are not the only enemies we must guard against," Cassandra reminded him, hoping to restore and renew his sense of purpose. "There are others who seek the Talismans. I've seen them in my visions.

"The flying huntress is still out there; she may still return. Or others may come in her place. Remain vigilant, and may the True Gods watch over you."

The Guardian bowed his head, and she couldn't tell if he took comfort in her words or not.

"The True Gods are dead," he said sadly. "But I will honor the vow I made to them. I will not surrender the Sword while I still live."

Cassandra hesitated for one last, lingering moment in the magical warmth of the cave before stepping out into the blizzard. Despite her preparations, her lungs flared with pain at the shock of the frigid air. Cold, hard pellets of ice stung her face, and the fierce wind threatened to rip her from the narrow ledge and send her toppling into the abyss below.

Pressing herself against the slick wall of frozen stone, she began to shuffle slowly along the treacherous path, a fugitive on the run once again. The pack with the Crown, still slung over her shoulder, swung wildly in the wind, striking her hard on the back over and over as if constantly trying to remind her of its presence.

Chapter 11

"TREASON IS A serious charge," Rianna said, speaking slowly and giving emphasis to each word. "I will not tolerate unfounded accusations."

"Andar intentionally tried to disrupt the summoning ritual," Orath insisted. "He willfully disobeyed my instructions and put us all in danger."

Though his voice was calm, in the empty council chamber his words seemed to echo off the walls.

"How do you know his actions were intentional?" the Danaan Queen asked. "You warned us the spell was dangerous, and the ritual used a type of magic my people are unfamiliar with. Perhaps Andar was merely overwhelmed by it."

Orath knew the High Sorcerer's actions were no accident. It wasn't just that he'd pulled away from the spell to save himself from being consumed by Chaos; that could be dismissed as an instinctive reaction. But when Andar realized what was happening, he'd somehow led the rest of the Danaan mages with him in his retreat.

He couldn't admit this to the Queen, of course. She would be outraged if she realized the Minions had intended to sacrifice Andar and his brethren all along, and Orath needed her now more than ever.

Technically, the ritual had succeeded. Consuming Gort and

Draco had given the spell enough power to bind the ogre though it had drained much of Orath's own strength as well. Even though the beast had groveled at his feet, he had felt a bitter resentment in its submission.

The ogre sensed its new master's vulnerability. The beast's allegiance was just barely held in check by invisible chains of Chaos fire. Each time Orath gave an order or command, it would test the chains, probing and prodding for weakness. If Orath's will wavered, the ogre would break free and turn on him.

He could still use the ogre as a tool, but the creature's resistance would limit its effectiveness. If he wanted to recover the Ring, he'd need the Danaan armies as well.

"I made the risks clear before the ritual began," the Minion explained, hoping he could still convince Rianna that Andar had betrayed her. "I warned your people of the consequences if they did not follow my instructions exactly. Had Andar done so, none of this would have happened."

For a moment he considered trying to use Chaos to make the Queen more susceptible to his arguments, but ultimately he decided against it. The more he used magic to try to influence or persuade her directly, the more likely she was to recognize what he was doing. If that happened, she would turn against him and his only recourse would be to crush her will and turn her into a mindless puppet. The cost and effort would be too great; he needed to conserve his strength so he could keep control over the ogre.

"Andar's defiance put the lives of everyone by the lake at risk," he continued, hoping to sway her with his words alone. "Gort and Draco were forced to sacrifice their lives to keep the beast from breaking free and slaughtering us all. Their blood is on Andar's hands."

"Your companions knew the risks when they joined in the ritual," the Queen answered, her tone icy. "Like Andar and my people, they chose to participate despite those risks. Their deaths, while tragic, do not condemn Andar as a traitor.

"Based on your logic," Rianna continued in the same cold manner, "if it had been my people who perished during the ritual, then you would be the one now accused of treason."

Orath hesitated, wondering if the Queen knew he had intended to sacrifice her people all along.

She might suspect, but she doesn't know for sure, he decided. *She's clinging to the doubt because she knows I am her only hope of revenge.*

"Andar's actions nearly unleashed the ogre on your kingdom," Orath said, hoping an appeal to her sense of duty might be more effective. "He put your subjects at risk."

"That was never his intent," the Queen countered, though some of the steel had gone from her tone.

"Intent is irrelevant," Orath argued. "You've seen the destruction that the Ring can unleash. The only way to get it back is to call upon powers even more dangerous.

"You know Andar cannot lead you down this path. That is why you turned to me."

Orath paused, letting his words sink in. Rianna stood silent, her face emotionless and impassive.

"I asked what you were willing to do to reclaim the Ring," the Minion reminded her. "You said 'anything.' Do you really believe Andar feels the same?"

When the Queen didn't reply, Orath knew he'd won her over.

"If you still want my help," he told her, "then your people must give me the same absolute loyalty they give to you. If they hesitate or refuse or disobey—as Andar did—then the powers we are calling upon could destroy us all. If Andar—"

"Enough!" Rianna snapped, holding up a hand to cut him off. "Your point has been made."

"Andar must pay for his insubordination," Orath whispered. "You must make an example of him."

"Do not tell me what I *must* do," Rianna warned him. "I am still the Queen; I will not take orders from one of my advisers. Even you."

Orath shrugged an apology, aware she was lashing out in frustration because she knew he was right.

"I have offered my counsel, Your Highness," he said in his most ingratiating tone. "I trust you will make the right decision."

When the Royal Guards came for him, Andar didn't resist. When they told him he was being arrested for treason, he didn't speak. When they led him from his private chambers to the dungeons beneath the castle, he offered neither objection nor complaint.

He'd seen the confusion and uncertainty in the eyes of the guards. Andar was well respected, both among the common citizens and the castle staff. His reputation was unimpeachable; it was difficult for them to even imagine he was capable of treason.

Yet unlike me, Andar thought, *they follow orders despite their questions and doubt.*

Left alone in the small, unlit cell, Andar couldn't help but wonder whose orders they were following: the Queen's or Orath's?

In the cold darkness, it was difficult to follow the passage of time. A few minutes could seem like an hour, and Andar had no idea of how long it would be before someone would come to see him. Fortunately, the guards hadn't felt the need to shackle his hands and wrists, so he was able to find a somewhat comfortable position sitting in one corner of his cell.

He understood the gravity of his situation. Treason was a serious charge, one the Queen could not ignore. Rianna was a just ruler, but her heart had grown hard. She had banished her own son for similar crimes; it would be foolish to expect her to grant clemency to the High Sorcerer. If found guilty, he would be sentenced to either exile or execution.

And I am guilty.

When questioned, he wouldn't deny it. He could argue that when he broke away from Orath's ritual, he had acted in the heat of the moment, trusting his gut. But the truth was, he had been fully aware of the implications and possible consequences. Even now, with time to look back and reflect, he was confident he'd make the same decision again.

But does that make it right? Or am I still a traitor?

Eventually the steel door opened, the light of the dim lantern on the other side as blinding as the heart of the midday sun. Andar was forced to look down and shield his eyes, unable to see who had been sent to try to force a confession out of him.

"Leave us and close the door," a familiar woman's voice ordered.

At the sound of the grating hinges, Andar dropped the hand over his eyes and braved the lantern's light to meet the gaze of Rianna standing over him.

"It is unseemly for the Queen to be alone with a prisoner," he told her.

"As the Queen, I decide what is unseemly," she reminded him. "Though I still expect my subjects to stand in my presence."

Abashed, Andar scrambled to his feet.

"You know why you are here?" the Queen asked.

"I do."

"Then explain yourself."

"Orath deceived us," Andar said after a moment's silence to collect his thoughts. "He didn't warn us of the true cost of his spell. I sensed the ritual was killing us; consuming us. I broke away to save myself, and I took the others with me."

"You didn't fear this would unleash the ogre on our people?"

Andar shifted uncomfortably.

"I hoped Orath would find another way to contain the beast."

"I'm disappointed in you, Andar," Rianna said, reaching out to place a hand on his shoulder. "You put the lives of you and your fellow mages ahead of what is best for our kingdom."

"With all due respect, my Queen," the High Sorcerer replied, his eyes fixed on the floor. "I don't believe anything that Orath can offer is what is best for our kingdom."

The Queen sighed and let her hand slip off his shoulder. Slowly she turned away from him and stepped toward the door. But instead of leaving, she stopped and turned back to face him once more.

"I cannot exile you," she told him. "Not after what happened with . . . my son."

She can't even bear to speak Vaaler's name.

"I will not execute you, either," she told him. "Already rumors are spreading of how you saved the lives of the other mages in the ritual. You have become a hero to the common folk, a symbol of someone who can stand against the deadly powers of Chaos.

"But you did put the entire kingdom at risk by refusing to follow Orath's instructions. For that, I must make an example of you."

Andar bowed his head, still confused as to what she intended.

"You are relieved of your position in my court," she told him, "and you will be held here in the dungeons until I decide on a fitting punishment."

You won't sentence me, but you won't absolve me, either.

Her reticence to pass judgment confirmed what Andar already suspected: Rianna was lost in a sea of self-doubt and uncertainty.

Orath preys on this vulnerability.

"Forgive my boldness," he said aloud, "but who have you chosen to take my place?"

"Lormilar will be elevated to the position of High Sorcerer," she informed him.

"A good man," Andar said, though he silently added, *but one lacking the confidence to stand up to Orath.*

"I don't trust Orath," the Queen assured him, almost as if she were reading his mind. "But in these dark times we must take whatever allies we can find. Our capital is in ruins and thousands are dead. The people are scared; they need leadership. They need to know I can protect them."

"Orath can't help you protect your subjects," Andar said, shaking his head emphatically. "All he offers is revenge."

"The most treasured heirloom of the royal family—the most sacred symbol of our kingdom—was stolen from us," Rianna snapped back. "Plucked from my neck while I slept by my own flesh and blood. Are you saying we should let this offense go unpunished? The savages in the East must be taught a lesson!"

"We don't even know for sure that Vaaler and the others are allied with the barbarian clans," he reminded his Queen.

"Whether they are or not, the Ring is too powerful to be left in the hands of another," she insisted, her voice defiant. "You saw the devastation it brought to Ferlhame. I cannot allow anything like that to happen again."

"The Ring is gone," Andar admitted. "But maybe we are better off without it."

You certainly seem to be, he thought. The Queen was still gaunt, but she looked much better than the haggard, skeletal creature she had become in the months leading up to Vaaler's betrayal.

The Queen shook her head, then looked at the floor.

"I saw the Destroyer of Worlds in my dreams before he came to Ferlhame," she said in a low whisper. "I did not heed the warnings. I did not have the strength to do what had to be done. I have learned my lesson."

"You've seen something," Andar noted. "More visions."

"In my nightmares I've watched the Destroyer of Worlds feasting with the barbarian tribes. I've seen the warriors of the East rise up, all the clans united against a common foe," she told him. "I've seen the Free Cities bow down to the Order and join the vast ranks of the Southland armies, their soldiers swarming like ants to every corner of the world. I've seen Danaan lying dead on the battlefield, the bodies stretched as far as the eyes can see.

"War is coming," she declared. "We cannot stop it. And we need the Ring to survive."

Andar wasn't a Seer, but he understood enough about Chaos to recognize the inherent perils in the Queen's visions.

"For centuries we have survived by staying hidden in the North Forest," he cautioned. "We have defended our borders, but we have never gone beyond them. Assembling an army and marching against the barbarians of the East will compel others to see us as a threat.

"It will force them to mass armies of their own. It may even cause the Destroyer of Worlds to unite them and use the Ring against us again."

"You dare to lecture *me* on the dangers of a self-fulfilling prophecy?" the Queen snorted. "Do you really believe I have not already considered this a thousand times over?

"When I foresaw the Destroyer of Worlds coming to Ferlhame, I did not know what to do," she explained. "So I did nothing, and what I saw came to pass.

"When I realized my son walked with the enemy," she continued, "I could have had him killed. But I chose to show mercy instead, and Ferlhame paid the price.

"There is no way to be sure I walk the right path now," she admitted, her voice once more slipping into the low whisper. "But this is the path I have chosen, and I will not waver."

With that, she spun on her heel and thumped her hand on the door. It opened a second later and Rianna stepped through, taking the lamp with her. The guard on the other side closed the door behind her, once more plunging Andar's cell into utter blackness.

Chapter 12

KEEGAN WAS STANDING close enough to Scythe to see her reaction when she learned Shalana was Norr's wife. She didn't say anything else—not to Shalana and not to Norr. But in seconds her expression went from confusion to shock to dismay before settling into a tight mask of cold, hard anger.

He could read Norr's expression as well—regret and shame. The big man started to reach out his hand toward Scythe, only to think better of it and let it drop away as she turned ever so slightly away from him.

If Shalana saw the exchange, she made no reaction. Instead, she started issuing commands to the rest of her patrol, and within minutes they were on the move again. The pace was steady, but not too taxing, and Keegan was able to keep up without much difficulty. As they marched, his attention kept going back to Scythe.

The Stone Spirits had formed a loose ring around Norr and his companions. The big man was up front, hobbling slightly but managing to stay only a few steps behind Shalana as she led the way. Surprisingly, they didn't speak.

What kind of wife doesn't have anything to say to her husband after years apart?

Vaaler was walking close behind Norr, as was Jerrod.

He's still keeping his distance, Keegan noted of the monk. *Still worried about drawing unwanted attention my way.*

Scythe had dropped back beside Keegan, though she kept her gaze fixed straight ahead, as if she was trying to burn a hole in the back of Norr's skull. He turned around only once to check on her, then quickly snapped his head back to the front on seeing the look in her eyes.

Keegan couldn't stop himself from constantly looking over at Scythe, but she was so intent on Norr she didn't notice his attention. It was hard to imagine what was going through her head right now. He didn't fully understand the relationship she and Norr shared, but he knew they were physically and emotionally close.

But not close enough for Norr to tell her about Shalana, I guess.

Keegan didn't know what it felt like to be betrayed by someone you trusted. He had gotten over the anger and resentment he'd felt over his father's brutal death, and since then he'd been too busy studying under Rexol to develop any close attachments besides his friendship with Vaaler. And even though several years had passed, when he came to the Danaan prince for help his friend had done more than Keegan could have ever asked of him.

Perhaps that was why he was so infatuated with Scythe. He'd known several women, but nothing had ever developed beyond a single night or two of physical passion. He'd never felt any kind of real emotional or spiritual connection to any of them. But in Scythe he sensed a kindred soul, a woman who could understand him, someone he could imagine a future with.

You're being foolish, he chided himself. *You barely know her.*

It was possible his attraction to the young Islander was born of envy. He sensed the feelings Scythe and Norr clearly had for each other. Maybe he just wanted to feel that passionate about someone himself and have someone—anyone—feel the same way about him.

Yet even now, marching wordlessly beside her across the frozen tundra, he felt there was some kind of chemistry between them. He still remembered the spark he'd felt when he first set eyes on the young woman outside the inn where their lives became intertwined.

Stop this. She's with Norr, and she's made it clear she isn't interested in anybody else.

He knew that Scythe was hurting, stung by Shalana's unexpected revelation. Norr was upset, too, and clearly just waiting for a chance to speak with Scythe in private. Keegan felt bad for both of them. In their short time together they had all been through so much that he already considered them friends. It pained him to see them suffer.

But part of him—a small, dark, twisted part he didn't want to admit existed—couldn't help but hope this would drive a wedge between the two lovers.

Scythe had hoped the day's march would let her work out some of the emotions raging inside her. But the pace was too slow to push her physically, and when they finally reached the patrol's temporary camp and stopped for the night she was still fuming.

It's Norr's fault we couldn't go any faster, she thought. *Limping along like a cripple!*

Petty and childish as the thought was, it stirred up conflicting emotions. On the one hand she was even more angry at Norr than before for holding them back. Yet at the same time, part of her was worried about him.

Why isn't he getting better?

She'd learned enough about medicine from Methodis, her adopted father, to know that minor injuries that took too long to heal could be symptoms of something much worse.

Probably not an infection; he wasn't cut. But he could have torn a ligament.

She'd have to examine him to find out the true extent of his injury. Unfortunately, that wasn't going to be possible. Shalana had been quick to lead Norr away right after they arrived at the camp while Scythe and the others were ushered off in the opposite direction.

Glancing back over her shoulder, Scythe watched them disappear into a small tent.

They haven't seen each other in years; of course she'd want to talk to him in private. That's all they're doing. Just talking.

To keep her mind from conjuring up crazy images of her lover and the tall, auburn-haired beauty, she turned her focus to the rest of the camp as their guards led them along. Though obviously temporary, it was large and well organized. In addition to the fifteen envoys who had gone to meet the Ice Fang contingent, there were another dozen Stone Spirit warriors who had been left behind to watch over the site.

Small, portable tents of animal skin had been arranged in clusters of four around the site, positioned so that they formed a tight ring, with the entrances all facing inward to offer some protection against the wind. Hides and blankets had been stretched between each quartet of tents, and a fire pit had been hollowed out in the earth in the center of each ring, the warmth of the smoldering peat captured by the makeshift animal-skin walls.

Beyond the outskirts, two long trenches had been dug to serve as latrines. Ample food and supplies—spare weapons, extra clothing, and more blankets—had been piled near the middle of the camp, along with several small sleds that could be used to haul their provisions across the permafrost terrain.

No dogs, Scythe noted. *They must pull the sleds by hand.*

They were led to one of the tent clusters near the edge, on the side closest to the latrines.

"Outlanders stay here," one of the warriors explained to them in a clumsy, halting version of Allrish. "Rest of camp forbidden."

He didn't bother to wait for their reply. Instead, he and the rest of their escort turned and headed back to the main hub, not even bothering to post a guard.

Guess they don't figure we're stupid enough to try anything when we're outnumbered five to one.

"We should get in from the cold," Vaaler said, pulling aside the hide flap so they could step into the tent ring and get closer to the fire pit's warmth.

Jerrod and Keegan were quick to take him up on the offer; now that they weren't on the move the chill of the air was more noticeable. Scythe hesitated, her gaze wandering over to the other side of the camp where Norr and Shalana had disappeared.

"Are you okay?" Vaaler asked. "Want to talk about it?"

Yes, but with Norr, not you.

"I'm fine," she mumbled, then ducked under the hide flap as Vaaler followed close behind.

The air inside the tent circle was hazy from the burning peat, but it was a small price to pay for shelter from the wind and cold. It wasn't exactly comfortable, but at least it was bearable.

Scythe hoped the others would have the decency not to say anything about Norr—as far as she was concerned, it was none of their business. Unfortunately, Jerrod felt like everything was his business.

"It is clear you did not know Norr was married," the monk said, showing his typical disregard for tact. "I'm worried what your reaction to this news will be."

"That's between me and Norr," she answered, her tone making it clear the conversation was over.

"I wish that was true," Jerrod countered, refusing to let the matter drop. "But in the eyes of the barbarians, we are all the same. Outlanders. If your emotions lead you to do something reckless, it might have consequences for all of us."

"I'm not a child," Scythe reminded him.

"We're just worried about you," Keegan chimed in. "This kind of betrayal can be hard to take."

What could a kid like you know about it? Scythe thought, momentarily forgetting that they were the same age.

"We shouldn't judge Norr until we hear what he has to say about all this," Vaaler cautioned. "Whatever's going on, I'm sure there's more to it than meets the eye."

"It could be that he has abandoned us now that he is back among his own people," Jerrod speculated.

"He wouldn't do that," Scythe insisted.

"Are you certain?" Jerrod replied. "Obviously you don't know him as well as you thought."

"I don't think he'd abandon us, either," Vaaler said. "I bet he'll show up any minute to tell us exactly what's going on. And when he gets here," he added, "we owe it to him to hear what he has to say."

The Danaan turned to look directly at Scythe. "Especially you. *Listen* to him."

Scythe didn't bother answering; she was in no mood to be lectured.

It didn't take long before Vaaler's prediction proved true, and Norr pulled aside the hides and blankets and squeezed his bulk in to join them. He had changed from the stitched-together Danaan robes he'd been wearing during their journey into an armless animal-hide vest, a leather kilt, and heavy boots.

"We wondered where you had gone," Jerrod said before the big man even had a chance to sit.

"It has been many years since I left my clan," he answered. "I had to speak with Shalana. There were things I needed to know and things I needed to tell her."

"What kinds of things?" Jerrod demanded, making no effort to hide the suspicion in his voice.

Norr ignored him and turned to his lover.

"Scythe," he said, "we need to talk. In private. I want to explain what's going on."

"This affects all of us," Jerrod protested. "We put our lives in your hands. We deserve to know what this is all about."

Scythe snapped her head around to shoot the blind monk a withering glare, but when she turned back to Norr her words surprised even herself.

"White Eyes is right. I think I've had enough secrets for a while. Let's get everything out in the open."

Norr hesitated, then sighed and nodded. He awkwardly lowered himself to the ground and began to speak.

"Shalana doesn't have cause to speak your language often, and she sometimes makes mistakes. We were betrothed, but we never shared the marriage feast."

"So you're not her husband," Vaaler clarified. "You're her fiancé."

"That was many years ago," Norr explained.

"Is that why you left?" Keegan asked. "To avoid marrying her?"

"Not exactly. My reasons for leaving were complicated."

"Did you love her?" Scythe asked.

"I did, once," Norr said softly. "We grew up together; since we were children, we have been very close. There was a time when we shared our hopes and dreams; when just the sight of Shalana would make my heart race."

"Do you still love her?" she whispered.

"I will always care about Shalana," he admitted, "but you are the only one I love, Scythe."

She knew Norr well enough to recognize the powerful emotion behind his plain and simple words. She was still hurt and angry, but in that instant she knew this was something she'd get over.

The others were silent, waiting for her to reply. But romantic declarations weren't her style, especially not in front of an audience.

"Let me see your knee," was all she said, coming over and sitting close beside him and placing her hand on his arm.

From the look in Norr's eyes, she knew he understood exactly how she felt. In their relationship actions spoke louder than words.

"What happened with you and Shalana?" Keegan wanted to know. "Why did you leave your clan?"

"And how does all of this affect us now?" Jerrod added.

"Shalana's father was Terramon, Chief of the Stone Spirit clan. He was a great warrior in his youth, and a brilliant tactical and political leader. He's also arrogant, stubborn, and sometimes even cruel."

Scythe was listening along with the others, but her focus was on Norr's injury. His knee was so badly swollen that the skin around it was stretched and discolored.

Fluid building up; his body's trying to immobilize the joint to protect it. No wonder he can barely walk.

Gently, she began to poke and prod the area with her fingers, trying to feel through the bloated flesh to find the full extent of the damage.

"Thirty years ago, when Terramon took over as chief from his father, the Stone Spirits were already a large and fierce clan, with a dozen other clans paying regular tribute to us. But Terramon wanted more.

"Over the next three decades he led a campaign of conquest. Stone Spirit warriors swept across the tundra, forcing more and more clans to bow down and swear fealty to Terramon until we were one of the largest and most powerful clans in the East.

"In the early years, my father was Terramon's most trusted thane, fighting by his side in each and every battle. Until the sickness."

"Sickness?" It was Vaaler who asked the question though Scythe knew they were all thinking it.

"I don't remember it well; I was only a child. It started with a simple cough. In a few days, those infected would be choking on thick, black phlegm."

Scythe recognized the symptoms from the medical texts Methodis had made her study as a child. In the south it was called lung rot.

But lung rot thrives in warm, humid climates. How did it end up in the Frozen East? she wondered.

She'd heard stories of adventurous traders from the Free Cities and the Southlands dealing with some of the barbarian tribes. If one of them had been carrying the disease, he could have passed it on to Norr's people accidentally.

Or not so accidentally if they knowingly gave them infected blankets and clothing during the trades.

"Many clans suffered," Norr continued. "Dozens of Stone Spirits died."

"It could have been worse," Scythe told him. "Lung rot wiped out entire villages in the Southlands. The cold must have weakened the disease and kept it from spreading. You were lucky."

"The sickness took my mother," Norr said quietly. "Shalana's, too."

Mortified, Scythe felt herself flushing with shame.

"I'm sorry, Norr," she gasped. "I didn't mean to . . ." She trailed off, unable to think of anything to say that could make up for her callous stupidity.

He reached out one of his giant hands and wrapped it around both of hers, momentarily stopping her from tending to his injury.

"It's okay, Scythe," he told her, gazing deep into her eyes. "You didn't know."

The simple gesture lasted only a few seconds before he released her hands and resumed his tale. Yet that was all it took for Scythe to realize he had forgiven her.

"My father took ill, but he survived," he continued. "But his lungs were ruined. Even walking across the camp left him gasping for air; his days of being a warrior were over.

"Out of respect for what he once was, Terramon let my father keep his title as thane. While Terramon led our war parties on their forays deeper and deeper into enemy territory, my father stayed behind and oversaw the day-to-day welfare of the clan.

"He also took over the responsibility of raising Shalana. Knowing she would be the one to succeed her father as leader of our clan, he taught her the ways of our people even as he taught them to me: our traditions; our customs; how to track; how to hunt; how to fight.

"When we came of age, we joined Terramon's raiding parties, fighting for the glory of the clan and spreading the reach and influence of the Stone Spirits. Shalana had heeded my father's lessons well, and over the next few years she became a great warrior, forging her legend in the fires of battle."

Knowing Norr's nature, Scythe guessed that he had also created quite a reputation for himself but was simply too humble to mention it.

"Back then Shalana and I were close, but our feelings were only those of good friends. But when my father returned to the earth something changed.

"He was taken too soon; after the sickness his health was always poor. His death left a void in Shalana's life . . . as it did in mine. In our loss and sorrow we turned to each other for comfort. We drew closer. Eventually we became much more than friends."

Norr grunted in pained surprise as Scythe's examinations found a tender spot.

Luckily the ligaments aren't ruptured, she noted, trying to recall

Methodis's lessons about anatomy. *But he needs to stay off his feet for at least a week to heal properly.*

Norr looked down at her, his eyebrows raised inquisitively. Scythe indicated for him to continue his tale with a subtle tilt of her chin.

"That summer we approached Terramon and told him of our feelings. We asked for his blessing on our union, both as Shalana's father and as leader of the clan. He granted our request without hesitation. At the time, neither of us knew him well enough to suspect the trouble he would bring upon us."

"He didn't actually approve of you?" Keegan asked.

"Terramon and my father saw the world differently," Norr said after a long pause to gather his thoughts. "Terramon believed in conquest and expanding our empire. Battle was all he knew. But though my father had once been a warrior, he learned that there was more to life. He believed there comes a time when it is more important to defend and protect what you have, when one must set aside the sword and keep close the very things you once fought for: family, friends, and clan.

"He had spoken to Terramon and the other thanes of this, and many agreed with him. Terramon's never-ending wars had spread the Stone Spirit influence and brought us wealth and prestige, but there was a heavy cost: many warriors had lost their lives, and those who lived spent many months of each year away from their families.

"After thirty years of war, the clan was weary. Many hoped Terramon would step down and let Shalana become chief. That is the way of my people when the chiefs enter the twilight of their years. They step aside and take on the role of councillor to the new chief.

"Many expected that, even with Terramon serving as one of her advisers, Shalana would take them down a different path. But

Terramon was not a man of peace; he had built his reputation on conflict and strife. Perhaps he feared what would become of him once he stepped down; perhaps he feared his counsel would be ignored. Maybe it would have been."

"So he refused to step down?" Vaaler asked.

"That would have been a temporary solution," Norr explained. "Eventually, the thanes would have forced him to name a successor. Or one would have risen and challenged him for the right to be chief. Terramon knew this, so he devised a more cunning solution.

"He called a meeting of the entire clan. There, in front of his thanes and all his people, he named me to be his successor instead of his own flesh and blood. Shalana was devastated. Humiliated and shamed in front of everyone."

"I don't get it," Keegan said. "Couldn't you just refuse?"

"The damage had already been done," Norr explained. "Terramon had cast a cloud over Shalana's name. He had publicly questioned his own daughter's ability to lead our people. Even if I refused, there would still be those who doubted her, especially among the other clans.

"By stepping aside, I would make the Stone Spirits seem weak and some of the chiefs who paid us tribute would challenge Shalana's authority. The thanes would have to set aside their desire for peace to defend the glory of our clan."

"And Terramon would have what he wanted all along," Jerrod noted. "More battles. More war."

"I tried to speak with Shalana," Norr continued, "hoping we could find some way to put things right. But she wouldn't listen to me. She was bitter and angry.

"There had already been whispers among some of the thanes that I should be the next chief. Because of my size and strength, my reputation had spread across the East, and my father had been a great warrior in his youth and a respected voice of wisdom in his later years. And while it is not unheard of for a chief to name a female successor, it is uncommon.

"By publicly naming me, Terramon strengthened the resolve of those who wanted me to take over. Shalana saw this as another betrayal, another slight against her reputation and her pride. So she turned to the old ways, and challenged me to single combat to prove which of us was worthy of becoming chief."

"That spiteful bitch!" Scythe snarled, instinctively jumping to Norr's defense even after the fact. "It wasn't your fault her father's an ass, but she turned on you the second she didn't get what she wanted!"

"She's not like that," Norr insisted. "You just don't understand."

"I think I do," Vaaler said quietly. "Terramon took away her birthright. As long as she could remember, she'd been told she would one day rule her people. That identity defined her. Everything she did and everything she learned was centered around it. She spent her entire life trying to prepare herself for the responsibility; to make herself worthy of being a leader. And then in a single humiliating moment it was all stripped away from her. You can't imagine what that feels like."

His words gave Scythe pause, and in light of the former prince's obvious pain she decided to keep any further arguments to herself.

He's right—I don't know what that feels like. But Vaaler didn't turn on his friends when it happened to him. Shalana did.

"According to our customs, Shalana needed at least a third of the thanes to support her claim before she could challenge me," Norr continued. "She found them, though there were many who still supported my claim as well. Terramon had driven a wedge between the thanes, forcing them to choose sides and stirring up bitter animosity in our clan."

"Who won the duel?" Keegan asked, eager to hear the end of Norr's tale.

"We didn't fight," Norr answered. "The duels are rarely lethal; typically one of the combatants would yield once the other gained the upper hand. But I feared Shalana wouldn't yield. I feared she would force me to kill her."

"What if she defeated you?" Jerrod asked.

Norr paused before reluctantly admitting, "Shalana was a great warrior, but she was no match for me. Few were. My strength and size gave me too great an advantage. We had sparred enough times for us both to know this."

"Yet she challenged you anyway," Vaaler noted. "She was desperate. She would rather die than face the humiliation of what her father had done to her."

"Even if I let her win," Norr said, "many of the thanes would suspect what I had done. Some of those who supported me would continue to urge me to become chief, constantly pushing me to challenge Shalana to a second duel for leadership of the clan. And my presence would be a constant reminder of Shalana's shame.

"I realized that as long as I remained with the clan, there could be no true resolution. The only solution was to disappear; to vanish. So I fled the night before our duel, slinking away like a coward in the night, renouncing my people and my status as a warrior."

That's why you refuse to carry a weapon now, Scythe realized. *You don't think you're worthy of one anymore!*

"You could have told us this before you led us into this frozen wasteland," Jerrod growled. "Instead of delivering us into the hands of a bitter political rival."

"It's not like we had a lot of other options," Scythe reminded the monk.

"I'm sorry for keeping this from you," Norr apologized, though Scythe wasn't sure if he was speaking only to her or to the entire group. "I struggled for the proper way to bring this up, but I thought I'd have more time.

"Shalana is the clan chief now; I didn't expect her to be part of the delegation that came to parlay with the Ice Fangs."

Scythe shook her head at Norr's naïveté. "Did you really think disappearing for a few years would make her forget everything that happened between you?"

"This might not be a bad thing," Vaaler pointed out. "She doesn't seem to hate Norr. Not that I can tell, anyway. Maybe she regrets what happened. Maybe she wants to try to repair your relationship."

That could be even worse, Scythe thought.

"Well?" Jerrod demanded. "Is she an ally or a foe?"

"I don't know," Norr admitted. "She is keeping her feelings hidden, at least until we reach the clan's main camp.

"When we get there I will confront her," Norr promised. "I will tell her of Keegan's importance; I will explain that he is the chosen savior of the mortal world and I will ask for her to help us."

"Maybe don't just blurt it out like that," Keegan cautioned. "It can be a lot for someone to take in all at once."

"Good advice," Scythe concurred. "Maybe don't say anything for a while. At least until we know if she's on our side or not."

"How much longer until we get to the camp?" Jerrod asked.

"Three or four days," Norr said. "Depending on the pace Shalana chooses."

"No matter how tight I wrap your leg, you can't handle three more days of marching," Scythe warned him.

Remembering how Jerrod had helped heal Norr's wounds after they'd escaped Torian, she decided to swallow her pride.

"Anything you can do?" she asked the monk.

"Something about this land limits and restricts my abilities," he reminded her. "I can try, but the results will be minimal."

"Don't worry," Vaaler assured them. "I've got a better solution."

Chapter 13

THEY SET OUT early the next morning at Shalana's command. The air was cold, but the wind had died and the sky above was a clear, cloudless blue.

Perched atop the sled, Norr sat with his arms crossed and a petulant scowl etched on his face, glaring at the backs of the four Stone Spirit warriors tasked with dragging him along. When Vaaler had first suggested he ride while everyone else walked, he'd voiced his objection—traditionally only the very old, the very young, and the infirm rode in the sleds. But the others had supported the idea, especially Scythe, and he quickly realized it was better to submit than risk angering the fiery young woman. She was already upset with him for not telling her about Shalana.

We've always said the past doesn't matter, but that's not really true. Especially not when my past jumps up and slaps her in the face.

He'd been planning to tell Scythe everything, of course. But he just hadn't found the right time to bring it up. Before they were taken by the Pack Masters, there hadn't seemed to be any reason to dredge up his past relationship. And once they were in the Ice Fang camp, he was afraid telling her might upset her enough to do something rash that might jeopardize the exchange with the Stone Spirits.

I could have told her while we were heading to the Stone Spirit camp if Shalana hadn't blurted it out.

Seeing her in the Stone Spirit delegation had caught him completely by surprise; clan chiefs rarely went out on such expeditions.

But she decided to come and see me with her own eyes.

He wasn't sure if that was good or bad. It was possible she had forgiven him after all this time; she wasn't a vindictive person.

At least, she didn't used to be. Who knows what happened to her after I left?

Shalana had readily agreed to Vaaler's suggestion that Norr ride on the sled.

She didn't just agree. She jumped at the idea.

Shalana knew how humiliating it would be for him. She wanted to shame him. Punish him.

Maybe I deserve a little punishment.

He had abandoned her without a word, sneaking off in the night like a coward instead of meeting her in battle. At the time, he'd convinced himself that he had acted out of love—sacrificing his place in the clan to spare her the embarrassment of possibly losing to him in combat. Now, however, he knew that wasn't the truth.

Shalana and I were close friends, but I never really loved her. Not like I love Scythe.

For years they had both known their betrothal was inevitable, but when it was officially announced he hadn't felt any joy. Yet he never voiced his reservations for fear of upsetting Shalana and the thanes.

Our engagement was founded on momentum and the expectations of the clan. After seeing us grow up together, everyone just assumed we would marry.

He had no idea if Shalana had felt the same way or if she had cared for him more deeply than he cared for her.

Instead of having the courage to ask her and find out, I chose to disappear. She has every right to be angry with me. She has every reason to want to shame me.

If his embarrassment was the cost of winning Shalana's cooperation, Norr was more than ready to pay. But what if this petty revenge wasn't the only price? What if this was just the start of something much more? Something much darker?

Shalana isn't like that. Whatever ill will she bears me, she's still a fair and decent person.

But as much as he wanted to convince himself everything would work out, part of him couldn't help but worry. He was assuming she was still the same woman he had grown up with.

People change, he reminded himself. *And not always for the better.*

After several hours, Shalana called for a brief rest stop. While most of the group were still fresh enough to press on, Jerrod could sense that the warriors pulling Norr's sled were growing fatigued.

As they were about to set off again, the monk caught Vaaler's eye and nodded in the sled's direction. Taking the unspoken cue, the Danaan joined him in taking a turn on the tow ropes, along with two fresh Stone Spirits.

Grunting with exertion, Jerrod and the others struggled and strained against the ropes. The thin layer of ice and snow helped the sled glide smoothly over the ground, but it also made it difficult to find any traction. The first few steps were slow and difficult, but as the sled gathered momentum it became much easier to keep it moving. Even though Shalana set a brisk pace, Jerrod and the others were able to keep up, and they made better progress than they would have with Norr limping along on foot.

Throughout it all, Norr sat atop the sled like a petulant child, not speaking but making his discomfort and displeasure obvious with his sour expression. Jerrod, however, cared little for what the big man thought about his current situation. He was far more interested in what the Stone Spirits thought about Norr.

Shalana was difficult to read. Given their history, she probably harbored some bitterness toward him. But she hadn't shown any outright hostility, and she had agreed to let Norr ride on the sled. Jerrod chose to take that as a good sign: had she wanted her former fiancé to truly suffer, she would have forced him to walk on his wounded knee.

Maybe she's forgiven him for what happened between them.

The rest of the Stone Spirits didn't seem to bear Norr any grudge, either. In fact, it seemed the opposite was true. Even though most of the Stone Spirit warriors with her were clearly too young to have ever fought at Norr's side, several had been quick to volunteer to take turns helping pull his sled.

He is well liked among his people. Even after being gone for years his reputation still inspires their loyalty. That could help win the Stone Spirits to our cause . . . unless Shalana sees this as a potential threat to her position.

Unfortunately, there really was no way to know for sure until they reached the main camp.

The journey was grueling but otherwise uneventful. During the day a steady rotation of men and women helped drag Norr along, and at night the Stone Spirits set up makeshift camps with impressive efficiency.

Norr stayed with Keegan, Jerrod, and the others at night, but there was little talk among them. By the time the convoy stopped each day they were all too exhausted to do little more than collapse into a deep sleep, wrapped up in the blankets and bedding provided by Shalana's people.

Even with the relentless pace Shalana set, it still took them three days to reach the Stone Spirit settlement. When they did, Jerrod couldn't help but be amazed at its size.

Norr had told them the Stone Spirits were among the largest and most powerful of all the clans, but the monk had assumed his words were born of partisanship and pride. But on seeing the hundreds of tents and dozens of single-story mud buildings stretching off for almost a mile into the distance, he realized the massive barbarian hadn't been exaggerating.

The Ice Fang clan had numbered around fifty human members. Of those, about thirty had appeared to be warriors; the rest either too young or too old to fight effectively. In contrast, Jerrod's highly attuned senses estimated the Stone Spirit camp to house in excess of five hundred souls.

The larger population would mean less urgency to conscript warriors—they could afford to have members of their society who focused on other skills. However, it was probably safe to assume they had at least two hundred members who would be able to take the field of battle.

That doesn't include the clans that pay them tribute, either, Jerrod reminded himself. *They might be a lot smaller, but Norr said over a dozen chiefs paid the Stone Spirits tribute. If Shalana needed to raise an army, how many could she call on? A thousand? Two thousand? More?*

The Order had always been aware of the potential threat the Eastern savages represented, but their attention had primarily been focused on the Southlands, the Free Cities, and the mysterious, Chaos-blooded Danaan. Nobody had ever attempted to get an accurate count of the clans; the assumption had always been that the nomadic tribes were too few to ever represent any real danger.

How many other clans wield the same kind of influence as the Stone Spirits? Jerrod wondered. *If they united against the Southlands, would the Order be able to raise an army large enough to keep them at bay?*

Based on the most recent census, taken shortly after the Purge almost twenty years ago, each of the Seven Capitals had populations approaching or exceeding fifty thousand. It was safe to assume there were at least that many more subjects in the smaller cities, villages, and hamlets under their jurisdiction. But most of those were untrained, unarmed civilians: actual soldiers made up only a fraction of the population.

The Order had always feared a Danaan invasion: an army supported by Chaos mages emerging from the North Forest. Seeing the Stone Spirit village in all its glory made Jerrod realize that their inherent fear of a kingdom built on Chaos magic had blinded them to the nomadic empire lurking in the Frozen East.

As they drew closer to the makeshift village, people came rushing out to meet them. Men, women, and children poured out in a wave, clapping and cheering as the delegation, with Shalana at its head, marched into the center of the city. A number of dogs came with them, but these were not the deadly trained killers of the Ice Fang packs; rather, they were the random assortment of pet mutts and curs one would expect to find in the streets of any small Southern settlement.

At first, Jerrod assumed the crowd was coming to pay homage to the return of their chief. He didn't understand Clan-speak, but amid the cacophony of shouts and chants he could clearly hear Shalana's name rising up. But as he listened more closely, he also heard Norr's name being called out. The language barrier made it foolish to assume context, but given the festive atmosphere it almost seemed as if the crowd was welcoming back a long-lost hero.

Unfortunately, there was no way to predict whether Norr's popularity would win his people over to their cause or compel Shalana to see him as a threat to her authority.

Vaaler's command of Verlsung wasn't perfect; he'd had little chance to practice what his tutors had taught him in the real world. The shouts and cheers of the crowd overlapped and ran into each other, making it difficult to pick out what was being said. Shalana's name was being called out, as was Norr's. Most everything else was lost in the rumble of the crowd. But there were two words he was able to pick out, being said over and over: red bear.

Are they talking about Norr?

It would certainly fit, given his size and the color of his hair and great, bushy beard.

He said he's been gone for five years. How popular was he before he left?

The Eastern culture valued strength and prowess in battle. It wasn't hard to imagine a giant like Norr becoming a legendary warrior. One who had earned the nickname of the Red Bear and won the hearts and minds of his people.

Norr's account of how he had left his people made it seem like he'd deserted them; slinking away in the night to avoid a duel with Shalana. If anything, he should be reviled as a coward. In his own eyes, he wasn't a warrior anymore: he didn't even deserve to carry a weapon.

Clearly the people who'd come out to welcome them didn't share that opinion. As they entered the village itself, the crowd swarmed them. Men and women fell on Norr: shaking his hand, patting him on the shoulder, embracing him in firm, quick hugs.

Realizing it was pointless to try to keep the sled moving in the throng, Vaaler let the tow rope drop and stepped back from the crowd. Jerrod and the warriors who had been helping pull Norr along did the same. Two large, middle-aged men reached down to help Norr up, each grabbing ahold of one meaty wrist and hauling him to his feet.

The big man was smiling and laughing with his old friends in a joyous reunion. Watching him, Vaaler couldn't help but feel a bit jealous as he remembered his own homecoming after his years studying under Rexol. The citizens hadn't lined the streets of Ferlhame to welcome him; instead, he'd been greeted by an honor guard and a handful of his mother's most trusted advisers. Drake and his mother had been the only ones genuinely pleased to see him; the others were stoic and glum. He was supposed to return as a great wizard, but word had already spread of his failure to learn the mage's art.

He noticed Scythe and Keegan standing apart from the crowd

as well, watching with a bemused expression. Like him, they were clearly taken aback by Norr's popularity. But Jerrod, still standing close to Vaaler's side, wasn't watching Norr. Following his blind gaze, he realized the monk was studying Shalana.

Unlike the rest of the crowd, she wasn't laughing or smiling. Her features were frozen, carefully set in a reserved, neutral mask to keep from betraying her emotions. But her body was tense, her shoulders back, her head moving slowly from side to side as she took in her people's reaction. Her left hand clenched tightly around the shaft of her spear, the long, lean muscles of her arm taut and firm.

She wasn't expecting this, Vaaler realized, and a picture began to paint itself.

From his account, it was clear Norr had assumed Shalana had always been the natural successor to Terramon. But maybe that wasn't the case. Norr was humble and modest; even if others saw him as a potential clan chief, he wouldn't have thought of himself that way. Yet it wasn't hard to imagine. He'd been the clan's greatest warrior—the legendary Red Bear—and the son of a well-respected thane.

The people wanted him all along. They were certain Terramon would name Norr as the next chief, and Terramon probably knew it. It was only Norr and Shalana, blinded by their feelings for each other, who were surprised.

When Norr vanished without warning or explanation on the eve of his duel with Shalana, it would have led to rumors and speculation. Some would condemn Norr as a coward, but others would wonder if Terramon had driven the clan's greatest warrior away so his own daughter could become chief. And if Shalana's reign was troubled or difficult for any reason, it would be inevitable for at least some of her people to imagine things would have been better under Norr.

Their resentment of Shalana had probably simmered quietly

below the surface, whispers and secrets that never reached her ears. In her eyes Norr had acted like a coward and abandoned his people. She probably thought she was being merciful and magnanimous by agreeing to the Ice Fang ransom. She probably imagined she was bringing home a fallen, broken hero, a man who would have to work long and hard to redeem himself in the eyes of the clan.

In the face of Norr's triumphant return it would be impossible to keep clinging to that illusion.

"Enough!" Shalana suddenly called out, her voice rising above the crowd as she brandished her spear above her head.

Everyone fell silent, all eyes turning to their chief.

"The thanes are waiting for us in the great hall," Shalana said, directing her words to Norr. "We must decide the fate of you and your Outlander friends."

Clever, Vaaler thought. *Remind everyone that he has allied himself with those outside the clan.*

"There will be time for catching up later," she added in a softer tone. "But we will do it right. A proper feast to honor the return of the Red Bear."

Another smart move. Don't paint yourself as the villain.

"What's happening?" Scythe asked, coming over to Norr as the mollified crowd slowly dispersed.

"Shalana is taking us to meet with the thanes," he answered, speaking loud enough for Keegan, Jerrod, and Vaaler to hear.

"Right now?" Scythe protested. "We don't even get a chance to rest or eat?"

"We go now," Shalana told her in Allrish.

The two Stone Spirit warriors who had helped pull Norr on the sled bent down to grab the tow ropes, but the big man shook his head.

"I've rested long enough. I can walk to meet the Thanes without help."

With Shalana at the head, they were escorted through the camp by a half dozen warriors to a long, narrow, low-roofed building made from mud and stone.

I guess once a clan becomes as big and powerful as the Stone Spirits, they don't have to be nomads anymore, Vaaler thought.

They approached the building from the broad side, where a single door stood in the middle of the wall. Shalana pulled it open and went in first. The rest of their escort stepped aside, indicating for Norr and his companions to follow. The big man had to duck to get through the entrance, but inside, the ceiling was just tall enough for him to stand upright.

Is that coincidence, Vaaler wondered as he and the others shuffled in, *or did they build this tall enough for the Red Bear to stand up in on purpose?*

The interior was a single open room—the distance to the back wall was only twenty feet, but the hall extended at least thirty feet off to either side. A large table ran almost the entire length, with benches lining either side. There was probably room for sixty or more, but currently there were only about twenty seated at the table, all on the opposite side so they could face the door.

Those inside rose as Shalana made her way along the length of the table, around to the other side, and eventually to a seat in the middle, directly across from where Norr and the Outlanders stood, waiting and anxious. The other thanes took their seat only after she sat down, and Vaaler heard the door close behind them.

The Danaan scanned the faces of the thanes staring curiously back at him. Most were men; he counted only six women besides Shalana. The men were all bearded, so it was difficult to judge their ages, though Vaaler guessed they ranged from mid-twenties to well into their sixties. Seated immediately to Shalana's right was a stern-looking man of about fifty, clutching a rough-hewn cane in his left hand. Based on his position at the table, Vaaler guessed this was Terramon. The last two fingers on the hand clutching the cane were missing, probably lost to frostbite on a long winter campaign. Between the weathered lines of his face and his beard, it was hard to see any resemblance to Shalana, but he shared her cold blue eyes.

In contrast to the unbridled enthusiasm of the men and women in the camp, the thanes showed little emotion as Norr stood before them.

They probably know what really happened when he left. And they know the reality of being chief is a lot harder than most realize. They don't imagine a world where everything is perfect just because Norr is in charge.

An awkward silence settled over the gathering. Norr shifted, trying to find a more comfortable stance. One of the thanes cleared his throat, and another coughed, but none dared speak. The silence dragged on, becoming an oppressive weight on the room. Finally, after what seemed like hours but was probably less than five minutes, Shalana rose from her seat and addressed her followers.

"Five years ago, the man before you disappeared. We did not know what happened or why he left. We did not know whether he was alive or dead. We only knew he was gone. Now he is back, and we must decide his fate."

She sat down, yielding the floor. Vaaler noticed Scythe, Keegan, and Jerrod all wearing concerned, confused expressions, unable to follow her Verlsung speech but fearing the worst.

Beside her, Terramon was quick to rise and let his voice be heard, using his cane to help him get to his feet.

"I think we all have the same questions," he said, addressing Norr. "Why did you abandon us? And why have you come crawling back?"

"I make no excuse for the actions of my past," Norr said, speaking slowly. "What is done cannot be undone. What happens now, and will happen in the future, is all that matters."

"Fine words," Terramon sneered, "but they tell us nothing."

"I left because I could not bear the burden of becoming clan chief," Norr replied.

Vaaler felt the words came easily from the big man; if he felt any shame over what he had done, he had come to terms with it long ago.

"My actions were rash, and I know there are some who were hurt by what I did," he continued, his eyes glancing quickly to Shalana, then back to Terramon. "But at the time I felt it was best for the clan."

"Do you no longer feel this way?" Terramon pressed. "Is that why you returned?"

"I am not here to reopen old wounds," Norr explained, his voice deep and calm. "I turned my back on the clan, and I was wrong. But now I hope the Stone Spirits will not turn their back on me and my friends."

"Friends?" Terramon replied with a smirk. "You have chosen these Outlanders over your clan! Why should we help you after you turned your back on us?"

"What's going on?" Scythe hissed in a loud whisper, unable to follow the conversation but sensing from the tone that Norr was being challenged.

"I am not the only one on trial here," Norr said, switching to Allrish. "My friends have a right to know what is being said. I ask that I be allowed to translate for them."

"Now you wish to turn your back on our language, too?" Terramon snarled, still in Clan-speak. "Their fate is tied to yours. Nothing they say matters!"

"Peace, father," Shalana said, reaching up from her seat to place a hand on his arm.

An awkward silence fell over the room. It was Norr who broke it, addressing himself directly to Shalana.

"We need your help," he said, still speaking so his companions could understand. "We have nowhere else to turn. We have many enemies, and I ask you for the protection and aid of the clan on behalf of me and my friends."

"We already have enough enemies of our own," Terramon answered before Shalana could reply. He obviously understood All-rish well enough to grasp what Norr was saying, but he refused to speak any language but his own.

The old man turned to his daughter. "I warned you no good could come of Norr's return. I warned you not to pay the Ice Fang ransom."

"But you did pay the ransom," Norr said. "And we are grateful for our freedom."

"You are not free yet," Shalana curtly responded, rising to her feet. Like Terramon, she was only using Verlsung.

Her father begrudgingly took his seat, yielding the floor to his daughter.

"You are here as a prisoner," she reminded Norr, "not as one of the clan. You gave up that right when you abandoned us."

"Banish them," Terramon spat from his chair. "Send them away. They have no place here!"

"Is that how the rest of you feel?" Shalana asked, turning her attention to the other thanes. "Should Norr be cast out?"

Her question was met with another awkward silence.

They really don't know how they feel about him anymore, Vaaler thought. *They're hurt and betrayed, but they remember the man he used to be and they don't want to turn their back on him.*

Shalana nodded slowly in understanding.

"I will grant you and your friends safe haven," she said to Norr, "if you meet my terms."

"Name your terms," Norr said, though he hesitated before speaking.

"You swear allegiance to me as Chief of the Stone Spirits. You promise to once again be a warrior and protector of the clan. And you become my husband, as you promised long ago."

She still spoke in the language of her people, so there was no immediate reaction from Scythe.

Good thing. She'd probably leap across the table to try to tear out Shalana's throat in a jealous rage if she knew what was being said.

The former prince, however, recognized that the offer was more political than romantic. Bringing Norr back into the clan would appease the masses, and having him marry her would leave little doubt that she had his full support as the new chief. In this one symbolic act she could seal the rift she had created five years ago by challenging Norr, solidify her position, and eliminate a potential future rival.

"You know I can't do that," Norr answered, switching back to his native tongue. His eyes glanced down at Scythe, then back up to Shalana. "I told you why that first night."

"If you refuse," Shalana said, her eyes narrowing, "then you and your friends will be cast out with no food or supplies. How long will you survive with winter coming?"

"Would you really condemn us to death out of jealousy and spite?" Norr asked her, his voice low and hard. "Are you really still so bitter?"

"Don't think you know me," Shalana shot back. "Much has changed since you've been gone. You have my terms. Make your choice!"

"You brought this on yourself," Terramon declared, rising from his seat to stand beside his daughter and slamming his cane hard against the floor for emphasis. "You know the ways of our people!"

"I do," the big man agreed, then turned his head to address the other thanes in the room. "I left to keep from tearing this clan apart. I thought Shalana would lead you down the proper path. Now I see I made the wrong choice."

A murmur of surprise swept through the thanes. Scythe, Keegan, and Jerrod reacted as well, though only with confusion.

Unable to follow what was going on, they had no way to know what Norr had said to draw the startled reaction from the thanes.

"I have returned to fix my mistake," Norr continued, his voice gaining strength. "I have returned to reclaim what is rightfully mine. I have returned to challenge Shalana for the right to rule the Stone Spirits!"

All the blood drained from Shalana's face, and Terramon's jaw dropped as the big man made his declaration. Some of the thanes gasped aloud, but Vaaler noticed others nodding faintly.

Norr raised his massive arms up and held them out toward the assemblage.

"Who among you will stand with me?" he bellowed, his cry echoing throughout the Long Hall. "Who among you will support my claim?"

At first, none of the Thanes made any motion. Then one near the far end of the long table—a man of about Norr's age—slowly rose to his feet. Another, a man as old as Terramon, joined him a moment later. Then another followed, and two more.

Before any others could rise to their feet, Shalana slammed her fist on the table.

"Enough!" she shouted. "I accept your challenge. We will settle this in the old way; three days from now."

"If you lose," Terramon added, waving a gnarled finger in Norr's direction, "you and your friends will be stripped of your weapons and clothes and turned out naked on the tundra to die shivering and helpless!"

"That is not for you to decide," Shalana snapped at her father.

Chastened, the old man sat down.

"I am not as bitter and spiteful as you seem to believe," she said, addressing Norr but clearly speaking for the benefit of her thanes. "I did not cast you out of this clan—you left of your own free will. You have also returned of your own free will, and it is not my place to cast you out now.

"If you lose your challenge, my first offer still stands. Swear allegiance to me as a warrior and husband, and your friends will be kept safe from harm. Is this acceptable to you?"

There was a murmur from the assemblage, and Vaaler had the feeling they approved of Shalana's moderated response.

Norr hesitated before finally realizing there wasn't any way to refuse. "If I lose, I will accept your terms."

Shalana nodded and called for the guards.

"Take Norr and his Outlander friends to their tents," she said when the door opened.

"Three days," she reminded Norr.

As the guards led them away, Vaaler could just make out Scythe whispering to Norr under her breath.

"I don't know what just happened in there," she hissed, "but I'm pretty sure I hate that bitch."

Chapter 14

Yasmin's eyes snapped open as the first rays of dawn crept through the windowsill. Disentangling herself from the cross-legged lotus position she had slept in, she rose from the thick, carpeted floor to her full imposing height.

The room was empty, though only a week before it had been lavishly furnished. Lord Carthin, ruler of Brindomere—largest of the seven capitals—had graciously offered his most luxurious guest quarters to the new Pontiff when she and her entourage of Inquisitors and Seers had arrived in his city. Yasmin had accepted, but only on the condition that the goose-down bed—and all the other ornate trappings of luxury and wealth—be removed from her chambers. Lord Carthin had, of course, complied.

His unhesitating obedience was more than just political savvy. Brindomere had always been a stronghold of the Order's influence in the Southlands; its ruling family steadfast and earnest in their faith. For this, the True Gods had looked favorably upon the city, granting it wealth and power that had endured for centuries. With the fall of the Monastery, Brindomere was the most logical place for the Pontiff to relocate.

But Yasmin understood there were still dangers lurking, even here. In these dark times she could ill afford the sins of complacency and contentment. That was why she had demanded the removal of the bed and why she continued to sleep on the guest chamber's floor.

Opening the door, she left the room behind and made her way down the staircase to the main floor. She passed through the kitchen, grabbing a single slice of stale bread to nourish her body. Tearing into it with grim resolve, she continued on, ignoring the mix of reverence and fear on the faces of the household staff as she passed them by without even acknowledging their existence.

In the courtyard outside she found the Seers already waiting for her. They also had private chambers, though these were located in the servants' quarters in the buildings at the rear of Lord Carthin's estate. Like their leader, they rested only a few hours each night—just long enough to give birth to their nightly visions.

Recently, all the Seers had shared the same dream: a wave of blood sweeping across the Southlands, devouring all in its path. For three days Yasmin and the Seers had tried to interpret the dream, seeking understanding and guidance.

Nazir had been a master of interpreting the Seers' visions, but Yasmin lacked her predecessor's talent. Her strength was in her unwavering resolve and her willingness to take action—traits necessary now more than ever. And yet, ever since the dream of blood, she had been unwilling to act, paralyzed by the fear of leading the Order—and the entire Southlands—down the wrong path.

If Cassandra had not stolen the Crown, I could use its power to interpret the visions.

A pointless sentiment. Yasmin had patrols roaming the Southlands, the Frozen East, and even the Danaan forests searching for Cassandra, but so far they had failed to reclaim the Crown. The Pontiff was confident they would eventually track her down, but until then there was no use in lamenting the Talisman's absence.

The patrols were also searching for the heretics: Jerrod and Rexol's apprentice. They had nearly captured them in the Free

City of Torian, only to lose them when they unleashed a fiery destruction upon the defenseless city. Another had nearly captured them in the wastelands of the Frozen East, only to fall victim to the barbarian savages that roamed that Gods-forsaken land. Yet despite these setbacks, Yasmin never doubted for an instant that Jerrod would one day pay for his crimes.

Unfortunately, the unshakable certainty that both Cassandra and Jerrod would eventually be found did nothing to help her make sense of the Seers' most recent dreams.

On sensing Yasmin's arrival, Xadier, the newly appointed head of the Seers, rushed over to greet her. The young man was eager, excited. It was unbecoming; he lacked the dignity and gravitas suitable to someone in such an important and revered position.

Too many of our best were lost when the Monastery fell. Those who remain are weak and inexperienced, their visions only coming when they work in concert. It limits them, makes them all see the same thing over and over.

"Good news, Pontiff," Xadier gushed, not even waiting for Yasmin to make a proper acknowledgment of him. "The dream has changed!"

"Tell me," she instructed, not quite ready to share his exuberance.

"The wave of blood still sweeps across the Southlands, but now it shifts and changes during the journey, becoming an army of marching soldiers."

When he finished, Yasmin waited silently, hoping there would be more. Of course there wasn't.

The vision is still unclear. Is it a warning of something we must stop or a prophecy showing us something we must do?

"Is something wrong, Pontiff?" Xadier asked, his elation fading given her lack of response.

Had he been an Inquisitor, Yasmin would have unleashed the full fury of her rage on the hapless young man. She demanded results from the Inquisitors; failure was unacceptable, and she held them accountable for their actions. But the Seers were different. Their visions were born from Chaos; unpredictable and unreliable. Berating Xadier for things beyond his control was neither fair nor productive.

"I am considering the implications of this new vision," she explained.

"Of course, Pontiff," Xadier said with a slight bow of his head.

Blood and armies. War is coming. Against the Danaan? Against our own people? What wisdom would Nazir have drawn from this?

Despite her faith, Yasmin didn't believe in divine inspiration. She believed in preparation and planning; success came through cold, hard resolve. When the sudden spark of understanding flared up within her, she was momentarily stunned by its force.

The Purge. The blood of wizards, witches, and heretics. The armies of the just.

"I understand the visions," she declared. "It is time for another Purge."

Xadier knew better than to question her openly, but she caught a glimmer of doubt in the young man's eye. Nazir had openly cautioned against another Purge, believing it could destroy the Order. He had feared the Free Cities would unite against them, and the public executions and harsh laws against magic would drive the people of the Southlands to rebellion. Perhaps he had been right, once. Times were different now.

"For too long we have sat idly by while those with Chaos in their blood have spread their vile teachings," Yasmin began. "We have allowed them to practice their foul arts openly, without fear of punishment and retribution, and they have brought death and destruction to the land.

"Chaos has been unleashed upon the mortal world," she continued. "The rumors have spread throughout the Southlands: The

Monastery has fallen; Chaos Spawn wander the depths of the Danaan forest; Evil walks the earth.

"The devastation in Torian has rekindled the fear of rogue mages, especially among the Free Cities," she explained. "The people there are scared. Helpless. Powerless. They need someone to lead them, someone to hold back the Chaos.

"This time the Free Cities will not oppose us—they will flock to our cause, along with the entire Southlands. They are eager to follow, and it is our sacred duty to guide them down the righteous path!"

"Yes, Pontiff," Xadier agreed, his expression changing to one of rapturous joy as he was swept up in her holy fervor. "Now I see! Now I understand!"

"We will finish the job we began forty years ago," Yasmin vowed. "In the name of the True Gods, we will cleanse this world of Chaos in all its forms!"

Cassandra's mind floated in a meditative fog somewhere between waking and sleep. The semiconscious state allowed her mind to rest as her body continued its slow but steady progress, instinctively placing one foot in front of the other as she marched through the ankle-deep snow.

Meditation was a poor substitute for true sleep, but she didn't have the luxury of allowing herself to stop. The ones who hunted her—the Crawling Twins—didn't sleep. She could sense them scuttling along in her wake, tireless and relentless as they tracked her across the frozen plains. They were still at least two days behind her, but they were gaining.

Her journey was made more difficult by a steady stream of wandering Easterners crossing her path. Their numbers were far greater than when she had first crossed the tundra on her way to the Guardian's cave. Instead of a few scattered hunting parties or scouting patrols made up of three or four individuals, she was seeing processions numbering twenty or more, all heading in the same northeasterly direction. It almost seemed as if there was some kind of mass migration or gathering under way, though Cassandra had no idea what could be behind it.

Each time one of the barbarian bands drew near she had to take steps to hide her presence. Sometimes she would have to change direction to avoid running into them, other times she would have to temporarily slow or pick up her pace. In every instance, she had to call on the power of the Talisman she carried in the sack slung over her shoulder, obscuring their sight so they wouldn't notice the signs of her passing.

She had long since stopped wondering at how she knew to do this; it had become almost second nature. The principle was the same as the one she'd used to cast out false trails to confuse and mislead the avian huntress during her initial flight with the Crown. It wasn't something she consciously tried to do; it seemed to happen instinctively, as if something deep inside her—or inside the Talisman itself—sensed the danger and took steps to protect her.

Unfortunately, the Crawling Twins were not fooled by such tricks. Even at this great distance, she'd felt their minds brush up against hers: They shared a simple, almost bestial, intelligence. Their thoughts were primitive and direct, but focused to the point of obsession. They had her scent, and nothing she could do would throw them off it. All she could do now was keep moving and hope she could stay ahead of them.

That isn't all you can do, the now-familiar voice that wasn't her own said inside her head. *You already draw upon the power of the Crown just by being near it. Think of what you could do if you dared to put it on!*

Cassandra ignored the voice as she always did. But its insistent presence jarred her from her meditative state. She shook her head from side to side as full awareness reluctantly returned, taking quick stock of her surroundings.

Nothing had changed. The temperature was dropping and her belly was empty, but she was still strong enough to ward off the worst of the cold and hunger through sheer force of will. Hopefully by the time her strength began to falter, she would be in more hospitable surroundings.

Her mission was still the same: get to Callastan and find a ship to take her to the Western Isles. Ahead of her were leagues and leagues of bare, frozen plains, populated by traveling tribes of savages. Beyond that was the breadth of the entire Southlands, swarming with Yasmin's Inquisitors. And behind her were the Crawling Twins, inexorably getting closer and closer.

Dwelling on all the obstacles in her path could only weaken her resolve, so Cassandra pushed them from her mind. Calling on her monastic training, she let herself slip back into a semiconscious meditative state, her thoughts slipping away until all that remained was the steady rhythm of her feet crunching on the snow.

The Crown was a prison without walls, but it was still a prison. One Rexol was determined to escape.

The great mage hadn't been strong enough to contain the Chaos unleashed when he dared to put the Talisman on. Its power consumed his physical form; incinerating his flesh and turning his bones into a pile of burned ash. Yet though his body was gone, Rexol's mind and essence—his awareness and his identity—had survived.

Through sheer force of will, he had kept himself from being swallowed up into the infinity of knowledge swirling inside the Crown. The ordeal had left his disembodied consciousness floating aimlessly inside the vastness of the Talisman's power, weak and virtually helpless. But over time his strength slowly returned, and he realized that his connection to Cassandra—forged through the invisible mark he had burned into her arm when she had been his ward—still existed.

Even trapped in the Crown, he was still able to exert an influence on the mortal world through the young woman. Using her as a conduit, he had channeled the power of the Crown to create the false trails that had allowed Cassandra to reach the safety of the Guardian's cave during her flight from the Monastery. In her current exodus he was the one twisting and altering the perceptions of the wandering barbarians to keep her hidden.

And he was the one who kept urging her to use the Crown.

Cassandra felt his presence. He knew she could hear his words in her mind; she had even recognized Rexol's influence in them. But he doubted she understood what was really happening. She thought his words were a mixture of memories and recollections—ideas formed in some deep, dark recess of her own mind. She had no idea he still lived, and he was eager to preserve her misconception. Yet even though he'd tried to make his suggestions seem like her own, so far she had rejected them out of hand.

Rexol wasn't discouraged. He could sense he was beginning to wear down her resistance. She was getting weaker and he was growing stronger; eventually she would stop ignoring his suggestions, give in and use the Crown.

When she did, he would be ready. And his imprisonment would end.

Chapter 15

SHALANA SAT STILL and quiet in the darkness, listening to the walls of her tent rustle and snap as they were battered by the wind.

As clan chief, her domicile was the largest in the camp. Nearly fifteen feet on each side, there was enough room for her to stand fully upright, though for now she was seated cross-legged on a small fur blanket in the center.

After five long years as chief, the tent still felt strange to her. She had lived here as a young girl with her mother, but she could barely remember those days. After the sickness took her, Norr's father had taken her in. With only the three of them, they hadn't needed much room: a cluster of small tents near the center of the camp was where she spent most of her youth.

Even when Terramon had been around, she hadn't lived with him. Her father had never remarried, and he was rarely in the main camp for more than a month at a time. He was always eager to begin the next campaign, eager to lead the next raid, eager to force the surrounding clans to bow down and pay tribute to the Stone Spirits. He had little time or concern for the needs of a young daughter; growing up, it was just easier for everyone for her to stay with her adopted family.

When she came of age she joined the Stone Spirit war parties in their battles and raids, as did Norr. But that didn't bring her any closer to Terramon. Norr's father had taught her that glory in battle was only a means to an end, a way to protect and secure the things that truly mattered: clan and family. She cherished her time in the camp; that was the reason she fought.

Terramon felt differently. For him, conquest was a goal in and of itself. When he wasn't leading his warriors into battle, he was restless and sullen. He scowled and glared at everyone in the camp. He took little pleasure in the stories and songs shared over drinks in the Long Hall. He had elevated the Stone Spirits to one of the largest and strongest clans in the East, earning the respect and admiration of his thanes and his people. But they never loved him.

Shalana had vowed her reign would be different than her father's. She wouldn't make the same mistakes. She wouldn't force her thanes into an endless succession of battles against neighboring clans like her father had. She would be the chief to bring peace and prosperity to the Stone Spirits. Instead, she sat alone in the cavernous tent, knowing that many of her people would be cheering against her when she faced Norr in three days.

Why did you come back now, you great oaf? Dragging your Outlander friends and your Islander harlot with you? After all this time, why reopen these old wounds?

In the first year after he left, she—like everyone else in the clan—kept expecting him to return. She had challenged him for leadership, but she'd borne him no ill will. Being chief was her destiny; it was her birthright. She wasn't willing to surrender that to anyone, not even Norr. She thought her betrothed would understand that. She thought he would give her the honor of meeting her challenge.

Maybe we didn't know each other as well as I thought.

As the months rolled by and he didn't return, Shalana came to realize the truth: Norr had turned his back on her and the Stone Spirits. She accepted the truth for what it was and moved on. But the future she envisioned for her people never came to pass.

When Terramon stepped down, the Black Wings—a recently conquered clan—refused to pay their promised tribute. The Red Bear was gone, and the new chief was a woman whose own father had not deemed her worthy of being named his successor. She was perceived as flawed and weak, and it made the Black Wings bold.

Shalana had no choice but to rally her thanes and bring the rebel clan to heel. She broke them easily, proving her skill as a warrior and a leader on the field of battle. But when it came time to punish them for transgressions, she faltered.

Her father would have doubled their tribute. He would have made prisoners of their warriors and hunters, and taken most of their weapons and food stores. But Shalana knew such a sentence would mean starvation and suffering when winter came. She was not hard-hearted enough to condemn scores of men, women, and even children to a grim, slow death.

Terramon warned me not to be lenient, she recalled. *He warned me the other clans were watching.*

What Shalana considered mercy, others saw as a lack of resolve. By failing to impose brutal consequences on the Black Wings, she inadvertently encouraged others to rise up against the Stone Spirits. More clans refused to pay tribute. Some even banded together, forming alliances in the hope they could become the dominant clan in the region.

Shalana broke them all, one by one. Just like her father, she led her thanes in a seemingly endless cycle of war and bloodshed against the other clans. But instead of gaining power, influence, and glory for the Stone Spirits, her campaigns were a desperate struggle to hold together the fraying corners of Terramon's empire.

In the Long Hall and in the war councils, her thanes gave her their support. Yet she knew there were whispers and rumors that things would have been different if Norr had been chief.

Maybe they would have, Shalana admitted to herself. *But I had no choice. I did what had to be done.*

She tried to ignore the whispers. In battle after battle she fought to forge her own legend—one to rival the stories still told in whispers of the Red Bear. Through her actions, she thought she could win the respect and admiration of her thanes and the loyalty and obedience of her clan. But now she understood that nothing she did would ever be enough. Norr was something she would never be: beloved.

She knew that the Red Bear had proved himself too many times in battle to ever be branded a coward. Yet his sudden flight in the face of her challenge should have cast some aspersions on his reputation. Instead, the opposite had happened.

Many believed he had done something noble by leaving, sparing Shalana the shame of defeat, or sacrificing himself to keep the loyalties of the clan from being divided. His exploits—along with his prowess in battle, his incredible strength, and his great courage—became more and more legendary in the retelling. The myth and legend of the Red Bear became greater than the man himself. His absence only made them love him even more.

She had stayed to lead and serve the clan, and they resented her for it. It was irrational, illogical, unfair. She knew some even thought that Shalana was to blame for driving away the Stone Spirits's greatest champion.

And in a way, I did. But I'm also the one who brought him back. Somehow, she doubted she would ever be given credit for that.

She heard a familiar thumping coming from outside the tent—the sound of Terramon rapping his cane against the tent's hide entrance flap, pulled taut to keep out the winter chill. Her father didn't visit often, and when he did he only came to criticize. But at least he came. The same could rarely be said of her thanes or the rest of the clan. Outside of the official business of the Long Hall, they rarely sought her counsel or company.

Gritting her teeth, she rose from the warm pelts lining the ground and pulled aside the flap to let him in.

"Why are you always sitting in the dark?" he grumbled as he made his way inside, leaning heavily on his cane.

Shalana didn't answer but left the flap open a sliver so the dim light from the peat fire outside could shine through.

"You are the clan chief," Terramon reminded her. "You should have a lamp and oil to light this tent."

"Why waste the oil?" she countered. "I can find my way around in the dark."

Terramon gingerly lowered himself to the ground. He was only in his fifties, but nagging injuries from a thousand battles and three decades of campaigns through the dead of winter had taken a harsh toll on his joints and bones.

"I warned you not to pay Norr's ransom," he said once he was settled.

"The Ice Fangs would have killed him," she said, her voice flat and tired.

"So? He abandoned us. He abandoned you. Why is his fate your responsibility?"

"I'm not so bitter that I would let a good man die out of spite."

"There are more important things you should be focused on," Terramon reminded her. "Hadawas has called a Conclave. We shouldn't be wasting time with this foolishness!"

"The Conclave is still two weeks away," she reminded her father. "We will be there. We have time."

"The clan must always come first," her father insisted, as if he hadn't even heard her words. "We must look after our own."

"Norr is one of our own," Shalana reminded him. After a moment she added, "The clan still loves him."

"Do you?" her father demanded.

Shalana didn't bother to answer.

"Is that why you paid the ransom?" Terramon pressed. "Is that

why you tried to force him to marry you? Because your head is
still ruled by a young girl's foolish heart?"

"He made a promise," she whispered, her voice too low for her
father's aged ears to hear. "He should honor it."

"Speak up!" Terramon chided.

"I knew there were some among the clan who would rather
see Norr as chief," she answered in a louder voice, trying to use
logic to defend her actions. "I thought if we were wed, they would
look at us as a united front."

"And you believed Norr would simply bow down to your
demands?" Terramon snorted. "He didn't come back to serve; he
came back to rule!"

I don't believe that, Shalana thought. *He's not like you.*

"You should have told me you were going to bring him before
the thanes," her father chided. "I could have warned you this
would happen. We could have prepared and planned instead of
walking into his trap!"

"Such a tragedy that I lack your great wisdom," Shalana sneered.

"You are in no position to mock me," he reminded her. "Not
after you left yourself open to being challenged in the Long Hall."

"What other choice did I have?" Shalana asked. "Bring him
bound and gagged like a prisoner to stand trial for deserting us?"

"Yes!" Terramon blurted out. "You let the clan and the thanes
see him as their long-lost hero making a triumphant return! You
should have brought him in on his knees, like the cur he is!"

"Humiliating him would not win me any friends."

"You care too much what others think of you," her father lectured. "A clan chief doesn't need friends. The thanes answer to
you, not the other way around. You worry to much about pleasing
them."

Shalana laughed, harsh and bitter.

"This, coming from the man who chose Norr to be his successor over his own daughter!"

"Is that why you think I picked him?" Terramon asked, clearly surprised. "To appease the thanes?" Now it was the old man's turn to laugh.

"Then why?" Shalana demanded.

"I knew my days as chief were over, but you were not ready to take my place.

"Living with Norr's family had made you soft," he continued. "You had the physical skills to be a great warrior but lacked the will to lead. As did Norr.

"We are born in the winters of the Frozen East," he continued. "We are the Stone Spirits: We must be hard and cold to survive.

"Your feelings for Norr made you weak. Foolish. But I knew you were my daughter; I knew my blood still flowed in your veins.

"I knew you would challenge Norr. I knew you would fight for what was rightfully yours. And I knew it would make you strong."

"You thought I could beat him?" Shalana asked, taken aback. Despite Norr's size and strength, she'd always believed she was the more skilled warrior. Yet she'd always felt the rest of the clan, including Terramon, underestimated her.

Terramon shrugged. "Perhaps. Perhaps not. In the end it did not matter which one of you was the victor. By pitting you against each other, I forced you both to see the truth. Your feelings were weak and childish. Strength is the only thing that matters. No matter who emerged victorious, the clan would have a leader who was strong."

"But Norr refused to play your game," Shalana muttered wearily. "He left instead."

She wasn't shocked by her father's admission. She wasn't surprised by his indifference to her feelings or his callous manipulation of her emotions. She wasn't even angry. Too much time had passed for her to be upset by what he had done, too much had changed.

I've become too much like him.

"My plan still worked," Terramon insisted, his voice smug. "When Norr left, you hardened your heart and became the leader we needed. You continued the work I began. You made the other clans bow down and fed the glory of the Stone Spirits.

"Now that Norr is back," he added after a brief pause, "I only hope you stay strong enough to defeat him."

Shalana snorted. "Did you see his leg? He can barely stand."

"Don't underestimate him," Terramon cautioned, leaning on his staff as he struggled back to his feet. Shalana made no effort to help him up.

"Norr may appear vulnerable," her father added, "but he consorts with Outlanders. They are devious people who have no honor. Beware of their treachery."

As he left the tent, the irony of his warning was not lost on Shalana.

Scythe reached out a trembling hand and placed it on Keegan's naked shoulder, sending a shiver down his spine. In the night shadows she was little more than a silhouette, but to the young man's eyes she had never been more beautiful.

Too overwhelmed to speak her name, he reached out and drew her naked body in close to his, his heart beating so fast it ached in his chest.

"Keegan," she breathed in a soft whisper, "can you hear me?"

The question seemed odd, given the situation. It caught him off guard and caused his romantic anticipation to falter.

A confused, "What?" was all he could reply.

"Keegan," Scythe said again, still whispering but louder and more insistent. "Are you up?"

In an instant, the dream was shredded and torn apart, the pieces falling away like the tatters of an old blanket.

Keegan rolled over, his eyes trying to pierce the darkness of his small tent as he pushed away the last vestiges of sleep. The hide flap keeping out the night's chill was open, and by the dim light of the smoldering peat fire outside he could just make out Scythe's lithe form crouched near the entrance.

"It's cold out here," she said. "Can I come in?"

The young man nodded and scooted over to give her room, grateful the darkness hid the bright red flush of embarrassment he felt crawling across his features.

She doesn't know you were dreaming about her. That you dream about her most nights.

There wasn't much room in the tent, and her leg brushed up against his as she crawled inside, causing his pulse to race. He felt a familiar stirring below his belt and began to blush even harder, praying to the Old Gods and the New that Scythe wouldn't notice the effect her presence was having.

It's the middle of the night, he thought, trying to calm himself by keeping his breathing slow and steady. *Why is she here?*

"It's Norr," she said. "If we don't help him, he's going to lose."

Keegan knew exactly what she was talking about. In two days Norr was scheduled to face Shalana in single combat, a duel to determine who would be Chief of the Stone Spirit clan. Immediately after the meeting with Shalana and her thanes, the big man had explained to all of them what was to come and what was at stake.

Scythe had made it very clear she wasn't happy about it, but there didn't seem to be any other options.

"I don't think we're allowed to help him," Keegan said, his mind still groggy from being woken up in the middle of the night. "It's a duel. Single combat."

"You don't seem that worried about it," Scythe said, her tone exasperated.

Even if he loses, Shalana has promised to help us, he thought, but he knew better than to say it out loud. That wasn't why Scythe was here.

"He's going to lose that duel," she insisted. "And when he does, he's just stupid enough to keep his promise to marry that spear-carrying cow!"

Keegan wanted to put a comforting hand on her arm or give her a reassuring hug. But he didn't trust his body not to betray him if he made physical contact. Instead, he had to resort to awkward, empty words.

"Norr knows how to fight," Keegan offered. "Maybe he'll win."

Scythe gave a dismissive snort.

"Not with that bad knee. That's the only reason Shalana ever agreed to it. She knows he can barely stand."

"And he hasn't even picked up a weapon in five years," she added. "I don't care how great a warrior he used to be—he's out of practice. He doesn't stand a chance."

"We've been over this, Scythe," Keegan reminded her. "Norr doesn't have a choice. None of us do. He has to fight."

"Yeah," Scythe conceded, "but he doesn't have to fight fair!"

"What do you mean?"

"You know," she said, and through the darkness he could just make out her silhouette holding up her fingers and twiddling them in the air. "Maybe you can cast a spell to help him out."

"Even if we could get the Ring away from Jerrod," Keegan cautioned, "I think it's too dangerous to use it for something like this."

"Not the Ring. Just you. You're a wizard, right? You know how to do magic."

"Barely," Keegan admitted sullenly. "I'm still an apprentice." *And now I'm a cripple, too,* he thought as he rubbed the stump of his missing hand.

"That storm that almost wiped out Torian wasn't something an apprentice could pull off."

"That was different," Keegan said. "I didn't control that. It just . . . happened." *Because you poured a massive overdose of witchroot down my throat and almost killed me,* he silently added.

"Please," Scythe implored, reaching out and placing a hand on Keegan's bare shoulder, stirring up memories of his recent dream.

Struggling to ignore his body's eagerness to respond, he paused to collect his thoughts. Even if he wanted to help, there wasn't much he could do. They didn't have any witchroot to open his mind and they had no talismans or charms he could draw on. Plus, he had no idea what kind of spell or ritual would be able to shape the Chaos to help Norr win the duel without alerting the entire clan.

And if Norr loses, we still get the clan's help. He just has to marry Shalana.

In some ways, that was the perfect outcome for Keegan. Scythe would be upset at first. But with Norr out of the way she might someday start to feel for Keegan what he already felt for her.

It's like fate is bringing us together. I just have to tell her there's nothing I can do.

Instead, when he opened his mouth he told her, "We can't do this alone. We need to speak with someone who knows way more about magic than I do."

"I'm not a wizard!" Vaaler protested. "You know that, Keegan. We studied together for two years!"

"And in that time you memorized everything Rexol taught us: every chant, every rune, every ritual."

It had been difficult to avoid physical contact with Scythe while the two of them shared Keegan's small tent. Now, with all three of them crammed into Vaaler's, it was impossible to avoid pressing up against her. But Keegan was excited enough about their plan to stay focused on why they were really here.

"It took me weeks to learn a new spell," he continued, trying to build up his friend's confidence. "But you could do it in a single day. You know how to summon, shape, and control Chaos better than I ever will.

"With Rexol gone," Keegan concluded, "you probably understand the fundamental theories and tenets of magic better than any mage in the Southlands."

"But all that knowledge doesn't help me," Vaaler insisted, "because I'm not a wizard! I can't summon Chaos!"

"You don't have to," Scythe chimed in. "You just have to show Keegan how to do it, then he casts the spell."

"If I'm ever going to learn to control the Ring, then I need someone to teach me all the things Rexol never got around to," the young mage added.

Vaaler was silent for a few seconds before trying another argument against them.

"Scythe, you know that Norr doesn't love Shalana anymore, right?"

"What does that have to do with anything?" she snapped, a bit too quickly.

"If he marries her, it will be in name only," Vaaler assured her. "It's purely political. She just needs him as her husband to legitimize her claim as chief. That's all it is. You two can still be together."

"You don't know Norr like I do," Scythe replied. "He's got this weird, stupidly stubborn sense of duty. If he takes that marriage vow, he's going to honor it. He won't put it aside just so we can still be together.

"And that heifer's going to want him to stay here and become part of the clan again. Even if Norr was willing to keep me around as some kind of mistress or concubine, I can't spend the rest of my life living with these people. Not even for him."

"I'm sorry, Scythe," Vaaler said, shaking his head. "Even if I wanted to help, there's nothing we can do. A wizard can't do anything without taking some witchroot first. It opens up the mind so it can summon the Chaos."

"I dumped a whole bottle down Keegan's throat back in Torian," she said hopefully.

"And almost killed him," Vaaler reminded her. "Anyway, it's cleared his system by now," he added.

"Maybe not," Keegan said. "That overdose did almost kill me, but I survived. I was lost in the Sea of Fire, but I found my way back. The journey changed me."

"What are you talking about?" Vaaler demanded.

"When that patrol found us in the forest," Keegan said, speaking quickly as the vague idea that had been lurking in the back of his mind slowly began to coalesce, "I was able to use Chaos to warp their arrows and snap their bows."

"And that almost killed you, too," Vaaler reminded him. "That one small act of magic left you huddled and helpless on the ground."

"But I did it," Keegan insisted. "And I didn't need any witchroot to make it happen."

"There still could have been some lingering traces in your system," Vaaler objected. "And the Danaan Forest is special. The trees hold the power of Old Magic. It's easier to summon Chaos there. That's why the Danaan mages don't need to use witchroot like they do in the Southlands."

Vaaler was right. The Danaan Forest was special; Keegan had almost been able to feel the power of Old Magic hanging in the air. That feeling had vanished once they left the forest behind. But that wasn't the only time he'd summoned Chaos without the mind-altering effects of witchroot flowing through his veins.

"I've done this before," Keegan said softly. "The night my father died, I unleashed Chaos on the bandit who murdered him.

Killed him instantly. That's how Rexol found me and took me to
be his apprentice."

Scythe didn't say anything, but she reached out and placed her
hand on Keegan's shoulder from behind, giving him a gentle, con-
soling squeeze.

"Remember what Jerrod told us," Vaaler warned, still not convinced. "Chaos is thin here in the Frozen East. If he could sense
that, then you can, too."

Keegan reached up and placed his hand on top of Scythe's, still
resting on his shoulder. He patted it twice and took a deep breath.

"I have to try," he said. "If I can't even help one man win a duel,
how can I save the world from an army of Chaos Spawn? Trust
me, Vaaler. I can do this. I need to do this."

The Danaan reached up and rubbed the back of his neck as he
thought it over, forcing Keegan to lean back to keep from catching an elbow in the side of his head. The movement caused him
to release his grip on Scythe's hand as it dropped from his shoulder.

"If you can actually manage to summon Chaos without the
witchroot, then you should be able to use Rexol's staff as a talisman to channel and focus its power," he mused. "We might be
able to put some kind of curse or hex on her."

"Perfect," Scythe said, leaning in close over Keegan's shoulder
in her exuberance.

"It would have to be subtle," Vaaler cautioned. "Something
small so the Stone Spirits don't know we cheated. Something to
give her a little bad luck during the fight."

"Will something that small be enough for Norr to beat her?"
Scythe fretted.

"At least it'll give him a chance," Keegan said. "That's more
than he's got now."

"It'll be easier if we have something to use as a fetish," Vaaler noted. "Something personal from Shalana. Hair or blood would work best."

"Could Norr get that from her without raising suspicion?" Keegan asked, turning back to look at Scythe over his shoulder.

"Norr can't know about this," Scythe said. "He'd never go along with it. But I can get what you need."

"We don't need much," Vaaler said. "Don't shave her head bald or slice off her finger or anything crazy like that. We don't want to attract any attention."

"Nothing like that ever crossed my mind," Scythe assured him, though Keegan got the sense she wasn't being completely honest.

"What about Jerrod?" the young mage asked. "Should we tell him what we're planning?"

"Not unless you want him to try to stop us," Scythe shot back. "You really think he'd let his precious savior do something this risky?"

"He can be a little overprotective," Vaaler agreed. "But in this case he might be right. Summoning Chaos is always dangerous. Don't take this lightly."

"I won't," Keegan promised.

Vaaler let out a long, heavy sigh. "Okay, I guess that's it. Let's meet tomorrow night on the far side of the camp near the latrines after everyone else is asleep. We'll want some privacy for this.

"Now let me get some sleep," the ex-prince said, lying back down and turning his back to them.

Scythe backed out of the tent, then Keegan did the same, tying off the door flap. They stood up and he turned to head back to his own tent, but stopped when Scythe grabbed his hand.

"Thank you," she whispered, leaning in close so he could hear. "This means a lot to me, and I know how hard this is for you."

She squeezed his hand, then let go and vanished into the darkness, leaving Keegan standing alone in the night.

Chapter 16

THE NEXT NIGHT, Vaaler was already waiting for Keegan when he arrived. Inside the perimeter of the camp, peat fires and lanterns provided plenty of illumination and heat. Here beyond the edges, however, it was both dark and cold, and the young wizard used Rexol's staff to help feel his way across the frozen, uneven ground.

At least the cold keeps it from smelling too bad, Keegan thought, remembering the nearby latrines. The fact that they'd been built just west of the camp, so that the prevailing winds would carry the stench in the opposite direction, probably didn't hurt either.

"Any trouble slipping away?" Vaaler asked, as his friend approached.

Keegan shook his head. Ever since Norr had challenged Shalana, the Stone Spirits had stopped treating the Outlanders like prisoners. There were no guards assigned to watch over them, and—as far as Keegan could tell—no restrictions on their comings and goings.

He'd expected to be regarded with either suspicion or curiosity by the clan, but instead the barbarians mostly just ignored him. Few of them spoke Keegan's language, or if they did they weren't interested in making conversation. They weren't even interested in making eye contact.

Vaaler had already begun to make preparations for the ritual, tracing a two-foot diameter circle on the ground. Around it he'd inscribed several arcane symbols. Some of them Keegan recognized from his studies with Rexol, but others were unfamiliar.

Let Vaaler worry about the symbols, he reminded himself. *You just make sure to get the words right.*

He'd spent most of the day alone in his tent, memorizing and rehearsing the tongue-twisting syllables Vaaler had written down for him until he could recite them flawlessly. Fortunately, all the words were ones he'd used before, so he had some experience in saying them with the proper tone, inflection, and emphasis.

Is that coincidence, or did Vaaler compose this spell using only words he knew I'd be comfortable with? Does he know enough about magic to actually alter and modify a spell to make it easier for me, or did he just grab a simple incantation that only uses the most basic verbal components to bind the Chaos?

Keegan understood that his friend knew more about magic than he did; in their time together under Rexol it was clear Vaaler was the far superior student. What he couldn't be sure of was exactly how much more Vaaler knew. Unleashing Chaos on the mortal world in an explosion of destructive power was a relatively simple task; even Keegan could manage something as crude as that. Channeling and directing it to a specific purpose, especially something as subtle as the hex they were hoping to cast on Shalana, was far more difficult.

If Vaaler knows how to do this, then what else does he know? How much can he teach me? And how long will it take me to learn? And will it be harder because of my missing hand?

Rexol had never focused on the importance of using physical gestures to control and shape a spell, but Keegan had noticed that it was something that happened almost unconsciously whenever he unleashed Chaos. A clenched fist; a raised arm; a finger pointed at a specific target: small, subtle things. But even subtle things could have major consequences when dealing with the mages' art.

"Did you see Scythe anywhere behind you?" Vaaler asked, interrupting Keegan's train of thought.

"No," he said. "I haven't seen her all day."

What if something went wrong? What if she was trying to get some hair or blood from Shalana and got caught?

"I'm sure she's okay," Vaaler said, sensing Keegan's apprehension. "She knows how to handle herself."

As if on cue, a small, lithe figure scurried quickly toward them from the shadows near the camp's edge, crossing the treacherous terrain far more quickly than Keegan had dared to.

"Sorry," she whispered as she drew close. "Norr's nervous about the duel. Took me a while to get him calmed down enough so he'd drift off to sleep."

"Did you get what we need?" Keegan asked quickly, eager to keep his mind from imaging exactly what Scythe might have done to help her lover relax.

"Is this enough?" she said, holding up several strands of long hair.

"Perfect," Vaaler answered.

"How did you get it?" Keegan asked. "Are you sure Shalana doesn't suspect anything?"

"I may be out of practice, but I still remember a few tricks from my time on the streets," was all she said.

Vaaler took the hair and placed it inside the circle he'd drawn on the ground.

"What about Jerrod?" Scythe asked. "I thought he'd be watching you like a hawk," she said to Keegan.

The young man shook his head. "He's been spending most of his time in his tent meditating. Maybe he thinks it will help him regain some of his . . . well, whatever it was he's lost in this land."

"There is Chaos here," Vaaler said. "But it's faint and hard to draw on. He's not the only one affected by its absence, remember?" he added pointedly.

"I can do this," Keegan assured him though he couldn't help worrying about the effect of his missing hand.

"So you've said," Vaaler replied, before making a final inspection of his work, though it was clear from his tone he still had his doubts.

"I think we're ready. Scythe, let's back up and give Keegan some room."

The two stepped away, leaving the young mage standing by himself near the circle and runes Vaaler had inscribed on the ground. Keegan dropped to his knees, clutching Rexol's staff in his hand while resting his stump across the wrist of his good arm. He took a few seconds to collect himself and focus his mind, then he began to chant in a soft whisper.

"Saarash hamsha eethiss. Essthich suurra shevvish."

The incantation itself held no power, but the words helped shape and form the patterns of his thoughts to maximize the potency of the spell. The repeated mantra was carefully constructed to help a mage unlock his own potential, to stimulate and awaken the subconscious mind in ways that could draw on and manipulate Chaos.

"Saarash hamsha eethiss. Essthich suurra shevvish."

It was easier with the witchroot. The drug helped free the mind from the chains of consciousness. It made it easier to let go of the physical world, while simultaneously heightening his awareness and perceptions. Without the witchroot running through his veins, it was a struggle to let go of the familiar, mundane patterns, and Keegan could sense his conscious and subconscious in conflict, battling each other for control.

"Saarash hamsha eethiss. Essthich suurra shevvish."

He focused on the words as they fell from his lips. There was a softness to them, a soothing sibilance, like a zephyr brushing against his skin, or a lover's whisper in his ear.

"Saarash hamsha eethiss. Essthich suurra shevvish."

As he lost himself in the words, part of him seemed to break free and float away, hovering above him, watching. This was the essence of Chaos: to master it, one had to first surrender all conscious control. Allow it to wash over you like an ocean wave, then slowly try to contain it within the twisting, winding channel of the spell.

But as the Chaos began to gather, everything felt strange. Slow. Heavy. The power didn't flow through or wash over him like the tide; it crawled along like a river choked with mud.

Jerrod believed Chaos was thin in the East, but Keegan realized the monk was wrong. Magic was strong here; but it was bound to the earth and stones. Like it was trapped in some kind of stasis. Frozen still by something more ancient and powerful than winter's ice and snow.

"Saarash hamsha eethiss. Essthich suurra shevvish."

Slowly, drop by precious drop, Chaos was gathering. Directed by the repeated chant, his subconscious continued to call upon it, freeing his conscious mind to channel it through Rexol's staff. The runes painted along the oaken shaft became illuminated, shimmering with red and blue light as the Chaos ran along its length. The gorgon's skull suddenly came alive as an intense green light flared up in the empty eye sockets, pulsating with a steady rhythm that matched the cadence of Keegan's voice.

"Saarash hamsha eethiss. Essthich suurra shevvish."

Echoed and amplified through Rexol's staff, the trivial drops of Chaos Keegan had initially summoned were multiplied over and over, kindling a familiar heat in his veins. The heat intensified rapidly, and Keegan embraced the pain. It grew quickly then, a self-feeding circuit racing from wizard through the staff and back in an endless loop, a mounting pressure pushing him closer and closer to agony and ecstasy.

"Saarash hamsha eethiss. Essthich suurra shevvish."

Keegan fought the urge to scream or cry out. The ritual was at a critical stage; it was vital to limit and contain the spell. Careful not to alter his chant in any way, Keegan slowly rose to his feet, raised the staff above his head with his good hand, then drove the butt end into the ground.

There was a crackling blue flash as he discharged the Chaos in a sudden, single burst, releasing it into the rune circle. The locks of Shalana's hair were instantly vaporized, and the runes scrawled onto the earth vanished in a puff of turquoise smoke.

A hollow, empty darkness welled up inside Keegan, and he collapsed to the ground, silent and drained. The rush of gathering Chaos was equaled only by the crash when it was unleashed upon the mortal world. Normally the witchroot's high would help offset the crushing, crippling sense of loss and despair, but without the drug Keegan felt the full impact.

For several seconds he sat motionless on the ground, not even bothering to respond when Vaaler rushed to his side, saying his name over and over while shaking him by the shoulders.

"What's wrong?" Scythe asked, her voice higher and sharper than usual. "What happened?"

Her words cut through the bleakness, piercing it and causing it to fall away. And Keegan realized how foolish and fleeting it really was.

"I'm okay," Keegan said, trying—and mostly succeeding—to make his voice sound confident and strong. "I'm okay."

"Are you sure?" Vaaler asked, twisting him so he could look him directly in the eyes.

"Help me up," Keegan said, holding out his hand to his friend.

As Vaaler took it, Scythe rushed in and seized his other arm. Despite her small stature, she was wiry and stronger than she looked, and between the two of them they lifted Keegan to a standing position.

On his feet he felt better. He was still tired, but the utter exhaustion that had caused him to collapse at the end of the spell

was gone, just like the overwhelming sense of despair and emptiness. Instead, he felt a soft glow of satisfaction.

*I did it! I may only have one hand, but I'm still a wizard! I can still
control the power of Chaos!*

"I can stand," he assured them.

They each released their grip and stepped back cautiously, both
ready to jump forward should he stagger. Bracing himself with
Rexol's staff, Keegan was able to stay up on his own, and after a
few seconds they relaxed.

"Did it work?" Scythe asked once it became clear that Keegan
was okay.

"It worked," Keegan insisted. "I felt it."

"I'm sure you felt something," Vaaler conceded, "but there's no
way to know for sure."

Turning to Scythe, he added, "This was far more difficult than
you could possibly understand. Even if Keegan is right, the spell
will be subtle. Don't be shocked if Norr still loses."

"So what now?" Scythe asked, ignoring Vaaler's warning.

Still leaning on the staff for support, Keegan shrugged.

"We wait and see what happens tomorrow."

The morning of the duel was cold and clear. Even to Jerrod's
mystical second sight, it was odd to see the sun shining so brightly
in a clear blue sky yet not feel any heat coming from it.

Shalana had scheduled the battle for shortly after first light, and
despite the early hour virtually the entire clan had come out to
watch. They crowded in a large circle around an open clearing in
the center of the camp, thirty feet across. In the front ranks, closest
to the action, Jerrod recognized many of the thanes from the
meeting in the Long Hall. Behind them were mostly men and
women in their twenties and thirties—fit and muscular specimens

the monk assumed to be Stone Spirit warriors. The back rows were filled with the rest of the men, women, and even children who made up the clan's civilian population. Many stood on tables they had dragged outside, while others simply pressed in close to those in front, hoping to catch a fleeting glimpse of the two combatants.

Jerrod and the rest of Norr's companions had been allowed to stand among the thanes. He took that as a good sign; ever since Shalana had accepted the challenge they had been treated with nothing but respect by the clan. Hopefully that meant Shalana intended to honor her promise and give them sanctuary even if Norr lost.

It was hard for the monk actually to imagine the big man winning. His size and strength were incredible, and under normal circumstances he was much quicker and more agile than a man of his stature and bulk had any right to be. But Shalana knew all this; she had seen firsthand what kind of warrior Norr was—or rather, used to be—and she hadn't hesitated to accept his challenge.

As big and strong as he is, Jerrod thought, *she knows he's no match for her on one leg.*

She was probably right. Yet the monk had a suspicion the duel wouldn't go as Shalana expected.

Without bothering to turn his head, he shifted his awareness. Instead of studying the barbarians in the crowd eagerly waiting for the primaries to arrive, he focused on Keegan, Scythe, and Vaaler.

They were nervous, but it didn't seem to be the simple anxiety that would come from hoping Norr would win. They kept exchanging furtive glances, as if they knew something the others didn't. They had a secret, something shared among the three of them.

Jerrod didn't know what that secret was, but he knew they'd

been plotting something recently. He'd heard Keegan sneaking out of his nearby tent the past two nights, no doubt scurrying off to meet with his coconspirators.

His initial impulse had been to go after the young wizard: it was his duty to watch over and protect the savior. However, he'd fought against his instincts and allowed Keegan and the others to meet without his interference.

It was difficult to explain why, exactly—even to himself. He couldn't shake the sense that there was something more going on with the trio than he'd first realized; there was some kind of connection between them. Vaaler and Keegan had been friends for years, and Keegan clearly had a crush on Scythe. But it was more than that. Jerrod was beginning to suspect there was some kind of bond that went beyond their relationships as friends—even if they had been mortal enemies, they would all still have been linked in some way.

He didn't understand it yet, not fully. All he knew for sure was that he no longer believed random chance had thrown them all together. Fate and destiny were at work, and Jerrod was wise enough to step aside and let it unfold, at least for now.

A roar from the assemblage snapped his attention back to the crowd. Those in the back were parting, stepping aside to form a path for the combatants to enter. Both were wearing the clan's typical garments: fur vest, knee-length leather kilt, and heavy boots. Shalana's hair was tied in a long braid hanging down her back, but she had abandoned the silver circlet on her head and the silver bracers on her forearms. Despite the cold, both chose to leave their arms and shoulders exposed.

To Jerrod's surprise, they made their way through the crowd together. For some reason, he'd expected them to come from opposite sides, or at least for them to arrive at different times, one after the other.

They're trying to downplay the adversarial aspects of the duel, Jerrod realized. *This isn't war; they're both supposed to represent the same clan. Win or lose, they're both supposed to be on the same side afterward.*

Their weapons further reinforced the point that the duel was meant to be a challenge and not a battle to the death. Both were armed with thick, five-foot-long staves, though in Norr's gigantic hands his weapon looked like a child's toy.

Jerrod had assumed they'd be using swords, spears, or axes—the most common weapons he'd noticed around the Stone Spirit camp. But given the nature of the duel, the less deadly staves were a logical choice. Anyone who challenged for the title of chief would be a popular and skilled warrior. A fight to the death would remove a valued member of the clan.

And blood calls for blood, Jerrod thought. *The clans recognize this; they're smart enough not to tear themselves apart.*

Watching a friend or kin die—no matter the circumstances—could inspire an unquenchable desire for vengeance. A public defeat in a ritualistic duel could be humiliating, but it wasn't likely to spark a lethal feud between rival factions that would fracture the unity of the clan.

Although the heavy staves weren't designed to be lethal, there was still an inherent element of danger. In contrast to the thin, lightweight weapons favored by the Inquisitors, these were not designed for speed and maneuverability. They were heavy, almost cumbersome implements intended to bludgeon and beat an opponent into submission through brute force.

The quickest way to victory would be a blow to the head that knocked an opponent unconscious; even if the intention wasn't to kill, trauma to the brain was always risky. The chance of broken bones was also high; fracture an arm or leg and the opponent would almost certainly yield.

Even without a knockout or broken bone, Jerrod realized, an overmatched opponent might yield to a superior foe before any serious harm was done after taking a few hard, painful strikes. But more evenly matched foes—or those too stubborn or desperate to admit defeat—would continue to pummel each other until one was simply too injured and exhausted to continue.

This won't end with a quick cut or stab. It's going to be a war of attrition. Brutal and barbaric.

The cold, determined expression on each combatant's face made it clear they both understood the risks. Neither displayed any hint of the savage excitement that rippled through the crowd. The supporters might be eager for this contest, but the principals entered under the burden of grim inevitability.

Jerrod was expecting some type of speech or presentation before the battle began. In the Southlands, this kind of deeply ingrained cultural tradition would be awash in ritual and ceremony. To his surprise, though, once both combatants were inside the clearing the action began immediately.

As he'd expected, Shalana was the aggressor. She rushed forward, jabbing the butt end of her staff in quick thrusts at Norr's face. The big man took a clumsy step in retreat, but managed to deflect her assault to the side. Before he could counter with a return attack, Shalana stepped back and out of range, moving with a speed and grace that even Jerrod found impressive.

The crowd reacted with a roar, shouting and cheering to encourage their respective champions.

Shalana crouched low, jaw set and muscles in her bare arms flexing powerfully as she began to circle counterclockwise around her opponent. Jerrod appreciated the strategy: to keep facing her, Norr was forced to continually pivot around his bad leg.

The big man's face grimaced with pain as he turned awkwardly, taking small little hop steps to take pressure off the knee. But the steps kept him off balance, making it impossible for him to launch a sudden lunge or surprise attack against his foe.

The cries of the crowd slowly dwindled as the action slowed, the spectators saving themselves until they had something to cheer about again.

Shalana was patient, staying out of range and biding her time as she feinted and prodded, doing just enough to keep Norr on the defensive.

Norr can't win like this, Jerrod realized. *She's just wearing him down.*

As if in response to Jerrod's silent analysis, Norr let loose a mighty roar and rushed forward, grabbing the staff by one end with both hands like a club and swinging it in wide, waist-high arcs. Because of his leg, his charge didn't have the explosive fury to catch Shalana off guard, and she was easily able to backpedal out of reach.

She darted to the side and jabbed at Norr's flank as he staggered forward. He tried to turn to meet her attack, but couldn't stop his momentum with only one leg. His parry was an off-balance, ill-directed effort, and Shalana managed to ram the butt end of her staff hard into his unprotected ribs.

The force of the blow caused him to grunt and sent him stumbling sideways. Shalana leapt forward, seizing the advantage to put a quick end to the duel with a single, well-aimed stroke to the back of Norr's exposed skull.

At least, that's what should have happened. Jerrod's training allowed him to anticipate the moves of an enemy in combat an instant before they happened; he foresaw the inevitable outcome of the chain of events as they were unfolding in the ring. Except Shalana slipped.

Just as she prepared to deal the telling blow, her back foot landed squarely on a small patch of ice on the frozen earth. With no traction beneath her she wasn't able to lunge forward and finish Norr off; instead her foot shot out straight behind her, throwing her off balance so that her swipe went wildly askew and she fell hard to the ground.

The crowd reacted first with a roar of anticipation, followed by a gasp of surprise as they watched Shalana's victory snatched away by a bizarre stroke of ill fortune.

She sprang to her feet almost instantly, but her recovery gave Norr enough time to gather himself and turn to face her again. Shalana began to circle the big man once more, her icy gaze fixed on her opponent as she waited for another opening. She was angry at missing her chance, but she knew Norr's luck had only prolonged the inevitable.

Was it luck? Jerrod wondered, turning his attention momentarily to Keegan, Jerrod, and Scythe. Like the rest of the crowd, they were focused intently on the action in the duel ring, for all intents and purposes relegated to the roles of cheering spectators.

What were you three doing these past nights? the monk wondered.

Another lumbering charge from Norr pulled Jerrod's interest back to the fight. Shalana danced to the side again, but this time Norr was ready for it. Even before she started moving, he was changing direction to cut off her path.

Shalana seemed taken aback by the move, and she barely managed to get the shaft of her staff up in time to block Norr's strike. The big man kept driving forward, throwing his weight into his smaller opponent. Shalana was knocked backward, falling to the ground.

Norr's supporters roared approval; Shalana's groaned in despair.

Yet again, Norr's handicap kept him from fully exploiting his advantage. Before he had a chance to fall on her and use his massive bulk to pin her to the ground, she'd rolled out of the way and sprung back to her feet. Norr pressed gamely forward, trying to overwhelm her by raining down overhand blows in quick succession. Shalana was forced into a step-by-step retreat, driving the crowd into a frenzy.

Shalana blocked Norr's attack with her own staff, holding it crosswise with both hands above her head. Arms braced and her muscles straining, she grunted in pain as each impact sent shock waves shivering down her arms.

The relentless assault drove her down to one knee. When the next blow came, instead of trying to block it she ducked and rolled forward, sending her lean but solid frame into Norr's legs. At his full strength, she lacked enough mass to have any hope of knocking him off his feet. With the big man hobbled, however, the maneuver sent him toppling over so that they both ended up in a heap on the ground.

The crowd screamed and shouted, giving voice simultaneously to their anticipation, apprehension, and confusion as the two rolled around on the earth.

Norr released his grip on the staff with one hand, trying to grab hold of his smaller, quicker foe. But Shalana managed to wriggle free of his grasp and roll clear of the carnage. She sprang back to her feet and swung her staff like a club, bringing the shaft slamming down across Norr's back over and over as he tried to rise.

Amazingly, Norr shrugged off the vicious assault and somehow regained his feet, clutching his own weapon in one hand. But he was dazed and stunned, and when he retaliated with a wild, clumsy swing Shalana easily stepped aside and darted in at Norr's exposed flank.

Once again the crowd exploded, and once again Jerrod could foresee the inevitable end of the battle. The momentum of Norr's awkward attack had left him defenseless. Shalana had seized on the opening to deliver a single precise strike to the back of Norr's skull that would send the big man crashing down, unconscious and defeated.

For the second time, however, Shalana missed. This time she didn't slip, but as the fatal blow was coming in Norr's bad knee buckled slightly—just enough to send him tumbling forward. He fell awkwardly, bracing himself with one hand on the ground as

Shalana's blow came swooping in at an upward angle from the side. But she had aimed at where Norr's head would have been if he hadn't tripped. Instead of connecting with his temple, her staff whistled through the air a fraction of an inch above its target, drawing groans of disbelief from the crowd.

Expecting to feel the resistance of wood meeting skull, Shalana's follow-through sent her reeling and her advantage was lost. This time, however, when Norr recovered and got back to his feet it was clear he was favoring his bad leg far more than before. His weight was almost completely over his good knee, and he had jammed the butt of his staff into the cold earth to help him stay standing.

Shalana regained her balance and slowly turned to face Norr.

"You can't fight on one leg," she called out to Norr, trying to reason with him. "Yield, and we can end this now."

Norr didn't reply, but shook his head slowly from side to side.

"I have sworn to keep your friends safe," she added. "I offer them the protection of the clan."

"You know that's not enough," Norr grumbled. "Not with your other terms."

With an almost regretful slump of her shoulders, Shalana moved in to finish him off. Faced with a basically immobile opponent, she didn't bother with tactics or strategy. Instead, she stepped forward and delivered a series of hard two-handed chops, knowing Norr wouldn't be able to fight back. There was little the big man could do but throw his own staff up like a shield, bracing to meet the fury of her attack.

The crowd was screaming and shouting now, their voices so loud they drowned out the sounds of the battle. The first blow sent Norr reeling backward, hopping on one foot as he frantically tried to stay upright. The second and third sent him tumbling to the ground, where he landed heavily on his back, his weapon falling from his hands.

Shalana charged in to finish him off, gripping her staff by one end with both hands and raising it high above her head before bringing it crashing down like a hammer on an anvil. Still on his back, Norr's seized his fallen weapon. With one hand, he whipped the heavy wooden staff up and around in a desperate attempt to intercept her blow—an impossible move for anyone other than the enormous giant of a man.

The sound of the two staves meeting echoed like thunder, the sharp crack rising up above the noise of the rabid crowd as the shaft of Shalana's weapon sundered. It snapped clean off just above her hands, some unseen warp or defect in the wood giving way under the tremendous force of Norr's blow.

For an instant, Shalana stared dumbfounded at the few inches of useless wood still clutched in her grip, her mind unable to process the one-in-a-million fluke that had just disarmed her.

The hesitation was all Norr needed. Still gripping his own staff in one hand, he swung it again, slamming it hard into her side as she stood over him. The impact lifted her into the air; a second later she came crashing to the ground beside him where she lay gasping for breath.

Before she could recover, Norr rolled onto his side and grabbed Shalana's braid with his free hand. Using it like a rope he hauled her in, still coughing and choking as she feebly tried to pull herself away. A second later he had her facedown on the ground, his good knee in the middle of her back and his full four hundred pounds pinning her to the earth.

"Yield!" he shouted.

Shalana struggled vainly for a few more seconds, reaching back to ineffectually clutch and claw at the man on top of her before realizing the impossibility of her situation. Then her body went limp as hope vanished and defeat washed over her.

"I yield," she gasped, her lungs fighting for air under Norr's bulk. "I yield."

Bedlam erupted as the crowd surged forward to congratulate the winner. Through the mass of rushing bodies, Jerrod saw Scythe grab Keegan by the shoulders. Spinning the young man to face her, she gave him a hard kiss on the lips.

It lasted only a second, an unplanned act of raw emotion pouring out in a single spontaneous gesture before she rushed off to Norr's side.

Jerrod kept his attention on the young mage. Bewildered and bemused, Keegan stood frozen in place as the crowd shoved past him, the faint hint of a smile on his lips.

Interesting, the monk thought to himself, his mind slowly putting all the little bits and pieces together. *Very interesting.*

Chapter 17

NORR WAS SNORING so loudly, Scythe was worried their tent might actually collapse around them, but at least he was finally asleep.

The twelve hours since Norr's duel with Shalana had been a chaotic, hectic blur of frenzied activity. During the fight Scythe hadn't screamed and cheered with the rest of the crowd, too nervous to give voice to her emotions. Her stomach knotted with fear and worry, all she could do was watch and silently pray that Keegan's curse would work while trying not to throw up.

She remembered grabbing Keegan by the shoulders after Norr won and planting a fierce kiss on his lips before rushing off to her lover's side, an impulsive, instinctive act of gratitude for what the young man had done.

I just hope he saw it that way. Poor kid's probably more confused than ever.

Everything after that became a jumbled collage of images and emotion. The look of utter defeat and despair on the vanquished Shalana's face. The unbridled joy of Norr's supporters as they somehow picked him up and carried him to the Long Hall. The strained smile on her lover's face during their celebrations, his victory tempered by the emotional pain of what he'd done to Shalana and the physical pain of his injuries.

In addition to further aggravating his knee, he'd suffered dozens of deep, ugly bruises that would take weeks to fade. Scythe had done her best to tend to him, wrapping and splinting his leg to protect the joint from further harm, but there were precious few medicinal plants and herbs growing in the Frozen East. The only available method of dulling his pain was to pour flagon after flagon of mead down the new clan chief's throat; something his supporters had been all too eager to do.

A constant stream of men and women had come to the Long Hall to see Norr all day long. Scythe had stayed by his side, hovering anxiously and trying to make Norr comfortable. Vaaler and Keegan—and even Jerrod—had come by to congratulate Norr. But it didn't take long for the urgent crush of people around the big man to force them into retreat. The last she'd seen, the monk had wandered off outside and the two younger men were being coerced into raising mugs of ale in a salute to Norr's victory.

Scythe, however, refused to let the crowds drag her away from her lover's side. She still didn't know enough of the local language to follow the conversations of everyone who approached him, but based on tone and facial expressions, she assumed most of the visitors were simply congratulating him on his victory. The majority seemed sincere, but she suspected a few of simply trying to get into the new chief's good graces as soon as possible—even among the savages of the Frozen East it was impossible to escape the sycophants and political schemers.

She'd bristled when Terramon, Shalana's father, had dared to approach. His cane thumping heavily on the floor, he leaned in close to Norr and offered his hand. Norr had accepted it warily, eyeing the old man with suspicion. They'd exchanged a few whispered words in their native tongue before Norr nodded. Satisfied, Terramon then left, not bothering to stay and celebrate his daughter's defeat.

A handful of other visitors—more men and women she recognized as thanes from their first meeting in the Long Hall—had similar short but intense conversations with him during the celebrations. No doubt they were concerned about the direction Norr would lead them now that he was in charge, and Scythe suspected there would be many lengthy and contentious meetings in the Long Hall over the next week as they each tried to push their own agenda.

That's probably the last thing Norr wanted. If Shalana had just agreed to help us, he would have been perfectly happy to let her stay chief.

As far as Scythe was concerned, this was just one more reason to dislike the woman. Her selfishness had forced Norr's hand and put him—and Scythe—into an uncomfortable position.

Now that he's the chief, what does that make me? Am I still an Outlander? And what happens to us down the road? How long will Norr feel obligated to stay and lead his people? How long before he decides to step down and let someone else take over?

Important questions but ones Scythe didn't need to ask right away. Instead, she'd remained silent as the well-wishers came and went, letting Norr bask in the adulation of his victory. She'd stayed at his side, slowly nursing a large flagon of warm ale. Not drinking anything would have seemed out of place, but she wasn't about to abandon her long-standing practice of staying sober while others drank. Alcohol dulled the senses; it left you slow and vulnerable, and she'd seen too many bad things happen to those who let themselves get in that condition.

Finally, after many hours and many raised and drained cups by those in the Hall—especially Norr—the stream of visitors dried up. With the help of two strapping young warriors, Scythe had brought her lover back to their tent, where he'd collapsed on the bed almost immediately in an inebriated stupor.

Despite Norr's thunderous snoring, Scythe was exhausted enough that she wasn't worried about falling asleep beside him. Before she could turn in, however, she heard someone calling her name from outside the tent.

"Scythe, we must talk."

For a second she thought it was Keegan, and the memories of her ill-advised kiss sprang to her mind. Then she realized the voice was deeper.

Jerrod?

Knowing an entire army could traipse through the tent without waking the snoring giant, she lifted the entrance flap and ushered the monk inside.

"What do you want?" she asked, getting right to the point.

"The duel today was unusual," he said, choosing his words carefully. "Shalana seemed to have it won until her staff splintered."

"Bad luck," Scythe said with a shrug. "It happens."

"It does," Jerrod conceded. "But sometimes we make our own luck."

Scythe narrowed her eyes suspiciously.

How much does he know? Has he talked to Keegan?

She wasn't sure how Jerrod would react to what they had done, but she imagined he'd be upset about it. In his mind, the only thing that mattered was Keegan's supposed destiny as the savior of the world. He'd probably think that using Chaos magic to unleash a curse, even to help a friend, was an unnecessary risk.

"If you have something to say," Scythe told him, "just say it."

"I think you, Keegan, and Vaaler helped Norr win the duel somehow," he declared, though his monotone voice betrayed none of what he might actually be feeling. "I want to know what the three of you did."

"I have no idea what you're talking about," Scythe insisted.

She'd noticed the monk talking briefly with Keegan in the Long Hall. She didn't think the young mage would betray her intentionally, but a few drinks might have loosened his tongue. But if Keegan had already told the monk the truth, then there wasn't any need for her to fill him in. And if Jerrod didn't know yet, she wasn't going to be the one to tell him.

"Vaaler and Keegan won't tell me what happened, either," he admitted, and Scythe couldn't help but think back to her days as a thief on the streets of Callastan.

Well done, lads. Stick together and keep our mouths shut. Code of the underworld.

"I was hoping you would be reasonable, but I should have known better," Jerrod continued in his same emotionless tone. "Maybe Norr will be more forthcoming when I speak with him about this."

Bastard. He knows Norr wasn't involved.

"He's sleeping," Scythe answered coldly. "He had a long day."

"He will wake up eventually," Jerrod replied. "When he does, I'm eager to share my theories about what happened in the duel with him."

The monk had her, and he knew it. Norr could be naïve, but he wasn't stupid. If Jerrod started questioning him about the duel, he'd demand the truth from Scythe. She could lie to him, but his suspicions would be raised. He'd know something wasn't right; he'd probably even tell Shalana out of some misguided sense of honor and duty.

Then what? Will they fight again? Or will Norr be disqualified and Shalana declared the winner?

She didn't know a lot about the Eastern culture, despite her time with Norr. He'd always seemed reluctant to talk about his past, so she had never pressed him. But she was pretty sure cheating during a duel to determine who would become clan chief would be considered a serious offense.

The snores coming from her lover reassured her he was still fast asleep; there wasn't any risk of his waking up midconversation.

"If I tell you," she said, "you can't say anything to Norr."

"That was the implication," Jerrod agreed. His voice and expression never changed, yet somehow he still managed to sound smug.

"Keegan cast a curse," she admitted. "Something to give Shalana bad luck during the duel."

"How long will this curse last?" Jerrod wanted to know. "Any misfortune that befalls Shalana could affect us, as well. That is how Chaos works—there are always unforeseen consequences. Rexol called it backlash."

"I think it was just for the duel," she said, though she realized now that she wasn't exactly sure. "Vaaler took steps to make sure the magic didn't flare up out of control," she added.

The monk nodded, and Scythe silently cursed herself for inadvertently selling Vaaler out. Threatening to tell Norr had rattled her into revealing more than she'd intended.

"This was all my idea," she explained, hoping to at least redirect Jerrod's wrath away from the other two. "Vaaler and Keegan both tried to talk me out of it."

"But in the end, they listened to you," Jerrod muttered, almost as if he were talking to himself instead of her.

"Now that Norr's clan chief, he can use his influence to get the Stone Spirits to help us," Scythe added. "It was risky, but it worked out for the best."

To her surprise, Jerrod answered, "I agree."

"I thought you'd be mad," Scythe said warily, wondering if this was some kind of trick or trap.

"We all know Keegan's destiny, though exactly how he will fulfill it is still unclear," the monk explained, speaking slowly as if still trying to work the ideas out. "I feared you were a distraction—an impediment; an obstacle. Now I think I may have been wrong."

"I don't understand."

"You were born beneath the Blood Moon?"

"How do you know that?" Scythe demanded. She'd never talked about her birth, even to Norr.

"So was Vaaler," Jerrod continued, ignoring her question. "And Keegan."

Scythe was momentarily taken aback. The Blood Moon was a rare event; the last one had happened twenty years ago and lasted only a couple weeks. She knew the three of them were roughly the same age, but she hadn't guessed they'd all been born within days of each other.

"Coincidence," she finally said. "It's weird, but so what?"

"The three of you are linked by your untimely birth," Jerrod told her. "Some would call you cursed, but it is more accurate to say you have all been touched by Chaos in some way."

"I'm no wizard," Scythe assured him. "And neither is Vaaler, from what I can tell."

"Chaos manifests in many different ways," Jerrod explained. "We've all seen Keegan's power; with him it is obvious."

"Vaaler's parents were both blessed with the Sight, yet he is completely blind to its visions," Jerrod continued. "He cannot summon Chaos, yet his mind is quick to grasp the most complex and intricate theories of magic. Ironic, maybe even tragic . . . but not that surprising if you understand that Chaos usually defies expectations."

He paused, and Scythe knew he was waiting for her to ask, "What about me?" But she refused to give him the satisfaction. After a few seconds Jerrod resumed, undeterred by her silence.

"You are touched in a different way. You are driven by impulse and emotion. You are quick to act—rashly and often violently."

"That's all you've got?" Scythe laughed. "Based on that, everyone I knew back in Callastan was touched by Chaos."

"With you it goes deeper," Jerrod insisted. "There is an aura about you. I first sensed it in the encounter with the Inquisitors.

During the battle you were little more than a blur to my Sight. A random, unpredictable storm swirls around you. Most would be devoured by it, but you ride the storm. You embrace the Chaos. It makes you strong."

Scythe shrugged off the blatant appeal to her ego for what it really was.

"I know the games fortune-tellers play," she warned him. "Spit out some vague generalizations about human nature, throw in some compliments to make the mark feel good, then sit back and watch as the client twists the words to make them fit the specifics of his or her own life. It's just a con."

"There are charlatans who use such techniques," he admitted. "But in the Order there were true prophets. When they first dreamed of the Burning Savior, much was unclear. They saw a figure bathed in fire and flames, but little else. We did not know where our savior would be born, or even if we were searching for a boy or a girl.

"Now I understand their confusion," the monk continued. "Keegan is the savior, but he does not stand alone. There is a deep and powerful connection among Keegan, Vaaler, and you. To unlock his full potential and achieve Keegan's destiny, all of you must work together."

"Nice try," Scythe said, shaking her head. "But I'm not letting you drag me into your crazy plans."

"You refuse to see what is right in front of you," Jerrod admonished. "The curse Keegan placed on Shalana was the first step in a much greater journey. Keegan cast the spell, but it was you who urged him to take action. You inspired him to use his power, and Vaaler showed him how to direct and control the Chaos. This was only possible because all three of you worked together."

"I just wanted Keegan to help Norr," Scythe protested. "That's all it was."

"No," Jerrod insisted. "There are greater forces at work. Crossing paths with you wasn't just random chance. You were destined to become part of this."

"I wanted to kill you back then," Scythe reminded him. "Keegan, too."

"But you didn't," Jerrod countered. "And now we share a common purpose. I was blind to this at first; I stood in opposition to you. Now I realize you and Vaaler are as important to stopping the armies of the Slayer as Keegan. Now I see the truth."

Scythe knew there wasn't any point in continuing the argument; logic could never sway the mind of a fanatic. Jerrod wasn't actually interested in any kind of objective truth. Faced with facts that didn't match his original narrative, he wouldn't reconsider or reevaluate his position. Instead, he'd redefine and recalibrate his interpretations of his prophecy to make things fit. He'd twist his perception of events so that they supported his beliefs, regardless of what actually happened.

"Does this mean you're on my side now?" she asked.

"I always was," he told her. "I just didn't realize it until now."

"How much of this have you told Keegan?" she asked, worried the monk's crazy theories might heighten the young man's infatuation with her.

"Nothing," Jerrod answered. "I have not spoken to Vaaler yet, either. They are already both on the proper path; they have already accepted their roles in Keegan's destiny."

Now the real purpose of the meeting became clear: Jerrod was here to try to bring her into line.

Scythe was pretty sure his newfound loyalty wouldn't last. Keegan's role as the savior seemed to be the only constant in his religious delusions. Sooner or later she'd say or do something that contradicted the image Jerrod had so carefully constructed for her and he'd respond by redefining his prophecy yet again.

Probably decide I'm some kind of false prophet who needs to be cleansed from Keegan's life.

Until that inevitable betrayal, however, she was more than happy to make Jerrod think she was buying into his madness.

Keep your friends close and your enemies closer. Especially the crazy ones.

"I guess it's good to know you've got my back now," she said.

"I know you don't believe me," he said. "I hope in time you will come to see the truth for yourself though I don't believe it matters either way."

There were plenty of responses she could give, but she knew none of them would make the monk rethink his position. And she was too tired to argue, anyway. So she said nothing.

Much to Scythe's relief, Jerrod seemed to take the hint and turned to go. Raising the flap of the tent, he paused and looked back over his shoulder at her.

"You are part of something greater than you realize. You and Keegan share something deeper and more powerful than you can comprehend. Destiny will not be denied."

He vanished before Scythe could reply. Exhausted, she tied off the tent flap and curled up beside Norr.

Think whatever you want, but I'm more than just a pawn in your stupid prophecy.

She clung to that thought defiantly even as she felt sleep creeping in, the rhythmic rumble of her lover's snores washing over her as she slipped away into blackness.

Every breath Shalana drew was agony.

Norr had cracked at least two of her ribs with the blow that brought her low. Her left side was one giant purple-and-black contusion from her armpit to her hip. Her back ached, another dark bruise marking the spot where the big man's knee had kept her pinned to the ground and forced her to yield.

Her shoulder ached; she was lying awkwardly on her right side.

But she knew shifting positions would bring on a wave of new torments, so she ignored and endured her discomfort.

Physical pain was nothing new to her. She bore the scars of several battles—some much worse than what she'd suffered in the duel with Norr. But those wounds and injuries had always come in victory. The pain she felt in defeat was different: an inescapable reminder of her failure and humiliation.

In the aftermath of the duel, a handful of her supporters had forced their way through the celebrating crowd and helped her to her feet. They had guided their fallen champion through the bedlam of Norr's victory, ignored and forgotten, until she reached her tent.

No, not my tent. The clan chief's tent. It belongs to Norr now.

She wondered how long until he came to claim what was his. Hopefully not until tomorrow. For this night, at least, she just wanted to be left alone.

The thanes who had escorted her to the tent were gone, leaving her side hours ago to go pay their respects to Norr. She didn't resent them for abandoning her; it was important for them to show the new leader that he had their support and loyalty. Any claim she had over them had been forfeited in the duel.

He was hobbled. Crippled. Standing on one leg by the end. And I still lost.

She kept replaying the battle over and over in her head, watching as victory slipped through her hands time after time and trying to understand what went wrong.

It almost seemed as if fate itself didn't want her to win. As if destiny had chosen Norr to be chief, and her to be simply cast aside.

Or was it something else?

Terramon's final words before the battle rose up like an accusing spirit from her memory: *Now that Norr is back, I only hope you stay strong enough to defeat him.*

Her father was a cruel and heartless man. But he wasn't stupid. He had sensed something in her. Some flaw or failing that made him wary, despite Norr's vulnerability.

Weakness.

Was it really fate that snatched victory from her grasp? Or had she subconsciously sabotaged herself? Did some part of her feel sympathy or pity for Norr? Did some part of her feel bad about trying to force him into marrying her? Did some part of her actually want to lose?

These were questions she didn't want to face. Not tonight. So she rolled over onto her back, easing the throbbing in her aching shoulder but unleashing fresh agony in her ribs.

She gasped and gritted her teeth, but the pain cleared her mind. Unable to sleep, she let her consciousness drift, unfocused and free. Faint laughter and singing rose up from the night's silence, carried on the wind from the celebrations still going on in the Long Hall. And then another, all-too-familiar sound—the thumping of a cane against the flap of the tent.

For several seconds she ignored Terramon's presence, hoping he would just go away. Of course, that didn't happen.

"Shalana," his voice hissed in the night, the cane's rapping against the tent becoming more insistent. "Shalana, wake up!"

With a faint groan, she rolled back over onto her right side. It took several seconds before the fresh burst of pain faded enough for her to speak.

"I'm awake."

That was more than enough invitation for Terramon, and he quickly pulled the flap aside and thumped his way into the tent. She expected him to sit, but he chose to remain standing: a dim shadow in the blackness of the tent.

"Still sitting in the darkness," he muttered.

Shalana braced herself for the coming lecture.

"I tried to warn you," he said, with a weary shake of his head.

"I didn't listen," she answered, keeping all emotion from her voice.

"This isn't what I wanted," he assured her.

"I know." *You wanted me to win so you could stay in power. You were my right hand, first among the thanes. Now you are just one of many.*

The chief had the power to both name and reject thanes. By right, Norr could strip her father of his title. However, despite his personal dislike of Terramon, he wasn't likely to take such a drastic step. To preserve the unity of the clan, he'd probably let her father—and the rest of Shalana's supporters—keep their titles, though they would have far less influence over the new chief than those who had backed Norr's claim.

"I spoke to Norr," Terramon told her.

Of course you did. You know he doesn't trust you, but that won't keep you from trying to get close to his ear.

She wasn't surprised her father had already cast her aside. He was scrambling to forge new alliances, trying to secure his position so he could slowly rebuild his sphere of influence under the new chief's rule.

Norr wasn't a vengeful or spiteful man; at least he hadn't been when she knew him. He wouldn't openly speak out against Shalana or take any action against her or her supporters. But the Stone Spirits would still see her as his rival. Though technically still part of the clan, she was a fallen and defeated adversary in their midst, and anyone befriending her would be looked at with suspicion.

Eventually she could regain her status among the clan by proving herself in battle and through loyal service to Norr and his thanes. But it would take time—months or possibly even years. Until then she would be ignored and shunned, a pariah among her own people.

If that is what must be, it must be.

"I made Norr an offer," her father explained. "He accepted."

What kind of offer? Shalana wondered, though she didn't say the words aloud. *And why would Norr accept?*

Norr had grown up under Terramon's reign. He knew what kind of man her father was: ambitious, ruthless, cunning. Age had stripped him of his warrior's skills, but he could still use political manipulation to bring an enemy low. Surely Norr had to recognize that Terramon was the single biggest threat to the continued loyalty of the thanes. The glow of the Red Bear's triumphant return would fade in a few months. As winter settled in and the day-to-day realities of life washed away the luster of the new chief, there would be whispers of unrest. There would be questions about his long absence, his unexpected return, and his strange Outlander companions.

And what about Hadawas's Conclave?

The leader of the Sun Blades—a clan even larger and more powerful than the Stone Spirits—had called a meeting of all the clan chiefs. If not for Norr's arrival and unexpected challenge, Shalana and her thanes would already be making preparations for the journey.

Such a request was not made lightly; it had been forty years since the last Conclave: the time of the Purge in the Southlands. Hadawas was well respected among all the clans. The other chiefs knew he must have had a good reason to call them together in the last few weeks before winter gripped the East in her icy fist: some looming crisis or disaster.

Whatever it was, Shalana had no doubt it would be the first real test of Norr's leadership. And if he stumbled in any way, she had no doubt Terramon would try to turn the situation against him.

So whom will you back this time, Father? Who among the thanes will you chose to be your next puppet?

"You need to speak to Norr, too," Terramon continued when Shalana—lost in her own convoluted thoughts—failed to respond. "Tomorrow, if you are well enough."

"He doesn't need to hear from me," Shalana spat out, suddenly angry.

You destroyed me with your manipulation and your games. Now you'll try to destroy Norr. He doesn't deserve this!

"All the thanes are paying their respects to the new chief," Terramon reminded her.

"I'm not a thane."

"Not yet. But Norr will name you to his council if you come to him."

Shalana blinked in surprise.

"Why would he do that?"

"Because I told him I would step aside if he chose you as my replacement."

"I . . . I don't understand." Shalana's head was spinning as she tried to wrap her mind around his words.

"Norr promised to bring you to the Conclave," Terramon continued. "He has sworn to give you a position of honor and importance among his supporters."

"This is madness," Shalana gasped.

"Norr doesn't trust me," her father explained. "But he still admires and respects you. He always will. He wants you to be on the same side. He still has not learned the lesson I tried to teach you both."

"I won't betray him," she said, her voice cold. "Not for you. Not for anyone."

Terramon shook his head. "Why not? He turned his back on the clan and abandoned you when he left."

That was your fault.

"Now he has returned and taken away what is rightfully yours. He humiliated and shamed you in front of everyone."

"He won the duel," she muttered. "He earned the right to be chief."

"Don't be a fool," her father spat. "We both know he cheated!"

Shalana didn't answer right away. She didn't think Norr was capable of something so dishonorable . . . but she hadn't thought he would simply vanish five years ago, either.

"Do you have any proof for these accusations?" she asked.

"I saw what happened in the duel," he answered. "The victory was yours, and then it was somehow snatched away.

"The masses may be blinded by the legend of the Red Bear," he continued, "but I still see clearly enough to know he had no hope of beating you on only one leg. And yet, somehow, he was the victor. It was . . . unnatural."

As much as she hated to admit it, Terramon was right. Something odd had happened in the duel. But whatever it was, it wasn't something she could explain. Or prove.

"Even if you are right," she told him, "nobody will listen."

"No," he admitted. "Not without evidence to back our words. But Norr still has feelings for you. He will be looking for someone he knows and trusts to help him lead the clan. He will bring you into his confidence.

"Wait. Watch. Listen. In time, you will uncover his treachery. And then you can take back your birthright!"

"I don't want to play your games anymore," she said, rolling over so that her back was to him. The pain caused her to grit her teeth, but she managed not to cry out.

"This is not a game," Terramon said after several long seconds of silence. "When the truth is revealed, you will realize Norr is not worthy of being chief. It will be up to you to bring him low."

Shalana didn't bother to answer.

Her father endured the crushing silence for several long seconds before adding, "I know you better than you know yourself. You are my daughter; you are my blood. You will do what is necessary to keep the clan strong."

Then she heard him pull aside the hide flap and step out into the night, moving slowly while leaning heavily on his cane for support.

Shalana lay motionless in the darkness of her tent long after he was gone, her mind too busy thinking about what Terramon had said to notice the aches and pains in her body, until she finally drifted off to sleep.

Chapter 18

SURROUNDED BY HER dogs, the Pack Master raced across the snow-covered plains with long, loping strides, her body hunched so low the tips of her fingers grazed the frozen earth. The wind whistled in her ears and her long, dark hair trailed out wildly behind her. Her breath came in ice-fogged clouds as she panted heavily, her pounding heart pumping hot, eager blood through her veins to ward off the chill in the air.

She had no trouble keeping pace with her four-legged brethren; she had learned to run with them shortly after she had learned to crawl. Like all the Pack Masters, she could go days without stopping or slowing. To run with the pack was freedom; it was life.

Dusk was approaching; their third straight day away from the rest of the clan. Her pack had ranged many leagues, hunting for meat and patrolling the far-reaching borders of Ice Fang territory. As it always did a day or two after leaving the other humans of her clan behind, her mind had slipped into a semiferal state. She was one with her dogs, her identity subsumed yet also augmented by her inclusion in the pack.

The wind shifted, bringing new scents and smells to her eager nostrils. There was something foreign coming from the west, something *unclean*. The rest of the pack smelled it, too—she felt their unease, their fear. She felt the hair on her neck stand up and some of the younger dogs growled low as they ran, hackles raised.

But their fear was held in check by the strength of the pack and overridden by the deeply ingrained instinct to protect the clan and defend their territory.

She gave two low whistles, and as one the pack changed direction, moving toward the unfamiliar and unsettling scent. After several more miles they topped a small ridge, and the entire pack pulled up short.

Below them stretched an army of humans: thousands of interlopers marching slowly but steadily eastward. The shock snapped the Pack Master from her blissful semiprimal state, her rational, human identity rising to the surface.

She knew right away this was not some rival clan—none of the Eastern tribes could field an army of this size.

Not human, she thought, recognizing the same slightly alien scent of the strange young man traveling with the Outlanders they'd ransomed to the Stone Spirits. *Danaan.*

The odor rising from the distant horde wasn't the smell she'd noticed earlier; it wasn't the one that made her want to cower in fear or run away. That smell had faded, swept away by another shift in the cold winds.

She studied their slow but relentless progress for a few minutes, noting their general direction and numbers. The Danaan ranks were spread thin: rather than a single mass, they traveled in small groups of roughly a dozen individuals clustered closely together. These smaller units moved with varying speed, their relative positions constantly changing as some pressed forward and others fell back. The seemingly random ebb and flow reminded her of the subtle, shifting patterns of a pack on the run—a formless, freeform mass that somehow held together as a whole.

It didn't take her long to realize that the army's path would inevitably bring them to the clan's most recent campsite. She had no illusions about what would happen if the Ice Fangs crossed paths with the invaders.

And then she was spotted. The main force of the army was still on the plain below the ridge, but several scout patrols had already made their way to the top. One of them had emerged over the crest of a small hill, unnoticed while she had been studying the army below. Seeing the dogs, they let loose with a series of horn blasts.

From a distance, another series of calls signaled back. Based on where the sounds were coming from, the Pack Master realized some of the advance patrols had already forged many miles ahead—far enough that they could circle around and cut off the pack's retreat.

She gave three quick whistles: sharp, short, and high-pitched. *Danger! Home!* In response, the pack whirled around and set off in the opposite direction at a full sprint. The Danaan behind her set off in pursuit, but she knew they could outrun them. The real danger lay in front.

More horns rang out. The response came from multiple directions up ahead, and the Pack Master realized the net was closing in on them. Within seconds the enemy began to materialize in the distance: gray, shadowy shapes in the rapidly fading twilight.

Another whistle sent her pack scattering, spreading out in all directions in the hope that one or two might escape to warn the clan. The enemy responded with more horn blasts, and the patrols ahead fanned out to block their escape.

The Danaan were light on their feet, but their speed couldn't match the Pack Master or her dogs. For an instant she thought they all might make it. But she hadn't counted on the archers.

The air was split with the sharp twang of bowstrings, and a second later a rain of arrows engulfed them. Dogs yelped and squealed as the deadly projectiles pierced their fur and flesh. The first volley dropped nearly half the pack though the Pack Master herself wasn't hit. The second volley changed that.

She didn't hear the second twang; her ears filled only with the cries of her dying pack. But she felt the impact as the first arrow thudded into her shoulder, knocking her off stride and spinning her half-around. The second caught her thigh, taking her down. Another buried itself in her stomach, and she grunted in pain and shock.

Unable to rise, she looked up from the ground to see that all but two of her dogs lay dead or dying around her.

It only takes one to warn the clan, she thought, clinging to a last, desperate hope.

She saw the survivors break through the enemy ranks, running hard. Another volley of arrows took one down as he fled, impaling him through the back of the neck. But by some miracle the last—a young bitch, strong and fierce—wasn't hit. The archers fired again, but by this time she was out of range, and the arrows fell harmlessly to the earth well short of her.

Go! the Pack Master silently screamed, the world beginning to fade and tilt as her life oozed out from her wounds. *Go!*

Suddenly another shape appeared from over a nearby hill, far too large to be Danaan or human. It was nearly as wide as it was tall; standing upright on two legs but hunched forward to help brace its bulk with the knuckles of its forelimbs.

She didn't know what the creature was, but she recognized the stench coming off the mountain of dark, putrid flesh—this was the scent that had so unnerved the pack. The monster turned its massive head to the side, yellow eyes glowing in the fading light as it fixed them on the fleeing dog. It gathered itself for an instant, muscles coiling then exploding into a fury of action as it gave chase with unnatural, unfathomable speed.

The creature was little more than a blur as it raced across the plain, eating up the distance between it and its quarry in mere seconds. As its charge overtook the fleeing dog, the beast swung its meaty fist down like a hammer, pulverizing the canine's spine. The dog shrieked—a sound something between a human scream and a howl that ripped at the Pack Master's rapidly faltering heart.

The last thing she saw before she slipped away forever into darkness was the beast lifting the squirming, still-struggling dog up to its maw and beginning to feed.

Chapter 19

KEEGAN DIDN'T SO much wake up as grudgingly claw his way back to consciousness. He couldn't remember how many flagons of ale he'd downed during Norr's victory celebration, but clearly it had been more than his body could handle.

His head was pulsing, every heartbeat sending blood roaring and rushing through his temples. His eyes were heavy and itchy, as if someone had poured sand in them while he slept. His mouth was so dry and scratchy he actually wondered if he'd been chewing on the rough woven blanket that had kept him warm through the night.

Despite all his physical discomfort, however, he hadn't been able to drink enough to keep from dreaming about Scythe. But in his groggy, hungover state he wasn't sure if what he recalled was a vision or just an ordinary dream.

We were together, he remembered. *Naked. Close.*

In the dream, she'd leaned in close to kiss him . . . just as she'd kissed him after Norr won his duel.

She was just grateful for what you did. It didn't mean anything.

But she hadn't kissed Vaaler.

He'd been thinking about that kiss all night. Downing cup after cup of ale and celebrating Norr's triumph with his supporters, he kept glancing over in Scythe's direction. If she noticed, she hadn't acknowledged him—all her attention and focus had been on the new clan chief.

You're reading too much into that kiss, he warned himself. *At best, she's a friend. That's all she'll ever be. Nothing more.*

"Things can change," Keegan mumbled out loud. "The future isn't written in stone."

Vaaler knew Keegan well enough to see something was bothering him. Keegan was even more quiet and pensive than usual. The alcohol still cleansing itself from his system was probably partly to blame; the young wizard had downed far more drinks than Vaaler. But the Danaan felt there was something more. Keegan hadn't spoken a word since crawling out of his tent for breakfast; he just chewed quietly on the jerky the Stone Spirits had for seemingly every meal.

Winter is a hard time in the East, Vaaler realized.

The growing season was over; whatever fruits or vegetables could survive the inhospitable climate would have been harvested long ago. Fresh game would be scarce, and anyone out hunting would be at risk of getting caught in one of the fast-building storms that seemed to sweep through every few days. Until the spring thaw, the hard, leathery meat was probably the only source of reliable food for the clan.

"Something on your mind?" the Danaan asked, hoping to draw his friend out of his shell.

"Just thinking," he mumbled in response.

I'll bet.

Vaaler had been doing a lot of thinking himself. Norr had won his duel but the former prince was more anxious than ever. Despite downing several flagons of thick ale with Norr's supporters while celebrating the new chief's victory, he'd barely slept.

Keegan's magic was strong enough to change the course of that duel. But what other consequences will there be?

Vaaler had taken every precaution he could to make sure the backlash of the spell was contained. But the ritual he'd devised had been based on theory rather than actual experience, and Chaos was unpredictable.

Especially when Keegan's involved.

Before the duel, Vaaler hadn't even been sure their plan would actually work. Despite all he knew about Keegan's potential as a wizard and Jerrod's unwavering faith that the young man was destined to be the savior, he half expected to see Norr lose. Everything he knew and understood about magic told him the spell would fail. Watching the fight unfold, however, it was clear Keegan had actually succeeded in unleashing the curse.

Nobody else could have done that under these circumstances. Not even Rexol.

The spell hadn't been fueled by the latent energies of the Danaan forest; its power had come from some reservoir of Chaos deep inside Keegan himself. Even more amazing, he hadn't needed the mind-altering effects of witchroot to unlock it. The implications were staggering.

He can summon Chaos anytime he chooses. But can he control it?

From his studies under Rexol, Vaaler knew the arcane symbols and complicated chants recited during any ritual were mostly mnemonic devices. They were tools to focus and direct a wizard's mind, catalysts to trigger the thought patterns that allowed a mage to shape the Chaos to a specific purpose. The trappings of the mage's art made it easier to cast a spell, but theoretically, if a wizard was strong enough, he could accomplish the same thing through sheer force of will.

Keegan had proved beyond all doubt that the theory was correct. He had unleashed Chaos in a way nobody had thought possible since the Cataclysm.

He's like the great mages who practiced Old Magic.

It was an exhilarating, yet also sobering, thought. The Cataclysm was caused by Old Magic, or so the Danaan legends claimed. Rexol had spent his life searching for that kind of power, only to have it destroy him. Yet if Keegan was to fulfill Jerrod's prophecy, he would need to embrace his potential, despite the risks. Vaaler couldn't even imagine what it would feel like to bear that kind of burden.

He was also worried about Jerrod. The monk had been watching them very closely during the duel; Vaaler had felt his unseeing eyes on them the entire time. Jerrod was closely attuned to the ways of Chaos; maybe he had sensed something unusual during the fight.

If he did, wouldn't he challenge us about it?

Vaaler didn't know him well, but if Jerrod wasn't confronting them about what they'd done, there had to be a reason. With the monk's pupil-less eyes and unnatural sense, it was hard to know exactly what he was watching. But to Vaaler it had seemed like Jerrod was studying him and Keegan closely all night.

He has to suspect something. Is that what's bothering Keegan? Is he worried how Jerrod will react when he finds out?

"You can talk to me about anything," Vaaler assured his friend. "You know that, right?"

Keegan sighed, then took a deep breath.

"I can't stop thinking about Scythe," he admitted.

I should have guessed.

Vaaler was well aware of how his friend felt about the young woman; Keegan wasn't very good at hiding his feelings. It was understandable: she was an attractive young woman full of energy and spirit. But a simple crush was one thing; if Keegan was starting to obsess over her, it could lead to trouble.

"She's with Norr," Vaaler said, trying to keep from sounding judgmental. "You know that."

"I know. But when she kissed me after the duel it felt like ...
it's hard to explain."

"It's hard to explain because there's nothing there. So quit acting like a spoiled child."

"You said I could talk to you about anything," Keegan shot
back, offended. "Now you're mocking me?"

"I'm not mocking you," Vaaler protested. "I'm just telling you
not to get all knotted up because of one little kiss. She was just
excited for Norr. She got caught up in the moment."

"I think there was more to it," Keegan insisted. "There's a connection between us."

"You mean you want there to be a connection," Vaaler corrected. "I've seen her and Norr together; they mean everything to
each other. You don't want to get between that."

And if you keep trying, he silently added, *Norr might decide to
pummel you into oblivion.*

"Maybe I should just ask her how she feels," Keegan muttered,
more to himself than his friend. That didn't stop Vaaler from answering.

"Don't bring this up with Scythe," he warned. "You'll just em-
barrass yourself. You're making a big deal out of nothing. You've
got more important things you need to worry about, anyway."

"Like what?"

"Like Jerrod. Didn't you see him watching us last night? I think
he knows what we did."

"Now you're the one reading too much into nothing," Keegan
answered. "Jerrod's always watching me. He worries too much."

"Maybe he's right to worry."

"What does that mean?"

"It means you don't seem to be taking what happened seriously.
Your spell worked! You put a hex on Shalana, and it made her lose!"

"I told you it would work," Keegan reminded him. "I don't see
what the big deal is."

Vaaler gritted his teeth in frustration. Keegan was like a brother to him, but sometimes he could be so dense it was painful.

"You don't even realize what you did, do you?" Vaaler sighed, shaking his head. "You summoned Chaos without using witch-root."

"I've done it before," Keegan replied defensively. "I told you that."

"This wasn't some wild outburst of raw emotion! This was a cold, calculated act. Do you even understand the implications of what you've done?"

"Do you?" Keegan shot back. "This isn't the first time I have summoned Chaos. And it won't be the last."

"You take your power for granted," Vaaler snarled. "You don't appreciate how incredible and amazing your ability is. If I had the gift—"

"You don't!" Keegan snapped, cutting him off. "And you never will. So stop trying to tell me how to feel about it!"

Vaaler was stunned into silence. Keegan opened his mouth as if he was about to say something else, then closed it and turned his gaze down to the ground.

Disgusted with his friend, the former prince stood up and stomped away, leaving Keegan alone by the fire, gnawing away at his breakfast jerky.

He stormed through the camp, not heading in any particular direction, driven by anger and humiliation. By the time he reached the Long Hall near the far edge of the camp, the emotions clouding his mind had begun to clear. As they did, he couldn't help but wonder at how things had gotten so quickly out of hand. They'd had arguments before, but it wasn't like Keegan to lash out at him.

And it's not like me to overreact, he realized.

He'd spent his whole life dealing with his lack of magical ability; he'd learned to shrug it off. But for some reason the young mage's words had cut particularly deep.

We've been under a lot of stress. That's all.

But on some level, Vaaler knew there was more to it. Over the past few weeks they'd been through far worse situations than the one they were in now. Tempers had flared, but he and Keegan had never gone at each other before.

So why now?

Before he could analyze it further, the door to the Long Hall swung open, and Scythe came barreling out. She was walking fast: fists clenched, jaw set, and her face twisted into a mask of rage. Vaaler's first instinct was to step aside and let her pass; he'd seen the full force of her fury enough times to not want to get in her way. But at the last instant he changed his mind.

Why should I tiptoe around her? She's not the only one who has the right to get mad!

Besides, the irrational, petulant side of his mind chimed in, *Keegan and I wouldn't have started arguing if she hadn't given him that stupid kiss!*

"Where are you headed in such a hurry?" he asked, confronting her head on.

"Gotta pack," she snapped, pulling up short just in front of him.

"Pack? Are we leaving?"

"Apparently. A bunch of the clans are having some kind of big meeting."

"The Conclave," Vaaler said, recalling Shalana's words to the Ice Fang emissaries. "Someone named Hadawas is calling all the chiefs together."

"Well, Norr's decided to ask this Hadawas and the rest of the clans to join us in Jerrod's stupid quest to save the world."

"That's probably a good idea," Vaaler said, failing to see what had gotten Scythe so worked up. "We've made a lot of enemies already. We can use a few more allies."

"He wants to leave tomorrow," Scythe added, her voice dripping with contempt. "He's bringing all his favorite thanes with him."

Something about the way she said *favorite* clued Vaaler in. "Shalana?"

"Even after everything she did, even after she tried to force him into marrying her, that idiot still wants to bring her with us!"

"That actually seems like a smart thing to do," Vaaler countered. "Shalana still has supporters in the clan. Things will go better for Norr if he can get everyone to believe they're all on the same side."

"Should have expected a former prince to want to play politics," she sneered. "Guess I'm the only one around here who doesn't want to crawl into bed with my enemies."

"Shalana's not your enemy."

"Really? All she had to do was agree to help us and everything would've been fine," Scythe protested. "But she wanted to make trouble instead."

"Try to see things from her side," Vaaler urged. "Norr hurt her when he left. He abandoned her."

"Because she challenged him to a duel!" she spat out. "It's her own fault!"

"It's not that simple," Vaaler reminded her. "When her father chose Norr over her, Shalana was humiliated. Shamed. Everything she had worked her whole life to achieve was suddenly taken away. She's been struggling with that for the past five years, trying to rebuild what she'd lost. And when Norr suddenly showed up again, it all came crashing back down."

"Quit making excuses for her!" she snapped. "She needs to pay for what she did!"

"You won, Scythe!" Vaaler shot back. "Norr's the clan chief, and the two of you are still together. Isn't that enough?"

"No," she said. "She needs to suffer."

"She's already suffering," Vaaler assured her. "More than you can know."

"You feel sorry for her, don't you?" Scythe accused.

"Maybe I understand what she's going through better than you can," he said quietly.

"Pick your side carefully," Scythe warned. "You're either with her or me."

"I'm on your side," Vaaler snapped, jabbing a finger into Scythe's face. "I helped Norr win that duel, remember?"

"Get your finger out of my face before I slice it off," Scythe warned in a low whisper.

Vaaler hesitated, then finally dropped his hand and stepped to the side. Satisfied, Scythe pushed past him, gracing him with a parting scowl as she left.

First me and Keegan, now me and Scythe, Vaaler mused as he watched her go. *What's wrong with the three of us?*

He was still wondering about it when the door to the Long Hall opened a few minutes later and the thanes began to make their way out. They filed past him, most seemingly in good spirits. He noticed that Shalana wasn't among them.

Probably still recovering from the duel.

Norr was the last to exit, limping along on a splinted leg and using a makeshift crutch wedged under his arm to help support his weight.

Noticing Vaaler, he asked, "Did you see Scythe when she came out?"

"She wasn't happy," he replied.

"I've never seen her so mad," Norr admitted. "Maybe making Shalana a thane was a mistake."

"It was the right decision," Vaaler reassured him. "Scythe will see that in time."

"She can be stubborn," Norr noted. "She holds grudges. But even for her this was extreme."

"Just give her some space," Vaaler suggested. "Let her cool off during the journey to the Conclave."

"She told you?"

The Danaan nodded.

"We need to leave first thing tomorrow if we want to get there in time," Norr added. "Can you tell Jerrod and Keegan?"

"I don't think Keegan wants to see me right now," Vaaler told him. "We had a fight of our own."

"That is not like you two," Norr remarked.

No, it's not.

"I'll tell Jerrod, and he can tell Keegan," Vaaler offered. "We'll be there."

As he watched the big man limp away, he kept replaying his arguments with Keegan and Scythe over and over in his head, trying to figure out how they'd become so confrontational so quickly.

After a few minutes he gave up in frustration, convinced he was missing something very, very obvious.

Chapter 20

THE HEAVY IRON collar chafed at Andar's neck, as did the shackles on his ankles and wrists. The restraints weren't actually chained to anything; their role was mostly symbolic, marking him as a criminal.

The metal was inscribed with ancient runes meant to strip him of his power; glyphs to bar him from summoning Chaos. Had they still been in the Danaan lands, such safeguards might have been necessary, but now they were little more than ornamental. None of the Danaan mages—not even the former High Sorcerer himself—could call upon the power of magic here on the snow-covered plains of the Frozen East.

Moving slowly, but with purpose and precision, he made his way about the large tent that had been erected only an hour before, setting out the plates, cutlery, and cups for the Queen and her war council. The iron restraints made his movements awkward, their weight a constant reminder of his lowly station as he carefully set the table.

For his treasonous acts, Rianna had chosen an ancient and little-used punishment. Andar had been stripped of his former title and forced into the role of an indentured servant. The sentence was both merciful and particularly cruel.

It was better than banishment or execution, or even a long imprisonment in the dungeons beneath the castle, where he would suffer cold, hunger, and other physical torments. But the humiliation and shame of being forced to serve those who were once his equals was its own peculiar brand of torture.

According to the ancient laws Rianna had invoked, he wasn't permitted to speak to anyone but the Queen herself, on threat of having his tongue removed. Andar wanted to believe his monarch lacked the cruelty to enact such a barbaric price should he slip up and say something in the presence of the others, but he wasn't willing to risk it.

Doing so would also undermine the entire purpose of the sentence, and despite his seditious acts during the ritual at the Black Lake, he was still loyal to the Queen. Rianna needed him to be an object lesson to her still-loyal followers; an ever-present reminder that anything other than absolute, unquestioning loyalty would be met with harsh consequences.

Yet even though he was now a slave, there were advantages to his new position. He was the Queen's personal attendant, present at virtually every meeting of the war council. Despite being officially removed from any position of authority, he was still privy to the innermost workings of the monarchy and the Danaan campaign against the barbarians of the Frozen East.

Andar liked to believe Rianna had done this intentionally, that some part of her admired how he had stood up to Orath and wanted to keep him close so he could advise her and help guide her through her most difficult decisions.

And maybe even protect her from falling too far under Orath's influence.

Once the table was set, Andar began to place the food. Loaves of bread, bricks of cheese, and sides of meat were placed in the center of the table—simple fare, but the best that could be managed with the Danaan army on the move each day.

He then placed a cup at each of the six seats and filled it with wine, finishing just as the first councillors began to arrive. Andar bowed low and retreated into the far corner of the tent. In the shadows of the dimly burning lamps it was easy to remain unobtrusive and forgotten.

There were five councillors in all; Rianna had left the rest of her high-ranking advisers back in Ferlhame to oversee the rebuilding of the city. They were forbidden from acknowledging his presence, though as they entered he caught each of his former peers glancing over, then quickly averting their eyes before taking a seat at the table. Once, they had been Andar's friends. Now, they had to pretend that he didn't exist.

The Queen and Orath were the last to arrive, coming in together. Protocol dictated that the Queen arrive last, but Rianna had waived this bit of formality while they were in the field. She knew her advisers were uncomfortable in Orath's presence when she was not around.

They're uncomfortable even when she is here, though it's far worse when they must face the Minion alone.

The quartet of councillors rose as a sign of respect for their liege as she made her way to her seat at the head of the table. Unlike the others, neither Orath nor Rianna glanced in his direction. For the Queen, it was important that she shun him in front of the others to reinforce the gravity of his punishment. As for Orath, he simply didn't like Andar.

He'd rip out my throat and feast on my blood if he thought he could do it without incurring the Queen's wrath.

Fortunately Orath still needed the Queen, at least for now. Andar wasn't certain if that would always be the case.

Once Rianna was seated, the others joined her. As he always did, Orath remained standing, looming over the Queen's shoulder at the back of her chair. Unlike the Danaan advisers, he wouldn't partake of the food.

When and what does he eat? Andar wondered, then decided it was better not to know.

After a moment of silence, Rianna took a small sip of wine—the ceremonial start of their nightly feast. The meal was a grim and silent affair. The councillors she had chosen to join her on the campaign all had served in the patrols; they understood that in the field when it was time to eat, you ate quickly and efficiently in case the opportunity was interrupted.

Standing over them, Orath studied the subdued diners with an implacable, unreadable expression.

Andar also watched them carefully, ready to swoop in with the wine if any of the cups should run dry. But none of the assembled were in a mood to drink, and his services weren't needed.

Once everyone had finished, Andar was compelled to step forth from the shadows and clear away the plates and cutlery. As he did so, the meeting began in earnest, the councillors doing their best to talk around him as if he weren't there.

"Status reports," the Queen ordered.

"We found the main camp of the dog clan," Greznor, her grizzled senior military adviser, informed her. "We caught them completely unprepared. The archers finished them off without any casualties on our side."

Greznor had no practical experience in large-scale battles—none of the Danaan did. But he was considered the kingdom's foremost academic expert on the subject and had served two tours in the Danaan patrols during his youth. Limited as they were, those credentials were enough for him to be given the title of general and command over the entire Danaan force.

"Were you able to take any prisoners?" the Queen asked.

"Unfortunately not. They fought like animals, and we had to put them all down," Greznor said, his voice betraying no emotion.

"They are barbarians, my Queen," Lormilar, the newly appointed High Sorcerer, chimed in.

"It would be useful to interrogate some of them." The speaker this time was Pranya, the middle-aged woman who oversaw the

Queen's espionage and spy network. "We need to learn the numbers and location of other nearby tribes."

"I doubt it would do much good," Lormilar countered. "The clans are nomadic and very insular. They would only be able to tell you about the clan they came from, and most would die before betraying their own people."

He's studied the Easterners, Andar realized. *He knows his power beyond the North Forest is virtually nonexistent, and he's eager to make himself useful.*

Unfortunately, Lormilar's knowledge would be limited to what was available in the royal archives—a collection of stories, tales, and very limited firsthand accounts that would be woefully out of date.

The truth is, we know almost nothing of these people beyond myths and legends. And now we are at war with them.

The Danaan had always seen the Southlands as the real threat to their kingdom. For generations spies and informants had been gathering whatever information they could about the Seven Capitals and the Order. The tribes of the Frozen East had been nothing but an afterthought—they never dared venture into the Forest, and the Danaan never crossed the icy tundra.

Until now.

"One of my patrols hasn't reported back yet," Hexiff said. The young man was in charge of the army's advance scouts though ultimately he answered to Greznor. "It's possible they encountered an overwhelming enemy force."

"Or a blizzard," Lormilar noted. "This is a hostile land."

"The winter is making it difficult to replenish our supplies," Bassi, the female quartermaster, agreed. "We have been unable to forage for anything edible for our reserve stores."

"How long will our food last?" the Queen demanded.

"Six weeks," Bassi replied. "Two months if we start rationing now."

"Then start rationing," Orath intoned, his voice devoid of emotion.

Bassi looked to the Queen for confirmation, and Rianna gave a curt nod.

"Even if we ration our supplies, do any of us really believe this campaign will be over in only two months?" Greznor asked, unwilling simply to let the matter rest.

"You are being too cautious, my Queen," Orath said, speaking directly to her and ignoring Greznor. "The army is only advancing a few leagues each day. We should sweep across this land like a storm instead of creeping like thieves afraid of being discovered."

"We have no idea how many barbarian tribes there are, or how far their territory extends," Pranya cautioned. "Stumbling blindly into unknown terrain is a poor way to win a war."

"The scouting patrols should give us this information," Orath said, fixing his yellow eyes on Hexiff.

"We've scouted everything within a twenty-mile radius of the main force," the young man answered defensively. "It's the rest of the troops who can't keep up the pace."

A silence settled over the table as all eyes turned to Greznor. He shifted uncomfortably but didn't speak.

"General," Rianna said, "can your troops move faster?"

"If that is your wish, Your Majesty. Though I fear we will run into a trap."

"My scouts won't let that happen," Hexiff assured them.

"Does anyone have anything further to add?" the Queen asked after another moment of heavy silence.

When none of the councillors spoke up she dismissed them with a wave of her hand. Wordlessly, the five Danaan seated with her rose from their chairs and left. Once they were gone, Rianna turned to Orath.

"What of the ogre?" she asked him. "You told me the beast could track the Ring. Lead us to it and the Destroyer of Worlds."

"Patience, my Queen," the Minion assured her. "The trail is cold, but once the ogre picks up the scent of the Ring he will not lose it."

Rianna considered his words, studying them as if she sensed there was some deception or subterfuge in them. Ultimately, however, she accepted his explanation with a nod.

"Leave me," she said, dismissing Orath as she had the others.

The Minion cast a pointed glance in Andar's direction before gracing Rianna with a faint bow and exiting the tent.

Alone with just the Queen, Andar moved in and slowly began cleaning up the chairs, stacking them in the corner so they could be quickly loaded on one of the supply wagons when the army packed up camp and set out the next morning.

Rianna watched him for a few moments before saying, "I sense you do not approve of Orath's plan to increase our pace."

"There is nothing that creature says or does that I approve of," he replied even as he continued with his task.

"The slower we go, the more time we give for the barbarians to unite their forces against us," Rianna explained, as if she felt the need to justify the decision. "We must hit them hard and fast to minimize our losses."

"If you say so, my Queen."

Rianna chewed her lip.

"This is our only hope to get the Ring back," she insisted. "It's our only hope to stop the Destroyer of Worlds before he unleashes its power again."

"If he sees a Danaan army descending on him, he isn't going to surrender," Andar warned. "He will have no choice but to turn the Ring against your soldiers. Do you really think even an army can stop its power?"

"That's why we have Orath and the ogre," the Queen reminded him. "The beast will slay the Destroyer of Worlds while our armies wipe out his barbarian followers."

If he even has barbarian followers, Andar thought, but didn't bother to say.

"Even if you're right," the disgraced mage asked, "and the ogre destroys him, are you certain Orath will command it to deliver the Ring to you?"

"We have no choice but to trust him," the Queen said with a sigh. "There is no other way. We've come too far to turn back now."

Andar couldn't have disagreed more.

Chapter 21

THE STONE SPIRIT camp was a flurry of activity as the five thanes and two dozen clan warriors selected to accompany Norr to the Conclave made ready to depart.

Vaaler watched the activity with interest. At first it appeared to be a chaotic mess: men and women scrambling to load food, clothing, and other supplies haphazardly onto a half dozen large sleds. But soon it became clear there was a pattern and precision in their work: the sleds were packed in a specific order, layer by layer. Sacks and packs were stuffed tightly together to make the most efficient use of space before being tied off.

Norr had explained that each individual was expected to pack their own food, clothing, weapons, and other essentials. That way if anyone's supplies ran short on the journey, they had only themselves to blame. But, he'd added, an exception would be made for the Outlanders—someone would pack for them to make sure they didn't forget anything.

Vaaler still would have been happy to help load the sled. But being unfamiliar with the specific way the clan had of placing each bag, there wasn't anything he could do to help except stay out of the way.

Along with Jerrod and Keegan, he stood awkwardly off to one side while the sleds were loaded, not speaking. That wasn't surprising with Jerrod—the monk wasn't one for small talk. And he and Keegan hadn't spoken since their argument the day before.

Scythe and Norr were strangely absent. Vaaler had risen early, but the pair were already gone, the flap on their tent hastily tied from the outside.

Norr must have already packed for them. Now they're either meeting with the thanes one last time before we go, or Scythe and he are off somewhere private still fighting about Shalana's coming with us.

Standing idly by as the clan worked left plenty of time for Vaaler to think about his own recent argument with Keegan. The former prince knew he'd overreacted; Keegan's words were cruel but he'd heard far worse. So why did his friend's casual comments about Vaaler's failings cut so deep?

Because it's the kind of thing Rexol would say.

The thought that Keegan was slowly changing, becoming more like their former master, was more than a little troubling. Rexol was arrogant, selfish, and ruthless—a dangerous combination for someone who could summon Chaos.

Keegan isn't like that. At least, he didn't used to be.

Vaaler had initially dismissed the young mage's interest in Scythe as a harmless crush. But now he feared it would turn into an obsession. He wanted Scythe: what if he decided Norr was the only thing standing in his way?

He likes Norr. The old Keegan would never betray a friend. But Rexol wouldn't even think twice about using his power to eliminate a rival.

Vaaler looked over at his friend, wondering if he should try to talk to him again to smooth things over. As if sensing he was being watched, Keegan turned and glared at him, then looked away dismissively.

That's something Rexol would do. Like I'm beneath his notice.

It was possible he was overreacting. Keegan had used his talent to cast a curse on Shalana to help Norr. Rexol wouldn't have done that.

Or would he? What if Keegan didn't do it to help Norr but to impress Scythe? Or maybe he just wanted to see if he was strong enough to actually make the spell work.

Manipulation and egotistical overconfidence were part of Rexol's nature; had they become part of Keegan's? Was this an inevitable progression in the journey from apprentice to full-fledged Chaos mage? The corrupting influence of having un-imaginable power at your fingertips?

Or is it something else?

He remembered the rapidly deteriorating health of his mother and her descent into madness—a decline he blamed on the Ring the Queen always wore around her neck.

Keegan didn't just wear the Ring on a chain—he unleashed its full power!

He could say something to Jerrod about his fears, but he doubted the monk would listen. His belief in Keegan was too intractable to allow for the possibility of a flaw in his chosen savior . . . particularly if the flaw was triggered by the very Talismans they were trying to find.

He could always talk to Scythe once she returned. She seemed to care about Keegan, though clearly not in the same way the young man felt about her. But if she was still angry about Norr's inviting Shalana to the Conclave, she'd have trouble focusing on anything else. Recalling their last meeting, he decided the last thing he needed was another argument with her, too. And if he was right, Keegan's infatuation with Scythe was actually part of the problem.

If I tell her about that, she might decide to take matters into her own hands.

Scythe was just crazy enough to slit Keegan's throat while he slept if she thought he was going to hurt Norr.

You're overreacting!

Vaaler shook his head, surprised at the violent turn his thoughts had taken.

Scythe has a temper, but she's not insane.

Vaaler realized that brooding over the situation wasn't helping. Like it or not, he had to talk with Keegan.

Keegan watched Vaaler coming toward him with a mixture of relief and dread. He knew he'd crossed a line during their argument; Vaaler's greatest shame was his inability to summon Chaos. He had no right to throw it in his friend's face like he did, but the words were out before he'd even realized he was saying them.

Vaaler isn't an innocent victim here, the darker part of his mind chimed in. *He's the one who started lecturing you about how to use your power.*

Keegan ignored the voice. Vaaler was his closest friend; it was time to make amends.

"Keegan, we need to talk," the former prince said. "Alone," he added, casting a glance in Jerrod's direction.

The monk shrugged and wandered off to the other side of the camp. Keegan waited until he was far enough away that even his Chaos-heightened senses couldn't overhear them, then began before Vaaler could start.

"I'm sorry, Vaaler. I said things I didn't mean. I . . . I got caught up in the heat of the moment."

The apology seemed to catch Vaaler off guard for a moment, but then he forced a smile.

"I think we were both out of line. But everything you said was true. I don't have the Gift, and it's not my place to tell you how to live with it."

"You may not have Chaos in your veins," Keegan assured him, "but you're one of the smartest people I know. You were always a better apprentice than I was."

"Until it came time to actually cast a spell," Vaaler added, his smile slipping.

"It should have been you," Keegan said after a brief pause. "Rexol could have turned you into the greatest mage the world has ever known."

The Danaan shrugged. "Maybe. But I'm not sure I would have wanted that. Rexol was a cruel, heartless bastard. I wouldn't want to turn into someone like that."

Are you saying that's what's happening to me? Keegan thought, though he bit his tongue. Instead, he said, "I think he was like that to begin with."

Realizing the implications of his words, Vaaler quickly back-pedaled. "I'm sorry—that didn't come out right. I know you, Keegan. I know you're not like him. I know you want to use your power to help people. But Chaos has a way of twisting good intentions."

"Are you saying we shouldn't have cast that curse on Shalana?"

"No," Vaaler answered, though he seemed to think about it first. "I think Scythe was right—we really didn't have a choice. But I feel bad for what happened to Shalana. For what we did to her."

"She brought this on herself," Keegan reminded him. "She didn't have to try to force Norr into marrying her."

"Maybe," Vaaler conceded, though he clearly had his doubts. "We don't really know the politics of the clan that well, though. Marrying Norr might have been the only real way she could keep her position."

"Don't let Scythe hear you defending her," Keegan warned.

"Too late," Vaaler answered, flashing another smile that disappeared almost immediately. "She nearly tore my head off."

There was a long pause before Vaaler added, "I guess it's easier for me to understand what Shalana was going through. We were both raised to be leaders of our people, then we both had it torn away by circumstances beyond our control."

This isn't really about Shalana, Keegan realized.

"Are you saying it's my fault the Queen exiled you?" he asked, his voice more defensive than he'd intended.

"No, of course not," Vaaler assured him. "I'm the one who stole the Ring.

"But it's important to remember there are consequences for our actions," he added. "Ferlhame was nearly destroyed by the dragon. Thousands of my subjects lost their lives that night."

"I haven't forgotten," Keegan answered, his voice cold. "I carry the guilt of that night, too."

"I'm not blaming you," Vaaler insisted, and this time he was the one who sounded defensive. "None of us knew the Ring would awaken the dragon. That creature's the one who devastated the city. If you hadn't gone back to Ferlhame to stop it, nobody would have survived.

"If there was any justice in the world," he added, "my people should be hailing you as a hero. You saved them."

Keegan could have let his comments go. Nobody but Scythe knew the real truth: that he'd gone back to Ferlhame looking for revenge, only to be attacked by the wyrm that had gotten there first. But he didn't want to lie to Vaaler. Not about something like this.

"It wasn't like that," he said in a whisper. "I didn't go back to help them. I didn't even know the dragon was there."

"What do you mean?"

"I wanted revenge for the Danaan patrols that attacked us," Keegan explained, his voice still low. "I wanted to make them pay. I wanted to wipe Ferlhame off the map."

Vaaler's eyes went wide, his features twisting into a mask of horrified shock.

"You're no better than Rexol," he accused. "What kind of monster have you become?"

"I'm not a monster!" Keegan snapped at him. "And I'm not like Rexol!

"You don't know what it's like to have that kind of raw power rushing through you," he explained, his voice pleading. "It's overwhelming. Like an ocean that floods your mind, drowning out your very thoughts!

"You studied under Rexol enough to know how dangerous and unpredictable Chaos is," Keegan reminded him. "If it isn't properly contained, it can twist your emotions. Drive you into fits of insane rage."

"I don't remember Rexol's teaching us anything like that," Vaaler shot back. "It sounds like an excuse for a wizard to act without conscience. No responsibility. No accountability. Just deny the consequences of your actions and blame it all on Chaos!"

"You have no idea what you're talking about," Keegan snarled. "You've never felt it, so how would you know?"

Vaaler didn't bother to answer. Instead, he spun on his heel and stormed away.

Watching him go, Keegan realized they'd ended up exactly where they'd been in their last argument—Vaaler trying to tell him how to deal with his power and him throwing Vaaler's Chaos-blind blood back in his face.

Good thing we both apologized, he thought bitterly, wondering how things had gone so wrong.

Scythe was beginning to despise the Long Hall, mostly because she still didn't understand enough of the language to follow what was going on. Sitting by Norr's side listening to him talk gibberish with his thanes was a poor way to pass the morning.

It's your own fault. If you'd ever asked Norr to teach you Clan-speak, he would have done it gladly.

She knew Jerrod was already taking lessons; Norr had assigned one of his thanes the task of teaching the monk. She could have joined them, but that would have meant abandoning Norr's side, and she wasn't about to do that.

He'd told her that most of the thanes spoke Allrish, but she wasn't going to ask Norr to make them abandon their native tongue for her sake. It was bad enough their new chief had chosen an Outlander over Shalana; she didn't need to rub their noses in it.

They probably wouldn't have objected if Norr translated everything for her, but that would only make the meeting drag on even longer. And, to be honest, she didn't really care that much about what was going on. The main reason she'd come here was to keep an eye on Shalana.

Even after defeating her in the duel, Norr didn't believe she'd try to betray him. He was too trusting; he always wanted to see only the good in people. Fortunately, Scythe was there to watch his back.

Not that it mattered. That oversized heifer didn't even have the decency to show up.

Nobody else seemed bothered by Shalana's absence, at least not as far as she could tell through the language barrier. In Scythe's eyes it was a major insult, considering everything Norr had done for her. But maybe they were cutting her some slack because of the physical punishment she took during the duel.

But she gave as good as she got, and Norr managed to show up.

Her lover was covered with welts and bruises that would take days to heal, but instead of bed rest he was using a makeshift crutch to help support his weight.

At least he agreed to ride on a sled while we head for the Conclave.

The meeting droned on and on, but Scythe gritted her teeth and suffered through it with as much grace as she could muster. It wasn't like she had anywhere else to go or anyone she wanted to talk to, anyway. Keegan was still mooning over her like some love-sick puppy, and she wasn't in the mood to deal with that. She was still mad at Vaaler for taking Shalana's side the last time they'd spoken. And if she spoke to Jerrod, she'd probably have to sit through another of the monk's didactic lectures on how she'd become part of Keegan's great destiny.

Maybe I should go look for Shalana. Let her know that I'm watching her.

She dismissed the idea as quickly as it came. Norr wouldn't want her stirring up trouble. And if Shalana really was plotting something, there was no sense getting her guard up. It'd be easier to catch her in the act if Scythe stayed in the shadows.

Guess I'm here till the end.

There was a pause in the conversation, and she briefly hoped the meeting was over. Norr turned to look at her, and she knew him well enough to read his intent without words.

Are you holding up okay?

She forced a reassuring smile and a nod, and he turned his attention back to the thanes. Realizing they could still be some time, Scythe shifted in her seat until she found a more comfortable position.

Keegan's magic had made Norr the chief, but Scythe wasn't actually sure things were any better. Norr had the responsibility of the entire clan on his shoulders now, not to mention the danger of Shalana or her father plotting some kind of revenge. And she had the added worry of making sure Norr never found out about the curse. If Jerrod figured it out, others could, too.

That spell really didn't solve anything. Guess this is what the monk meant when he warned me to watch out for backlash.

Vaaler wasn't walking with any purpose or direction; he just needed to put one foot in front of the other as forcefully as possible. He focused on the physical act of slamming his boots onto the cold, hard ground in an effort to ignore the vicious anger Keegan's words had stirred up inside him.

He was going to slaughter my people!

Only they weren't really his people anymore. He wasn't their prince anymore. He was an exile. A fugitive. An outcast. So why did Keegan's admission make him so angry?

It's the Queen's fault. She's the one who sent Drake out to meet us. She's the one who sent the patrols after us. My mother gave them orders to kill us; Keegan only responded in kind.

His steps began to slow as his anger faded away. As his mind cleared, he thought back on the argument and realized Keegan wasn't some soulless monster—his friend had been deeply troubled by what had happened.

He opened up to you, and you instantly turned on him. Why?

Before he could come up with an answer, he noticed Shalana walking gingerly through the camp. The tall woman was bent over, a bulky sack thrown over her left shoulder. Her right hand clutched the long, feathered spear she'd carried when she first met them at the parley with the Ice Fangs. But now she was using the weapon more like a crutch to help her bear the weight of the bag as she made her way slowly to a large supply sled a hundred yards away.

Though she wasn't sporting the visible bruises and welts that covered Norr's face and arms, she was clearly injured. Vaaler recalled the final moments of her duel with Norr. The big man had brought her to the ground with a savage blow to her side, then pinned her to the ground with his massive bulk.

Probably broke her ribs.

It was only now, watching her hobble across the camp, that he realized things could have been worse.

We really had no idea what the curse would actually do to her. If she'd died, her blood would be on our hands.

Fortunately she'd survived, but Vaaler couldn't help feeling guilty as he watched her struggles. He'd cracked a rib once on patrol; he knew how painful an injury it was. Every step pulled on tender muscles that screamed in protest, every breath stabbed at the lungs with a sharp blade.

There were plenty of other Stone Spirits around, moving quickly and efficiently to load the sled. Yet none of them offered to help their former chief. They didn't even acknowledge her presence.

She's ostracized. A pariah among her people. That's on us, too.

Still fifty yards from her destination, Shalana paused to gather her strength and adjusted the pack on her shoulder, leaning heavily on her spear. Her jaw clenched to keep from crying out as she twisted awkwardly, sending a fresh wave of pain through her side.

Unable to bear it any longer, Vaaler jogged over to her side.

"Here, let me help you with that," he said, holding out his hands toward the pack.

Shalana didn't react at first; she just stared at him with suspicious eyes. If not for her injury, Vaaler suspected she would have turned her back on him.

"You speak Verlsung," she finally said.

"I do," he admitted. Vaaler couldn't tell if she was angry or just surprised.

"Should have kept that quiet," she told him. "A good way to learn our secrets."

"But not a good way to make friends," Vaaler countered.

She raised a skeptical eyebrow.

"Nobody here wants to be your friend, Outlander."

Vaaler looked around at the other Stone Spirits. They were still carrying on with the task of loading the sled, none of them paying any attention to their conversation.

"I could say the same to you," he noted.

Shalana snorted, then slowly started walking again, ignoring his offer. But Vaaler wasn't about to give up so easily, so he fell into step beside her.

He'd noticed most of the Stone Spirits were bringing two or three bags at a time when they emerged from their respective tents. In addition to bringing enough food for the journey to the Conclave, some of them were no doubt stuffed with clothes and other personal effects they might want during the trip. Because of her injuries, however, Shalana could only handle one pack at a time. And given how slowly she was moving, he guessed she still had to make at least one more trip.

"It's going to take you all morning to do this alone," Vaaler noted. "And none of us can leave for the Conclave until everything is loaded onto the sleds."

Shalana turned her head and fixed him with a scowl, clearly annoyed at his transparent effort to appeal to her sense of duty to the rest of the clan. But after a few more steps she stopped and let the bag slip from her shoulder and fall to the ground with a heavy thud.

"Do you even know where it goes on the sled?" she demanded.

"You'll have to show me," Vaaler said, groaning softly as he hefted his new burden.

The weight surprised him, and he staggered for a couple steps before finding his balance.

"You don't seem to be doing any better than me," Shalana said smugly.

From the corner of his eye, Vaaler swore he saw the hint of a smile touch the corner of her mouth. But when he turned to look it was gone, replaced by the same stern expression she'd been wearing since their arrival.

They made better progress with him carrying the bag, though Shalana still wasn't able to move much faster than a brisk walk.

"Lay it down at the back, on top and crosswise to the ones below," she instructed once they reached the sled.

Vaaler swung the bag back and forth a couple times to build momentum, then hoisted it into place. Shalana reached forward to make a small adjustment to its position, wincing as she did so.

"Try not to reach or twist," Vaaler advised her. "Or bend."

"Or breathe," she added in a surly tone. "I know."

"How many more bags?" Vaaler asked, hoping they'd be lighter so he could take more than one at a time.

"Did Norr send you to spy on me?" she suddenly asked.

"Does that seem like something he'd do?" Vaaler countered.

"Not unless his little Islander whore told him to."

"Don't let Scythe hear you call her that," Vaaler warned. "Be careful you don't make the same mistake I did and slip into the Southern tongue."

"Is that what she used to win Norr over? Her Southern tongue?"

Vaaler laughed, not so much at the crude joke but more at Shalana's deadpan delivery.

"You didn't answer my question," she said after a brief pause. "Are you supposed to watch me in case I'm plotting my vengeance?"

"If I say no, you'll just think I'm lying anyway."

Shalana nodded solemnly. Using her spear, she pivoted away and started walking back toward her tent.

"Come on, Spy. Three more bags to go. We don't want to keep the rest of the clan waiting."

Chapter 22

CASSANDRA COULDN'T STOP shivering. She'd left the Frozen East behind, but here in the sparsely populated farms that dotted the outer borders of the Southlands there was still a biting chill in the air when the sun went down.

She'd left the Guardian's cave feeling strong and determined, but the elements were taking a toll on her body's dwindling reserves. And for the past two nights, she hadn't slept at all, pushing her pace as she sensed the monstrous Crawling Twins getting ever closer.

They'll catch you tonight. It's time to use the Crown. You have no other options.

She shook her head, an unconscious gesture she'd adopted after rejecting the advice from the ever-present voice inside her mind.

She could still escape; she just needed to find a horse. She couldn't outrun the Twins on foot, but mounted she'd be able to keep ahead of them.

You had a chance to get a horse, but you passed it up.

Yesterday she'd noticed a small mare in a field near a lone farmhouse. The voice in her head had urged her to steal the animal, but instead she'd given the property a wide berth. No matter how dire her situation, she didn't want to inadvertently lead the Crawling Twins to an innocent family.

Sometimes we must sacrifice a few innocent lives to save thousands.

This time the voice in her head sounded different. It wasn't Rexol, her old Master, but rather the memory of something the Pontiff had told her long ago when she was still training to join the Order.

If you want to save anybody, Rexol's voice chimed in, *you have to save yourself first.*

Cassandra reflexively shook her head again, even as she refocused her mental energy to her physical form. She'd been traveling for two days without rest at a pace faster than most people could run, but she forced her body to release a fresh burst of adrenaline. Her weary legs redoubled their efforts, but she knew she couldn't sustain it for long. Her heart was already pounding and her lungs burned; in an hour or two she'd have to slow down again.

But at least it quieted the voices for a while.

Inside the Crown, Rexol raged against his prison. The link between him and Cassandra was steadily growing, but she still resisted his efforts to manipulate and control her.

Even when she was a child you sensed how strong her will was.

Though he was powerless to affect his former apprentice, Rexol was aware of the mortal world through Cassandra's senses. The monsters that hunted her were too close now; any hope of escape was impossible.

Rexol had recognized this much earlier than Cassandra. For the past few days, he'd known she wouldn't survive on her own. And so the disembodied wizard had sent out a call for help.

Using the Crown's power to affect the physical world was difficult, but he was getting better at it. He'd used it to lead the flying huntress away from Cassandra during her flight to the Guardian's cave. Now he was doing the opposite, using it to try to lead someone to them. Hopefully, someone would answer the call before it was too late.

Cassandra sensed the men ahead of her long before their torches were visible through the night's gloom. She'd changed course to try to avoid them, but when they matched her movements she realized they could sense her in the darkness, too.

Inquisitors.

As they drew closer, she realized they weren't alone. There were only three of her brethren from the Order, traveling on foot at the head of a small company of armed soldiers. Five rode on horseback and another fifteen marched along behind on foot.

The Inquisitors forged ahead, leaving the footmen to scramble along in their wake as they closed in on her. At the same time, the riders broke away from the main group, two circling out to the left and three to the right to keep her from trying to flee.

Even if she hadn't been near the limits of her endurance, Cassandra wouldn't have been able to escape. But she'd already given that hope up. Instead, she headed directly into the teeth of their trap.

I have to warn them!

The Crawling Twins were only minutes behind her now, and she didn't have any illusions of what would happen if they ran across the unsuspecting patrol.

"Cassandra!" one of the Inquisitors called out as they drew close. "Yasmin the Unbowed, forty-fourth Pontiff of the Order, has declared you to be a traitor to the True Gods!"

She recognized the speaker, a young man named Mirgul. He was only a few years older than she was; seeing him in a position of authority reinforced how badly the Order's numbers had been devastated when the Monastery fell.

The Inquisitors had blocked her path, their staves at the ready, but Cassandra didn't stop or slow down as she approached.

"Run, Mirgul!" she called out, drawing on the last reserves of her inner power to amplify her voice so the soldiers in the distance could hear her. "Everybody scatter!"

Unfortunately, the soldiers were too well trained to obey her shouted commands, and they didn't even hesitate as they continued toward her and the Inquisitors.

Mirgul and his compatriots dropped into fighting stances, convinced she was charging toward them with hostile intent. But before she came close enough for them to bring her down, their Sight saw what she was running from.

"Run!" Cassandra screamed again, and for a second she thought Mirgul might listen.

Then he raised his arms above his head, twirling his weapon as he shouted, "Destroy the Chaos Spawn!"

At the same time, Cassandra sensed one of the riders who had circled around charging in hard from behind her, unaware of the monsters lurking in the nearby shadows. In his hand he had a large cudgel, and as he closed the gap between them he brought it around in a wide, sweeping arc meant to knock her flying from her feet.

Without breaking stride, Cassandra ducked as the horse came alongside her, the heavy club whooshing harmlessly over her head. She let the pack with the Crown slip from her shoulder and fall at her feet. At the same time she spun and grabbed the rider's leg with both hands, then yanked him out of his saddle.

As he came crashing down to the ground his mount, confused by the sudden loss of its rider, circled around, then pulled up short.

The horse! Grab the Crown, get the horse, and flee!

The other riders were closing in on her now, too. The foot soldiers were coming up behind the Inquisitors, who stood poised

and ready for battle. And then the Crawling Twins arrived, bringing Chaos with them.

In the dim illumination of the soldiers' torches, the creatures
would look like little more than gangly, misshapen shadows crawling low to the ground. But though their eyes couldn't grasp the
true nature of the scuttling horrors that confronted them, the
Twins let loose with a long, baying howl that was clearly not of
the mortal world.

Somewhere between a roar and a scream, their cries rose to an
ear-shattering pitch that made everyone drop to their knees and
cover their ears. There was some malevolent magic in the howl; it
left Cassandra's head spinning and her senses disoriented. Even
her mystical second sight was blurred by the terrible sound.

It took only a second to recover, but by then the Twins were
charging forward, still crawling on all fours but moving with
alarming speed. Instinctively, Cassandra threw herself forward,
covering the bag containing the Crown as if her frail mortal body
could somehow protect it.

She braced for the agony of claws and teeth ripping her flesh
apart, but instead she felt a strange pulse of energy from the
Crown. At the same instant, the Twins leapt over her prone form
and threw themselves at the still-reeling Inquisitors.

Rexol recognized the power of Chaos in the unholy scream, even
from inside the Crown. Though lacking any physical form, he
somehow still felt a wave of pain and terror. But though the Minions were strong, so was Rexol.

He'd been praying for Cassandra to free the Crown from its
sack and place it on her head. He was convinced if she tried to
unleash the full fury of the Talisman, he could escape his prison
and destroy the Crawling Twins. But when she failed to do so, he
was forced to improvise.

The Crown's power was focused on the mental rather than the physical. Calling on it, Rexol reached out and brushed against the dark, fetid minds of the red and blue beasts as they charged their helpless victims. Trapped inside the Talisman, he couldn't stop their deadly assault; their wills were too strong. Instead, he manipulated their instincts and emotions, heightening their savage bloodlust while subtly pushing their fury away from Cassandra and redirecting it to the other enemies before them.

Cassandra didn't have time to wonder why the Twins had ignored her and the Talisman to go after the Inquisitors. She needed to get away from the battle before the creatures finished off the others and turned on her.

Though her Sight was still fuzzy, she was aware of everything happening around her. Several of the soldiers had fled into the night, driven away by the horrific scream, but most—inspired by zealotry or coin—were standing by the Inquisitors. Two of the riders had vanished, but the other two were driving their reluctant horses into the fray. The Inquisitors were flipping, spinning and whirling like living tops, their staves whistling through the air with blinding speed as they met the Twins' charge.

The monsters didn't bother unleashing more Chaos magic at their foes; instead, they tore them apart with brute strength and raw speed. The red one lashed out a foreclaw, hooking it deep into the belly of Mirgul as he tried to leap over the crouching demon. The muscles of its gangly arm flexed and with a flick of its malformed wrist, the beast ripped out his innards, sending bits of gore and viscera spewing across the battlefield.

Mirgul's face went white with shock and he fell to his knees, his staff slipping from his grasp as he fumbled at the entrails spilling from his belly. Ignoring him, the beast twisted to the side, its back leg jutting out at an impossible angle to grab the nearest soldier by the throat in its curved toes. His eyes bulged as the beast contracted its claw, crushing his windpipe.

One of the horsemen tried to run the blue Twin down as it scurried along. But instead of being trampled beneath the mount's hooves, the creature twisted its torso and leaned back so that it caught the horse's underbelly in its clawed hands. The creature then stood up, lifting both horse and rider high above its head.

Four soldiers took the opening and rushed in, hacking and slashing at the monster's legs, chest, and back with their swords. A dozen blows rained down, but instead of slicing the creature to bits, only a handful even managed to draw blood.

The Twin growled and slammed the upraised horse and rider to the ground, crushing two of the attackers beneath the animal's bulk. It then whirled around and seized the other two soldiers as they tried to run and slammed their heads together with enough force to crush their helmets and cave in their skulls.

The second rider had pivoted his mount away from the violence, realizing flight was a better option. But as he set his spurs to his horse's side, the blue Twin leapt forward, flying twenty feet through the air before landing on the horse's back.

The impact brought mount, rider, and the Twin down in a heap, and the Minion tore into them both with claws and the sharp fangs of its piglike snout. The man managed a single scream, and the horse thrashed violently for several seconds before lying still, blood pouring from ragged holes in their throats.

There's nothing you can do to save them! You have to get out of here now!

Cassandra forced herself to ignore the carnage as the other two Inquisitors fell on the red Twin, trying to drive it away from Mirgul. Their leader had collapsed onto his side, his body convulsing while a red froth bubbled up from his lips.

The animal she wanted to grab—the horse from the rider she'd dislodged at the start of the battle—was already gone, racing off in terror. The horse that had been thrown to the ground still lay on its side, whinnying and kicking frantically but miraculously uninjured. The rider was unconscious, his body tangled up in the saddle and harness so that his weight kept the horse from getting to its feet.

Cassandra scooped up the sack at her feet and raced toward the panicked beast, knowing it was her only chance of survival. Nearby, the blue Twin was taking deep chunks out of a still-living soldier's cheek with its tusks while using a long, sinewy tongue to lap up the geyser of blood.

As she reached the horse's side, she felt another pulse from the Crown and the thrashing animal suddenly became calm and docile.

The red Twin had already broken the neck of one of Mirgul's companions, and had seized the last surviving Inquisitor by the shoulders with its hands. Rolling onto its side, it pulled the Inquisitor to the ground, then used its rear claws to grab the flailing man's ankles. Then it arched its back and ripped him in half, separating upper and lower torso with a wet pop.

Cassandra pulled a knife from the unconscious soldier's boot and sliced the leather straps of the saddle and bridle. The instant it was cut loose, the horse scrambled to its feet. But instead of racing off, it waited calmly as if it somehow knew Cassandra would keep it safe.

The Crown, she realized.

She paused for only a second to see if the men pinned beneath the horse were still alive, but both had been crushed to death when the beast had landed on them.

The battle was effectively over—only a handful of soldiers were still alive, and they were all trying to escape. But the Crawling Twins had other ideas. Reveling in the brutal massacre, they were toying with those that remained: picking the soldiers off one by one as they tried to run, mutilating and maiming them out of sheer malice.

Go now! Once the soldiers are dead, they'll come after you!

Cassandra slung the pack over her shoulder, grabbed a fistful of the horse's mane, and swung herself up onto its bare back. She dug her heels into its side, and the beast took off.

Channeling her own power through the animal she rode, Cassandra was able to push the pace, racing over the gently rolling terrain and leaving the gruesome slaughter far behind them.

They won't catch me now, she realized after a few minutes with no signs of pursuit. *But they won't give up the hunt, either.*

Chapter 23

Keegan grimly raised the Sword above his head as the Chaos hordes rushed toward him, pouring through the breach in the Legacy. Time seemed to stop: the charging enemies becoming statues; the dark storm clouds above and the waves crashing against the sandy shore behind him frozen in place.

A young woman lay unconscious at his feet, but his attention was focused on the exquisite weapon clutched in his hand. The black handle tingled in his grasp; the silver blade shimmered and pulsed with power.

Armed with the Sword, he had the strength to stand alone against any mortal army. But the creatures bearing down on him weren't mortal, and they were legion. This was his desperate, doomed final stand against overwhelming odds. He could stain the beach with the blood of a thousand foes, but in the end he would fall. Death was inevitable.

And then the moment of stasis ended with a crack of thunder, and the horde fell upon him.

Keegan woke with a sudden start, his heart pounding and his breath coming in short, quick gasps. The terror of the dream clouded his mind, and he struggled to make sense of the darkness and bodies pressed close around him for several seconds before he realized where he was.

We're on our way to the Conclave.

They'd covered a lot of ground in only three days despite having to tow Norr in addition to the supply sleds. They left early each morning and marched well past dark, though sunset came quite early with winter looming in the east.

At night the sleds were arranged in a circle around the campsite, and several thick blankets were strung up between them to serve as makeshift walls to keep the wind out. Then each individual would wrap themselves in layers of furs and bed down for the night, all of them sharing the same space inside the ring. With nearly thirty men and women in their group it made for cramped quarters, but the heat from all the bodies huddled so close together did wonders to ward off the chill.

Jerrod lay close on one side, Norr on the other. He knew Scythe would be pressed up close against the big man, too. Despite Norr being the new clan chief, they were still Outlanders; they still stuck together. Even Vaaler still slept close to them; Keegan could hear him snoring just across from Jerrod.

Fortunately, none of them seemed to realize Keegan had woken up. Closing his eyes, he tried to slow his still-racing heart.

Despite never having seen it before, he recognized the Sword from his dream.

Not a dream. A vision.

Though he couldn't remember any of the details of the young woman lying at his feet, every detail of the perfectly forged blade was still absolutely clear. The power he'd felt coursing through him as he clutched the hilt left little doubt that the weapon was one of the three Talismans given to Daemron. Along with the Ring and the Crown, it had transformed him into an Immortal and given him the power to challenge the Gods themselves.

But it didn't give me the strength to stop the Slayer's army.

Jerrod would want to know about the dream, but Keegan wasn't sure he wanted to tell him. How would Jerrod react if Keegan told him he saw a vision of his own failure?

He'll probably just brush it aside.

It seemed as if nothing could shake the monk's belief. He'd be more likely to see the dream as something positive, like the Sword's calling to Keegan, just as the Ring had called to him in the Danaan forest.

When I answered that call, I woke a dragon and left Ferlhame in ruins.

The fanatical monk might not feel any regret over the Danaan blood he had spilled, but Keegan wasn't eager to bring similar destruction down on Norr's people.

This isn't like my vision of the Ring, anyway, he rationalized.

That dream had been so intense, it had burned an indelible image into his mind; even after waking he could still feel the Talisman's presence nearby. He didn't feel the same connection to the Sword, though he did feel something.

It was possible the Sword worked differently than the Ring. Or maybe it was simply too far away for him to sense it clearly.

So why did you dream about this now? Are we getting closer to it?

The more he thought about it, the more he felt the visions were more like the dreams he'd had in his youth. A prophecy. A warning. A glimpse into one of many possible futures, far in the distance.

A future I want to avoid.

Jerrod wasn't the only one he could talk to about it, of course. Vaaler might be able to help him interpret or better understand the vision. But he'd barely spoken to Vaaler since they'd left the main Stone Spirit camp three days ago. Even if he did tell Vaaler about the dream, the Danaan would probably just see it as more proof of how arrogant and selfish Keegan was becoming.

In the wake of their second argument, Vaaler had taken to spending most of his free time with Shalana. The former chief was almost as much an outsider as Keegan and his friends; none of the other members of the clan seemed to talk with her beyond what was necessary. Keegan half expected to see her sleeping next to Vaaler one night, but so far she'd stayed with her own people when bedding down.

Probably wants to keep as far away from Scythe as possible.

The thought brought his final option to mind, but there wasn't much point in telling Scythe or Norr. Norr already had enough on his mind, dealing with the pressures of being chief and speculating on the as-yet-unknown reasons behind the Conclave.

As for Scythe, Keegan admitted, he simply didn't want to tell her. She'd embraced the idea that he was a wizard; she'd been more than happy to have him use magic to help Norr. But he knew she was still uncomfortable around Jerrod and all his talk of Keegan's destiny as a savior. Telling her about the dream might unsettle her.

But what if the dream affects her, too? What if she was the woman on the beach?

Try as he might, Keegan couldn't remember anything about the figure at his feet. He couldn't recall her hair, or her skin, or any kind of identifying feature other than the fact that she was female. He didn't even know if she was alive or dead.

If he mentioned all this to Scythe, there was a good chance he might push her farther away.

How could she be any farther away? We've barely spoken since she kissed me.

On some level, he knew Vaaler was right—the kiss really didn't mean anything. And if he brought it up to Scythe, he knew she'd make that clear. So rather than have his illusion stripped away, he clung to it like a child with a favorite toy.

Nobody needs to know about this. Not yet.

Keegan rolled over onto his side, careful not to wake the others. His rambling introspections hadn't done much to help him understand his vision, but they'd distracted him long enough for his pounding heart to calm itself. Without the fear and adrenaline pumping through him, exhaustion from the day's march took over and he soon slipped back into a deep, dreamless sleep.

The sled was gliding smoothly over the snow, but Vaaler was still struggling to match Shalana's pace as they pulled it along behind them.

Everyone in the Stone Spirit company headed for the Conclave took a turn each day towing one of the supply sleds, except for Norr. However, it was his knee, not his rank as chief, that kept him from helping out.

The first couple days Vaaler had stepped in to help Shalana because he feared nobody else would. It was possible for one person to pull a sled alone, but it was a grueling task. And given Shalana's injuries, Vaaler was worried she might fall behind.

If that happened, someone else would probably step up to give her a hand, but Vaaler suspected that would only add to the shame and humiliation she was already carrying. It was possible having an Outlander helping you was just as bad, but if so, Shalana didn't say anything.

She hadn't said much at all the first two days, despite Vaaler's attempts to engage her in conversation. Vaaler chalked it up to the extra effort it required for her to keep up with the others while she was still recovering rather than resentment at his constant presence or confusion because of his imperfect command of her native language.

Obviously, though, Shalana was a quick healer. He'd noticed the spring in her step as soon as they took the tow ropes this morning, and her long legs were churning up the distance at a furious pace.

"Are we trying to ditch the others?" Vaaler asked once she had pushed them to the front of the caravan.

"Would they even notice if we did?" she countered.

He suspected there was an underlying bitterness in the sentiment, but it didn't creep into her voice. The words were delivered in an emotionless monotone that Vaaler was starting to recognize as her style of making a joke.

"For my sake, could we just slow down a bit?" he asked, already breathing hard.

"Of course, Spy. All I want is to make things easier for you."

Despite her words, she did pull back slightly.

"Why don't you use dogs for this?" Vaaler asked, once he'd settled into the new, more comfortable, pace.

"Dogs need to be fed. Trained. Cared for."

"The expense isn't worth it?"

"Not for stronger tribes who've established large camps," she explained. "But the weaker tribes can't defend a permanent settlement. They have to keep moving all the time. Some of them still choose to use dogs for the sleds."

"So it's a status thing, then? You'd rather pull the sled yourself than lose face by letting dogs do the work for you?"

"If you get too close to the dogs, they can take over the clan."

"Like the Ice Fangs?"

Shalana nodded. "The Ice Fangs love their animals too much. Calling a dog a 'pet' in their clan is insult enough to end in bloodshed."

"So what do they call them?"

"Brother. Sister. Husband or wife when the nights get lonely."

For a second Vaaler thought he'd misunderstood, then he realized Shalana was making another of her deadpan jokes.

Her expression doesn't really change, but her eyes get this little twinkle as she watches for a reaction.

"If that's how you talk about other clans," Vaaler said, smiling at the jest, "I don't think I want to know what you say about my people."

"I've heard that the Tree Folk men have a tiny twig where

there should be a mighty trunk," she shot back without missing a beat.

"Uh, let's change the subject," Vaaler suggested, blushing despite himself. "What do the clans say about the people in the Free Cities?"

"We call them butchers and wish for them to suffer a slow and painful death."

This time he was pretty sure there was no intended humor in her statement.

The Free Cities consider the Easterners to be barbarians and savages, Vaaler recalled from his history lessons. *They used to hunt them for sport or send out raiding parties to butcher as many as they could find.*

Shalana's grim reply effectively killed the conversation, and Vaaler cursed himself for saying something so stupid and culturally insensitive.

She was just starting to open up to me, too.

After a few minutes of silent trudging through the snow, however, it was Shalana who broke the stillness.

"I've never met one of the Tree Folk before," she admitted. "You're not what I expected."

"Really?" Vaaler said, trying not to smile. "And what did you expect?"

"I thought your skin would be green as grass, and your hair as tangled as a bird's nest."

There actually was a greenish brown tinge to the Danaan complexion, but it was rather subtle. Despite this, the green-skinned Tree Folk was a common stereotype in the Southlands. The hair thing, however, was something Vaaler hadn't heard of before.

"As children, we were warned never to go into the North Forest or the savage Dwellers would eat us," Shalana continued.

"So you thought the Danaan were monsters?"

"In some of the older legends," Shalana explained, "your people are described as too wild and uncivilized to even wear clothes."

"I guess that's where the whole twig-trunk rumor came from, right?" Vaaler noted with a grin.

Shalana didn't actually smile in response, but he caught the mischievous twinkle in her eye.

They lapsed into silence for a while before she spoke again.

"Norr said you were a prince among your people. He said you were exiled for helping him and the others escape the Forest."

Vaaler was momentarily caught off guard by her admission. He wondered how much more Norr had told her.

Surely he wouldn't be foolish enough to mention the Ring?

"I'd rather not talk about it," Vaaler muttered. As much as he was enjoying Shalana's company on the trip, he wasn't ready to go into something so personal and painful with her.

She glanced over at him, her expression softening slightly. But instead of offering empty words of comfort, she simply nodded, and said, "I understand."

I bet you do, Vaaler thought, grateful she let the matter drop. *I bet you do.*

Scythe's attention was split between the sled carrying Norr at the rear of the Stone Spirit convoy and the lead sled, where Shalana and Vaaler were getting far too friendly for her comfort.

She knew better than to say anything to Norr. Every time Scythe brought her up, her lover accused her of being jealous.

He still thinks of her as the childhood friend he grew up with. He can't even imagine her as any kind of threat.

Scythe knew better. Her gut told her not to trust Shalana, and she'd learned to trust her gut. And if Norr wouldn't listen to her concerns, she knew someone else who would.

"I'm going to check on Keegan and Jerrod," she told Norr.

He nodded but didn't reply. He barely spoke at all while riding on the sled; instead, he sat with his arms crossed and a miserable scowl on his face, glaring at the backs of whoever was taking a turn pulling him.

Despite the extra burden of her petulant lover, there was no shortage of volunteers eager to grab one of the three tow ropes hooked up to the supply sled he rode atop. The younger warriors chosen to join him and his thanes at the Conclave considered it an honor to drag the Red Bear across mile after mile of frozen wasteland.

For Norr, however, it was humiliating torture. Each morning he and Scythe argued about the need for him to stay off his knee. So far, she'd managed to win each time.

He's as stubborn about that as he is about Shalana, Scythe thought as she broke into a light jog and moved up the line of the caravan.

Jerrod and Keegan were walking off to one side, close to the middle of the line. She knew they'd taken a turn hauling one of the sleds already this morning before the group had stopped briefly for lunch. It hadn't escaped her eye that Vaaler and Shalana had spent the break sitting close together, chattering away as they downed their food.

Scythe took a quick look for Jerrod's language tutor, confirming that he was up near the front of the line, close to Norr—their lessons were usually limited to the evenings. None of the other Stone Spirits around them were those Norr had identified as understanding Allrish, meaning she didn't have to worry about someone's overhearing their conversation.

"I need to talk to you two," she said, forgoing any preamble.

"What do you want?" Keegan asked sharply.

"It's Vaaler," she said, ignoring the unexpected hostility of the young mage's tone. "He's spending a lot of time with Shalana."

"I noticed this as well," Jerrod said. "He seems to be avoiding our company for hers."

"So? Who cares who he's talking with?"

Scythe couldn't help but be taken aback by the peevishness of Keegan's reply. *What's gotten him in such a bad mood?*

"I'm worried he might be getting too close to her," Scythe explained after taking a second to compose herself. "I don't trust her. Not as far as I could throw her sorry ass."

"Maybe Vaaler feels the same way," Jerrod offered. "He might just be trying to keep a close eye on her."

"I don't think so," Keegan said. "I think he just feels bad for her because ..." He trailed off, glancing first at Scythe then over to Jerrod. "Because of what happened to her after she lost the duel," he concluded lamely.

Scythe rolled her eyes.

"He knows about the curse," she said, jabbing her thumb in Jerrod's direction.

"You know?" Keegan said, confused. "And you don't care?"

"You, Scythe, and Vaaler share a deep and powerful connection," the monk explained. "You are all touched by Chaos, you were all born under the Blood Moon."

Scythe groaned softly; she'd already heard this speech.

"Their fate is intertwined with yours," Jerrod continued. "They each have a role to play in your destiny."

"What does this have to do with the curse?" Keegan asked, glancing over at Scythe, then quickly looking away when she met his eye.

"The three of you worked together to call upon the Chaos for your spell," Jerrod told him. "Each playing a vital role. Vaaler brought you the knowledge of how to control your power, and Scythe was the catalyst that inspired you to attempt it."

"Give the prophecy pitch a rest for a few minutes," Scythe said impatiently. "We're talking about Vaaler, remember? What if he accidentally lets something slip while he's talking to Shalana? What if she finds out what we did?"

"He's not stupid," Keegan told her. "He's not going to just blurt something like that out."

"But if he feels guilt over what we did, it could eat away at him until he feels like he has to say something," Scythe argued. "Secrets have a way of bubbling to the surface."

"Sounds like you're really talking about you and Norr," Keegan noted.

"My relationship with Norr is just fine," Scythe disdainfully assured him.

"Then why did you kiss me?" Keegan shot back.

"Is that why you're mad at me?" Scythe demanded. "It was just a kiss. Stop being such a child!"

"Keep your voices down!" Jerrod warned.

Scythe glanced over her shoulder at the nearby Stone Spirits. Even if they couldn't understand what was being said, they had clearly noticed the tension between the Outlanders.

"You manipulated me into casting that curse," Keegan accused though he did lower his voice. "Even Jerrod just said so!"

"That's not exactly how I described it," the monk cautioned.

"How did this become about you?" Scythe wanted to know. "How come it always seems to be about you? You need to stop listening to White Eyes telling you what a big deal you are. It's gone to your head!"

"Stop it, both of you!" Jerrod snapped. "Don't you see what's happening?"

Something in his voice killed the snide reply in Scythe's throat. Keegan was similarly silent.

"Backlash," the monk whispered. "From the curse. It's turning the three of you against each other."

His words hit Scythe like a punch to the stomach, and the truth became painfully obvious. Suddenly, her suspicions about Vaaler and Shalana seemed ridiculous.

"You're right," she muttered, remembering how angry she'd

gotten at Vaaler the last time they spoke. "Vaaler and I had the stupidest argument. I was almost ready to fight him."

"Me, too," Keegan admitted sheepishly. "The last couple times I spoke with him he ended up storming away."

"I thought Vaaler prepared the ritual so this wouldn't happen," Scythe said.

As the words were leaving her mouth, she felt anger and blame toward the Danaan bubbling up inside her. *This is his fault!* But now that she knew her emotions were being manipulated by some kind of magical aftereffect, she was able to ignore them and they faded almost instantly.

"Backlash is unpredictable," Keegan said. "A wizard can try to minimize or contain it, but sometimes Chaos still breaks free to wreak havoc on the mortal world."

"We need to warn Vaaler," Jerrod said. "It could be the backlash that is driving him toward Shalana."

Guess my fears about him getting too close to her weren't so stupid after all, Scythe thought, though she bit her lip to keep from spitting the words out. *That's the backlash talking. Trying to start another fight.*

"Let me do it," Keegan offered. "I said things to him I had no right to say. I need to apologize."

"Just be careful you don't make things worse," Scythe warned, and she saw Keegan momentarily bristle. Then, just as she had, he seemed to realize the source of his anger and it vanished as quickly as it had come.

"I'll speak to him tonight," Keegan promised.

"This must happen now," Jerrod insisted. "If the backlash is left unchecked, there is no telling what it could cause Vaaler to do."

Vaaler was enjoying being able to walk without dragging several hundred pounds of food and supplies on a sled behind him. However, he knew Shalana would probably volunteer to take another turn on the tow ropes before they stopped for nightfall; it was like she was trying to re-prove her worth to the rest of the clan by taking extra shifts.

She's taking this harder than she lets on.

The other Stone Spirits were still basically shunning her, but Vaaler got the sense they were doing it more out of cultural habit than anything else. She had lost her position as chief; clan society demanded some kind of punishment. But from the way they spoke to her when they were forced to exchange words while setting up and taking down the camp, it was clear they still respected her.

Does she realize that? Vaaler wondered, glancing over at the tall woman loping along beside him.

"Can I ask you something?" he said aloud.

"You've already asked me lots of things, Spy," she reminded him.

It wasn't a no, so Vaaler plunged ahead.

"Are you bitter over losing the duel?"

Shalana didn't answer right away but tilted her head up and seemed to stare at the sky for several seconds.

"I guess you wouldn't be much of a spy if you didn't ask me that," she finally said with a heavy sigh.

"I'm not plotting some kind of revenge against Norr or your friends," she assured him. "I'm not like my father."

"That's not what I meant," Vaaler said. "Are you angry over what happened? Do you feel cheated because of what happened in the duel?"

Shalana turned her head and gave him a curious look.

"Cheated?"

"Your staff broke," Vaaler hastily explained. "If it weren't for that, it seemed like you were going to win."

"Norr bested me fairly," she answered, turning away. "He earned the right to become chief."

Vaaler already felt he knew her well enough to tell she wasn't being completely honest with him. Her answer was a stock reply—the kind of thing she had to say to keep others from seeing her as a sore and spiteful loser.

She doesn't want to talk about this. Just like you don't want to talk about getting exiled.

But Vaaler had chosen his own path. Shalana's fall wasn't her fault. Not really.

We stole what was rightfully hers. She deserves to know that, no matter what the consequences might be.

However, before he could think of a good way to tell her about the curse they had afflicted her with, he heard a familiar voice calling out to him from farther back in the caravan of sleds.

"Vaaler!" Keegan shouted as he ran toward them. "Vaaler, we have to talk!"

What more is there to say to each other?

He held his tongue until the young wizard came up alongside them, panting slightly from rushing to catch up.

"There's something you have to know," Keegan said. "It's important."

"So tell me," Vaaler insisted.

Keegan glanced over at Shalana, then said, "It's private."

That's not suspicious at all, Vaaler thought, annoyed at his friend. *If Shalana didn't actually think I was spying on her before, she probably will now.*

"Talk with your friend," Shalana said, trying to pass off Keegan's rudeness with an indifferent shrug.

She picked up her pace until she was well ahead of them and everyone else in the caravan. But even that wasn't good enough for Keegan, as he reached out and grabbed Vaaler's arm, slowing him down and directing him off to the side, away from where anyone could possibly overhear.

"Let go of me," Vaaler warned, his voice calm but cold.

Keegan snapped his hand back like he'd been bit.

"I'm sorry. Please, just listen for a moment. That's all I ask."

Vaaler narrowed his eyes and nodded, wary of some trick or con.

"The arguments we've been having . . . I know what's causing them."

Me, too. Your being a selfish, arrogant jerk.

"Backlash. From the curse."

Vaaler's head actually snapped back in surprise.

"No," he said. "That's impossible. I made sure the ritual wouldn't allow it."

"It's true," Keegan insisted. "Think about: the curse was only possible because Scythe, you, and I all worked together. Now the backlash of that spell is tearing the three of us apart."

He's right. That's how Chaos works.

"It wasn't just me you've been fighting with, right?" Keegan pressed. "It's Scythe, too. Every time any of us tries to talk to each other, we end up having a huge fight over the stupidest little things."

Vaaler still didn't say anything as the full implications of what Keegan was telling him slowly sank in. He hadn't even been sure Keegan would be able to summon enough Chaos to make the curse work. Was it really possible he'd unleashed so much power that it had been manipulating their thoughts and emotions for days?

I was on the verge of telling Shalana about the curse!

Looking at it now, he was able to see how bad an idea that would be. But only a few minutes ago, it had seemed like a perfectly logical thing to do.

"Vaaler," Keegan said, reaching out slowly to place a firm hand on the other man's shoulder. "I'm telling you the truth."

"I know," Vaaler finally answered. "I just . . . it's a little hard to wrap my head around."

"I guess you were right after all," Keegan said, releasing his grip on Vaaler's shoulder and dropping his hand.

"How so?" Vaaler's head was still spinning, making it difficult for him to follow Keegan's train of thought.

"You wanted me to worry less about Scythe and more about my ability to summon Chaos."

Vaaler vaguely remembered saying something like that, but at this point how could he be sure the idea was really his? What if it was something he only thought because of the backlash?

"So now that we know about this, what do we do?" he asked.

"I thought you'd know," Keegan told him. "I mean, you're the expert."

Vaaler shook his head. "This is beyond anything Rexol ever taught me. This might even be beyond anything he ever experienced."

"What do you mean?"

"That ritual wasn't that complicated. The safeguards were simple, but strong. There shouldn't have been any backlash from the curse."

"So what went wrong?"

A good question, Vaaler thought. He ran through the ritual one more time, checking and double-checking the safeguards. And in the end, there was only one explanation that made sense.

"It's you," he said to his friend. "Your power is growing. Maybe because of the witchroot overdose Scythe gave you in Torian. Maybe something happened to you when you used the Ring.

"Whatever the explanation, the runes and wards Rexol taught us aren't enough to contain your spells anymore. Even something small like a curse."

"The stronger the spell, the stronger the backlash," Keegan muttered after taking a moment to digest the idea.

Vaaler nodded.

"If you truly are destined to be our savior," Vaaler noted, "this could actually be a good thing. You need to be more powerful than Rexol ever was. As powerful as the legendary wizards who used Old Magic."

"But if that's true," the young mage asked, "then how do I stop something terrible from happening every time I summon Chaos? How do we control the backlash?"

"I don't know," Vaaler admitted. "But it's something you're going to have to figure out.

"Until then," he added, "think very carefully before you decide to use your power."

Chapter 24

As THE KEEP's drawbridge lowered a powerful oily stench wafted out to assail Yasmin's nostrils. She knew the smell of burning flesh well: tonight the Purge had truly begun.

A small company of Lord Carthin's soldiers marched out to meet her and the eight armed Inquisitors who traveled at her side; an honor guard to escort her into the central courtyard. There, three large bonfires were still burning, sending flames high into the night sky. Yasmin didn't need her Sight to pierce the veil of smoke and darkness to know the figures lashed to the stakes at the center of each blaze had already perished; the lack of screams told her that.

Lord Carthin stood imperiously off to the side, witnessing the proceedings in his official capacity as Justice of the Order. Normally the role of judging the unworthy would be reserved for Yasmin's Inquisitors, but their ranks had dwindled, forcing her to invoke a long-forgotten custom of granting divine authority to carefully chosen secular followers. The new title further strengthened Carthin's loyalty, and he seemed to enjoy the work.

We need his wealth, political influence, and soldiers. Keeping him happy is essential to our cause.

The announcement of another Purge had been met with mixed reaction. In some places, like Carthin's righteous capital of

Brindomere and the recently born-again Free City of Torian, the citizens eagerly set out to find and destroy those who practiced the foul arts of magic. But not everyone in the Southlands was as virtuous, and there were reports of minor nobles and various villages and towns who defied the Pontiff's will. Callastan had not only refused to uphold and enforce Yasmin's edict but had taken the drastic step of banishing all members of the Order from their city.

Callastan would be dealt with in due time, but first Yasmin was determined to snuff out those pockets of rebellion closer to home. Lord Fellmar had been a minor baron of little consequence: idealistic, educated, and impassioned about the plight of those less fortunate in the harmless manner of so many other bored young nobles. For several generations his family had ruled over a small estate a day's ride west of Brindomere's borders, and with his father's passing the previous year he had assumed the family title.

Though not an ardent supporter of the Order, he had never spoken publicly against them. But when Lord Carthin's spies informed the Pontiff that Fellmar's keep was secretly harboring a pair of fugitive wizards instead of turning them over to the Order as decreed, Yasmin decided to make an example of him.

She'd commanded Lord Carthin to lay siege to Fellmar's keep; his first act as a newly appointed Justice of the Order. In the end, though, no siege was necessary. On learning a force five times their numbers was en route, Fellmar's own guards had placed him under arrest, seized the rogue mages, and opened the drawbridge wide for the advancing army.

Beside Lord Carthin stood an old, grizzled soldier wearing the colors of Lord Fellmar; Yasmin assumed he was the guard who'd led the revolt against his former Master. Like Carthin, he was watching the bonfires, his face an unreadable mask of stone.

As Yasmin approached, both men turned toward her. The old

soldier took a half step back on seeing her blind eyes and the burned, scarred flesh of her bare scalp. Lord Carthin, in contrast, dropped to one knee and graced her with a florid bow.

"I did not expect you so soon, Pontiff," he said as he rose to his feet.

"Yet not soon enough to oversee the trial and execution of the heretics," Yasmin noted.

"I did not realize that was your intent," Carthin replied. "Forgive me if I overstepped my authority."

Yasmin waved off his apology. Technically, he had done nothing wrong. As the former Prime Inquisitor, she would have preferred to witness his first acts as a Justice to ensure he brought an appropriate measure of decorum and gravitas to the position. However his overzealousness could be considered more of a strength than a flaw, and she had no wish to chastise him for it.

"The reports said there were only two wizards hiding here," she noted, "yet there are three bonfires."

"Lord Fellmar was put to the flame for blasphemy," Carthin explained. "Even in chains, he spat out vile insults and called upon his followers to reject your authority."

"Regrettable," was all Yasmin said, though she realized she would have to speak with him privately about the value of discretion later.

Executing those of noble blood is a dangerous game.

It was important for the nobility to fear the consequences of the Purge; not even a king was above divine will. But nobles also expected the Order to protect them and even offer mercy if they surrendered. If those in power feared too much for their lives, many would resist to the bitter end, stretching the limited resources at Yasmin's disposal.

"Lord Fellmar was an only child, and he had yet to produce an heir," Lord Carthin mentioned, speaking as lightly as if discussing the weather.

"Then by right his land and holdings shall pass on to you, Lord Carthin," Yasmin replied, adopting a similarly casual tone.

She had no doubt Carthin was already well aware of the ancient laws of which she spoke. Had Lord Fellmar still been alive when Yasmin arrived, he might have recanted and offered a portion of his wealth to the Order as atonement for his wicked ways. With his death, however, Carthin was free to lay claim to everything.

Sometimes we must suffer such small evils for the greater good.

"There are some who might think you acted too harshly," Yasmin cautioned. "But we can quell such criticisms by entering his blasphemy into the official records."

She expected Carthin to hesitate, but if he had any reservations about his actions, they didn't manifest themselves.

"He said the Purge exposed the Order as blind fools. He accused the Seers of being false prophets leading us to our doom. He said if they could truly see the future, they would have warned us about the Danaan army instead of turning us against each other."

"The Danaan army?" Yasmin asked aloud, remembering Xadier's vision of battle and bloodshed sweeping the land.

"It's true, my lady," the old soldier chimed in. "A messenger arrived from Lady Fellmar's cousins last night. They have holdings near the barbarian lands, but they've fled their estate. They claim a massive Danaan force emerged from the North Forest last week. They're laying waste to all the tribes that cross their path."

Yasmin didn't say anything at first, weighing this new information. She could think of no good reason for such a message to be sent as a deception or jest. But if it was true—if the Danaan had formed an army—why hadn't she heard about it earlier?

The unrest of the Purge had caused some lines of communication to break down, particularly on the far fringes of the Southlands. It could take a week or more for news from the borders to reach the heart of the Southlands, particularly if the scouts who'd spotted the Danaan army were ordered to silence. Lady Fellmar's family wouldn't want to cause a panic while the nobles and their households made their clandestine flight to safer lands.

The Order had its own spies and agents in the Free Cities who always kept one eye out for a potential Danaan invasion, but their limited knowledge of the Dweller kingdom ended at the southern edge of the impassable forests. If the Danaan hadn't marched south—if they'd massed their legions deep inside their borders and entered the wastelands of ice and snow far to the north of the Free Cities—it wasn't likely any of her people would know.

Was this what Xadier's vision showed? Was it a warning of a Danaan invasion?

But if the reports were accurate, the Danaan weren't invading the Southlands—they were going to war against the Eastern savages. Why, Yasmin had no idea.

And then, in a flash of divine inspiration, she realized it didn't even matter. Xadier's vision had led them down the proper path after all.

"The Dwellers and barbarians will slaughter each other," she said, knowing Lord Carthin and the old soldier were both waiting for some reply. "While they spill each other's unholy blood, the Purge will cleanse the Southlands of those who do not follow and accept the true faith.

"And once the Purge is over, the righteous will be joined in a great army that will wipe away the tattered remnants of the savages and the Tree Folk in a single glorious battle!

"This is the vision of our Seers. This is the manifest destiny of the Order and all who follow it. This is the will of the True Gods!"

Yasmin had instinctively raised her voice as she spoke, her words echoing over the courtyard so that any and all could hear. She had no doubt the rumors of the Danaan army would spread quickly, but so would her message of the Order's inevitable victory and triumph over the pagans and apostates. Her own people would see to that.

The old soldier didn't say anything else though she had seen him nodding during her speech. Lord Carthin was even more enthusiastic; by the end he was grinning from ear to ear.

"You have done well, Lord Carthin," Yasmin told him, his smile stretching so that she thought his head might actually split in two. "But there is still one matter to be dealt with."

"What is that, Pontiff?" he asked, and she couldn't help but take some small satisfaction in his suddenly worried expression.

"What of Lady Fellmar? The one who received the message from the east?"

"She was only recently joined to Lord Fellmar in union," Carthin explained, his voice carrying a hint of guilt. "Until a year has passed, she cannot claim to be his heir."

"I am well aware of the law," Yasmin reminded him sharply. "And I care nothing for your claim to these lands."

Carthin only stared at her in silent confusion.

"What have you done with her?" Yasmin said, speaking as if to a child.

"I have taken her into custody," the Justice replied, speaking slowly as he carefully choose each word. "She is young and naïve, and I do not believe she shares his heretical views.

"I will question her carefully before I decide her fate," he assured Yasmin, and the Pontiff realized Carthin hadn't been confused before—he'd simply been doing everything he could to keep from admitting he had taken the young woman prisoner.

Yasmin understood what kind of interrogation Carthin intended to inflict upon the scared and vulnerable young woman.

"You have already done more than enough for us here, Justice Carthin," she informed him. "Let my Inquisitors relieve you of this final burden. We will take Lady Fellmar with us when we go."

There are some evils we will not suffer, even for the greater good!

Carthin did well to hide the disappointment on his face as he bowed yet again.

"Of course, Pontiff. I only live to serve."

Chapter 25

As THE SUN set and the temperature began to drop, the Danaan army was already making camp. In another hour the troops would wolf down their meager rations and wrap themselves in whatever cloth and blankets they could find as they huddled in small groups seeking shelter against the cold. Sometime in the night, fatigue would triumph over cold and they would slip into a dreamless state of unconsciousness.

The weakness of the frail mortals that surrounded him sickened Orath. He felt the cold, but it did not leave him shivering and helpless. He felt the physical toil of their march, but it did not leave him exhausted and bone weary. And he never slept.

Yet even he could not go on forever without rest. A few hours in a brief meditative trance would reinvigorate his body and refresh his mind. But doing so brought risks; the trance would dull his awareness and his focus.

The ogre was constantly fighting him, its savage mind pushing and pulling on the puppet strings he used to control it. There was little chance it could completely break free of his control, even if Orath allowed himself to slip into a trance, but the beast was eager to test the limits of its constraints.

The creature fed on savagery and violence, and it had precious little to slake its hunger over the past week. After the first few encounters with unprepared clans, the Easterners had finally be-

come aware of the invading army. It had been inevitable: an unseen scout spotting the advancing horde would rush off to warn
his people; they in turn would send messengers to the neighboring clans. Faced with an overwhelming enemy force, the nomadic
tribes would gather what they could and flee long before the
enemy came upon them.

The Danaan troops had picked up the pace of their relentless
progress, but an army this size still moved more slowly than the
clans fleeing before it. Instead of skirmishes or battles, all they
encountered during their march were deserted camps on the barren ice.

Each day that passed with no one to kill made the ogre's frustration grow. The beast could move much faster than the Danaan,
but Orath had kept it close to the main force of the army. Partly
to maintain control over the monster, partly as a visible reminder
to the Danaan of his power, and partly as protection in case they
stumbled across the mortal with Daemron's Ring.

But there was little chance of that happening tonight. And
rather than struggle to keep the ogre at heel all through the night,
Orath decided to give it a small taste of freedom. In the darkness
he couldn't see the ogre on the other side of the camp, but through
the bonds that held it enthralled he felt it leap up and rush off as
he loosened his hold.

Careful to maintain enough control to keep it from slaughtering the sleeping Danaan—and, more importantly, to call it back
once he was rested—he allowed himself to slip into his trance.

The ogre could still feel the invisible chains that kept it tethered
to its hated master, but the awareness of servitude was drowned
beneath the rush of cold air as it loped across the snow-covered
plains.

It could smell fresh meat far to the east: a full day's march for the army, but less than an hour away at the speed it was moving. The sliver of moonlight reflecting off the snow was more than enough light for a creature bred from the slime and darkness in the depths of the Chaos Sea to see the way, and it wasn't long before the dark outlines of a small cluster of tents came into view.

Figures scurried about the camp. Men, women, and children hurriedly packed in the night's darkness so they could leave at daybreak and stay ahead of the Danaan army, unaware a far greater threat was rushing at them faster than they could imagine.

A half mile from the camp the ogre bellowed—a twisted roar of hate and anger that froze the milling barbarians in their tracks. As the echo of the ogre's hunting call faded, the paralysis broke and the mortals panicked. Some fled off in random directions, others clutched at loved ones and collapsed to the ground weeping. The bravest men and women—a dozen warriors—gripped their weapons and turned to face in the direction of the awful sound.

A minute later the ogre fell upon them: little more than a small mountain of claws, teeth, and putrid flesh in the gloom. They stabbed at it with their spears, they hacked at it with their blades. But their weapons could not penetrate the thick, slime-covered hide of the monster in their midst.

The ogre reached out and grabbed the nearest warrior with one massive hand, crushing the bones of the screaming man's chest while lifting him up, then smashing him to the ground.

One woman stepped in close and jabbed the tip of her spear at the beast's left eye—the one vulnerable spot. But the ogre was too quick; it shifted to the side and twisted its massive neck so that the spear struck harmlessly against the thick muscles of its shoulder.

Before the woman could step back, the ogre lashed out with a long arm. The woman tried to duck; the claws meant to rip open her torso instead tore her head from her shoulders and sent it skittering across the snow.

The ogre laughed at the sight: an evil, guttural sound. Another warrior threw himself on its back, hacking repeatedly with a heavy axe in a futile attempt to injure the behemoth. The ogre calmly reached back with one of its grotesquely disproportionate limbs and slapped him off. The blow stunned the barbarian; he lay gasping in the snow. Before he could recover, an enormous foot stomped down on his chest and stomach, instantly pulverizing his internal organs.

Faced with a horror they could never defeat, the remaining warriors tried to run, scattering in all directions. But the ogre had their scent, and it chased them all down one by one, taking sadistic glee in each gruesome kill. The rest of the clan was not spared its fury: they, too, were hunted down. And once it was done—once every man, woman, and child had been stalked, caught, and killed—it began to feed.

Finally, its bloodlust and hunger both sated, the beast felt the pull of its master once again, calling it home.

Waking from his meditative trance, Orath focused his awareness on the ogre. The beast was thirty miles away, gorging itself on the remains of its victims. Steeling his will, the Minion reached out and gave a strong mental pull. The ogre tried to resist, fighting him in the hopes that the distance might allow it to break free.

But Orath had bested the creature once already; he had proved his dominance over it. The outcome of the struggle was inevitable, and after only a few seconds of defiance he sensed the ogre's submission.

Lowering its head, it turned and headed back toward the Danaan forces, leaving behind the remains of its fresh kill for the advance patrols to stumble across the next day.

Chapter 26

"WHAT'S WRONG, SPY?" Shalana asked, her words snapping Vaaler out of his silent stupor.

Two days had passed since Keegan had told him about the backlash. Things had been better between the two friends since then, but Vaaler was still spending most of his time alongside the tall, fair-skinned warrior. But he was careful around her now, watching his words in case some residual effect from the backlash caused him to say something stupid.

He was pretty sure Shalana had noticed the change, but she hadn't asked him about his more guarded attitude toward her.

"Nothing's wrong," he said by way of reply to her question. "I'm just thinking."

"Spies shouldn't think so much," she noted.

"I'm just worried about what will happen when we reach the Conclave," Vaaler lied. "What if the other clans don't like your bringing Outlanders with you?"

"Norr won't let anything happen to you, Spy," she promised. "Neither will I," she added with a playful wink.

Vaaler smiled. At first he'd been drawn to Shalana because he felt sorry for her. *Or was it the backlash that drove you to her?* Whatever the reasons behind his initial interest, he realized he had actually grown to like her. She was smart and funny and self-assured, despite losing her title as chief.

In some ways, she reminded him of the young women he'd served with in the patrols. The Danaan women were thinner and smaller—and a few years younger—but, like Shalana, they were fit and strong and blessed with a natural athletic grace.

And she's attractive, too.

Shalana's features were sharp but symmetrical, and he found the contrast between her pale skin and her striking blue eyes exotic and intriguing.

He was pretty sure she liked him, too. She seemed comfortable around him, and he thought she actually enjoyed his company during their long trek.

Or maybe she's just happy someone will talk to her even if he's an Outlander.

There was another possible explanation, but it was one Vaaler didn't want to dwell on. He'd been on the verge of telling Shalana about the curse just before Keegan had arrived and told him about the backlash. Vaaler hadn't given away their secret, but he was pretty sure the questions he'd been asking had raised Shalana's suspicions.

I wanted to know if she felt cheated by what happened, then Keegan showed up and I haven't mentioned it since. She has to wonder about that, doesn't she?

Shalana teased him about being a spy for Norr, but what if she was the one hoping to draw information out of him? She seemed to have accepted Norr as the new chief, but what if she was just biding her time? Did he really know her well enough to say for certain she wasn't harboring some deep resentment, just waiting for a chance to get even?

She's not like that.

But he honestly couldn't say whether that was true or simply what he wanted to believe. People were unpredictable. His own mother had sentenced him to exile; even if Shalana did like him, she might jump at the chance to reclaim her title.

So what if she does? I should be used to betrayal by now.

Yet even as he thought it, he knew that wasn't the case.

"How many more days until we reach the Conclave?" he asked, hoping to distract his mind from its dark turn.

"Probably late tomorrow at this pace," Shalana told him. "We're making good time because of the mild weather."

As if mocking her words, a sudden gust of wind swept in, stirring up icy flakes of snow from the small drifts that covered the ground.

"Why didn't Hadawas wait until spring to call the Conclave?" Vaaler asked.

"A good question, Spy," she answered. "Maybe you should ask Hadawas when you meet him."

"I doubt I'll get the chance," he answered. "Why would a clan chief want to talk to an Outlander?"

"You're not just an Outlander," Shalana reminded him. "You're a prince. A leader of your people."

"Not anymore," Vaaler reminded her. "They took that title away from me."

"There's more to being a leader than a title," Shalana insisted.

"Careful," Vaaler warned. "That almost sounds like you're criticizing Norr."

"Some might see it that way," she agreed. "But only time will tell if they are right."

Vaaler was tempted to just let her comment slide; he didn't want to upset her and risk the fragile friendship growing between them. After a few seconds, however, he realized he owed it to Keegan and the others to try and find out if Shalana was a threat they had to worry about.

"You have to be bitter about everything that's happened," he said.

She didn't answer right away, and Vaaler was beginning to think he'd pushed her too far. When she finally spoke, the familiar teasing, mocking tone she used with him was gone.

"I'm the one who challenged Norr," she said. "I put him in a position where he had no other choice. If I am to blame anyone, I must only blame myself."

"What about before, though?" Vaaler pressed. "You and Norr were going to be married. You were in love, and he abandoned you."

"We were never in love," she said. "Not in the way you mean. We cared for each other; we were close. But I see how he looks at Scythe. I see how he acts around her; how she is at the center of his thoughts at all times. He was never like that with me."

"Are you jealous?"

Shalana shook her head. "They feel something for each other I have never felt. If I had loved Norr, I wouldn't have challenged him when my father chose him as successor. If I loved him, I would have accepted the decision. I would have been happy for him.

"And if he had loved me—truly loved me—he would have never left," she added. "Norr and Scythe will never abandon each other. Even I can see that. Only death will tear them apart."

"How do you feel about Norr now?" Vaaler wanted to know. "Do you think he will be a good leader for the clan?"

The tall woman cocked her head to one side and gave him a sly smile. "That remains to be seen, Spy." The teasing lilt had returned to her voice. "But you can tell your friends I'm willing to give him a chance."

"They'll be glad to hear that," he answered with a smile of his own.

They continued on without speaking after that, unconsciously matching each other step for step.

Keegan could feel the creature in the shadows, watching him with bright red eyes that burned like fire. He was surrounded by Easterners—armed men and women wearing fur vests and heavy boots—but he didn't recognize any of them as members of the Stone Spirits.

Daemron's Sword was clutched in his hands, the perfectly balanced blade held out in front of him as he scanned the darkness for the monster stalking him.

The crowd shifted, and suddenly the creature in the shadows was standing right beside him—a naked woman with wings and the head of a bird. The crowd around him seemed oblivious to the monster in their midst, however—none of them reacted in any way.

Keegan tried to swing the weapon, but his arms wouldn't move. The woman didn't speak, but she reached out toward Keegan with both hands, her fingers ending in long, hooked talons . . .

Keegan woke from his dream, barely stifling the scream that was building in his throat. Several of the Stone Spirit early risers were already up and eating their breakfast, tearing into strips of jerky with a grim efficiency. Vaaler and Shalana were among them, as was Jerrod. Scythe and Norr, however, still slept.

Shaking off the last vestiges of sleep, Keegan stood up and stretched, the dream already fading.

His body was sore, but it wasn't in agony as it had been the first few days of the journey. Now his muscles simply felt tired, a familiar dull ache that he'd come to accept as simply part of his life since he and Jerrod had first fled the Monastery.

He was sick of traveling; right now he wanted nothing more than to spend a week in the same place, even if it was a half-frozen field of snow. Fortunately, Norr had said this would be the last day of the journey: they'd reach the Conclave before nightfall.

And then what?

Norr had spoken of trying to recruit Hadawas and the rest of the clans to his cause, but Keegan didn't even know what that meant. Since joining up with Jerrod, he'd been in a constant state of flight, trying to stay one step ahead of the Inquisitors.

It didn't seem to bother Jerrod, or if it did, he kept his concern hidden. But Keegan was starting to feel frustrated at not having some type of plan of action.

And whenever we do plan something, it goes horribly wrong.

They'd sought shelter with Khamin Ankha in Torian, only to have Rexol's former apprentice betray them. They'd left Torian in shambles as they fled into the North Forest, hoping Vaaler could help them get Daemron's Ring while offering them the protection of the Danaan people. Instead, they'd been forced to flee yet again after waking a dragon and leaving Ferlhame in ruins.

Is it just bad luck, or is it my destiny to spread death and destruction everywhere I go?

He hadn't told Jerrod about his talk with Vaaler yet. He doubted the monk's faith would be rattled by learning that the backlash from Keegan's magic couldn't be controlled anymore—he'd probably just see it as further proof Keegan was the all-powerful savior he was looking for. But if he knew Vaaler couldn't do anything to help Keegan master his talents, he might think the Danaan was an unnecessary distraction.

He won't mind Vaaler's being around if he thinks he still has some role to play in his prophecy.

He hadn't told Scythe about it yet, either. He'd stopped obsessing about her kiss, but he couldn't blame all his feelings for her on the backlash. He didn't want her to leave, and he was afraid she might decide she and Norr were better off keeping their distance if she knew the truth.

It had actually been Norr who'd insisted he and Scythe join Keegan's quest. Now that he was back with his own people, would he be willing to risk everything—not just his own life, not just that of the Stone Spirits, but the lives of all the clans answering Hadawas's call—to help Keegan if he knew the real risks?

Better to just keep quiet about it until after the Conclave. That's what Jerrod would do.

Knowing that didn't make him feel any better about his decision as he gnawed on his jerky.

There was less than an hour of daylight left when they finally came into view of the Conclave—several hundred Easterners scattered across a wide, open plain. Had they been in the Southlands, Jerrod would have noticed the massive barbarian horde much earlier, but in the East his Sight was limited to a more modest range.

As they drew closer, more details began to emerge. What had first appeared to be a single large group of Easterners was actually many smaller groups gathered together in separate camps at the base of a large, rocky hill.

Each clan must have set up its own camp.

The size of each camp varied greatly. The smallest were only five or six individuals, most had somewhere between a dozen and twenty, and a handful matched the thirty that made up the Stone Spirit delegation. In total, Jerrod estimated their numbers at close to three hundred.

Far toward the rear of the gathering, butting right up against the base of the hill, were six large buildings that resembled the size and shape of the Long Hall in the Stone Spirit camp. Instead of being made from mud and rock, however, these were constructed entirely from a single unfamiliar type of smooth, dark stone.

As the Stone Spirit convoy drew closer a welcome party marched out to meet them—ten large, heavily armed warriors. Seeing them approach, Norr held up his hand and called out for his people to stop.

Ignoring Scythe's objections, he hefted his bulk up from the sled he'd been riding on and strode to the front of his followers. Spitting out a curse, Scythe took her spot at his side. The pair were quickly flanked on either side by the five thanes Norr had chosen to bring with him. Behind this group the rest of the Stone Spirits stood in a seemingly haphazard collection, though Jerrod noticed they all had their weapons in easy reach.

At the front of the welcome party were two hard-looking men. One was huge—only a few inches shorter than Norr and heavily covered in muscles. But it was the other who spoke.

"My name is Roggen," the man said. "This is Berlen. On behalf of Hadawas, venerable Chief of the Sun Blades, we welcome you to this Conclave."

Jerrod's study of Verlsung had progressed quickly; the Order had trained him to focus his mind so he could absorb new information at a remarkable rate. By concentrating on not only the words but also the facial expressions, vocal cues, and body language of the speakers, he was able to follow the entire conversation.

"I am Norr, Chief of the Stone Spirits. We are honored to hear the wisdom of Hadawas."

Roggen eyed Norr's group with open suspicion, but Norr offered no explanation for the Outlanders in his entourage. Berlen, on the other hand, was staring only at Jerrod, who stood near the rear of the group.

The big man's gaze was unsettling in a way Jerrod couldn't quite explain. There was something in his eyes that went beyond mere suspicion of Outlanders or even hatred of the Order. His gaze was hungry, almost predatory.

Without even realizing he was doing it, Jerrod reached his hand up and closed his fist around the Ring still dangling from his neck. As he did so, Berlen licked his lips, then quickly looked away.

Jerrod dropped his hand, realizing nobody had spoken for several seconds. The men and women with Roggen were anxious and tense. They shifted their weight restlessly, their hands clenching the shafts of their spears and the hilts of their swords tighter as they glared at the unwelcome foreigners.

"The Conclave is a place of parley," Roggen said, though whether he was directing the words at Norr or his own nervous followers wasn't clear. "There is to be no bloodshed—is this understood?"

"The *Stone Spirits* will honor the sanctity of the Conclave," Norr answered, the emphasis making it clear he had his doubts about the other clans.

"Hadawas has promised the protection of the Sun Blades to any who answered his summons," Roggen assured him.

"He will speak in two days," he continued. "Until then, you may make camp wherever you can find space."

"I wish to speak with Hadawas before the Conclave," Norr said.

"Hadawas is not well," Berlen answered quickly before the other man could reply. "He must conserve his strength. He will see no visitors."

Roggen cast an annoyed glance at his larger companion before turning back to Norr.

"Berlen is right. You will have to wait until after the Conclave to meet with our chief."

Norr grimaced but nodded his agreement. Roggen and the others turned away; the Stone Spirits stood motionless, watching them leave. Once they were gone, Norr began issuing orders to his people, directing them to an open area on the edge of the assemblage with enough space for all of them.

Jerrod joined in with the others as they made camp. There was something odd about Berlen, but for some reason the more the monk tried to think about it the harder it became to pinpoint exactly what felt so wrong about him. By the time the camp was set up, his suspicions were gone, lost like a shadow in the darkness of the night.

Chapter 27

NORR WAS LOST deep beneath the ocean of sleep when he heard Scythe's voice close to his ear.

"Get up!" she hissed. "Hurry! Something's wrong!"

He opened his eyes to find his lover standing over him, brandishing the twin blades she always kept close by.

"What is it?" he asked, his mind still groggy.

"Fifty warriors, all armed," Jerrod said, the monk materializing from just behind Scythe. "We're surrounded."

Adrenaline kicked in, tearing away the final cobwebs clouding his mind. He sprang to his feet and saw that Keegan and Vaaler were also up. Jerrod must have roused them when he sensed the danger, leaving Scythe to drag Norr from his typical heavy sleep.

He peered out into the night but saw nothing. However, he knew better than to doubt Jerrod's abilities. He'd posted several sentries around the Stone Spirit camp, but if the enemy had crept up on them under cover of darkness they might not see them until it was too late.

Fifty warriors? Norr thought, realizing the number was too high to be from any single clan. The only explanation was that someone had united several of the clans against the Stone Spirits, though he couldn't imagine why.

"We are betrayed!" Norr roared, his booming voice shredding the silence of the night. "Prepare for battle and hold your ground!"

In response to his cry, the entire camp came alive as his thanes and warriors scrambled to their feet and grabbed their weapons. As they did so a dozen torches flared to life around the perimeter of the camp as the hidden enemy realized the element of surprise had been lost.

In the flickering light of the torches Norr saw that Jerrod was right—an enemy force had completely encircled the Stone Spirit camp, cutting off all hope of retreat. He held out his right hand to the side, and one of his recently roused thanes slapped the hilt of a heavy sword into his palm. Hefting the massive blade, he carefully shifted his weight onto his injured leg. The knee felt good; strong—the rest had done wonders.

Reassured his own body wouldn't fail him, the big man braced himself for battle, certain the enemies would charge. Instead, Roggen's voice rang out from somewhere amid the throng.

"We have no quarrel with the Stone Spirits. We have only come for the Outlanders!"

Norr felt an icy hand close around his heart at the words.

"Show yourself, Roggen!" Norr shouted. "I will not parley with a coward who hides in the shadows!"

Two figures stepped forward from the shadowy army surrounding them, one much, much taller than the other. Roggen carried a torch in one hand, a heavy spear in the other. Berlen, the second figure, held no torch; instead, each of his hands hefted a large axe.

"You promised us your protection," Norr sneered. "I did not know the Sun Blades were oath-breakers!"

"And we did not know the Stone Spirits were harboring spies!" Berlen shot back.

Norr hesitated, wondering if there was any value in further words. Was there any way he could convince Roggen his friends weren't spies, or was this going to end in bloodshed no matter what he said?

He doubted the Stone Spirits could win a fair fight; they were too badly outnumbered. But from the corner of his eye he noticed Jerrod had one hand on Keegan's shoulder and the other wrapped around the Ring hanging from his neck, ready to give the Talisman to the mage if there was no other way out.

He'll lay waste to the entire Conclave if they rush us.

As Norr tried to think of a way to end the standoff peacefully, Shalana spoke up to fill the silence.

"What proof do you have for these accusations?" she demanded.

"The proof comes from your own father!" Berlen sneered at her.

"A messenger from the Stone Spirits arrived an hour ago," Roggen explained, speaking loud enough for his words to carry across the entire camp. "Sent by Terramon himself.

"He told us a Danaan army is laying waste to our land. They slaughtered the Ice Fangs, killing the entire clan—even the children. Now all the clans are fleeing before the Danaan. Even the Stone Spirits have abandoned their camp and joined the exodus."

There were murmurs of shock and disbelief from Norr's followers.

"How do we know this is true?" Shalana asked. "And not some trick?"

Another figure stepped forward from the shadows to stand in the torchlight. Norr recognized him as Ullis, a young Stone Spirit warrior.

"I saw it myself, Shalana," he said. "They appeared on the horizon three days after you left. While the camp was being evacuated, your father sent me ahead to warn you because I'm the fastest. But I couldn't catch up before you reached the Conclave."

The young woman was stunned into silence, as were the rest of the Stone Spirits. They knew Ullis was telling the truth; he had no reason to lie. And in the face of the shocking news, Norr could sense their anger building.

"Runners have already been sent to warn all the other clans," Roggen added. "We must gather an army to meet the Tree Folk in battle."

"But first you will give us the Outlanders," Berlen added. "So Hadawas can question them and find out what they know."

"No," Norr said. "You cannot have them. They are with us!"

"Are you really so blind?" Roggen asked, clearly hoping to avoid a fight. "You bring a Dweller to your clan, and days later a Danaan army drives them from their homes. How can you not see what has happened?"

"These are my friends," Norr insisted. "I know them. They are not spies!"

"You spent too long away from your own people," Berlen accused.

"If the Red Bear is willing to throw away his life for an Outlander," he continued, now addressing Norr's followers rather than the big man himself, "then maybe he has forgotten what binds a clan together. Maybe he is not fit to be your chief."

"They are not Stone Spirits," an anonymous voice from the warriors gathered behind Norr whispered in agreement. "They're Outlanders."

The words weren't loud, but they hung in the air. Norr could sense the resolve of those standing with him slipping away. These warriors had welcomed Norr back and celebrated his victory when he became chief, but would they really be willing to die on behalf of his Outlander friends?

Will they blame me for the clan's having to flee our homeland? Will they turn on me if I refuse to surrender my friends? Are they right to?

"Take me, then," Vaaler said, suddenly stepping forward. "I'll surrender, but you must promise to let the others go."

Norr was momentarily caught off guard, partly by the self-sacrificing gesture and partly by the revelation that Vaaler understood their language. Shalana, however, was quick to react.

"No!" she said, stepping forward to stand beside Vaaler, drawing an audible gasp from somewhere in the ranks at Norr's back.

"The Stone Spirits do not bow down to the whims of the Sun Blades and their doddering, senile old chief!" she declared. "This is an insult to our honor!"

Shalana's bold words seemed to rally her companions, her appeal to clan pride strengthening their resolve.

"Do you think we fear you because we are outnumbered?" she pressed. "You could have a hundred warriors at your back, and they would not be the equal of the men and women you see standing before you!"

Shouts of affirmation and support rang out from the Stone Spirit ranks, and Norr could feel the energy of his followers building.

"The Sun Blades can make no demands on us!" Shalana shouted. "Hadawas can make no demands on us! We are the Stone Spirits, and we answer to no one but our own chief!"

She raised her spear high above her head as cheers broke out behind her.

The ranks behind Roggen and Berlen tensed, ready to surge forward in anticipation of the command to attack. But Roggen was silent, still desperately trying to find a way this could end without bloodshed.

Seeing his opportunity, Norr called out, "I wanted a meeting with Hadawas when we first came." He spoke loudly so that everyone on both sides could hear. "A meeting Hadawas refused.

"Now I demand another meeting. If he will agree to a parley, we will go to him—not as prisoners, but as guests. And after our meeting, he will know the truth: the Outlanders are here to help us!"

"Hadawas should meet with them," Berlen said, surprisingly throwing his support behind the idea. "We should accept the terms."

To Norr's great relief, Roggen finally nodded.

"Go back to your camps," he told the warriors he'd gathered, and the army reluctantly began to disperse.

"I will go wake Hadawas and help him prepare for your arrival," Berlen said, excusing himself, too. "He will see you in one hour."

"I will stay with you as your hostage as a sign of good faith," Roggen said, offering up his spear. "I give you my word no harm will come to you."

Norr shook his head.

"Keep your weapon. You will stay with us, but not as a hostage. If the Danaan have invaded, then we will not survive unless we are all on the same side."

As the small army surrounding them began to disperse, Keegan let out a long slow breath he didn't even know he'd been holding. He hadn't been able to follow the conversation, but it was clear Norr and Shalana had talked them out of a very tight spot.

Jerrod still had his hand on Keegan's shoulder; instead of letting go, he used it to draw the younger man in close.

"I think it's time for you to take this again," the monk said, handing over the Ring on the chain he'd been wearing since Ferlhame.

Keegan instinctively reached out for the Talisman with the stump of his left hand, then quickly pulled it back, ashamed. Jerrod lifted the chain and placed it over Keegan's head and neck, letting it fall so that the Ring disappeared beneath the collar of his shirt.

"Keep it close, but only use it as a last resort," Jerrod cautioned.

He's scared, Keegan realized. *He's afraid something will happen that he can't protect me from.*

The Ring felt strange rubbing up against his skin of his chest, and the chain chaffed at his neck.

The Talisman is meant to be worn, not carried.

The thought seemed to come out of nowhere, startling Keegan with its intensity. But by the time Roggen was ready to lead them through the camp for their parley, the young mage had almost forgotten the Ring was there. Almost.

Keegan had expected the Stone Spirit thanes and warriors to come with them; they had already been betrayed once by the Sun Blades. But Norr took Roggen at his word, and it was only the five of them—Norr, Scythe, Vaaler, Jerrod, and Keegan himself— who went to meet with Hadawas.

It was still too dark to see much beyond the small circle of light cast by Roggen's torch, but it felt like the eyes of every man and woman gathered for the Conclave were upon them as they slowly trekked across the meeting grounds. Eventually they reached the six stone buildings at the base of the hill, but this was not their destination. Just behind the permanent structures, hidden from sight, was a large tent. It was fashioned from hides in the same style as the ones the Stone Spirits used, though it was much larger than any of the ones Keegan had seen so far. Outside two women stood guard, each armed with the heavy spear that seemed to be the most common weapon in the East.

"Hadawas's great-granddaughters," Roggen whispered as they approached, speaking in Allrish so that the Outlanders could understand.

The women were both older than Keegan. If they were his great-granddaughters, it meant that Hadawas had to be well into his eighties or nineties.

The women nodded to Roggen as he approached.

"Hadawas is ready for you," Keegan guessed the one on the

left said, while the one on the right pulled back the flap to let them in.

Roggen went first and Keegan and the others followed. A dozen small lamps had been scattered about the ground, though they gave off more heat than light. It wasn't just warm inside the tent; it was actually hot enough that Keegan began to sweat.

The ceiling was high enough that even Norr could stand up fully, but inside the massive space looked bare and empty. A pile of unfolded bedding lay in one corner, and a small table stood in the other. Hadawas was sitting alone in a low, wide chair in the middle of the tent, leaning to the side to rest against one of the thick, padded arms.

His body was covered by a heavy fur blanket, leaving only his head exposed. His hair was thin and gray, his skin lined and weathered. But his eyes were still sharp and focused as he watched them enter.

Norr and the others stepped forward until they stood in front of Hadawas, who stayed silent, studying them carefully. Once everyone was inside, Roggen tied off the flap to keep the heat from the lamps from escaping.

"Where's Berlen?" Roggen asked, making his way over to stand beside the old man's chair.

"I sent him away," Hadawas answered, speaking so the Outlanders could understand. He studied the newcomers closely, never taking his eyes off them.

His accent was thick, but Keegan was more surprised by how deep and vibrant his voice was.

"You sent Berlen away?" Roggen said in surprise.

"I told him to catch up with the scouts we sent out earlier. I want him to see the Danaan army with his own eyes, then report back to me."

Roggen didn't say anything, but it was obvious from his expression he thought his chief had made a mistake.

"You wanted this meeting," the old man said, addressing Norr. "So tell me—why has the Red Bear returned to his people? And why have you brought these Outlanders to my Conclave?"

Keegan felt Jerrod tense up beside him, but the monk remained silent, content to let Norr be the judge of exactly how much should be revealed about their true purpose.

"The Outlanders I travel with are my friends," Norr told him. "Scythe and I have been together for many years," he said, nodding in her direction. "And Jerrod and Keegan saved my life in Torian.

"Hunted by the Order, we fled the city and hid in the Danaan forests until Vaaler's patrol found us," Norr continued, pointing in the direction of the exiled prince. "He and Keegan were old friends, and we thought the Danaan Queen would give us sanctuary."

He's leaving out everything about Jerrod's prophecy and the Legacy and the Talismans, Keegan realized. *At least for now.*

"Instead, she condemned Vaaler for bringing outsiders into her forbidden kingdom and we were forced to flee for our lives."

He's also not saying anything about Vaaler being the Queen's son.

"We had nowhere else to go, and so I led us East, hoping we could find refuge with my clan."

Norr halted his tale, uncertain what else he should or shouldn't reveal.

"A simple tale," Hadawas remarked. "But one that does not go all the way to the core, I think.

"You say you are hunted by the Order, yet you have one of the blind monks with you. You say the Danaan condemned you, yet one of your companions is of the Tree Folk.

"They are outcasts," Hadawas declared. "Is that why you travel with them, Norr? Like you, they were exiled from their own people."

"There is some truth in what you say," Norr admitted. "And I fear we are the reason the Danaan army has invaded the East," he added, trying to turn the conversation to another topic.

"When we escaped the North Forest, we did not think the Danaan would mount an army to come after us."

"Not surprising," Hadawas noted, "if you brought down the same kind of destruction on the Tree Folk as you did in Torian."

Norr didn't say anything at first, no doubt weighing how much Hadawas knew that the old man wasn't saying.

"What happened in Torian will not happen here," Norr promised. "Not unless you turn against us."

"Are you threatening me?" Hadawas asked.

Norr shook his head.

"You've already brought destruction down upon the clans," Hadawas reminded him. "Unless you have some secret weapon to stop the Danaan army yourselves."

The old man looked straight at Keegan as he said it, his eyes focused on Rexol's gorgon-headed staff. The implication was clear, but Jerrod inserted himself into the conversation before Norr could answer.

"That isn't possible," he warned. "Chaos was unleashed in Torian and upon the Danaan kingdom, but Chaos is weak here. There is no power to draw on."

Hadawas sighed heavily. "As I feared. There are no wizards in the East; no shamans; no mages. Our land is different."

"You seem to know much of what happens beyond the borders of Sun Blade territory," Vaaler chimed in.

"I have learned that the things which affect my people often have their roots in far-off lands," Hadawas explained. "I have scouts and spies who keep me informed so I can see what the future holds for us. That was why I called this Conclave.

"When I heard about the destruction in Torian, I realized there could be retribution. The Free Cities have long hated the clans, and I feared they would join forces to send an army against us.

"I knew the only way to stand against them would be to unite all the clans. I have seen our future, and we cannot survive unless all the chiefs are joined in a single purpose."

"Others have tried to unite the clans before," Norr cautioned. "All have failed. What made you think your efforts would be any different?"

"Because I know where we can find Daemron's Sword," Hadawas replied.

Keegan's head snapped back as if he'd been slapped, his recent dreams springing into his mind.

"I thought the Sword was just a legend," Jerrod said, watching carefully to gauge the old man's reaction.

"Legends come from truth," Hadawas answered. "I have studied this for many years, and I know the Sword is real.

"They say whoever wields it cannot be defeated in battle. With the Sword, the clans would not have to live in fear of the Free Cities or the Southlands ... or the Danaan who now march against us."

There was a long silence, and Keegan knew his companions were all struggling not with the revelation that the Sword was real but that Hadawas knew about. Even more shocking, he had claimed he knew where to find it.

"I know this sounds like madness," Roggen said, misinterpreting their silence. "But I trust the wisdom of Hadawas."

"The Sword is real," Keegan suddenly blurted out. "I've seen it in my dreams."

Jerrod shot him an angry look and Scythe gritted her teeth in silent frustration; but Hadawas only smiled.

"You are the one who rained fire down on Torian?"

"Yes."

"You are a wizard? A prophet?"

"Yes."

"Is that the real reason you came East, Norr?" Hadawas asked the big man. "To help Keegan find the Sword?"

"It is," Norr admitted, as Scythe threw up her hands and let out a choked gurgle of exasperation.

Beside Hadawas, Roggen was shaking his head in stunned disbelief.

"Fate has brought us together," Jerrod said, beating a familiar drum. "We need the Sword, and without it you cannot stand against the Danaan. We walk the same path."

"We want the same thing," Hadawas conceded, "but I imagine for different reasons. It may not be in our best interests to help you if you only want the Sword for yourself."

"The Sword is a Talisman of ancient and terrible power," Jerrod warned him. "If any of your people try to use it, they will be instantly consumed by its power. You need our help because only Keegan is strong enough to wield this weapon."

Keegan felt Hadawas studying him closely, and he could easily imagine what the aging clan chief saw: a thin, almost frail, young man with only one hand. He was no one's idea of a great warrior.

"If I help you find the Sword," Hadawas asked him, much to his surprise, "do you vow to use its power to save my people?"

"I do," Keegan swore, though part of him wondered if that was even possible.

I couldn't control the Ring; what makes me think the Sword will be any different?

"The Sword is hidden on the far side of the mountains," Hadawas warned. "It will be a long and dangerous journey."

"What about the Danaan army?" Norr asked. "If they have already crossed into the Stone Spirit lands, they are only a few days from here. We will never be able to cross the mountains and return in time to stop them."

"And what about all the refugees fleeing before them?" Vaaler asked. "Where are they supposed to go?"

"The Danaan are moving east and north," Roggen said. "They've spread across miles of territory to prevent any hope of doubling around behind them."

"They're herding the refugees," Hadawas added. "Driving them toward the mountains. Eventually, those fleeing will have nowhere left to run."

"We need to buy more time," Scythe said, finally breaking her silence. "So far the Danaan haven't faced any resistance. But if you send some warriors against them, they won't cover as much ground."

"If the Stone Spirit scout was right, the Danaan force is too large to fight," Roggen objected.

"You don't need to defeat them," Scythe said. "Just slow them down so the refugees can stay ahead of them. Don't meet them on the battlefield; use hit-and-run tactics. Target their supply lines. Set ambushes and pick off their patrols. You know this land, they don't. That should give you the advantage."

Hadawas nodded in agreement, but Roggen still wasn't convinced.

"Your strategy requires the clans to all work together. Everyone would have to answer to a single leader. None of the chiefs will agree to it!"

"If they don't," Jerrod reminded him, "then none of the clans will survive."

Chapter 28

SHALANA COULDN'T BELIEVE Norr was abandoning them to go chasing after some wild fable.

"The Sword is just a legend," she protested. "A story for children. It isn't real!"

They were alone in one of the Conclave's stone buildings—Norr had brought her here so they could speak in private after his parley with Hadawas. Soon, the room would be filled with the thanes and chiefs from over twenty clans, gathering at Hadawas's command to choose one among them to lead an army against the Danaan.

The Stone Spirit's new chief wouldn't be among them. He and his Outlander friends, along with Hadawas and a dozen hand-picked Sun Blade warriors, were leaving at daybreak on their ridiculous quest.

"It is real," Norr insisted. "It was one of the three Talismans given to Daemron by the Old Gods."

"How can you believe that?"

"Because I've seen the power of one of the other Talismans," Norr told her. "Vaaler was exiled because he stole Daemron's Ring from the Danaan. The Queen sent her patrols after us, and Keegan used the power of the Ring to slaughter them all."

"If that's true," Shalana challenged, "then why doesn't he use the Ring to stop the Danaan again? Why do we even need the Sword?"

"The Ring is dangerous," Norr explained. "The last time he used it, he woke a dragon. The beast destroyed an entire city before Keegan brought it down."

Shalana laughed; there really wasn't any other suitable reaction.

"A dragon?"

"I saw it," Norr said. "It was real—fifty feet from wing to wing, breathing fire and raining death from above."

"And Keegan killed it? He's just a boy!"

"He's a powerful wizard, Shalana. He's destined to save the world."

"From what?" she asked.

The big man ducked her question. "It's complicated. But he needs all of Daemron's Talismans to succeed. Including the Sword."

Norr's time away had changed him, but not as much as Shalana would have expected. Since coming back, she'd recognized the same traits that had once drawn her to him. He was loyal. Brave. And much smarter than people gave him credit for. He wasn't one to act rashly or foolishly.

He really believes finding the Sword is our only hope.

But even if he was right, the Danaan army was still rolling across the frozen plains, crushing anyone and everything in its path.

"So let Keegan and Hadawas cross the mountains," Shalana suggested, "and you stay here with us."

"Keegan needs my help."

"So do we!" she snapped. "Hadawas wants us to join forces to fight the Danaan. But you're the only one all the chiefs will listen to! You're the Red Bear! You're a legend!"

"They don't need a legend," Norr countered. "They need a leader. They need you."

"I can't even lead my own clan," she reminded him.

"That's not true," Norr said, grabbing her shoulders and staring directly into her eyes. His grip was firm but not painful.

"You were the one who rallied the thanes when Roggen threatened our camp. You were the one who inspired them and gave them courage. You were the one they followed, not me."

She brought her arms up, slapping his hands away and breaking his grip on her shoulders.

"That was different. The thanes know me."

"All the clans know you, Shalana. You are Terramon's daughter; you led the Stone Spirits—one of the largest and strongest clans in the East—for five years!"

"And how many of the chiefs that paid tribute to my father rebelled against my rule?"

"But you brought them back in line," Norr reminded her. "And you did it without destroying their clans. The other chiefs admire you, Shalana. They respect you. They trust you. None of the others can say the same."

Shalana sighed. Norr thought others saw in her what he saw, and she knew she wouldn't be able to convince him otherwise.

"Our people need you," Norr implored. "Not just the Stone Spirits, but all the clans. Please, Shalana—it has to be you."

"I'll try," she promised Norr. "But they won't listen."

Inside the perimeter of the Stone Spirit camp, Vaaler was busy packing for their upcoming journey with Hadawas. Beside him, Jerrod, Keegan, and Scythe were doing the same while the Stone Spirits looked on, their faces a strange mix of emotions. Norr had gone off to speak with Shalana alone, and for once, Scythe didn't seem jealous. In his absence, none of the clan felt comfortable approaching the Outlanders.

Time was of the essence, but for some reason Vaaler felt no

urgency as he filled his pack. Part of him wished Shalana was coming with them, though he understood why Norr had wanted her to stay behind. Scythe, of course, had agreed wholeheartedly with that idea.

As vital as our quest might be, she can do more good here than she can by coming with us.

Of course, he could argue the same thing about himself. Jerrod was convinced that Vaaler had some role to play in Keegan's destiny, but what if his role had come and gone?

I helped him get the Ring. Maybe that's all I was supposed to do.

There was another reason he was reluctant to go, though. He was scared. Not just for his own life but for what might happen if they actually succeeded. The Talismans were forged with Old Magic from Chaos itself; it was impossible to know what would happen if Keegan actually tried to use the Sword against the Danaan army.

We couldn't even control the backlash from a simple curse.

The Ring had roused a dragon, and Jerrod feared they might awaken more Chaos Spawn by using it again. The Sword could do the same. But Vaaler was beginning to suspect that was only the most obvious consequence of using the Talismans.

How much Chaos was unleashed when Keegan fought the dragon? Enough to cause a backlash that could drive an entire kingdom to war?

He didn't blame Keegan for what had happened. Not anymore. He was the one who'd stolen the Ring from the Queen. Everything that came afterward could actually be traced to that one act; all the death and destruction could just as easily be laid at his own feet as Keegan's.

I don't have the power of a mage, he thought bitterly, *but I still suffer the same consequences for my actions.*

Even if Shalana was able to slow the Danaan army down, how many men and women on each side would lose their lives? Their blood was on his hands.

The more he thought about the coming battle, the more he realized it would probably be a disaster for the clans even if the Danaan battle mages weren't able to use their magic in this land.

The Danaan have archers—will Shalana know how far she needs her troops to stay back to be out of range?

Vaaler's kingdom had never gone to war; they knew little about the logistics of waging war on a massive scale. But neither did Norr's people—even a battle between the largest clans would pale compared to this.

Will they understand how to use the terrain to their advantage? Will Shalana know the best way to deploy her units to minimize the Danaan numbers advantage?

It was likely the Danaan would operate in small, semiautonomous bands, mirroring the command structure of the patrols that kept outsiders away from the North Forest. It wasn't a great strategy, but the Queen's advisers knew no other way.

Vaaler had studied the military histories of the Southlands during his apprenticeship with Rexol. But when he tried to share his knowledge with the Danaan, they had dismissed his efforts.

They never thought they'd be the aggressors in a war, so they never saw any need to learn how to fight in any other kind of environment.

The tactics that worked well in the forests left them vulnerable on the wide-open plains. But Shalana wouldn't know how to exploit their weakness.

Both sides were stumbling in blind. Instead of precise, effective strikes to cripple the enemy, they'd engage in long, ineffective battles with staggering casualties.

This is madness! There has to be another way!

And then suddenly it hit him. He stopped packing, his hand clutching some extra clothes he had been about to shove into a small sack.

"Hurry up," Jerrod said, noticing him standing there frozen in place.

When he didn't move, Keegan came over to him, and asked, "Vaaler, what's wrong?"

He opened his fingers and let the clothes drop to the snow-covered ground at his feet.

"I'm not going," he declared.

"What?"

"I'm not going," he repeated. "I'm going to stay with the clans and advise them on military strategy."

Keegan's jaw gaped. "I . . . I don't understand."

"This war is partly my fault," Vaaler told him, speaking quickly. "I know the ways of the Danaan. I can help the clans. Give them a fighting chance."

"You come with us," Jerrod said flatly, overhearing his words. "Your place is with Keegan."

"No," Vaaler informed him. "It's not. I've done everything I can for him; he doesn't need me anymore. But if I stay here, I can save lives. Lots of lives."

"You have to teach Keegan to control his power," Jerrod insisted. "You have to continue the training he began with Rexol."

"He's gone far beyond anything Rexol ever taught him."

"He's right," Keegan said. "About everything."

Jerrod shook his head. "Your destiny is bound with Keegan's. If you abandon us now, you put the entire world in peril!"

"You don't know that," Vaaler shot back, suddenly sick of the monk's stubborn refusal to accept anything that didn't suit his own plans.

"How many times have you reinvented your prophecy since I met you?" he demanded. "How many times have you been wrong about something? You're just as lost as the rest of us; you just can't admit it. Not even to yourself."

"I have never wavered from my belief in Keegan's destiny!" Jerrod said, his normally calm and even voice betraying more emotion than Vaaler expected.

"You keep talking about Keegan's destiny, but what about my destiny? Maybe I have my own path to walk!"

Jerrod opened his mouth to say something else but closed it when Keegan put a restraining hand on the monk's arm.

"He's made his decision," the young man told him. "Nothing you say will change his mind."

Realizing it was true, Jerrod simply turned away from them both and resumed his packing. Keegan cast a quick glance over his shoulder at the monk, then shrugged apologetically.

"Don't worry," Vaaler told his friend. "Scythe and Jerrod will take care of you."

"I'm more worried about you," Keegan said. "You're right about this. I know you are. But will the chiefs even listen to you?"

"Shalana might," Vaaler said after thinking about it.

"What if she's not the one in charge?"

"Then I'll probably be executed as a spy."

The hall was very crowded and very loud. The echoes of the chiefs' angry shouts, protests, and arguments echoed off the stone walls, causing Shalana's head to ache.

By the time they had all gathered, most of the chiefs had heard rumors of what the meeting was to be about. But when Roggen addressed them and spoke of the mystical Sword of Daemron, scornful bedlam had erupted.

"Our people are being slaughtered, and you speak of fairy tales?"

"Has Hadawas finally gone senile?"

"Myths and legends won't stop the Tree Folk army!"

Shalana knew there was nothing to do but let their anger run its course. Eventually they'd realize that no matter what they thought of Hadawas and the Sword, it did little to change the stark reality of the situation.

After several minutes the shouts and curses began to die down, and Roggen once again dared to address the group.

"Whether you believe in Hadawas or not is up to you," he told them. "I know his mind is right; I know he would not speak of such things without good cause. But that is not why you are here.

"The Danaan army is real—on that we can all agree. We cannot stop it alone. Our only hope is to join together against this common enemy."

"You mean join together under the Sun Blades!" a voice called out from the crowd, causing another round of angry shouting.

Roggen held his hands up, pleading for silence that grudgingly came.

"Hadawas is still the Sun Blade Chief, and he is not here. You must choose another from among your ranks to lead you."

This time the reaction was so loud it actually made Shalana wince and turn her head away from the cacophony of voices, as every man and woman in attendance tried to shout out the reasons for their own candidacy.

This won't end well, she thought.

There was no love lost among any of the Eastern tribes. Stronger clans used violence and threats to extort tribute from the weak, but the tribute brought no loyalty or allegiance with it. It was hard to imagine any of the smaller tribes willingly following a chief from the Sun Blades, Wind Walkers, or even the Stone Spirits—being forced to bow down to them had bred too much resentment and mistrust. On the other hand, none of the larger clans would ever follow a chief from one that was smaller and weaker—it was an insult no warrior would accept. And the medium-sized clans were either growing, which made them too ambitious for others too trust, or shrinking, which made them desperate.

Listening to the dozens of arguments raging all around her, Shalana realized that some of the chiefs were trying to form alliances. But the wounds of generations of discord ran deep, and the negotiations failed time and time again.

It wasn't just ego that got in the way, however. Whoever was chosen to lead them would decide where the warriors from the various clans would be placed during battle. There was a legitimate fear that the chief in charge would put the safety of his or her own people above all others.

How could any war party function if the warriors had no confidence in their leader? How could they fight without fear and doubt if they believed that the chief valued the lives of some more than others . . . or even more than victory?

Maybe Norr is right, Shalana realized as an idea began to form. *Maybe I am the only one who can unite them.*

The shouting had fallen to a dull roar as the chiefs slowly wore themselves out. Knowing she would have only one chance to win them over, Shalana decided the time was right to act.

Striding quickly to the center of the room, she jumped up on the long, waist-high table. Tilting her head back, she placed two fingers against her teeth and blew a long, shrill whistle. The piercing wail reverberated through the hall, causing nearly everyone to bring their hands up to their ears.

"Do you think the Tree Folk generals waste their time fighting like dogs over a bone?" she called out in the moment of silence that followed. "Do you think their army will wait idly by while you bicker like children?"

She braced for a scathing response, but her words had momentarily shamed the others into speechlessness. Seizing the advantage, she charged into the breach.

"This is not about honor. This is not about clans. This is about survival! The Danaan do not want tribute; they want our lives!

"If we do not pick someone to lead us tonight—this hour— then everyone you know and love will die! Do you fools understand this?"

"You are not even a chief," someone called out. "Why are you even here?"

"You all know me!" Shalana shot back. "I am Terramon's daughter. For five years I ruled the Stone Spirits, and I never lost a battle!"

"You lost to the Red Bear," another voice called out.

"The Red Bear is gone," Shalana told them. "He has gone with Hadawas to find Daemron's Sword. He would rather chase after a myth than listen to the pathetic mewling in this room!"

Shalana snapped her head from side to side, her icy glare daring anyone else to speak up.

"None of you is worthy of leading us against this foe," she spat. "You are blinded by prejudice and self-importance, and your duty to your own clan. That is the burden of being chief—I know for I was once like you."

She paused, waiting for someone else to speak.

"But I am not a chief anymore. I have been humbled. I have been brought low. I have been shunned by my own people. That is why you must choose me to lead the clans."

Another angry roar rose up from the crowd. Shalana let it rage for several seconds, then killed it with another ear-shattering whistle.

"If you choose me," she told them, "I promise the Stone Spirits will be on the front lines of every battle, and I will be at their head. If a life must be sacrificed, it will be mine or one of my people.

"I make this vow to you because I know this is the price of victory. If I am not willing to risk my own life, then all our lives will be forfeit. Can any of you make the same promise?"

There was a long, heavy silence in the air. Then Qarr, Chief of the Black Wings, climbed up on the table to stand beside her.

"When we refused to pay tribute to the Stone Spirits," he said in a deep voice, his words carrying to the farthest reaches of the hall, "Shalana and her thanes broke our ranks.

"She could have punished us for our defiance. She could have doubled or tripled our tribute and left us to starve through the winter. But she did not do this. Instead, she showed us mercy."

He turned to face Shalana, then dropped to one knee.

"The Black Wings owe you our lives. I pledge my clan to you."

On the floor just in front of the table where Shalana stood, a broad-shouldered woman dropped to her knee, and declared, "The Moon Eyes will follow you."

Beside her, the Wind Walker chief did the same. "My clan is yours."

As if on cue, every chief in the room dropped down, their voices rising up one after the other as they all pledged themselves to Shalana.

Elated as she felt, Shalana knew there wasn't time to relish her victory.

"Rise, my thane-chiefs," she told them, inventing the new title on the spot. "Go to your camps and tell your thanes what has happened. Send runners to spread the news to all the clans.

"Tell your people who cannot fight—the mothers and children, the artisans and craftsmen, the old and infirm—to head to Giant's Maw at the foot of the mountains on the easternmost borders of our land. Tell them to bring food, tents, blankets, and any other supplies they can carry. As much as possible. The Maw will be our place of final refuge, a camp far from the path of the invading horde where they can seek shelter through the winter.

"But tell your warriors to gather here at the Conclave," she added, her voice rising slightly. "Tell them to bring their weapons and courage! Tell them all the clans will fight side by side. Tell them the battle for our land has begun, and we will drive the Tree Folk back into the forests!"

A great cheer rose up from the chiefs, and they saluted her with raised fists and chants of her name for several seconds before they began filing out of the hall. Shalana stayed on top of the table, watching them go until only she and Roggen were left.

"An impressive performance," he told her, holding out a hand to help her down from the table. "I did not believe it could be done."

Shalana ignored his hand and jumped down to the floor beside him.

"Would you rather see us all ground under the boots of the Danaan?" she asked.

"On behalf of Hadawas, I pledge the Sun Blades to you," he said in answer though he didn't bother to drop to his knee.

He turned to go, then suddenly stopped. Without looking back, he said, "They will hold you to your promise, you know. The Stone Spirits—and you—must lead us into battle."

"The Stone Spirits will lead you," she replied.

Satisfied, he walked out the exit, leaving her alone. Or so she thought until she noticed Vaaler sitting in the farthest corner of the hall, half-hidden by the shadows.

"How long were you there, Spy?" she asked.

"Long enough," he said, getting up and coming over. "Norr said the chiefs would pick you. I'm glad to see he was right."

"Why are you still here?" she wanted to know. "I thought Hadawas and the others had already left."

"They have," Vaaler said. "But I'm staying with you. I know the Danaan ways. I can help you."

"The others won't like it," she warned him.

"That's why I waited until everyone was gone to tell you."

"Be honest with me, Vaaler," she said, noting the young man's eyes go wide upon hearing her use his real name. "With your help, can we defeat them?"

"No," he said sadly. "Probably not. But that doesn't mean you shouldn't fight."

Chapter 29

IT HAD TAKEN two days for Hadawas and his entourage—six handpicked warriors, plus Scythe, Norr, Keegan, and Jerrod—to reach the edge of the mountains. The entire way, they'd fought a steady headwind: an endless wave of frozen air rolling down the mountains and across the plains. The temperature steadily dropped until even the exertion of their march couldn't keep Scythe from shivering.

As they drew closer, the jagged rock faces looming ahead seemed to shoot straight up into the air. Scythe could see that halfway up the smaller peaks the gray rock turned white with a covering of ice and snow. On the taller mountains the top simply vanished into the thick clouds high above.

According to their guide, the Sword lay on the other side of this formidable range. The old man had ridden on a sled for the journey, just as Norr had done earlier. But no amount of rest could heal old age, and as they made camp at the mountain's base she wondered what would happen with their guide as the way become too steep and rugged for the sled.

With night falling, the small group huddled around a hastily dug fire pit, positioning Hadawas's sled to block some of the wind. They'd brought extra clothes for the journey: heavy gloves, blankets, and bits of cloth they could wrap themselves in from head to toe. But even wearing so many layers that she could hardly move, Scythe still felt the sting of the cold.

Norr tossed a small brick of peat moss into the pit, and one of Hadawas's warriors lit it with his flint and tinder. Scythe and the others pressed in close, eagerly absorbing the dull heat while ignoring the heavy, cloying smoke curling up.

"We will never be able to climb these peaks," Jerrod noted once everyone had settled in. "Even if the weather holds."

Scythe didn't normally agree with the monk, but in this case she felt the same way.

"There are passes through the mountains," Hadawas informed him. "Narrow, treacherous, and well hidden. But I know where to find them."

"And what about the Sword?" Jerrod pressed. "Where is it?"

"For centuries it has been hidden away in a small cave, watched over by the Guardian—the last surviving servant of the Old Gods."

Of course, Scythe thought. *Why wouldn't there be an ancient, magical protector taking care of the Sword?*

A few months ago she would have dismissed the Guardian as an imaginary character in a folktale. Now, given all she had seen, she would actually be more surprised if the Guardian weren't real.

"How do you know all this?" Jerrod demanded.

"Most clans have forgotten the tales of our forefathers," Hadawas said. "But some—like the Sun Blades—have kept the history of the East alive. These stories were told to me by my mother, who learned them from her father. They have been passed down generation to generation since the Cataclysm, preserving the ancient knowledge.

"I have spent many years gathering the stories from any who preserve and protect the knowledge of our past. This is how I learned of the Sword and its protector."

"So do you know how we can defeat the Guardian?" Scythe asked.

"Maybe we don't have to," Norr suggested. "Keegan is destined to save the mortal world. Maybe if we explain this, the Guardian will give him the Sword willingly."

"Perhaps," Hadawas said, though he clearly didn't think that would happen.

From somewhere far away and high above them a strange cry echoed through the night, sending a shiver down Scythe's spine. The sound fell somewhere between a howl and a scream before trailing off in a maniacal, throaty laugh.

"What was that?" Keegan asked, clearly as unsettled by the strange noise as Scythe, though she did a better job of hiding it.

"Yeti," one of the warriors whispered.

"Twisted half-human monsters that stalk the mountains," Hadawas explained. "Legends hold that they were once a clan who sought Daemron's Sword shortly after the Cataclysm split the world, though they never found it.

"The power of the Sword changed them, transforming them from men and women into beasts while driving them mad."

Another of the bizarre howls rang out, answering the first. Though it was difficult to pinpoint a location, it clearly came from another direction than the first.

"How many of those things are there?" Keegan wondered.

"Nobody knows the yeti numbers," Hadawas said. "Maybe a few dozen. Maybe hundreds. Maybe more."

Several more cries echoed over the peaks. Despite what Hadawas had said about the yeti's origins, Scythe heard nothing intelligent or human in them. Even the cackling laughter at the end was bestial and unnatural.

"Should we post a guard?" Jerrod asked.

"The yeti never leave the mountain," Hadawas assured him.

"What about once we enter their territory?" Scythe wanted to know.

"The yeti do not hunt humans," the old chief stated confidently. "They will not bother us."

Despite his reassurances, Scythe barely slept that night, shivering uncontrollably even with Norr's great bulk pressed close against her and snapping awake each time a yeti howled.

The camp woke next morning to a light snow flurry; large flakes swirled around them, dancing in the air that had dropped another twenty degrees.

By focusing his mind, Jerrod was able to regulate his body temperature and protect against the chill. Instead of blood flow to his extremities being cut off, it continued to circulate through his fingers and toes, keeping them from going stiff and numb. But that didn't mean he couldn't feel the cold, and he knew how much discomfort it brought the others.

They'd debated whether to continue, but Norr had insisted they needed to press on for the sake of the clans—every day they waited represented more casualties for those who tried to stand against the Danaan army. And so, despite the weather, they had continued.

By midmorning, the path they were following became too steep and slick to continue with the sled. The provisions they'd packed were quickly divided up, with each member of the expedition taking as much as they could carry, stuffed into packs they threw over their shoulders. Remarkably, Hadawas vowed to continue as their guide even though it meant he must travel on foot.

The old man moved slowly, but when the trail they were following came up against a sheer rock face he proved his value.

"There's a crevice along the right side that cuts through the rock," Hadawas told them.

In the snow it took several minutes to find the passage, but in the end he was proved right. The endless cycle of ice melting and refreezing had carved a fissure in the otherwise impassable face. Without Hadawas, they would have had to either attempt to scale the fifty-foot rock wall blocking their way or turn back and seek out another route.

Even so, it was a tight fit for Norr. His back and belly scraped along the rock wall even after he'd shed all but the last layer of his clothes.

"How far does this passage go?" he asked, his teeth chattering.

"It opens up on the other side of the wall," Hadawas promised him. "A few hundred feet ahead."

They edged through the narrow crack single file, dragging their supply packs along the ground behind them on short straps of leather tied to their belts. Jerrod took the lead and Keegan followed right behind him, leaning on Rexol's staff for support. Norr brought up the rear. A few feet in the ground began to slope upward, the fissure continuing to climb at a sharp angle. At the halfway point it became noticeably darker, and looking up, the monk saw that the channel narrowed dramatically above them, cutting off the light.

In that moment he suddenly realized they were surrounded on all sides by thousands upon thousands of tons of rock and ice. He could feel it beneath his feet, and he could sense it pressing in on him from in front and behind.

If the snow and ice on the peak above us gives way, it will pour into the fissure and we'll be buried alive!

He tried to push the thought from his mind, but it was impossible to ignore given their surroundings. Yet there was nothing he could do at this point but continue onward. When he finally reached the other side and stepped out from the narrow passage, he felt a major sense of relief . . . until he looked down.

The tunnel ended on a narrow ledge, no more than five feet wide. Beyond it was a drop of at least fifty feet to the jagged rocks below. The snow had stopped falling by the time he emerged, but the wind had picked up. The rock beneath his feet was covered with a layer of ice, making the footing treacherous.

The ledge continued in only one direction: upward. Repositioning his pack, Jerrod pressed his back against the edge of the mountain and inched his way along it to give everyone else room. One by one the others crawled out of the crevice. From their expressions and gasps, the monk could tell they had a similar reaction to his own—claustrophobia followed by a short-lived relief that was replaced by mild vertigo.

"How far does this ledge continue?" Norr asked once they were all outside. As he spoke, Scythe helped wrap him back up in the clothes he had shed to fit through the fissure.

"A quarter mile up the side of the mountain," Hadawas answered. "It will bring us to a plateau at the top of this peak."

Jerrod noted that the old man was breathing heavily though he was the only one not burdened by a supply pack. The air here was already thin, making physical exertion even more difficult.

"Maybe we should use ropes to tie us together," Scythe suggested, peering over the edge of the trail.

"There's nothing to secure them with," Jerrod countered. "If one of us falls, the others would all be dragged over, too."

"Tread carefully," Hadawas advised them, "and you have nothing to fear."

Jerrod's senses were focused on his balance and footing, reducing his awareness to a small circle that included only himself and Keegan. He didn't know if he would be able to help the savior if he fell, but he knew he'd give his life trying.

"What was that?" Scythe suddenly called out.

"What?" Norr asked her.

"I thought I heard something."

"How can you hear anything over this wind?" one of Hada-was's soldiers asked.

A good question, yet all of them stood still and listened for several seconds before Scythe declared, "I guess it was nothing."

Jerrod, however, wasn't so sure. As they inched their way farther along the ledge, he slowly expanded his awareness, reaching out with his Sight. And then he sensed the yeti.

The creature clung to the stone of the mountainside twenty feet above them, using the claws on its hands and feet for purchase. It was about two-thirds the size of an average man; even smaller and slighter than Scythe. Its face was simian, its eyes set in a deep, protruding brow. It was completely covered in white fur, allowing it to blend in perfectly with the snow-covered surface of its perch.

The creature didn't move, and Jerrod realized it had been there for some time, watching their progress. The monk turned his head up toward it, and it scuttled higher up the mountain and vanished, the sound of its claws scraping on the icy rocks covered by the wind.

Not wanting to alarm the others unnecessarily while they navigated the precarious trail, Jerrod kept silent. But now that he knew what to look for, he decided to split his focus between the path ahead and the rocks above.

A few minutes after the first yeti vanished, several more appeared. Like the first they clung to the rocks above, watching. This time Jerrod didn't look up to scare them away, and slowly their numbers began to grow. Soon there were a dozen of the white-haired humanoids prowling the path above them. They were silent as ghosts, sliding easily along the mountain's face as they tracked the progress of the humans below.

They're stalking us, Jerrod realized.

Hadawas had said they were drawn to the power of Daemron's Sword; if that was true, it was logical to assume they could sense the Talisman Keegan wore around his neck as well. But something was holding them back. Despite their growing numbers, they never came too close, and they seemed more wary than violent.

Are they afraid of us? Or is it the Ring itself they fear?

It took almost two hours for them to reach the plateau though it wasn't Hadawas who slowed them down. The venerable chief was the most sure-footed of them all, and though he never hurried, he had no trouble keeping up with the others as they took tentative, cautious steps on the slippery surface.

The yeti had stalked them through most of the journey, but once Jerrod was close enough to the end to actually see the plateau above them they vanished en masse. Only once everyone was safely on the plateau did he tell them what he'd seen.

"The yeti were following us. Watching us."

"I knew I heard something!" Scythe exclaimed.

"How many were there?" Norr wanted to know.

"I counted twenty," Jerrod said. "But there could have been more higher up where I couldn't sense them."

"And all they did was watch us?" Keegan asked.

"The yeti are no threat to us," Hadawas assured them. "They will not keep us from claiming the Sword."

"How much farther is it, anyway?" Scythe asked.

"The Guardian's cave is beyond the valley that lies over the next peak," Hadawas told them. "Another two or three days. Maybe more—the way becomes harder from this point."

"Good to know the easy stuff is behind us," Scythe grumbled.

"We should rest here for a few hours," Hadawas told them. "There is a cave nearby where we can take shelter from the wind."

Once again, their guide was right. On locating the cave, the entire group squeezed inside. The ceiling was low enough that even Jerrod had to duck, and Norr was bent over nearly double. As they pulled blankets from their pack and spread them on the floor, the heat from their bodies quickly warmed the cramped quarters.

How could he know about this cave unless he's been over these mountains before? Jerrod wondered. *And how did he know the yeti wouldn't attack us?*

There was something Hadawas wasn't telling them. They couldn't have come this far without his help, but Jerrod was starting to wonder if the Sun Blade chief would betray them before it was all over.

He was planning to go after the Sword before we came. Will he really just surrender it to Keegan, or will he try to take it for himself?

The Crown had destroyed Rexol when he dared to use it; Jerrod assumed the Sword would do the same—its power too great for most mortals to endure. But what if he was wrong?

What if Hadawas knows something about the Sword that we don't?

Keegan and the others were already bedding down, the mental and physical strain of the day's climb having left them completely drained. Hadawas's eyes were already closed, his breath coming in a slow, steady rhythm.

Jerrod was tired, too, but when he closed his sightless eyes he kept his mind alert and his awareness focused on the entire cave, keeping watch over Keegan and his friends while everyone else slept.

Chapter 30

LYING FLAT ON their stomachs almost completely buried beneath the snow, Shalana and the thirty Stone Spirit warriors with her waited anxiously for the Danaan patrol to draw close enough for them to strike.

The scouting reports confirmed what young Ullis had told them—the hostile army marching across the Frozen East was massive. Traveling in small, loosely organized bands, the Tree Folk forces created a front that extended for several miles. Even united, the clans were badly outnumbered. And at the head of the invasion was some kind of enormous beast—a massive, heavily muscled creature that seemed to be formed of slime and sludge and rotting gray flesh.

If Vaaler's plan doesn't work, we'll all be slaughtered.

The exiled prince had shared everything he knew about the strengths and weaknesses of the Danaan army with her and the chiefs from the other clans. He'd even recognized the description of the strange monster that walked with the enemy from his childhood fables: he called it an ogre.

Yet several of the chiefs were suspicious of his motives, especially when they found out Vaaler wasn't willing to take up weapons against his own people. Shalana had explained his reluctance to fight by pointing out that in the confusion of battle, he could easily be mistaken for the enemy, but she knew that wasn't the only reason.

He still feels a kinship to them. He doesn't want to put himself in a position where he must spill the blood of those he once called his own.

Loudest among the voices opposing Vaaler was her own father. Despite his body no longer being fit for battle, Terramon had come to the Conclave with the Stone Spirit warriors in answer to her summons. But in the end, the direness of their situation finally won others over to her side. Despite his reputation as a great conqueror, Terramon could offer no strategy or battle plan that could save them—they simply didn't have enough warriors to meet the Danaan head-on. And so they had gone with Vaaler's tactics.

Our only hope is to harry and harass them, he'd explained. *Slow them down long enough for your people to seek shelter near the mountains.*

From Roggen's daily reports, Shalana knew hundreds of children, elderly, and other noncombatants were already pouring into the Giant's Maw each day. He hadn't been pleased when Shalana assigned him the task of overseeing the refugee camp; he was a warrior who wanted to be part of the battle. But the Sun Blade thane was well-known among many of the clans, giving him the authority and respect necessary to be in charge. He was also smart enough to understand the importance of the camp at the Giant's Maw, and he was organized enough to manage the food and other supplies as the population swelled.

Thinking of Roggen reminded her of Berlen. They could have used his great strength on the front lines, but he had disappeared. Nobody had seen the Sun Blade's mightiest warrior since the night Norr met with Hadawas and they left to seek out Daemron's Sword.

She was still angry at Norr for leaving when they needed him most. To Shalana's surprise, however, as news of their mad quest spread among the warriors and refugees, it kindled hope among the people.

They're scared and desperate. They need something—anything—to cling to.

But Shalana and the chiefs knew better. Their survival didn't depend on a long-lost mythical weapon. It would come from the spears and blades and blood of the men and women who dared to risk their lives against overwhelming odds.

They'd plotted the course of the Danaan march and laid their trap on the Frozen Sea, a wide plain covered with long lines of rolling, snow-covered hills that were said to resemble the ocean waves. The hills and uneven terrain would cut off lines of sight between the Danaan forces, giving the clans the cover they needed.

The enemy patrol was close now, less than twenty feet away. Any closer and they'd see through the Stone Spirit camouflage. Shalana sprang to her feet, rising from the snowdrift and unleashing a fierce battle cry. In response, her warriors burst from their concealment and charged the startled Danaan, closing in on them from all sides.

The patrol's archers scrambled to fire at the onrushing enemy, but their fingers were numb and the drawstrings on their bows stiff from the cold. They managed only a single ineffective volley before the Stone Spirits fell on them.

Shalana felt the tip of an arrow graze her cheek, leaving a thin furrow that quickly filled with blood. But the wound was superficial, and she ignored it as she drove her spear deep into the chest of the archer who had fired it.

Spinning away from the mortally wounded foe, she yanked the spear free from his ribs and swung it around like a club, the butt end of the heavy shaft slamming into the skull of the Danaan who had rushed in at her from behind.

All around her the Stone Spirits stabbed, hacked, and slashed at their enemies, their savage fury taking full advantage of the element of surprise. She felt a rapier slash against her side, but the thin blade lacked the force to slice through the thick, fur-covered hides protecting her torso.

She spun on her assailant as the Danaan woman struck again, plunging the point of her blade deep into Shalana's makeshift armor so that the tip bit into the flesh of her hip. Enraged by the pain, Shalana brought her spear slamming down on the other woman's weapon, and the thin blade bowed and snapped beneath the force of her blow.

A quick jab with the spear to the woman's throat ended the battle. In the snow around her all the Danaan lay dead and all the Stone Spirits were still standing.

"Find the horn!" Shalana ordered, and in response her warriors began rummaging through the bodies of their fallen foes.

"Here," one shouted a few seconds later, tossing the horn over to her.

It was carved from the curved horn of some unfamiliar animal; hollowed out and fitted on the small end with a thin reed. According to Vaaler, the Danaan used the horns so the far-ranging patrols could communicate quickly even when separated by great distances. Shalana put it to her lips and blew a series of short and long blasts in the pattern he had taught her.

A few seconds later she heard similar calls ringing out across the fields. Some were from the other ambushes, others were actual Danaan patrols hearing her call and relaying the message to the rest of the troops: *Enemy forces attacking the left flank. Send all available reinforcements.*

Tucking the horn into her belt in case they needed it later, she and her warriors set off at a run in the opposite direction. A few minutes later they reached the rendezvous point; shortly after, they were joined by all the other groups that had staged similar ambushes: nearly three hundred in all. There wasn't time for a head count, but she noticed a few had come back missing one or two of their people—apparently not all the ambushes had been as successful as hers.

She waited a few more minutes to give Qarr time to get into position. The false alarm Shalana had sent out to lure the Danaan away wouldn't work unless they actually saw enemy forces massing. The Black Wing chief had volunteered to lead several hundred clan warriors in a dangerous feint intended to keep the Danaan attention focused on the far side of the battlefield while Shalana and the others flanked the enemy and hit their supply wagons from the rear.

You're not there to engage them, Vaaler had reminded Qarr several times. *You just want them to chase you. Stay out of range of the archers and run them around in circles.*

Soon she heard another series of horn signals: the Danaan had spotted Qarr's company and were giving pursuit. With a hand signal she set her troops in motion. Using the hills for cover, they ran in a long, wide loop in the opposite direction, away from Qarr and the Danaan reinforcements until they could come at the enemy from behind.

Unlike the patrols that stumbled into the ambush, the Danaan assigned to guard the supply wagons were tense and ready; they'd heard the horns and knew the enemy had come. But they were not expecting the barbarian horde that poured down from the surrounding hills, and once again the archers scrambled to ready their arrows.

Running at a full sprint with Shalana at their head, the howling, screaming horde closed the gap quickly ... just not quite quickly enough. A volley of arrows rained down on them, the deadly missiles killing at least a dozen and wounding many more. But the Easterners never faltered, and seconds later they slammed into the Danaan ranks.

The battle lasted only a few minutes. With the Danaan patrols so spread out and most of them over a mile away chasing after the Black Wings, those left to guard the supply wagons were badly outnumbered. They put up a fierce resistance, but in the end they were quickly overwhelmed. Still they managed to get off several horn blasts calling for help before they were hacked down.

When the last defender fell, the clan warriors turned their fury on the supply wagons—breaking the axles and wheels, smashing the frames, and slicing open or chopping up any sacks, packs, and containers within reach.

"Find their oil!" Shalana shouted, knowing they didn't have long before reinforcements arrived. "And the torches!"

By the time the Danaan forces showed up, Shalana and her people were gone. All they left behind were enemy corpses and dozens of shattered wagons, their contents engulfed in flames.

Vaaler didn't want to take pleasure in war, but it was hard not to be swept up in the congratulations of Shalana and the others. His plan had worked brilliantly: men and women on both sides were dead, but the clan casualties were a fraction of what they had inflicted on the enemy.

I wonder how many of the fallen Danaan I knew personally? he thought.

After burning the supply wagons, Shalana's force had scattered in all directions, making it harder for the Danaan to pursue them. By now most had made it back to the temporary camp they'd used as their initial staging point, though a few stragglers were still coming in.

Shalana had chosen to make camp several miles from the site of the battle, far enough away that the Danaan wouldn't stumble upon it by chance. A handful of small lamps provided just enough light to see but did little to ward off the chill of the night. The others were used to the cold, but even covered in furs, Vaaler was shivering.

The vast majority of the clan warriors had remained at the camp during the battle. Vaaler's initial plan wouldn't have worked any better with a larger force, and he knew the more warriors Shalana sent, the more likely they'd be to try to engage the Danaan in a real fight. Fortunately, she'd seen the wisdom of his fears and agreed to hold them back.

Better to hide our true numbers for as long as possible anyway, Vaaler thought.

Of those who'd been chosen to go with Qarr, most had already returned. To confuse the Danaan pursuit, they'd split their force up into smaller groups, each led by one of Shalana's thane-chiefs. Only the Black Wings and their chief had yet to return, though that wasn't surprising. To draw the Danaan as far away as possible, he and his clan had gone in the exact opposite direction of the camp. Even if the Danaan had abandoned their pursuit after realizing Qarr's attack was only a ruse, it would take some time for the Black Wings to weave their way through the Frozen Sea's hills and back to their hidden location.

Several skeins of wine and mead had been unpacked from the supply sleds and passed around to the troops, but their celebrations were subdued. Individual tales of bravery from the recent battle were recounted, along with toasts to honor those comrades who would never return.

But far fewer had died than any of them had expected, and they all recognized who was responsible. Vaaler had the honor of being personally thanked and congratulated by each and every chief and thane who entered the camp. At first he thought Shalana had ordered them to do it, but it quickly became clear their gratitude was sincere.

A person is judged by his actions among the clans, he realized.

Even Terramon came over to see him.

"A great victory," the grizzled warrior grudgingly admitted. "But this was only the first battle. Your trick with the horns won't fool them again."

"Maybe with their supplies ransacked, they'll have to turn back," Shalana said, having come over to stand by Vaaler protectively when she noticed her father's approach.

"Is that the way of your people?" Terramon asked Vaaler. "Can you so easily be forced into retreat?"

"My people have changed," Vaaler told him. "Before, they never would have sought out this war in the first place."

Terramon scowled, then turned and wandered off.

"Ignore him," Shalana said, placing a comforting hand on Vaaler's shoulder.

This close to her, he could see the angry red slash on the pale skin of her cheek. She'd laughed off the injury, but Vaaler knew she'd come inches away from losing her eye . . . or her life.

"You have proved yourself this day," she told him as he stared at the wound that somehow enhanced rather than marred her beauty. "The chiefs will not forget."

Before Vaaler could reply a young woman stumbled into the camp. Even in the dim light of the lamps it was clear from her expression that something was wrong.

"Qarr?" Shalana whispered.

The young woman shook her head.

"He wasn't supposed to fight!" Vaaler said, more angrily than he'd intended. "What happened?"

"The ogre," the young woman muttered. "We followed your instructions. Once the Danaan began to chase us, we split up into smaller group. We stayed beyond the range of the archers. We led them in circles, listening to their horns to know which directions they were heading to try and cut us off. Everything was perfect.

"And then that monster appeared out of nowhere. It was fast— too fast to outrun. So Qarr ordered us to stand and fight."

She was speaking in a dull, emotionless monotone, and Vaaler realized she was in shock.

"A trap?" Shalana guessed. "The Danaan used the ogre to lure you into an ambush?"

The woman shook her head.

"The beast was alone. Qarr died first. It tore his head off with a single blow.

"Our weapons couldn't harm it," she continued, still talking without any visible emotion. "Our spears bounced off its hide and our swords bent and snapped when they struck it.

"Every blow from its fists left another dead. Those of us still alive tried to run, but it chased us down. It was fast. So fast."

"How many of you got away?" Shalana asked softly.

The woman shrugged.

"I don't know. I heard others screaming, but I didn't stop to look back."

A pall fell over the camp; Qarr had over thirty Black Wing warriors with him.

She can't be the only one who survived, Vaaler thought. *They can't all be dead!*

"Get the sleds ready," Shalana ordered. "We break camp now."

Andar watched silently from the corner of the tent as the Queen's war council debated what had gone wrong in the day's battle.

For the first time since entering the Frozen East they had been faced with real resistance, a devastating counterattack that had left them short of supplies and crippled morale. Now each of the councilors was desperately trying to shift the blame as they gave their reports.

"We should have been warned to expect a possible attack in that location," General Greznor declared. "It was the perfect environment for an ambush."

"My scouts aren't being given enough time to survey the territory," Hexiff countered. "You're advancing too quickly.

"And your troops should never have been spaced so far apart," Hexiff added. "It makes it difficult for them to provide support and reinforcements."

"We were trying to cover as much ground as possible to make sure none of the smaller clans slipped through our lines," Greznor shot back. "If I'd known all the barbarians had joined together, I would have used different strategies," he added, casting a dark look at Pranya.

The Queen's spymaster scowled.

"How are my people supposed to infiltrate the clans? They'd kill us on sight. We'd need some way to hide our true nature. A charm or illusion to alter our appearance."

"You know that isn't possible here," Lormilar snapped, his insecurity over his impotence making him even more defensive than the others. "We must focus on the things we can control—like the number of soldiers protecting the supply wagons!"

"Half my guards were called away by the horns," Bassi, the quartermaster, reminded everyone.

"And the vanguard patrols closest to you were too busy walking into barbarian ambushes to help," Greznor added.

"That wouldn't happen if our spies had given us proper warning!" Hexiff protested.

"If your patrols are too stupid to watch for an ambush, there's nothing I can do to save them!" Pranya fired back.

"Enough," the Queen commanded, her voice weary. "How bad are our losses?"

"The actual casualties aren't the issue, my Queen," Greznor said after clearing his throat. "It's the supplies that concern me the most."

"We salvaged what we could," Bassi told her. "But even with the rationing, we'll run short of food in another week."

The Queen nodded grimly, then dismissed the councilors with a wave of her hand. Slowly they rose and bowed before leaving the tent, each wondering who would bear the brunt of her—and Orath's—wrath for this catastrophic failure.

Eventually only Andar, Rianna, and the Minion remained in the tent. Only then did Rianna say what they all knew but none of the others had the courage to voice.

"My son is helping the enemy. He has chosen to stand with the Destroyer of Worlds rather than his own people."

"We will change the signals," Orath answered, as if that would somehow solve the real problem.

The Queen didn't speak but simply sat in her chair, staring down at her hands.

"Can you blame Vaaler for this betrayal?" Andar said, daring to speak up despite knowing it could cost him his tongue. "You cast him out. You drove him into the arms of these savages, then you unleashed this army on them! What did you expect?"

"Silence, slave!" Orath barked. The Queen, however, didn't speak.

Ignoring the minion, Andar approached Rianna and dropped to his knee beside her chair. He reached out and placed his hand gently on her wrist, and she finally raised her eyes to look at him.

"We have no supplies. The soldiers are exhausted and frozen and reeling from this defeat. If you press on, this can only end in disaster."

Orath reached out and seized Andar by the shoulder and hauled him to his feet, his grip strong enough to make the former High Sorcerer gasp in pain.

"If the Destroyer of Worlds has united the savages under a single banner," the Minion hissed in the Queen's ear as he shoved Andar aside, "then our victory will come even more quickly.

"Hexiff's scouts have spotted a mass exodus of refugees, all heading in the same direction. They are gathering in one place. If we follow them to it, we can wipe out your enemy in a single battle!"

"Slaughtering defenseless refugees won't stop the warriors who attacked us today!" Andar protested.

"It will draw the warriors out," Orath insisted. "Instead of scattered patrols, tell Greznor to transform your troops into a real army and we can meet them head-on!"

"We don't even know their true numbers," Andar cautioned. "The farther east we go, the greater the toll it takes. Our bowstrings freeze and the wood warps in the cold, rendering the archers useless. Frostbite takes the fingers and toes of too many soldiers each night, further thinning our numbers. Add in starvation and the threat of a winter storm, and your army might be a mere fraction of what we have now by the time the savages make their stand!"

"We still have the ogre," Orath reminded her. "It slaughtered dozens of the savages today; they are powerless to stop it. With the beast under our command, the enemy cannot stand against us. The Destroyer of Worlds will fall and the Ring will be yours once again."

Rianna turned her head slowly from Orath, to Andar, then back to Orath.

When she finally said, "Tell Greznor to gather our forces and change course for the refugee camp," Andar's heart sank.

Chapter 31

JERROD STILL DIDN'T trust Hadawas, but the physical ordeal of the second day of their mountain trek left him little time to focus on his suspicions. Hadawas led them through a frozen labyrinth of ice and stone, somehow finding every nook and cranny they could use to go farther and farther into the otherwise impassable mountain range.

Encumbered by the extra layers of cloth wrapped tightly around their bodies and the packs strapped to their backs, they crawled on all fours through twisting, seemingly endless dark and drafty tunnels. They hugged the cold mountain face, buffeted by fierce winds while creeping along slick ledges so narrow their heels dangled over the edge. They scaled sloping rock formations so steep that Hadawas's warriors had to go ahead and use a harness to hoist the elderly chief to the top, then half climbed, half slid down the other side, always on the verge of losing control and careening over the precipice at the bottom.

Once again the yeti followed them the entire way, growing more numerous and more agitated as the humans forged deeper and deeper into their domain. They came closer and closer until it wasn't just Jerrod who noticed them lurking above. Norr let out a cry of anger and surprise as one reached down to paw at the big man's arm, triggering a round of the howling laughs from the others as the offender bared its teeth then scampered away up the sheer side of the mountain, taking the others with him. The clawed swipe didn't leave a mark, but it shredded the top layers of Norr's thick clothing.

By the time they reached the relative safety of the wide, flat plateau at the bottom of the peak they'd just crossed, the light was fading. Darkness came early as the sun disappeared behind the massive mountain peaks, but Jerrod felt it was for the best—they desperately needed to rest.

It was obvious Keegan could barely walk another step; his missing hand making all the crawling and clambering through the mountain passes even more difficult. Norr was grimacing in pain, having pushed his knee too hard. Scythe was exhausted and shivering uncontrollably, her small, lithe form lacking any natural insulation against the cold. The Sun Blade warriors carried themselves with the herky-jerky motion of men so tired they had trouble controlling their limbs. Even Jerrod felt as if his body were ready to shut down.

How is Hadawas still on his feet? the monk wondered. *Even being lifted up the worst of the slopes, a man his age shouldn't even be able to stand after all this.*

And then, almost as if Jerrod's thoughts had triggered it, Hadawas collapsed face-first in the snow.

One of the Sun Blades cried out in dismay, and two of them dropped down and gently rolled the old man onto his back.

"There's a cave close by," he gasped, each word struggling to escape his lips, then his eyes rolled back into his head, and he lost consciousness.

Knowing they had to get Hadawas—and the rest of them— shelter quickly, Jerrod pushed out with his awareness. His head began to ache from the effort, a throbbing in his temples that he feared would last for hours. But he finally sensed what Hadawas was talking about—a small opening in the ground, almost completely buried beneath the snow.

Norr and two of the Sun Blades swept the snow clear to reveal the mouth of a sharply sloping tunnel leading down into the rock below their feet.

"It extends for several yards, then opens into a larger chamber," Jerrod assured them. "There's room for all of us. The ceiling is even high enough for Norr to stand up."

Once they were all inside, Norr took out the last of their peat supply and lit it. The smoke made everybody's eyes water, but as the heat spread slowly through the cavern nobody complained. The warmth seemed to revive Hadawas, who opened his eyes after a few minutes. With the help of one of his warriors, he managed to sit up.

"I can go no farther," the old man wheezed. "But you must continue on without me."

"How will we know where to go?" Norr asked.

"The worst is over," he told them. "There is a trail on the other side of this plateau. It leads down into a small valley. On the other side you will see another peak—much larger than any of the others. The Guardian's lair is on the other side, but you will not have to scale the mountain.

"There is a trail. Follow it up and around the peak; it will bring you to the Sword."

"What about you?" Scythe asked. "We can't just leave you here."

"You have enough food to spare," he told them. "Leave some with me and I will rest in this cave. Bring the Sword back to me here and I will lead you back down the mountains."

"We won't leave you here alone," one of the Sun Blades declared.

"Two of you stay with me," Hadawas ordered. "The rest go with Norr."

"I think that's a mistake," Jerrod cautioned, seeing a chance to eliminate any chance of Hadawas's double-crossing them. "You saw that yeti strike at Norr. The creatures are growing bolder. If they attack this cave, you will need all your warriors to protect you."

"Why are you so eager to leave my people behind," Hadawas wondered aloud, as if reading Jerrod's true motives. "Is this a trick to steal the Sword for yourself?"

Norr knelt down beside the old man and gently took his bundled hand in his own.

"We have our own need of the Sword," he admitted. "But I made a vow to the clans. I will not leave my people defenseless against the Danaan. This I swear to you."

Hadawas looked deep into Norr's eyes, then nodded.

"Tomorrow you four will go on alone," he said. "And we will wait here for you to return with the Sword."

Then he lay back down gingerly and closed his eyes, exhausted by the effort of speaking.

Keegan woke in the middle of the night from a familiar dream. Once again he'd been standing on the edge of the ocean, the waves lapping on the shore at his back as he brandished Daemron's Sword and faced the onrushing army of Chaos Spawn. But this time he'd recognized the woman lying unconscious at his feet before the ravaging horde tore him apart.

Cassandra, Rexol's old apprentice. The one who helped us escape the Monastery.

Identifying the woman with him did little to clarify the meaning of the dream, however. The vision of his own death—and failure—was troubling enough to keep him awake for several minutes, but in the end his body's fatigue won out and he drifted back to sleep.

It seemed only a minute later that Jerrod was shaking him back to consciousness. The peat had burned itself out in the night, but the cave was still warm enough that Keegan was glad he'd stripped off most of the layers of clothing before he fell asleep.

"It's time to go," the monk told him.

Once he, Jerrod, Scythe, and Norr were ready and about to leave, Hadawas said, "Remember—I will be waiting here for you to return. You made a promise, Norr. Do not betray your people."

The big man nodded and the four of them set out, climbing up the steep tunnel and back out onto the plateau above. Keegan's body still ached from yesterday, but they kept an easy pace and slowly his limbs and muscles began to loosen up. It helped that the weather was milder than before, and they had no trouble finding the path Hadawas had told them to look for.

The descent into the valley was steep, but compared to what they had already faced it almost seemed pleasant. A second mountain range rose up on the other side of the valley, and it was immediately obvious which peak Hadawas had referred to. Though the top was hidden high up in the clouds above, the base was three times around as any of the others.

"We better find that path Hadawas mentioned," Scythe noted, "or it's going to take us a month to climb that monster."

The temperature slowly warmed as they continued to descend, until Keegan was sweating beneath all his layers.

You'll need them soon enough when we start going up that mountain.

"The yeti are gone," Scythe noted.

"They stopped following us as soon as we began our descent into the valley," Jerrod noted.

"That doesn't make any sense," Norr said. "Not if they really are descended from ancestors who were seeking the Sword."

"Maybe in their madness they've forgotten what they once looked for," Jerrod hypothesized.

"Or maybe they're afraid of the Guardian," Scythe chimed in.

"Whatever we are about to face," Jerrod assured them, "we will prevail. We have the Ring, and this is Keegan's destiny."

Even if you're right, Keegan thought, *there's nothing in your proph-ecy that says all of you will survive.*

"I'm only going to use the Ring as a last resort," Keegan vowed.

"If we go in expecting the Guardian to oppose us with vio-lence," Norr warned them, "then that is what we will find."

The conversation came to an end as they reached the valley's floor. It was still cold enough for snow to cover the ground, but it was a pleasant relief from the bone-numbing chill atop the peaks, and Keegan savored their walk across it.

They found the trail without much trouble but decided to make camp in the valley that night rather than tackle the great peak with darkness coming. For the second night in a row, Keegan dreamed of him and Cassandra on the beach, but this time she was standing beside him . . . though it had the same violent end. This time when he woke from his nightmare, he wasn't able to fall back to sleep for a long, long time.

The morning brought the threat of another storm, but Norr insisted they had to risk the ascent anyway.

"Every day we wait the Danaan army carves deeper into clan territory. Every day more people die. If we cannot stop them, they will eventually march upon the refugees hiding in the Giant's Maw and slaughter my people to extinction."

"Norr's right," Jerrod said, much to Keegan's surprise. "There is no point in waiting."

He's actually eager for this, Keegan realized. *He's excited about claiming the Sword.*

As they began to climb the long, winding trail Keegan couldn't share Jerrod's enthusiasm. Instead, he felt an ominous foreboding that grew steadily worse as they made the long ascent.

The first part of the climb was simple, but as the path rounded the mountain's face they were hit with the full force of the wind howling on the other side. The mountain was so large its shadow blocked out the sun, and the path was covered in ice and snow.

The higher they went, the colder it became. The once-wide path narrowed sharply until they were again creeping cautiously along. But high above them they saw a faint flickering glow that seemed to emanate from the mountain itself.

Like a fire tucked away inside a cave, Keegan thought, and he knew without any doubt that the Guardian—and the Sword—waited within.

The others had also noticed the glow, and they redoubled their efforts, drawn to its promises of warmth and shelter. When they finally reached it, after several hours of inching their way closer and closer, Jerrod suddenly stopped them with a raised hand, wary of what they might encounter.

From inside the cave a deep voice intoned, "You have come this far already. What is a few more steps?"

The words rang clearly in Keegan's ears despite the wind, but it was hard to gauge the emotion of the speaker.

Angry? Sad? Resigned?

The four of them entered the cave in quick succession, just far enough to escape the elements outside. Inside, the Guardian was waiting for them.

Twice as tall as Norr, he looked like a sculpture of the perfect human form chiseled from some remarkable blue stone. He was naked save for a loincloth and boots, and he held a massive spear at his side—not raised for battle, but poised and ready. His face seemed almost ageless, though Keegan noticed a few wisps of gray in the pitch-black hair of his beard.

The second thing Keegan noticed was that it was warm in the cave; far warmer than the small fire burning at the back could explain. And then, finally, he saw the Sword, the silver blade embedded in a thick stone pedestal and the magnificent black handle pointing toward the ceiling.

"I know why you are here," the Guardian told them. "But I cannot give you what you seek."

There wasn't anything overtly threatening about what he said or how he said it. Rather, he seemed implacable, immovable as the mountain in which he had built his home.

"An army is marching across the East," Norr pleaded, "driving my people before it. The Sword could save them."

"It could," the Guardian conceded. "But you may not have it."

"You are a servant of the True Gods," Jerrod told him. "As am I. Now the Legacy is crumbling and the Slayer seeks to return. We need the Sword to stop him."

It seemed as though his words gave the Guardian pause, but when he replied his refusal was as steadfast as ever.

"Even Immortals can die. The Old Gods have faded from existence, and Daemron can sense his own end is near. The Legacy can be preserved until he is gone."

"No," Jerrod told him. "It can't. I've seen the visions of his Chaos Spawn armies pouring through the Legacy's breach. Without Daemron's Sword, we cannot hold them back."

"If the Legacy falls," the Guardian replied, "the Sword alone will not be enough to defeat the Slayer."

"I have the Ring, too," Keegan said. "And soon we will get the Crown."

"The Crown is not meant for you," the Guardian growled, showing anger for the first time. "It belongs to another."

"Cassandra," Keegan gasped, remembering his dream and putting the pieces together. "She was here, wasn't she? She has the Crown!"

"I offered her the Sword," the Guardian admitted. "But she refused. She did not believe any one mortal should possess all the Talismans. Their power is what drove Daemron to turn against the Gods."

"We will not leave without the Sword," Jerrod said, his voice hard.

"Then you will not leave at all," the Guardian said, raising his spear.

And then suddenly Scythe was lunging at him, her supply pack slipping from her shoulders to fall on the floor. She came in low to the ground, her blades flickering in the light of the fire. The Guardian seemed momentarily caught off guard by her attack, but at the last second he managed to pivot to the side as Scythe went hurtling past him.

She barely came up to his thigh, but she lashed out as he turned away and sliced one of her knives along his exposed skin just above the knee. For any normal man the wound would have opened up the femoral artery, causing him to bleed out in seconds. But her weapon barely left a scratch on the blue flesh.

Norr and Jerrod were already joining the fray, springing into action a split second after Scythe, their own packs hastily cast aside. The monk threw himself into the Guardian's leg, trying to knock the giant off balance, only to bounce off without even moving him. Norr grabbed hold of the massive spear with both hands, trying to wrench it out of his enemy's fist to no avail. With his free hand the Guardian picked the big man up and hurled him through the air so that he slammed hard against the wall on the other side of the cave.

Knowing they were completely overmatched, Keegan grabbed for the Ring around his neck, fumbling to get it off the chain and slip it over his finger with only one hand.

As he struggled, Scythe was literally crawling up the Guardian's back. With a bloodthirsty scream, she drove both her knives at the same time into the grooves on either side of his neck, just inside the collarbone. But instead of plunging in, the blades ricocheted off the muscle and sinew, twisting out of Scythe's grip and clattering to the floor. She stared at her suddenly empty hands in stunned surprise, but recovered in time to spring clear as the Guardian threw himself backward against the nearest wall, narrowly avoiding being crushed.

Jerrod was coming at the Guardian again, unleashing a series of spinning roundhouse kicks in rapid succession. The Guardian simply blocked them with the shaft of his spear, then sent Jerrod flying with a backhand slap. He landed beside Norr, who was still down. But unlike the barbarian, the monk rolled with the impact and came to his feet unharmed.

Keegan finally felt the Ring slide over his knuckle. He threw his head back and raised his fist high, opening himself up to the infinite power of the Sea of Chaos. But instead of an overwhelming wave of magical fire, he felt almost nothing.

The Sword! he realized. *It absorbs Chaos. Traps it. Keeps it frozen deep beneath the ice and stone.*

But though it was faint and hard to reach, he knew the power was still there. He'd summoned Chaos to unleash the curse on Shalana; he knew with the Ring he could summon enough magic to blast their enemy into ash.

Jerrod was on his feet again and rushing toward the Guardian, only to have his attack repelled and be sent reeling once more. Scythe—unarmed, with her knives still lying on the ground—had turned her attention to Norr, who lay motionless in the corner.

Focusing his mind, Keegan reached deep and found a hidden wellspring of Chaos. Steeling his will, he gathered it with the Ring, channeled it through Rexol's staff, and unleashed it against the Guardian.

A jet of blue flame shot from the empty eye sockets of the gorgon's skull to completely envelope his fifteen-foot-tall form. The mighty titan screamed in pain and staggered back as Keegan poured everything he had—everything the Ring could give him—into the searing flames.

The Guardian braced himself against the onslaught, ignoring the flames that covered his flesh. He cocked his arm back and hurled his spear. Keegan saw it coming but was powerless to stop it. And then suddenly Jerrod was there, leaping across the room with superhuman speed to knock Keegan aside. The spear passed through the air where he had been standing an instant before and buried itself deep in the rock wall.

The impact destroyed Keegan's concentration and ended his spell. The Guardian's flesh was discolored and badly blistered, his hair had all burned away—but he was still standing. With three great strides he crossed the cave and yanked the enormous spear loose from the wall and turned on Keegan, who still lay on the floor.

Jerrod threw himself between them, but the Guardian knocked the monk aside with a disdainful flick of the wrist as he raised his spear above his head. Keegan tried to call upon Chaos to save himself, but there was nothing left—the power of the Ring was spent; here in the cave where the Sword had lain for centuries it was no match for the other Talisman.

The spear came down in a blur, but instead of pinning Keegan to the ground it was deflected aside at the last moment by Scythe, wielding Daemron's sword.

The Guardian turned his rage on the young woman who had dared to lay hands on the sacred blade. Moving so fast he seemed a blur, he wheeled and stabbed at her with the tip of his spear. But fast as he was, Scythe was even quicker. She stepped aside and brought the Sword around in a tight circle. It sliced clean through the heavy spear, severing the tip.

Undeterred, the Guardian swung the shaft at her head like a club, the weapon moving so fast it carved a high-pitched whine through the air. Scythe calmly ducked under the blow and darted in, using the Sword to sever the tendon running down the back of his leg.

The Guardian howled and fell to the ground, his cry so loud it brought down bits of debris from the cave's roof. Before he could roll out of the way, Scythe plunged the blade deep into his stomach. She pulled it back as the Guardian's eyes went wide with disbelief and she raised the blade high above her head to deal the killing blow. And then suddenly Norr was there, standing between them.

"Don't," he said, holding up a hand as if the Talisman couldn't slice cleanly through his entire body and into the helpless foe on the floor.

He was on his feet, but he was hunched over and his other arm dangled uselessly at his side, the shoulder separated from his impact with the cave wall.

Scythe stared at him with an unreasoning madness in her almond-shaped eyes. And then recognition suddenly washed over her features and she turned away, letting Daemron's Sword fall to the ground as she walked away as if in a daze.

With his good hand Norr bent over and picked it up off the cave's floor, casting a single glance at the prone Guardian, who held one hand pressed tightly against the wound in his belly. Then the big man limped over to where Scythe was sitting huddled in the far corner of the cave, her eyes staring at something that seemed to be very far away. He lay the Sword down beside her, then sat down and wrapped his good arm around her shoulders and pulled her close.

Keegan slowly rose to his feet and slipped the Ring off his finger with his teeth, then spit it into his palm and clutched it tightly. Jerrod slowly made his way over beside him.

"Are you okay?" he asked.

Keegan nodded.

"Why did you spare me?" the Guardian called out across the cave, gasping slightly from the pain of his wound.

His question seemed to snap Scythe out of her daze, and she looked over at him.

"It wasn't me," she said, tilting her head in her lover's direction. "It was him."

"How come Scythe wasn't killed when she grabbed the Sword?" Keegan asked. "When Rexol used the Crown it devoured him. When I used the Ring in Ferlhame it almost destroyed me."

"The Sword must be different," Jerrod surmised. "It keeps the Chaos trapped within the blade. Anyone can use it." He turned his gaze to the Guardian, who still lay on the floor. "Is that right?"

At first the titan simply glared at him. Then, reluctantly, he nodded.

"Our legends held that the Sword had the power to heal as well as harm," Norr noted. "Is that true?"

Again, the Guardian nodded.

Norr picked up the Sword with his good hand, rose to his feet, and closed his eyes, concentrating. A faint silver nimbus surrounded him, and then suddenly his shoulder popped back into place and he stood up straight. He crossed the cave, no longer limping, and stood over the Guardian, then placed the flat of the blade gently against the titan's shoulder.

The silver glow was brighter this time, more intense. And then the Guardian took his hand away from his stomach. The flesh underneath was completely healed, pristine and perfect. He rose to his feet, his severed tendon healed as well, though the hair that had burned away did not return.

"I see that I was wrong about you," he said, though which one of them he was actually speaking to wasn't clear. "You are a worthy champion to carry Daemron's Sword. And I am not strong enough to stop you anyway. The Talisman is yours.

"But," he added, "I must also ask you for a favor."

"What?" Jerrod said before anyone else could speak.

"Cassandra. Go to her. She needs your help with her burden."

"She was also born under the Blood Moon," Jerrod whispered reverently, as if he was suddenly coming to some great understanding. "She has been touched by Chaos."

"You said this Cassandra person has Daemron's Crown," Scythe reminded him. "Why does she need our help if she's got one of the Talismans?"

"She is hunted by Chaos Spawn that have entered the mortal world," the Guardian said. "They seek the Crown for themselves, and she is reluctant to use its power . . . with good reason."

"The Slayer's Minions," Keegan said, remembering his vision of the Monastery in ruins.

"They will kill her and take the Crown for their master," the Guardian insisted. "Unless you can find her first. She is heading for Callastan."

"Callastan's a big place," Scythe pointed out.

"If we get to the city, I'll be able to find her," Keegan said, remembering his dreams. *They'll lead me to the Crown. Just like they led me to the Ring and the Sword.*

"We can't go to Callastan," Norr declared. "Not yet, at least."

"This is meant to be," Jerrod tried to reassure him. "This is the destiny the prophets of the Order saw though they didn't understand it.

"Everything is falling into place. Once we find Cassandra, we will have all three Talismans. With them Keegan will be able to drive back the Slayer's armies and the world will be saved!"

"What about my people?" Norr demanded. "The Danaan will slaughter them if we don't bring back Daemron's Sword!"

"This is more important," Jerrod insisted. "If the Slayer returns, no one will survive. Not the clans. Not the Danaan. Not the Southlands. No one!"

"I made a vow," Norr said, crossing his arms defiantly across his chest. "I will not break it."

"If Norr's not going, neither am I," Scythe said.

"Then Keegan and I will continue without you," Jerrod said flatly.

"I thought you said I was linked to Keegan's destiny," she reminded him.

"Maybe, like Vaaler, you have now played your part. He helped us acquire the Ring; you helped us find the Sword."

"You can go," Scythe told him, "but you're not taking the Sword!"

They stared at each other without speaking, wary and tense, neither willing to back down. The Guardian watched the standoff with obvious concern though he, too, was silent, as was Norr.

"There is another way," Keegan said quickly, an idea springing into his head that could solve everything.

"Norr," he said, turning to the big man, "you promised Hadawas you would give him something to defeat the Danaan army. So what if the Guardian vows to help the clans win the war?"

"Do you have that kind of power?" Norr asked after considering it for a few seconds.

"I have guarded the Sword for seven centuries," the Guardian told him. "Its power flows through my veins. I can use it to bring victory to your people if that is what you wish."

Norr looked over at Scythe.

"Whatever you decide, I will stand with you," she told him, turning away from Jerrod to place a hand on Norr's arm.

He took a deep breath and held it a long, long time before letting it out.

"Go to Hadawas," he told the Guardian. "Tell him you will help my people. And we will go after Cassandra and the Crown."

Chapter 32

RAVEN'S EYES SNAPPED open, and she knew something had gone very wrong with her plan. The Guardian had left his lair and was coming in her direction.

Did Jerrod see through my disguise?

She'd been switching back and forth between the forms of Hadawas and Berlen for weeks; ever since she'd given up hope of getting the Crown. Surrounded by the gullible Easterners, she'd become sloppy and careless. Instead of taxing her waning strength with a true spell of transformation, she'd started hiding her identity with a simple illusion—one the monk's Sight had almost seen through when he she had first greeted him as Berlen.

During the trek over the mountains she'd been more careful, but she knew Jerrod had sensed something unusual about Hadawas. He was suspicious of her, constantly on guard and watching for betrayal. That was one of the reasons she hadn't tried to take the Ring by force though she'd sensed it dangling from the young wizard's neck.

The Guardian was the other reason. The Ring couldn't help her defeat him; in his lair the power of the Sword would dull and mute the other Talisman, making it almost useless. So she had tried to manipulate Jerrod and his companions into doing what she couldn't: getting the Sword from the titan. She'd led them through the mountains, using her power to keep the savage yeti at bay, before sending them on ahead alone once she was certain they would reach their goal.

She'd planned to take the Ring and the Sword both when the four mortals—bound by Norr's promise—returned. With two of Daemron's three Talismans in her possession, Orath would have no choice but to welcome her back . . . assuming she didn't simply use their power to destroy him and become the Slayer's new right hand.

But something had gone wrong with her plan, and it was the Immortal titan—not the humans—who was coming for her.

There isn't much time.

The Sun Blade warriors escorting her were milling about the cave, not paying any attention to the frail old chief resting in the corner. But when she stood up, they turned to her with looks of confusion and concern.

There was no longer any point in continuing the charade, so Raven didn't bother to say anything to them. She simply reached up to her face and began to peel away the outer shell of flesh and blood that enveloped her true form.

The Sun Blades stared in horror, then began screaming, unable to understand what was happening. As the last bits of muscle and skin fell to the floor with a wet plop, Raven fell on them.

In the close confines of the cave they never stood a chance. She tore into them with her hooked beak and the long talons on her fingers, a dark shadow moving too quickly for their pitiful mortal senses to follow. Blood splattered and sprayed the walls of the cave, the warriors' shrieks echoing off the walls as she gashed open deep, ragged wounds and ripped off their limbs. The carnage lasted only a minute, but Raven didn't kill her victims. Instead, she left them in mutilated, quivering—but still living—heaps on the floor.

She needed magic to stop the Guardian, but the Chaos in her blood had grown thin after so much time on the mortal side of the Legacy. To summon enough power, she'd need to perform a ritual to pierce the Legacy and draw on the flames of the Burning Sea. And for the ritual, she needed six still-beating hearts.

The Guardian had hunted this territory for centuries; the Sword kept him young and strong, but he still needed food to sustain himself. He knew every inch of every mountain in a twenty-mile radius, and when Jerrod described the cave where Hadawas was waiting for them he recognized it immediately.

He hadn't told the mortals that giving them the Sword would cause him to rapidly age and die. He hadn't told them that once he left his lair, his body would no longer be impervious to weapons. It had no relevance to their quest, and the Guardian had grown weary of the mortal world. In passing the Sword on to them, he had served his purpose. And though he could already feel his strength slowly ebbing away, it would be weeks before his body began to falter.

Yet it wasn't just his physical strength that would aid the clans. After so many centuries watching over the Talisman, some of the power of Daemron's Sword now flowed through him. He projected an aura that would inspire his allies and demoralize their foes—a power that could turn any mortal battle though doing so would weaken him further. But the Guardian had sensed their cause was noble; sacrificing himself for their victory would be a fitting way for him to end his long, long life.

He loped across the valley, the powerful muscles in his legs propelling him across the terrain with incredible speed. In his right hand he clutched his heavy spear, the end now sharpened to a point where the Sword had sliced off the metal tip. When he reached the mountain on the other side he climbed straight up the face, leaping thirty feet in the air and using the massive fingers of his free hand to clutch and grab at holds, his grip never faltering on the uneven, ice-covered rock.

It was only when he stepped onto the wide, windswept plateau that he felt something was wrong. There was a foul stench in the air; a smell he recognized from when Cassandra had first come to him.

The winged huntress!

Suddenly alert, he sensed the dark presence of Chaos—a powerful spell had been unleashed on the plateau. And then the trap was sprung.

An army of yeti swarmed down from the cliffs surrounding the plateau, their howling laugh drowning out all other sound. Hundreds and hundreds of the creatures poured in from all sides, their bloodlust enraged by the Chaos that hung like smoke in the air.

With his retreat cut off, the Guardian realized escape was impossible. The yeti barely reached up to his knees, and he met the first wave with a mighty roar. Swinging his spear in a wide swath, he sent their bodies flying.

Normally the yeti were cowardly scavengers who would flee a superior foe. But driven by the spell, even his Immortal fury could not slow their advance. They leapt at him with suicidal recklessness, using their claws to latch on to his arms and legs, then clambering up his chest and back. First five, then ten, then twenty.

Dropping his spear, the Guardian flailed wildly, clutching and grabbing at the savage beasts as they bit and scratched his now-vulnerable flesh. Each time he seized one of the creatures and hurled it away, two more would take its place. They covered his massive body like a squirming blanket until the sheer weight of their numbers dragged him down.

Unable to stand, the titan rolled, turning himself into a living juggernaut and crushing the yeti with his bulk. The unexpected move threw the howling mass of bodies into momentary disarray, and the Guardian sprang to his feet. Bleeding from a hundred bites and gashes, he began to run, swatting furiously at the creatures as they flew at him.

He couldn't bat them all away, and once again they threatened to overwhelm him. But somehow he kept his feet until he reached the mouth of the large cavern below the plateau's surface. The entrance was barely wide enough for him to fit, and he wouldn't be able to stand up inside. But if he made it to the cave, the yeti would only be able to come at him from one direction and with limited numbers.

Stumbling, he managed to pull himself into the steep tunnel, sliding face-first down the incline to the floor below with a dozen of the creatures still clinging to him. He quickly shook them free, snapping their necks with his bare hands and crushing the skulls of those that lost their grip and fell to the floor beneath his boots.

To his surprise, the yeti didn't follow him in. There was only a sliver of light in the cave, spilling in from the tunnel's mouth above. Yet it was enough for the Guardian's eyes to see.

The walls were stained with blood. Six freshly slain bodies were scattered about the room, five arranged at the points of a pentagram traced in blood on the floor and the last in the center. The bodies had been dismembered and their chests torn open, as if their hearts had been ripped out while they watched on in helpless horror.

The stench of death filled the cave, and he knew this was the epicenter of the spell that had driven the yeti to madness. He could feel them out there, prowling anxiously around the mouth of the cave, howling in frustration but too afraid to enter.

He was safe, for the moment. Or so he thought. And then the cave collapsed, burying him under countless tons of ice and stone.

The yeti scattered as Raven approached the mouth of the now-sealed cave. She could sense the Guardian below her, entombed but miraculously still alive.

He knows I am here, she thought. *Just as he sensed me near his lair, he can feel me standing above his grave.*

And then suddenly the earth beneath her feet began to tremble. At first she thought it was an aftershock of the quake she had unleashed. But when it happened again, she realized with amazement that the Guardian was trying to dig himself out.

Ignoring the yeti army that now covered the entire plateau, she began a soft, rhythmic chant, calling on the last few drops of the Chaos she had summoned with the gruesome ritual in the cave.

A cloud of fine green mist formed around her, settling slowly to the snow which melted at its touch. The mist seeped into the rock, working its way down toward the still-struggling titan.

"Sleep," Raven whispered, calling on the same magic the Old Gods had used to send the Chaos Spawn into deep hibernation centuries ago. "Sleep forever."

After a few more seconds the ground stopped shaking under her feet as the Guardian succumbed to the spell.

Exhausted, Raven knew she needed to rest before she dared use any more magic to track the Ring and the Sword. But she had a suspicion as to what had happened to them.

"Find the humans!" she called out to the yeti army that filled the plateau. "Find them and tear them apart!"

Chapter 33

SCYTHE AND THE others didn't set out immediately from the Guardian's cave. They rested for half a day, recovering and recuperating before setting off in pursuit of Cassandra.

They headed west: the only thing east of the Guardian's lair was an impassable range of mountains that marked the edge of the mortal world, just as the ever-thickening forest, the seemingly infinite desert, and the whirlpools and krakens of the sea bordered the north, south, and west respectively. But while the Guardian was angling north to meet Hadawas in his cave, they were heading south in the hopes of picking up the young woman's trail before she reached Callastan.

The way was difficult, but not as arduous as the journey Hadawas had led them on. Jerrod was leading the way, with Keegan following close behind. Scythe and Norr brought up the rear, the big clan chief carrying the legendary blade across his back.

Jerrod had wanted to carry the Sword himself, of course, but Scythe had strenuously objected. The fanatical monk was already arrogant and dangerous enough; the Sword could push him over the edge.

She'd tasted the Talisman's power when she used it against the Guardian—she'd felt invincible, unstoppable. But she'd also felt the hunger for battle, for what use was it being invincible if you had no enemy to defeat?

It was unlike anything she'd ever experienced before—an adrenaline rush amplified a thousand times, combined with a heightened awareness so sharp it felt like she could see through time, peering into the future to anticipate and counter her enemy's attacks before they happened.

She'd also been filled with a fierce confidence that bordered on the irrational; even the mighty Guardian had seemed like a helpless child before her. It was exhilarating, intoxicating and—looking back on it—a little bit terrifying.

It's no wonder Daemron felt like he could challenge the Gods, she thought. Then, a second later, *Does Keegan get that same kind of rush from using the Ring?*

Norr had suggested that Keegan carry the blade, but Jerrod had worried that the young man was still mentally drained from using the Ring. The Sword could heal most physical wounds—though it couldn't restore the young mage's lost hand—but it wasn't able to replenish his will.

Having felt the Sword's power, Scythe had to agree with the monk. And based on what the Guardian told them, if they caught up to Cassandra, they'd need the combined power of both Talismans to defeat the demons hunting her. It was hard to imagine Keegan's using the Ring and the Sword at the same time.

She'd been the one to actually suggest Norr carry it. Partly because she knew Jerrod would object simply on principle if she offered up her own name, and partly because she was a little afraid of what the Sword had made her feel. She didn't like the idea of surrendering herself to an inanimate object, even one created by the Old Gods.

Norr won't lose himself in the Sword's power. It won't consume him like it might with the rest of us.

Out of all of them Norr was best suited to carry the Talisman. He was a warrior, but he was humble and self-sacrificing. He put others before himself. Scythe imagined the Guardian shared many of the same characteristics as Norr, which was probably why he had been chosen by the Old Gods to watch over the weapon.

Was Norr the reason he changed his mind about us?

Norr had put himself in harm's way to defend their fallen foe from Scythe's wrath. If he hadn't stopped her, she would have removed the Guardian's head with a single blow of the very blade he was sworn to defend.

Norr's always doing that. Reining me in. Keeping me from doing things in the heat of the moment that I'll regret. He doesn't just save others from my anger; he saves me from myself.

Fortunately, Jerrod had agreed with her suggestion, a further testament to Norr's character. And in the end her lover had, reluctantly, accepted the burden.

For years he refused to carry a weapon, now he's armed with the greatest weapon ever forged. No wonder he's hesitant.

After several hours the massive peak that housed the Guardian's lair was already behind them, though according to the directions they'd been given, they wouldn't reach the Serpent's Tongue— a narrow, twisting pass that would finally leave the mountains behind them—until sometime tomorrow.

Then we still have to cross the frozen plains and the entire breadth of the Southlands, Scythe reminded herself.

But at least they wouldn't have to worry about squads of Inquisitors anymore—not while they had the Sword. Having felt the weapon's power, Scythe knew it would take an entire army to stop them now.

Keegan woke the second morning from a mercifully dreamless sleep. He'd feared the presence of two of Daemron's Talismans might trigger an endless onslaught of dreams and visions, but that hadn't happened.

Chaos is nothing if not unpredictable.

Despite this, he couldn't shake a sense of foreboding as they set out. The sky was dark and the wind was both strong and cold, but it wasn't a storm he feared.

Though it had been muted in the Guardian's lair, he'd unleashed the power of the Ring. He'd summoned Chaos into the mortal world and set it free, and he feared the consequences of the backlash.

Maybe there won't be any. Maybe the Sword somehow absorbed it.

A reasonable assumption, but one Keegan couldn't quite get himself to believe. Part of him still believed something terrible was about to happen. And then they heard the distant howling of the yeti, rising over a brief lull in the wind tearing at their clothes.

Jerrod looked back, his normally expressionless face registering both surprise and concern. The Guardian had told them the yeti stayed only in the north; he'd assured them they wouldn't have to worry about the creatures if they went south after Cassandra.

Backlash!

"Everybody else heard that, right?" Scythe asked, and the others nodded.

The wind had picked up again, drowning out the cries for the moment. But there was no mistaking the insane, gibbering laughter.

"Any idea how close?" Jerrod asked.

"Their cries echo strangely in the mountains," Norr said with a shake of his head. "But it would be wise to pick up our pace."

The monk didn't need to be told twice, and they pushed on. Without saying it, they all knew the yeti were coming for them; probably drawn far from their natural territory by the irresistible call of the Sword itself.

Each time the wind died, they could hear the disturbing calls.

There must be hundreds of them, Keegan realized. *The howls are constant. They don't ever stop; we just can't hear them unless the wind is down.*

That changed after another hour. The mad, keening laughter was now strong enough to rise above the wind in a constant, endless wail. There was no doubt they were getting closer.

"The Serpent's Tongue is just ahead," Jerrod called out, hoping to inspire them to greater speed with a few words of encouragement. "If we get clear of the mountains, the yeti might not dare to follow us onto the plains."

Keegan didn't necessarily believe that was true, but he didn't object as they picked up the pace yet again, moving at almost a full run, their packs thumping against their backs.

Heavy black clouds blotted out the sun and a thick, wet sleet began to fall. It turned the ground under their feet into a treacherous trail of ice and slick rock, impeding their efforts. The yeti grew steadily louder, and Keegan realized that even driven by fear and desperation, they weren't going to make it.

The sleet turned to snow as the temperature dropped. The wind gusted and swirled, whipping up snow and ice that stung their eyes. But it wasn't strong enough to drown out the howls of their pursuers.

"There!" Jerrod shouted, pointing up ahead. "The Serpent's Tongue!"

Ahead of them stood an enormous heap of rock, ice, and snow. It looked as if two great mountains had been smashed together, crumbling into a pile of debris hundreds of yards thick. It stretched for miles to the left and right, and upward as far as the eye could see.

Maybe that's what actually happened, Keegan thought. *The Cataclysm reshaped the land.*

It would take days, if not weeks, to climb or go around the obstacle. But as they drew closer, Keegan saw a single hairline crack running through the center—a fissure in the rock that went all the way through to the other side. The Serpent's Tongue.

Glancing back over his shoulder, Keegan realized the yeti were now close enough to actually see. They rolled down from the rocks and slopes behind them, a writhing, twisting, screaming mass of white fur, claws, and teeth.

Calling on the final reserves of their strength, the four made a final sprint for the pass. When they reached the mouth of the pass, the yeti were only a few hundred yards behind and closing fast.

The Serpent's Tongue was only a few yards across, hemmed in on either side by walls of ice and snow too tall to see the top. It twisted and turned sharply, and the ground was littered with piles of ice and rock that had dislodged from the high walls and shattered on the ground below.

It's hopeless, Keegan saw. *The yeti move faster than us over this terrain. They'll climb along the walls and come at us from above. We'll never make it.*

Instead of plunging into the winding pass, Keegan stopped at the entrance and turned back to face the horde.

"What are you doing?" Scythe screamed as she almost ran into him.

"Go!" he shouted, waving her and Norr on past. "Go!"

The pair hesitated, but as he reached up for the Ring on his neck they understood and took off. Once again Keegan struggled to get the Talisman over a finger with only one hand, but it was easier than the last time.

The power of the Ring ripped through him, knocking him off his feet. It wasn't as strong as it had been in the Danaan Forest, but it was far, far greater than what he had felt in the Guardian's lair.

For a second he thought the Ring would overwhelm him, and he teetered on the brink of insanity. But he had used the Ring before. He knew he was strong enough to master it, and he slowly dragged his consciousness back from the precipice. Then, still lying on the ground where he had collapsed, he began to gather Chaos.

The yeti horde was closer now—only fifty yards away, their

shrieking laughter almost deafening. There wasn't time for sub-tlety or precision, and even if there was, Keegan's entire focus was on trying to keep the Chaos building inside from breaking free in a single explosion that blew his frail mortal shell apart.

Gritting his teeth against the energy threatening to burst through his skin, he grabbed Rexol's staff from the snow at his side and used it to haul himself back to his feet. Then he opened his mouth and screamed.

His voice was transformed into a blast of blinding blue light that rippled out in a concussive wave, washing over the onrushing yeti. The front ranks were pulverized, hit so hard the fur was ripped from their flesh as their bones shattered into dust. Those close behind were lifted from their feet and thrown a hundred feet through the air, spewing blood from their nostrils and throats as their internal organs liquefied from the impact. Those farther back—by far the greatest number—were knocked back and sent sprawling to the ground, shaken and stunned but not mortally wounded.

In the wake of the spell Keegan toppled forward, still conscious but too weak to break his fall as he landed face-first in the snow.

Jerrod didn't hear Keegan's scream—the spell directed it at the yeti and away from his friends—but he felt its power as the ground beneath his feet heaved and shook, sending a shower of snow and small rocks to rain down on the narrow pass.

Scythe and Norr, like Jerrod, had retreated into the safety of the first few feet of the Serpent's Tongue as Keegan unleashed his spell. Now they turned and rushed back to help their fallen com-rade. But Jerrod got their first, his limbs propelled by the internal-ized Chaos he had spent decades in the Monastery learning to control.

The yeti were no longer howling; those that survived were

dazed, temporarily paralyzed by Keegan's spell. How long that would last, the monk had no idea.

Reaching the young mage's side, he yanked the Ring off his finger lest the Talisman's power run wild and destroy the Savior. Keegan's eyes were open and alert at first, but they fluttered closed as Jerrod removed the Ring.

He was instinctively keeping the Chaos in check, Jerrod realized. *He's getting stronger!*

But that would mean little if the yeti decided to continue their pursuit once they recovered. Jerrod shed his pack and stripped off Keegan's own, then effortlessly slung the young man up over one shoulder. With his free hand, he scooped up the supply packs, knowing that without food and extra blankets to stay warm they'd never survive the journey. And then he raced off back into the Serpent's Tongue. As he expected, Norr and Scythe were quick to follow.

Even carrying Keegan and both packs, Jerrod was able to navigate the uneven ground faster than the others, and Scythe and Norr were soon left far behind. The Frozen East limited his abilities, yet his Sight still gave him surer footing, and his training still gave him far greater reserves of energy than those outside the Order. Yet he was only halfway through the Serpent's Tongue when he heard the howls of the yeti begin once more.

He'd hoped the beasts would flee in terror after witnessing Keegan's power, but something compelled them to ignore their fear.

Is their hunger for the Sword really so great? Or is something else to blame?

Their cries were tentative at first, confused and disoriented. But they quickly transformed into the familiar call of the hunt, and Jerrod didn't need his Sight to know they were being followed into the pass.

He reached the other end a few minutes later, the rock walls on either side stopping abruptly as the Serpent's Tongue spilled out onto a wide, snow-covered plain of gently rolling hills. He tossed the packs to the ground, then lay Keegan down before turning and rushing back to aid the others.

Norr and Scythe were three-quarters of the way through the pass, standing shoulder to shoulder with their backs to Jerrod. They had shed their supply packs; the bags lay at their feet as the pair braced themselves for the inevitable battle. The young woman had her daggers out, and Norr held the hilt of Daemron's sword with both hands, one clasped overtop the other. The silver blade seemed to pulse with a barely visible red glow.

The monk raced up to stand with them, the pass just wide enough at this point for all three to stand abreast.

"Thought you ditched us," Scythe snarled, not taking her eyes from the pass ahead.

"I had to get Keegan to safety," he answered. "We cannot let any of these monsters get past us—he is still unconscious."

There wasn't time for Scythe to say anything back before the first few yeti—those that had recovered quicker than the rest—suddenly materialized around the closest bend in the pass.

Six of the creatures threw themselves at the three humans, snarling and spitting. Scythe, in the unusual situation of facing an opponent even smaller than herself, abandoned her usual helter-skelter tactics and held her ground to meet the charge head-on. She used her blades to slap away the swiping claws of the first beast then drove her knives deep into the fur-covered belly and sliced it open. The corpse fell at her feet, a wispy cloud of steam rising from the wound as warm blood met the cold air.

Jerrod employed a similarly direct method, driving his foot straight forward in a front kick that caved in the face of the nearest yeti before it was close enough to use its claws.

But it was Norr who truly blunted the assault. Instead of standing to meet the charge, he stepped forward, Daemron's blade carving a wide arc in front of him. The front stroke decapitated one yeti and chopped another in half diagonally from shoulder to hip. The backswing took out two more with similar ease.

"Fall back!" Jerrod shouted, and the three of them scampered backward through the pass.

They got around the next bend before another five yeti reached them. Three came straight for them, but the other two scampered up the sides of the pass, their claws easily finding purchase on the sheer vertical surface. In seconds they were thirty feet up, high above the heads of the humans on the ground. But instead of attacking from above, they kept on going, heading for the exit of the Serpent's Tongue and the unconscious young man just beyond.

"Keegan!" Jerrod shouted, wheeling off in pursuit.

"Go help him," Norr shouted at Scythe. "I can hold the pass!"

Scuttling along the wall the yeti were fast, but Jerrod was still able to run them down. He caught them just as they reached the end of the pass, and when they dropped back to the ground he was waiting.

A quick flurry of punches broke the ribs of one, driving a splinter of bone into its heart as it crumpled in a heap. The other leapt on Jerrod's back and sunk its teeth into his shoulder as he targeted its companion, but couldn't pull out fast enough to keep the monk from seizing it by the fur. He dropped to the ground, twisting so that his weight came down on top of the yeti, momentarily stunning it. Then he spun so that his feet were facing the other way and scissored his legs around the yeti's head. Squeezing with his knees and arching his back, he snapped the beast's neck.

As he sprang to his feet three more yeti appeared; like their brethren they had gone up and over Norr rather than face the big man's wrath head-on. But Scythe was hot on their heels, and she dropped two with her blades in the same amount of time it took Jerrod to eliminate the third.

The battle had drawn them past the mouth of the pass and out onto the plateau beyond. Peeking back into the Serpent's Tongue, Jerrod saw Norr slowly making his way toward them in a fighting retreat under the crush of the relentless assault. He was drenched in blood though almost none of it was his own. Daemron's Sword was a blur of motion, even to Jerrod's mystical Sight, raining death down upon the enemy. But though scores were falling, hundreds more pressed forward, clogging the pass with their numbers. Several dozen had taken to the walls, crawling above Norr's reach and past him like a swarm of insects about to be disgorged onto the plain.

The barbarian glanced back over his shoulder and in his gaze Jerrod could see what he meant to do.

"Norr!" Scythe screamed as she turned and saw him surrounded on all sides—front, back, and above—by the gibbering, laughing yeti.

She took a step toward him, but fell forward as Jerrod dropped her from behind with a quick blow to the back of her knee. The strike wasn't meant to injure; it was only meant to slow her down.

At the same time Norr raised Daemron's Sword high above his head then chopped down into the side of the pass. The rock exploded where the blade hit, sending a cloud of debris raining down and a thunderous boom echoing through the pass.

Norr struck a second time, ignoring the enemies all around him, releasing the power of Old Magic. The noise that followed was so loud it caused the earth to tremble, and instead of a cloud of shattered rock the blow unleashed a shower of bright red sparks. The reverberations shook the entire mountain, bringing down a deluge of ice and stone as the walls of the pass began to crumble.

The climbing yeti stopped their advance, clutching desperately to their perches to keep from being dislodged.

Scythe was back on her knees, but instead of turning on Jerrod she stared in horror at the man she loved. For the third time Norr raised the blade and brought it crashing down into the rock. A brilliant flash of crimson exploded out and a wide fissure erupted in the stone as it split. The crack raced up the side of the rock face, spiderwebbing outward with a high-pitched, earsplitting shriek that sent the yeti into a frenzied panic.

"No!" Scythe screamed as Norr turned toward them and threw Daemron's Sword.

It hurtled toward them, spinning end over end before landing tip down in the snow a few feet away. And then, with a great roar, the entire pass collapsed on itself, burying Norr and the entire yeti army under an avalanche of rock and snow.

Chapter 34

DESPITE BEING TRAPPED inside the Crown, Rexol saw everything. Far more than Cassandra, at least. For even though his perceptions were limited to the people and places close to her, the young woman was blinded by the exhaustion and terror of her desperate flight.

Distracted by their slaughter of the Inquisitors, the Crawling Twins had once again fallen behind. Even the Minions weren't fast enough to keep up with Cassandra on horseback. But horses needed to eat and sleep; they grew tired after days of endless travel. The abominations chasing them did not.

To keep ahead of them, Cassandra had gone without sleep for days. She'd switched her horse twice, but the mount she was on now was already starting to tire. And still the Crawling Twins were coming.

Cassandra had given in to her most primal fears, and Rexol knew he was partly to blame. The spell he'd used to drive the Twins into a frenzy so they'd attack the Inquisitors had affected the young woman as well. There was still a powerful connection between her and her former Master, and he had inadvertently sent her into a prolonged state of almost mindless panic.

At first, Rexol had thought this might make her easier to control. He'd tried to convince her to place the Crown atop her head, inserting his own words and ideas into her mind. But the fear response he'd triggered made her instinctively reject the foreign presence, her consciousness fleeing from him just as her body fled from the Twins.

Yet some part of her was still rational and sane. She was still heading toward Callastan. And she was still careful to give a wide berth to towns and villages when possible, lest she unwittingly throw more innocent victims into the path of the Minions. And little by little, her sanity was returning.

How long until she realizes Yasmin has begun another Purge? he wondered.

Through Cassandra's senses, he'd smelled the oily scent of burning flesh as she crept past villages in the dead of night. He'd heard the crackling of massive bonfires. And he'd noticed a distinct lack of any other Chaos users once they entered the Southlands.

Like calls to like. I should be able to sense them—the echo of briar witches casting spells in their camps outside town, or the faint stirrings of a court mage enacting a ritual to bring good luck to a wealthy patron's latest business venture.

Rexol had always looked on such people with contempt and scorn; they were not true wizards. What they could do barely counted as magic in his eyes. But despite the frailty of their power, he'd always felt their presence in the background. The touch of Chaos was unmistakable and hard to ignore. Now, however, those with any kind of power had gone into hiding. Any magic they used would only be to hide their true nature from the Order's Inquisitors.

Perhaps this is a good thing, Rexol realized.

If the Order was busy hunting down rogue Chaos users, they wouldn't be looking for Cassandra. And average folk would be less likely to approach or even speak about a lone woman riding through little-used paths and trails—despite what the Order believed, most people would rather not expose others to the wrath of the Inquisitors.

If Yasmin was too busy with her own petty political wars to
interfere in what truly mattered, Cassandra might actually make it
to Callastan without getting discovered. Though what would happen once they reached the city even Rexol couldn't guess.

Vaaler could see the exhaustion on the faces of the clan warriors
as he slopped food into their bowls. It had become a permanent
feature, not just for the ones coming back from the battlefield, but
also those heading out to fight again.

For days they had been engaged in an endless series of hit-and-
run battles with the Danaan, rotating their warriors in and out in
a desperate attempt to halt the enemy progress before they reached
the massive refugee camp at the Giant's Maw. But nothing they
did seemed to slow their progress.

The Danaan army had changed tactics after the first battle,
abandoning the widespread patrols and moving as a single, tightly
bunched unit that marched inexorably forward, day after day. It
quickly became clear they were following the trail of the refugees,
plotting a direct course for the Giant's Maw. There was no sub-
tlety or tactical genius in this decision, and at first Vaaler thought
the enemy was making a critical mistake. He knew exactly where
the Danaan were headed, and—given their near-constant rate of
progress—he knew exactly how long it would take for them to
reach any given point along that journey.

Without having to worry about enemy patrols scouting ahead,
the clans were able to set devastating ambushes, carefully choosing
the perfect terrain at various points along the route and setting up
their warriors in precise locations. Each of these traps had been an
incredible success, with Danaan casualties outnumbering those of
the clans by nearly five to one. But still the enemy refused to
change course.

The Danaan were only a few days' march away from the Giant's Maw, and their numbers were still too many for the clans to meet in a full-on battle. So Shalana had redoubled their efforts, sending her troops out in rotating wave after wave. Each group was only able to grab a few hours' rest before having to rejoin the fight, and the relentless battles were taking their toll.

Had they been fighting any ordinary foe, they would have broken the Danaan ranks and routed them long ago. But no matter how he tried, Vaaler couldn't think of a way to overcome the ogre. Each time the clans began to gain the upper hand on the battlefield, the beast would come loping over and single-handedly turn the tide. So many had fallen to the beast in the first few encounters that the clans were now instructed to retreat at first sight rather than attempt to engage the slime-covered monster.

Someone tapped him on the shoulder as he continued to ladle thin stew into the bowls of the endless line of hungry, weary soldiers.

"Shalana is back," the young man told him. "I can do this if you want to see her."

Vaaler nodded his thanks and abandoned his post. He still couldn't bring himself to fight his own people; he didn't know if he could look them in the eye as he spilled their blood. So he had taken to supporting the warriors in other ways besides offering tactical advice to Shalana and her thane-chiefs. He helped with the food; he helped set up and take down the mobile camp they used as their staging operation; he helped haul the supply sleds to each new location.

But I won't fight for them. Do they resent me for that?

He found Shalana huddled by a peat fire, warming herself with the flame. Seeing Vaaler, she motioned him over. Reaching her side, he saw that her eyes were sunken. Her face and clothes were caked with dirt and grime. She smelled of sweat, blood, and death.

"How many this time?" he asked as he sat down beside her.

"Forty on our side before the ogre came and we scattered. A few hundred on their side."

"They can't go on like this much longer," Vaaler said, shaking his head. "Not with those kinds of losses. Not with winter coming and no supplies.

"They can," Shalana answered sadly. "Even with their losses, they still outnumber us more than two to one. Without the ogre we might have a chance, but with that creature in their ranks . . ."

She trailed off, not saying what they both knew.

"Maybe Norr and Hadawas will bring back the Sword," Vaaler said, though he knew Shalana still doubted the Talisman's existence.

"I realize why so many of the rank and file cling to that ridiculous idea," she whispered. "In the absence of all hope even a fool's tale was welcome."

"What other choice is there?" Vaaler asked.

"The Giant's Maw borders the mountains at the edge of the world. We could tell Roggen to start leading the refugees up into the peaks. They could hide up there for weeks."

"That only means they will starve or freeze before the enemy slaughters them," Vaaler noted.

Shalana sighed.

"After our first victory, I truly thought we could win this war," she said.

"So did I," Vaaler admitted.

"I thought the Danaan would turn back by now," he said, his voice rising with anger. "I don't understand how the Queen can keep driving them forward with so many dying each day!"

"She is bent on revenge," Shalana said simply. "It poisons our hearts and minds. It makes us do things that make no sense."

"She wants to punish me," Vaaler said, bowing his head. "I betrayed my people. My own flesh and blood. Maybe if I surrender, they will turn back."

"You know that's not true," Shalana told him. "If it was, you'd have already done it. I know you."

Vaaler expected her to say something like, "Don't blame yourself," but she didn't bother to waste her words. She understood platitudes couldn't heal the complicated mixture of guilt, anger, and shame that churned inside him. Instead, she just sat with him, offering the comfort of her companionship.

Without allowing himself time to reconsider, Vaaler suddenly reached out and clasped her hand in his own. He'd never acted on his feelings for her in any physical way before, and she stiffened at his touch. But just when he thought she was going to pull away, he felt her relax and she leaned over to rest her head on his shoulder.

Despite their grim surroundings and the crushing inevitability of their fate, Vaaler's heart suddenly felt lighter.

"The Sword is real," he promised. "It can save us. There is still hope."

"Sitting here with you," she whispered softly in his ear, "I can almost believe it."

Orath resented having to answer the Queen's summons; he was not some pet that ran each time the master called. But he still needed the Danaan army. If the wizard who had stolen the Ring was waiting for them in the refugee camp, the ogre would need to focus all its power on stopping him. As devastating as the beast was, it couldn't defeat the Destroyer of Worlds and an army of barbarians at the same time.

If the Destroyer of Worlds is even still with them.

The trail of the Ring had gone cold, and Orath was no longer completely certain they were heading in the right direction. Rianna's vision had shown the Destroyer of Worlds in league with the Eastern clans, but Orath now wondered if she had been misled or deceived.

He'd expected the Danaan army's wanton destruction of the Eastern lands would draw the wizard out. But the mortal was either a coward too afraid to show himself, or too cunning to fall for such a ploy, and he stayed hidden.

Or he's abandoned the clans to their fate and fled into the mountains.

If that was the case, then once the clans were wiped out Orath would command the ogre to hunt the fugitive Chaos mage down.

And then I will have no further use for you, my Queen.

He entered her tent without rapping on the outside and waiting for her to invite him in, a breach of protocol none of her mortal subjects would ever have dared. But either she didn't notice or she knew better than to take him to task for it. The Queen was standing with her back to him, staring at the blank canvas wall at the rear of the tent.

"I wanted to speak with you alone," she said without turning around.

To Orath's surprise, he and Rianna were actually alone. Not even the ever-present Andar was lurking in the shadowy corners.

"You seem troubled, my Queen," he said in his most ingratiating voice, coming up close behind her.

"I was walking among the troops," she said, still facing away from him. "Hoping to lift their spirits."

"Their spirits will be lifted once we crush the armies of the clans and defeat the Destroyer of Worlds."

Rianna didn't answer at first but brought her hands up to rub her temples.

"The soldiers say the ogre feasts on the corpses of the fallen immediately after each battle," Rianna whispered, and from behind Orath saw her shiver.

"The creature has to feed," he said. "Why do you care if he defiles the bodies of your enemy?"

"They say he eats both barbarian and Danaan flesh. Some even say they've heard screams and cries as he feeds on the wounded before we can find them and bring them back from the battle-field."

The ogre likes his meat fresh and warm, Orath thought, but he had the sense not to say it aloud.

"You told me you could control the beast," Rianna said, suddenly spinning around to face him. "I want this to stop!"

"That is not possible," the Minion explained. "Andar's interference in the summoning ritual weakened my mastery over the ogre. If I keep the beast from feeding, hunger will make it turn against us."

Rianna nodded slowly, as if she had expected this answer.

"My war council believes we should turn back."

Orath tilted his head to the side and reached up to run his long fingernails over his bald, batlike skull.

"You had a meeting of the war council without me?" he asked.

"I feared they would not speak openly in your presence," she told him.

You mean Andar feared it, Orath thought, realizing where the idea must have originated.

"In only a few days this will be over," the Minion reminded her. "Victory is too close to turn back now."

"Each day hundreds of my people die," she said, her voice rising. "Starvation and exposure take as many as the savages kill in their raids. And in this frozen wasteland we cannot even bury or burn our dead. We must leave the bodies of friends and family for a monster to devour!"

"You told me you were willing to do anything to get back the Ring," Orath reminded her, his voice calm and cold. "This is the price you must pay to stop the Destroyer of Worlds."

"I fear the Destroyer of Worlds is no longer with them," the Queen said softly. "I cannot feel the Ring's presence anymore. I no longer dream of his face."

"Chaos is weak in this land," Orath cautioned her. "And your connection to the Ring is fading with each day it is no longer in your possession. You must not rely on your visions to guide you."

"But what if the Destroyer of Worlds is no longer with the clans?" she pressed, echoing his own earlier thoughts. "Then all this will be for nothing."

"Once the barbarians are crushed," Orath promised, "we can find the Destroyer of Worlds at our leisure. He cannot hide; the ogre has the scent of the Ring. The Talisman will be ours once more if you listen to me."

He could see indecision in the Queen's eyes. She was hesitant. Uncertain. Lost. The fury that had burned inside her was gone, snuffed out by the brutal reality of waging a winter war against the Frozen East. But with her resolve fading, her spirit was now weak.

Orath's hands lashed out and seized her by the shoulders, pulling her close. He leaned his face in toward hers; the Queen's eyes went wide with horror and her face twisted up in revulsion. She opened her lips to scream, and Orath breathed deep into her mouth—a black cloud that crawled down her throat and into her lungs, smothering her voice.

He let go and Rianna stumbled back, coughing and choking on the Minion's vile essence. Orath watched her struggle, patiently allowing the spell to take effect. Using magic to bind her completely to his will wasn't something he wanted to do—every time he called upon Chaos on this side of the Legacy, he grew a little weaker. But her current mental state made her vulnerable; she wouldn't be able to fight him like she could have earlier. And even though controlling both the Queen and the ogre at the same time would further tax his slowly waning power, it would only be for a few more days. The reward was worth the risk.

Rianna had stopped coughing and was standing up straight, her eyes unfocused and her head slowly turning from side to side as she stared around the tent without any hint of recognition.

"Tell the war council we will go on," Orath said, reaching out with his mind to twist and bend her now-malleable thoughts. "Tell them we will see this through to the end. We will not turn back until every last barbarian is dead."

The Queen nodded, the glazed look in her eyes slipping away as her reeling mind latched on to and embraced Orath's projected will.

"The savages gave sanctuary to the Destroyer of Worlds," she said, snarling out the words. "For that they must be exterminated!"

Chapter 35

KEEGAN COULDN'T STOP looking over at Scythe as the three of them trudged across the empty, snow-covered plains. The weather here was slightly warmer than it had been in the mountain peaks, and they'd shed their outermost layer of clothes. They hadn't bothered to repack them; they'd simply left them behind, knowing they could make better time by traveling light.

Their pace was slow enough already, their minds unfocused as they struggled with the shock of Norr's loss. Yet he knew she was taking it far harder than he and Jerrod, and he was worried about her. He also couldn't help wondering if this was his fault.

I used the Ring twice. What if the backlash caused Norr's death?

Two days had passed since Norr's sacrifice had let the rest of them escape the yeti at the Serpent's Tongue. In the immediate aftermath of the avalanche, Scythe had thrown herself against the mountain of ice and snow, digging frantically at it with her daggers as if she could somehow reach Norr through the hundreds of tons of debris.

Keegan would have rushed to her side, but unleashing the Ring against the yeti had left him too weak to stand. He could only watch, helpless to offer any kind of support or comfort.

Eventually Jerrod did go to her, but only, Keegan noted, after first picking up Daemron's Sword.

"He's gone, Scythe," the monk had told her, reaching out to

put a restraining grip on her shoulder while still clutching the blade in his other hand.

She'd wheeled on him with hatred in her eyes, her razor-sharp blades held poised and ready for combat. Jerrod didn't even flinch.

"Why did you knock me down?" she demanded. "I could have gone to him! I could have helped him!"

"Then you would be dead, too," the monk had answered, his voice emotionless as ever.

"Maybe that's what I wanted!" she shouted.

"That's not what Norr wanted," Keegan had called out, still lacking the strength to stand.

"Use the Sword and get Keegan on his feet," Scythe had suddenly snapped, turning away from both of them and slipping her knives out of sight. "There's no reason to stay here."

Those were the last words she had spoken to either of them. Jerrod did use the Sword to help Keegan, placing the blade gently on his shoulder. The young mage had felt the strength returning to his limbs—enough to walk again. But he knew he was still too mentally spent to attempt calling on Chaos again anytime soon.

Fortunately, there were no signs of pursuit. Virtually all of the yeti had been trapped in the pass with Norr when it collapsed. And the handful that weren't would have had to spend days either going around or over the mountains that were falling farther and farther behind them.

After the first day, however, Keegan wasn't certain that was a good thing. If one or two of the yeti had somehow made it through to attack them, Scythe's warrior instincts might have kicked in and snapped her out of her fugue. Instead, she'd been completely uncommunicative.

For the past two days she hadn't spoken, made eye contact, or even acknowledged them with a nod. She simply walked along beside them, stopping when they stopped, eating when they ate, sleeping when they slept. But she didn't seem to be aware of what she was doing; everything was automatic and instinctual, as if her conscious mind had completely shut down.

Keegan understood the numbing emptiness of her grief; he'd gone through the same thing when his father had died. Vaaler had pulled him out of that black abyss, but he'd done it slowly. He'd given Keegan time to grieve. They needed to do the same for Scythe.

But you also need to let her know that she's not alone.

Jerrod was leading the way, Daemron's Sword lashed diagonally across his back with leather straps and each hand clutching one of the two remaining supply packs. He and Scythe followed close behind, walking side by side, though Keegan was giving her plenty of space.

He slowly sidled a few feet closer to her, then in his most comforting tone said, "It's okay to cry, Scythe. It might even help."

She didn't respond, but she turned her head to look at him with narrowed eyes, never breaking stride.

"I know how you feel," Keegan assured her. "I felt the same thing when I lost my father. Frustrated, helpless, angry. It's a terrible thing to watch someone close to you die and know you couldn't help them."

"You could have helped him," Scythe growled, coming to a sudden stop.

"I—there was nothing I could do," he stammered awkwardly, caught off guard not by the resentment in her voice but by the fact she had replied at all.

"You're a wizard. You could have used the Ring."

"I couldn't," Keegan protested, suddenly feeling guilty. "I was exhausted. Drained."

I couldn't help him. But his death could be my fault.

He opened his mouth, ready to admit his fears about the backlash from the Ring. But at the last instant he thought better of it and snapped his jaw shut.

"Some savior," Scythe snorted, turning away from him in disgust.

"Keegan is not to blame for Norr's death," Jerrod said, having dropped back to join the conversation. "You know that."

Unlike Keegan, there was no compassion or sympathy in his words. As always, his voice was cold and emotionless. The wizard also noted that Jerrod had dropped the supply packs he'd been carrying, leaving his hands free and ready.

"I do," Scythe agreed, turning back to them as a grotesque smile spread across her lips. "He's just your pawn. We all were. And it cost Norr his life."

"Norr recognized the truth," Jerrod countered. "After we fled Torian, he saw that Keegan was special. He chose to help him find his destiny."

"That's not true!" Scythe shouted. "He wanted to take the Sword back to Hadawas. But you convinced him to go after the Crown—and now he's dead!"

"We all cared for Norr," Keegan said, sensing her rising anger and trying to calm her down. "None of us wanted this to happen."

"But it worked out good for you, didn't it?" she snapped. "Norr's gone and now you get to swoop in to offer me comfort. Is that your plan, Keegan? Use my grief to make me fall in love with you?"

"I don't ... that's not what this is, Scythe!" he assured her. "Norr was my friend! I would never do anything to hurt him!" *Not on purpose.*

"And what about you?" she barked, wheeling on Jerrod. "You still think Keegan and I are connected somehow, don't you? You think we're both part of this prophecy you follow!"

"I do," Jerrod admitted.

"But Norr was just getting in the way," Scythe continued, her voice having risen to a yell. "He wasn't part of your plan. Now that he's gone, everything is just the way you always wanted it!"

"Norr's loss is a tragedy," Jerrod told her. "He was a great man, and he knew the value of our cause. He understood that compared to Keegan's destiny, his own life meant nothing."

"Nothing?!" Scythe shrieked, a wail of equal parts suffering and rage. "Nothing? He meant everything to me!"

From seemingly out of nowhere, the deadly twin razors materialized in her hands and she threw herself at Jerrod, moving so quickly Keegan didn't even have a chance to scream out a warning.

Jerrod sensed Scythe's growing anger, but he was still caught off guard by her sudden assault. He barely managed to avoid having his throat sliced, throwing himself back and turning his head to the side so that the first blade narrowly missed carving open his windpipe. The second blade managed to gouge a deep groove in his shoulder, but though painful, the wound was neither lethal nor incapacitating.

Scythe was still coming at him, her blades flickering and flashing in seemingly random patterns that confused and confounded his Sight. Unable to match her blow for blow, he threw himself into a succession of three back handsprings to get clear of her savage fury.

For an instant he feared she would turn on Keegan, and he cursed himself for leaving the young man exposed.

Something about the way she fights throws me off balance. Forces me into foolish mistakes.

Fortunately, her anger was focused on Jerrod, not Keegan, and she charged forward even as the wizard cried out after her to stop. But instead of resorting to his usual array of acrobatic punches, kicks, and flips, Jerrod reached over his shoulder and wrapped his hand around the hilt of Daemron's Sword.

With a flick of the wrist he severed the leather ties that bound it to his back and brought the weapon around to meet his foe. And instead of being faced with a disorienting, blurred figure of unpredictable violence and fury, the power of the Talisman allowed him to see Scythe with total clarity.

She seemed to be moving in slow motion: darting, ducking, feinting, and lunging as if the chill in the air had left her muscles half-frozen. Jerrod easily parried her blades, swatting them aside as nonchalantly as he would brush off a speck of dirt from his sleeve.

He turned to let Scythe's momentum send her careening past him, leaving her back completely exposed. As if it had a mind of its own, the blade thrust forward. But at the last instant Jerrod's Sight noticed the horrified expression on Keegan's face, and instead of running Scythe through, he turned the weapon so that he struck her between the shoulders with the flat of the blade.

The blow carried far more force than it should have, given the awkward angle of his thrust. Instead of a light tap, it drove the small woman forward and down, sending her hard face-first into the snow.

She was up in an instant though it seemed like an eternity to Jerrod's newly heightened senses. Spinning around, she rushed him again. This time Jerrod used Daemron's Sword to slap the blades from Scythe's hands with a pair of lightning-quick yet incredibly precise strokes that didn't even draw blood.

Stripped of her weapons, she kept coming at him like an animal, throwing herself toward his throat. Jerrod admired her tenacity, but he'd anticipated her move and had already reacted. Stepping to the side he once again brought the flat of the blade to bear, catching Scythe in the stomach and knocking the wind from her lungs.

She dropped to her knees with a loud grunt, clutching at her midsection and gasping for air. Then she raised her eyes and fixed Jerrod with a look of pure hatred.

"Do it!" she screamed. "Do it! Run me through! End this!"

Jerrod simply shook his head and stepped back, giving Keegan room to rush in and wrap himself protectively around the young woman.

She thrashed in his grasp until he reluctantly pulled away, then she slowly crumpled into a ball, tears flowing from her eyes and sobs racking her body.

Once again Keegan knelt and wrapped his arms around her, cradling her shoulders and rocking her gently back and forth. He didn't speak, and eventually she cried herself out, exhaustion overcoming grief as she closed her eyes and drifted off to sleep.

"Thank you for sparing her," Keegan said, looking up at Jerrod as he clutched the sleeping woman to his chest.

"I'll try to find somewhere close by where we can rest for the night," Jerrod said.

"She'll be better in the morning," the young wizard assured him. "You'll see. She'll be better tomorrow."

Jerrod didn't sleep that night. His awareness was intently focused on the two youngsters huddled together under the spare blankets, shivering in the hollow he'd carved out in the leeward side of a snowbank. And he prayed to the True Gods that Keegan was right.

Chapter 36

ANDAR COULD SEE there was something very wrong with the Queen. She spoke too slowly and she moved with jerky, unnatural motions. He'd first noticed it a few days ago and wondered if some strange illness had befallen her. Now, however, he suspected Orath was to blame.

The Minion never left Rianna's side anymore. Even when she slept, Orath stood watch outside her tent, like some deformed, nightmarish bodyguard.

He's done something to her, Andar realized, recognizing the signs. *Some type of foul magic that binds her to his will.*

But there was nothing Andar could do; not unless he could think of some way to get the Queen alone.

And then what? You have no power in this land.

The war council sensed it, too. He could see it in their eyes as they relayed their reports to the Queen. Before she had reacted to the reports of Danaan losses with a stoic concern; though she had never wavered from the course of war, it was obvious she understood the terrible cost.

Now she no longer seemed to care about what they said. Most of the time she seemed distant and distracted, as if she wasn't even really listening.

"The barbarians have nowhere left to run," Hexiff was explaining. "We've got them pinned up against the mountains."

"By my best estimates we still have nearly double their numbers," Pranya added. "They don't stand a chance, and their leaders know it."

"Perhaps if we offer them terms of surrender, we can achieve our final victory without further bloodshed," General Greznor suggested.

"Terms?" the Queen echoed, her eyes blinking rapidly as she seemed to snap to a sudden awareness. "What terms could they possibly meet that we would care about?"

"They have supplies," Bassi, the quartermaster, chimed in. "Food. Fuel for their fires. Extra blankets. We are out of everything."

"Even if we defeat them tomorrow—" Lormilar began, but the Queen cut him off.

"We *will* defeat them tomorrow!" she snapped. "We have an overwhelming force, and we have the ogre on our side!"

"Even so," the High Sorcerer continued after a respectful pause, "we do not have enough provisions to make it back to Ferlhame. Not without suffering heavy losses on the trip back home."

"Then we will crush them and take their supplies," the Queen insisted.

"If defeat is inevitable, they could destroy their own stores as a final blow against us," Pranya warned.

"The tribes often pay tribute to each other," Lormilar added. "The barbarians are used to buying off a superior foe. If we make this offer, they will accept."

"We are here because of the Destroyer of Worlds," the Queen reminded them, her head cocked to one side as if listening to a voice only she could hear. "They will never surrender him to us."

"Surely we can at least approach them," Greznor suggested. "Make the surrender of the Destroyer part of the terms."

"No!" the Queen snapped. "Parleys and negotiations only delay the inevitable. They will give the Destroyer a chance to escape!"

A heavy air of resignation settled over the war council.

"Then I suggest we attack at dawn," Greznor sighed. "With luck, the battle will be over by sundown."

Satisfied, Rianna dismissed them all with a curt nod. Wordlessly, her advisers shuffled out, leaving only Andar, the Queen, and Orath.

Andar scuttled forward to clear away the dishes, pointedly keeping his eyes away from the other two, hoping they would simply forget he was there.

I can't leave her alone with Orath. I can't!

Despite his best efforts to remain invisible, it wasn't long before the Queen addressed him.

"Leave this for tomorrow," she said. "I'm tired, slave. I need sleep."

Slave? She has never called you that before.

Andar bowed his head and slipped outside the tent, his mind racing. Instead of going back to the sleeping blanket and bare patch of ground that served as his own quarters, he made his way to where Lormilar, the man who had replaced him, was staying. Glancing around quickly to see if anyone was watching, he ducked inside.

Lormilar was sitting alone in a chair next to a small table in the corner of his tent, his head buried deep in one of the texts Andar used to call his own.

We don't have enough food to feed the troops, he noted in disgust, *but we're still transporting tables and chairs for each member of the war council's private chambers?*

"Andar?" Lormilar gasped, looking up from his book in surprise. "What are you doing here? The Queen will have your head!"

"The Queen is not in her right mind," Andar insisted. "You need to convince Greznor and the others to ignore her orders. Send someone to parley with the barbarians."

"You're mad," Lormilar said, shaking his head. "She is the Queen! If we disobey her, we'll all end up in chains like you. Or worse."

"You know this isn't right," Andar told him. "All of you. She's fallen under Orath's control. Surely you can see it!"

Lormilar shifted uncomfortably in his seat.

"We have discussed it," he conceded.

"So why has no action been taken?"

"There is no proof," Lormilar began. "At least, nothing we could bring forth as evidence to justify our actions."

"What do you mean?"

"The ogre is ... different these past few days. It seems less focused. Distracted. Even in the heat of battle it will sometimes stop and suddenly stand still as stone, ignoring everyone around it."

"It's trying to break free from Orath's will," Andar blurted out excitedly. "He's losing control!"

"That is what I believe," Lormilar agreed. "But as I said, there is no way to prove it."

Andar didn't answer at first; he was thinking back to the way the Queen had unexpectedly dismissed him. *When she sleeps, Orath doesn't have to fight to maintain his dominance. He needs to rest and regain his strength for the battle tomorrow.*

"Maybe if we attack Orath, the Queen will find the strength to break free," Andar suggested, sudden hope springing up in him.

"Another idea the war council considered," Lormilar noted. "But after much discussion we thought better of it."

"Why?" Andar demanded.

"If Orath loses control of the Queen, he could lose control of the ogre as well."

Andar nodded in understanding. "The beast could turn on our own troops, slaughtering them as it slaughters the clans."

"That was not our greatest fear," Lormilar corrected. "If the

Destroyer of Worlds does appear, we will need the ogre to stand against him."

The former High Sorcerer shook his head, not certain he had heard correctly.

"It sounds like you actually support Orath. Like you think the Queen was right to drive us into war."

"You saw what happened at Ferlhame," Lormilar answered, quick and defensive. "We have no way to fight an enemy like that."

And suddenly Andar realized the truth; the real reason none of the others had tried to break Orath's control of the Queen. *They're so afraid that they actually agree with what he's doing!*

They might take issue with the specifics of his plan: they still cared about all the Danaan soldiers losing their lives and sought ways to minimize the losses. But though they might complain and grumble about the methods, they would never actually try to oppose Orath because—on some level—they approved of his war.

None of them has ever actually suggested to the Queen that we go back, he realized. *Even earlier tonight, when pleading with her to offer the barbarians surrender, they all backed down once they realized the terms wouldn't deliver the Destroyer of Worlds.*

"Orath has you all under his spell," Andar said, shaking his head in disbelief. "He's blinded you to what we've become."

"You're the one who is blind," Lormilar spat at him. "You can't see past your own self-righteousness and martyrdom! Do you think you're the only one who cares about the Danaan? Hexiff and Pranya have located the clan food stores. During the battle tomorrow, Greznor will lead troops there first thing to secure enough provisions so we can return home after the battle!"

"What about all the soldiers who will lose their lives *during* the battle?" Andar wanted to know. "What about the innocent men, women, and children our own forces have been ordered to butcher?"

"Not everyone can be saved," Lormilar said, his voice lowering with regret.

Or shame, Andar realized.

"We are doing whatever we can to help as many as we can," the new High Sorcerer told him, trying to justify the actions of the war council. "Anything that stops short of treason," he added pointedly.

"Go back to your tent, Andar," his former friend said, dismissing him like the lowly servant he was. "If anyone sees you here, it will end badly for both of us."

Andar did as he was ordered, realizing there was nothing he could do to stop the massive slaughter that was only a few hours away.

Shalana made her way through the massive camp in the Giant's Maw, now filled with not just refugees but the warriors of all the clans. The Maw was named for the semicircular ring of small but sharp-peaked mountains that marked the eastern edge; some claimed they looked like the teeth of an enormous mouth. To Shalana, however, all they represented was the point at which they could no longer retreat.

They'd arrived a few hours after sunset, and she'd immediately given her warriors leave to seek out their loved ones. The Danaan army was massing only a few miles away, and they all knew it was the last night any of them would see. Better to spend it with family, friends, and clan then trying to devise last-minute strategies of hopeless desperation.

Yet she knew it was important that her warriors see her this night, tall and unafraid, striding among the fires of all the different clans. It wouldn't bring them victory, but at least it might bring them hope and take away some of the darkness that weighed so heavily over them all.

But now she was finished with her rounds; it was time for her to get back to the Stone Spirits and those who mattered most to her. Arriving at the section of the camp that had been claimed by her own clan, she spotted Vaaler and her father standing beside each other near one of the smoldering peat pits. They stood in silence, neither speaking—her father had still not come to respect Vaaler as many of the thane-chiefs did, and Vaaler still didn't fully trust her father.

Just another sign of his intelligence and excellent judgment of character.

The two men noticed her approach at the same time, but it was Terramon who spoke first.

"Why haven't you put any guards around the camp? What if the Tree Folk attack in the middle of the night?"

"Why would they?" Vaaler said with a shrug. "They already have the numbers to annihilate us without resorting to tricks. And their soldiers aren't trained to fight in the dark—a surprise attack now would only introduce an element of unknown risk.

"If victory is inevitable," the younger man continued, "why do anything to mess it up?"

"Then why don't we attack them?" Terramon suggested. "Now, before the sun rises! Catch them off guard!"

"They'll have sentries," Shalana noted. "And we don't have the numbers for a full-scale assault on their army. We've been fighting hit-and-run battles, and now there's nowhere left to run."

"We knew this was a war we couldn't win," Vaaler told him. "That's why Roggen was supposed to take the elders and children into the mountains to hide."

Shalana could tell from Vaaler's tone he was still angry at Roggen for disobeying them. But seeing the reunions of her warriors with their husbands, wives, children, and parents, she was glad he had ignored her orders.

We're all going to die anyway. Better they had one last chance to say their good-byes.

Before she had a chance to try and explain this to Vaaler, however, her father chimed in.

"What would be the point? If the Danaan didn't hunt them down, they'd all be dead in a few weeks anyway.

"When the end comes," the old man added, speaking softly, "the elders will take care of the children, quick and painless. Then they will take up arms and join us on the battlefield."

Vaaler was clearly disturbed at the idea of a mass mercy killing for the hundreds of children in the camp, but Shalana knew her father was right.

"Better to fall quickly beneath a blade then die slowly of starvation and exposure," she said softly.

"The whole point of this war was to buy time for Norr and Hadawas to return with Daemron's Sword!" Vaaler protested. "We knew we couldn't stop the Danaan; we just wanted to slow them down.

"If all the warriors laid down their lives tomorrow, those who flee into the mountains might survive long enough for Norr to return. They could still be saved!"

"That's your plan?" Terramon snorted. "Wait for Daemron's Sword?

"I don't believe in legends," the old man added with a scowl.

"Hadawas did," Shalana reminded him.

"And where is he now?" her father replied, shaking his head and wandering off in disgust.

"He never fought a battle he couldn't win," Shalana said by way of apology once he was gone. "This is difficult for him."

"I still believe Norr and the others will return," Vaaler told her. "If you saw what Keegan was able to do with the Ring, you'd believe in the power of the Sword, too."

He was quiet for a few seconds, then said, "You think I'm a fool, don't you?"

"Yes," she said, reaching her hand around the back of his neck and pulling him close. "But you're my fool," she said, planting a quick, tender kiss on his lips.

Despite the grimness of their situation, in the dim light of the fire she could see that Vaaler was smiling when she pulled away.

She was suddenly struck by how young he was. He seemed so wise and worldly, it was easy to forget he was almost a decade younger than she was.

"Tomorrow when the battle begins," she said, suddenly fiercely protective of the young man, "you can lead the refugees up into the mountains. It will buy a few more days. Just in case you're right and Norr really is coming back."

"I can't do that," Vaaler told her. "I'm not leaving you. I've decided to stay and fight by your side."

Shalana was touched by the gesture, but she knew how much it would cost him.

"You said it yourself—you can't raise weapons against your own people."

"They cast me out," Vaaler insisted. "And the clans took me in. I want to stand with them. And with you."

"Silly boy," Shalana teased him. "So young and foolish."

"I'm not a child," Vaaler told her, suddenly serious and earnest. "I'm a man and I know what I'm doing."

"I'll be the judge of that," Shalana said wickedly, pulling him close and tearing at his clothes.

Vaaler looked around, embarrassed. But there was nobody near them.

"Tonight?" he said, even as his hands began to fumble at her own clothes. "Are you sure?"

"If this is our last night alive," Shalana told him as she dragged him down to the cold snow, "then let's make it count."

Chapter 37

CASSANDRA FELT LIKE she was moving through a dense fog. The world around her had dissolved into gray. Exhausted, her Sight was barely able to focus on her and her horse, let alone her surroundings.

She knew it was night, of course—even in her current state she could feel the gloom pressing in on her. And she knew she was close to Callastan: she could smell the sea and the docks of the port city on the breeze blowing in from the west. Beyond this, however, she was aware of little else.

The Crawling Twins were somewhere still behind her though they weren't close enough for her to sense them. Despite this, she still felt the cold grip of fear slowly crushing her. Her stomach was twisted in knots and her heart couldn't stop racing. It had been that way ever since she'd fled the gruesome massacre of the Inquisitors. The images of the Twins literally ripping her former brethren apart were burned on her psyche.

She didn't remember most of her journey across the Southlands. Her mind, scarred by the trauma of what she had witnessed, had abandoned her body for long stretches. Only instinct and dedication to her cause had kept her moving forward.

And me, the voice inside her head that was not her own chimed in. *I guided your steps. I kept you safe. Do not forget that.*

Cassandra had finally recognized the voice though she still

wasn't sure if it was really Rexol speaking to her or simply the memory of her old master bubbling up from her subconscious. In either case, she was determined to ignore it.

If it really was Rexol—if he was somehow still alive, despite his body's being reduced to ash—then her extreme reaction to the Crawling Twins' attack was more understandable: the wizard had used Chaos magic to save her, and the backlash had nearly driven her insane.

As terrifying as that option was, however, it was better than the alternative. If Rexol wasn't the cause of her emotional breakdown, then she was simply losing control—her sanity whittled away by the Crown itself.

The Talisman is too strong for any mortal mind, she told herself. *Even the Pontiff, with all his training, only dared to use it a handful of times.*

You are stronger than the Pontiff, Rexol insisted. *Chaos flows in your blood. Use the Crown and claim the power that is rightfully yours.*

Cassandra didn't bother to formulate a response.

She felt something looming ahead of her in the gray void. Concentrating, she pushed her awareness outward and was rewarded with the dim outline of Callastan's buildings rising up in the night, illuminated by lamps and torches scattered about the city streets.

You're here, Rexol declared. *Now what?*

She needed to find a ship, one that could take her someplace the Crawling Twins couldn't follow.

Even if you cross the entire ocean, they will still find you. Stop running. Use the Crown and destroy them!

Cassandra's horse had slowed to a weary walk; like all the mounts before, it was nearing exhaustion. Grateful for the animal's service, she swung herself down from the saddle to walk beside it as she approached the city.

Get off the main road! Someone will see you!

She understood the individual words, but her fragile mind still struggled with the message they were trying to convey. She was heading toward Callastan; that was all that mattered.

And then suddenly two armed soldiers were approaching her: city guards. Seeing normal, ordinary humans helped anchor Cassandra back in reality, and she shook her head, dispelling most of the fog that had enveloped her.

The men stopped a few feet away, lowering their spears and pointing them in her direction.

"Identify yourself!" one of them ordered.

Tell these fools to get out of your way! Rexol sneered. *The Purge has made everyone in the Southlands fear the Order. Tell them you are here on the Pontiff's business and watch them scurry off!*

Cassandra didn't like the idea of lying to the men, but she knew the longer she was delayed by them the closer the Crawling Twins would get. For their own sakes, she decided to follow the mage's advice.

"I do not answer to you," she told them, stepping forward into the light so they could see her pure white eyes. "I serve only the Pontiff."

The soldiers' eyes went wide with fear and their faces blanched as they recognized what she was. But instead of moving aside, they raised their spears and began to move slowly toward her.

"All servants of the Order are banned from Callastan," one of them said, licking his lips nervously. "You are under arrest!"

"If you try to resist, we will have to kill you," the other added, raising his spear for emphasis.

Cassandra was no Inquisitor, but all who trained in the Monastery were taught the basic martial arts. She might be able to disarm the soldiers without injuring them, but she knew it wouldn't be easy.

Use the Crown! The Talisman will give you the power to destroy them!

The Crown was tucked inside a bag strapped over one shoulder; with no saddle for her horse she had no other way to carry it as she rode. It might be possible to grab it before the soldiers realized what was happening, but even if she did, she still didn't dare to unleash the Chaos trapped inside.

The first soldier was advancing slowly, his spear lowered. Cassandra felt a sudden push on her emotions; rage flared up within her. Realizing Rexol was trying to drive her into a fury to attack the innocent guards, she pushed back against him.

Everything around her disappeared as the veil of gray mist fell over her, her Sight blinded as she battled the wizard for control of her own mind. Rexol was strong, but she refused to surrender. And then, as suddenly as the battle of wills began, it was over and she felt the wizard's presence retreating.

He's only regrouping. Getting ready to try again.

As her awareness returned, she was surprised to find herself in a small, dark room. The stone walls were damp and covered with moss and mildew, and a foul stench hung in the air. There was only one exit; a heavy wooden door with a small, barred window through which she could see the flickering light of a faint torch.

With horrified amazement, she realized her battle with Rexol had lasted more than just a few seconds. She had blacked out for minutes or even hours, completely unaware of anything that had happened.

The guards arrested you, Cassandra. They threw you in this cell while they wait for morning so someone with more authority can decide what to do with you.

But Cassandra knew that when morning came, it wouldn't be a judge or city official who came for her.

The Crawling Twins!

"Please!" Cassandra cried out, rushing toward the door and pounding on it with her fist. "You have to let me go! Please, somebody listen—you are all in danger!"

There was, of course, no answer.

There's only one way out, Cassandra, Rexol said, and she realized the bag with the Crown was still slung over her shoulder.

He used magic on the guards so they wouldn't notice it.

I called upon the power of the Crown, Cassandra. So can you. Place it on your head and free yourself before it's too late.

"Never," Cassandra vowed, defiantly speaking the word out loud. "Never!"

Keegan was up as the first rays of sun peeked over the horizon. He stood up slowly, reluctantly unwrapping himself from the warmth of the blanket as he brushed away the snow.

Jerrod was already up. The monk needed little sleep, and given Scythe's outburst yesterday, Keegan suspected he'd spent the entire night awake and alert, watching her in case she tried to attack him again.

I was holding her when I fell asleep, the young man remembered. *She must have woken and pulled away in the night.*

Ignoring the twinge of rejection he felt, he looked from side to side until he noticed Scythe. She was sitting on the snow several yards away from where they had slept, facing away from him.

Looking back the way we came. Back toward Norr.

"What time did she get up?" he asked Jerrod, speaking quietly so she wouldn't hear.

"Over an hour ago," the monk answered.

"How is she?"

"She's getting worse."

Alarmed, Keegan rushed to her side, his feet crunching over the windblown crust that had formed on the snow. She didn't react to his approach; not even when he gently laid a hand on her shoulder and crouched beside her.

"Scythe?" he said. "Scythe, can you hear me?"

She didn't answer. She simply stared off into the distance, her legs crossed and her hands folded in her lap.

Keegan sighed. He'd hoped after her emotional release last night she'd be feeling better. But she seemed to have slipped back into her catatonic state.

"Come on, Scythe," he said, standing up. "It's time to go."

She didn't move. Keegan looked over at Jerrod, who only stared back without expression. He reached down and gently slid his arms under hers, then tried to lift her up. It was like trying to move deadweight, made even more awkward by his missing hand, and he only raised her a few inches before his grip slipped and she fell back hard to the ground.

"I'm sorry, Scythe," Keegan gasped, but she didn't even seem to notice.

Without acknowledging his efforts or his presence, she readjusted herself until she was back in the exact same position as before.

Keegan walked back over to Jerrod.

"What do we do now?" he asked.

"There's nothing we can do," the monk told him. "We go on without her."

"We can't just leave her sitting there in the snow!" Keegan exclaimed. "She'll die out here!"

"Obviously that is what she wants."

Keegan shook his head. "Scythe's a fighter. She's hurt. Damaged. But she wouldn't ever give up. And I won't give up on her!"

He expected Jerrod to argue with him, but the monk didn't reply. Instead, he turned his head in the direction of a small hill in the distance.

"Someone is coming."

A few seconds later a figure emerged from behind the mound. Bent over nearly double, it moved toward them with slow, shuffling steps. As it drew closer, Keegan finally recognized who it was.

"Hadawas?" he called out, his mind boggled by the mystery of how their guide had somehow caught up with them.

"That's not Hadawas," Jerrod said, raising Daemron's Sword.

The old man suddenly stood up straight, laughing. But it sounded more like a woman; high-pitched and shrill.

No, not a woman. A bird!

The figure shimmered, the illusion wrapped around it falling away like pieces of broken glass to reveal a creature Keegan had seen in his nightmares of the Monastery being destroyed. Its skin was black and smooth, and it had the body of a lean, muscular woman. But its hands were claws, it had massive black wings growing from its back, and the head resembled that of some monstrous bird of prey.

Parting its hooked beak, the Minion spoke.

"I am Raven," it squawked, its female voice sharp and crackling with power. "You have taken what rightfully belongs to my master. Surrender the Talismans to me and you shall live!"

The compulsion of her words was so strong, Keegan took a half step forward before Jerrod stopped him by seizing his arm, breaking the spell.

"The Ring," the monk hissed. "Put it on!"

As he reached for the chain around his neck, Jerrod charged the creature. Raven threw back her head and lifted her arms to the sky, shrieking out arcane words that made Keegan's skin crawl.

In response, twin pillars of green fire came shooting down toward them from above. Jerrod dove to the side, avoiding the flames. Keegan—reacting instinctively—called on Chaos to save himself. He was instantly bathed in a soft blue glow, but he wasn't wearing the Ring yet, and he wasn't strong enough to ward off the Minion's magic.

The green flames devoured the blue barrier and engulfed him.

He screamed and collapsed to the ground as his flesh bubbled and blistered from the heat. And then the flames vanished as Jerrod fell on Raven, Daemron's sword a whirling blur of glowing red steel.

Keegan fell forward, the cool snow offering little relief to the hideous burns covering his flesh. He lifted his head to see Raven and Jerrod locked in a vicious battle, both combatants moving so quickly it was impossible for his mind to process the action.

A fresh wave of pain hit him, so intense he thought he would black out. Knowing he was going into shock from his injuries, he managed to roll onto his side so that he could see Scythe.

She hadn't moved at all, completely oblivious to the battle raging only fifty feet away. He tried to call out to her, but his burned lips and cracked, swollen tongue made the words stick in his throat. And then Keegan's eyelids fluttered, and the world went black.

Vaaler stood tall among the ranks of the clan warriors as dawn peeked over the mountains that made up the Giant's Maw. Like the others, he was clad in a haphazard assortment of hides and furs—a sharp contrast to the cured-leather vests and uniforms of the enemy.

The clans were arranged in a long, loosely bunched line a dozen rows deep: a wall of defenders determined to hold back the enemy from the refugee camp behind them for as long as possible. True to her vow, Shalana was in the front, immediately to Vaaler's left. Whatever happened today, whenever and however they met their end, they had both vowed to face it side by side.

As the sunlight crept across the battlefield, he heard a rising roar of anticipation from the gathered Danaan troops. But the warriors standing with Vaaler were silent.

They're used to fighting for honor and glory. But this is different. This is about survival, plain and simple. There is nothing noble in what we do here, and there will be no songs sung or legends told of what happens today.

A horn blew, the sound quickly echoed by a dozen others. And the Danaan surged forward. Shalana raised her spear and let loose a fierce battle cry as she, Vaaler, and the united forces of all the clans charged ahead to meet the enemy.

Vaaler had just enough time to realize the ogre hadn't joined the rush; the beast was standing still as stone near the back of the Danaan lines. But before he could wonder about it, the two armies met with a deafening crash, and everything descended into madness.

Armed with his rapier, Vaaler cut and jabbed at his enemies, moving nimbly among the soldiers from both sides chopping, hacking, slashing, and stabbing furiously at each other all around him. In the confusion he couldn't recognize the faces of friend or foe; there was too much happening too quickly for his mind to process such minute details. But even in the heat of battle, he was still aware of Shalana beside him, laying foe after foe low with her deadly spear.

The tide of battle swept them forward as there was a momentary break in the Danaan lines, and Vaaler and the others poured through. But reinforcements arrived almost immediately to seal the breach, and the clans were forced to fall back again.

Someone slammed into Vaaler from behind; in the crush of bodies he didn't know if it was friend or foe. The impact sent him staggering toward a waiting Danaan soldier, and Vaaler threw himself face-first to the ground to avoid being gutted by a wild slash of his enemy's blade. He rolled onto his back and thrust upward, the point of his rapier slipping through a seam between the jerkin and belt of the other man and plunging deep into his belly.

Clutching at his mortal wound, he toppled backward, and both of them were overrun by the mayhem as the ebb and flow of battle washed over them. Soldiers from both sides trampled them down, heavy boots kicking and stomping heedlessly as desperate men and women fought for purchase on the uneven ground.

Twice Vaaler managed to get to his hands and knees, only to be knocked down again each time. A toe caught him in the ribs, a heel struck the side of his head, leaving him woozy and disoriented. For a second the world swam in an ocean of silver stars.

Vaaler bit down hard on his tongue, the pain jolting him back to consciousness just in time to see a heavy axe swinging down toward him. He rolled to the side and the head buried itself deep in the ground. But before he could rise the man pulled out a short, thick sword and lunged toward his prone and helpless foe.

Instead of feeling the cold steel wedging itself between his ribs, however, Vaaler heard a heavy thud and the fatal blow went askew, knocked off line by the feathered spear protruding from the man's sternum.

As the Danaan toppled lifeless to the ground, Shalana yanked Vaaler back to his feet. Without saying a word, she wrapped her hands around the shaft of her spear, braced her foot on the corpse, and hauled her weapon free.

Vaaler looked around frantically, expecting to be assailed on all sides by more of the enemy. But he and Shalana were standing alone in a small pocket of calm.

Eye of the storm, he thought, as the battle continued to rage unchecked all around them. And then he heard a vile, sickening sound rising up over the din of battle: a wet, ravenous, rumbling growl.

"Run!" Shalana screamed, her eyes going wide with fear.

But it was too late. The monster had spotted them, fixing its baleful gaze on the pair that stood momentarily untouched by the fray. The ogre had joined the battle, and it was coming for them.

– – – – –

The walls that imprisoned her couldn't block Cassandra's Sight from sensing dawn as it rose over Callastan. She'd hoped someone would come to see her at first light, someone she could reason with. Someone she could convince to let her out of her cell before the Crawling Twins came.

But morning stretched to afternoon, and she realized she would have to find another way out of the cell.

"I need to speak to someone!" she shouted, once again pounding her fist on the door. "Please—lives are at stake!"

She knew the guards were out there; she could see them in a room at the end of the hall, three men seated around a table playing cards while pointedly ignoring the cries of their prisoner.

It's too late, Rexol told her. *The Crawling Twins have come.*

She sensed them in the same instant, their misshapen forms scuttling through an alley less than a block away.

"Please!" she screamed. "Please! I'm begging you!"

With a muttered curse one of the men threw his cards onto the table and got to his feet. He grabbed a key from a rack on the wall and began to walk down the hall toward her cell. Whether he intended to listen to her or simply unlock her cell to administer a beating she never found out.

The door to the street exploded as he walked past, the heavy wood blasted from its hinges with enough force to pin the unfortunate guard against the opposite wall, crushing the life from him.

The Crawling Twins spilled in, the blue-skinned one turning left and rushing toward the guards, the red turning right and coming for Cassandra. Memories of the Inquisitors' bloody slaughter filled her head; images of blood and gore that made her want to throw up caused her to start trembling in terror.

The Crown! Rexol shouted in her head. *Use the Crown!*

The red Twin paused outside her door, crouched low on all fours. Its limbs jutted out at strange angles as it rocked from side to side, then tilted back its snout to sniff the air. Behind it, the blue

Twin had already eviscerated the guards, pausing just long enough to lap up a small pool of the freshly spilled blood before joining the other outside her door.

The Crown! Do it now, or the Minions will take the Talisman for the Slayer!

Cassandra stepped to the side as one of the Twins smashed open the door to her cell with a single kick. As the door hurtled across the room to splinter against the wall, she was already pulling the artifact she had faithfully carried since she'd fled the Monastery from its sack. As the first Twin stepped through the door, she placed the Crown atop her head.

Cassandra's mind reeled as the power of the ancient Talisman poured into her, freezing time and all existence. Fueled by Chaos, her Sight exploded into omniscience, her awareness instantly stretching out to every corner of the mortal world, taking in every sight, sound, and even smell. Her consciousness recoiled as the thoughts of every living man, woman, and child bombarded her simultaneously. She was everywhere; she was everything. And the tiny, insignificant part of her being that was Cassandra was lost in the glory of infinity.

Chapter 38

REXOL WAS READY and waiting as Cassandra's essence and identity were overwhelmed by the Crown. The same had happened the first time he dared to use the Talisman; it had nearly destroyed him. But he was stronger now. Wiser.

Being imprisoned inside the Crown had changed him in ways far greater than the loss of his physical form. He had become attuned to the Old Magic used to forge it in ways even the great mages who predated the Cataclysm could not fathom. He had prepared for this moment; he'd yearned for it. And when Cassandra faltered, Rexol seized control of not just her mind but also her body.

It all happened instantly; at the speed of thought while the world outside crept along so, so slowly. In the entire time it took for Cassandra to lose her battle against oblivion and Rexol to seize control, the first of the Crawling Twins had only passed halfway through the door of her cell.

The Chaos was building, gathering so fast inside Cassandra's body that her flesh began to pulse and crack as the magical fire threatened to consume her mortal shell as it had consumed Rexol's. But this time the wizard was prepared, and instead of trying to contain and control the unstemmable tide, he let it pass through him and unleashed it on the mortal world.

Old Magic erupted like a geyser from Cassandra's body, an explosion of pure Chaos that sent ripples across the sky to every corner of the mortal world.

Dark purple clouds rolled in from the west, blotting out the cold winter sun that shone down on the empty, snow-covered plateau high among the mountain peaks. Bolts of silver lightning arced back and forth across the sky and deafening cracks of thunder echoed over the land. For several seconds the fury of the storm raged, and then it was gone, vanishing as suddenly and mysteriously as it had appeared.

Entombed beneath the earth, the Guardian felt the power of Chaos as it swept through. His eyes snapped open as he shook off his hibernating slumber, invigorated by the touch of Old Magic.

With a roar, he rose to his full height and thrust his fists toward the unseen sky, bursting through the avalanche of rock and ice that had buried him in the cave. A shower of debris rained down on the newly fallen snow as the surface of the ground exploded, leaving a gaping wound of a crater.

Freed from his prison, the Guardian leapt from the hole and up onto the surface of the plateau. He scooped his spear up from the ground, his muscles quivering with the crackling energy of raw Chaos. And then he felt it—a foul, hateful presence he had not sensed since before the Cataclysm.

The ogre has risen!

Turning to the west, he set off at a run toward the battle that raged on the other side of the mountain, devouring the ground with each massive stride.

Vaaler grabbed Shalana's arm and turned to flee, but the ogre was already charging toward them. Despite its size, it moved with in-

credible speed, leaping forward on squat, powerful legs and clawing at the ground with its long arms to help propel it along.

It closed the distance between them in seconds. In their frantic
flight, Shalana stumbled over a fallen body and tumbled to the
ground. Unwilling to let go of her arm, Vaaler was dragged down
with her.

The ogre landed beside them, the ground shaking and shud-
dering from its massive bulk. It raised its fist above its head, and
Vaaler threw himself on top of Shalana as if he could somehow
save her from being crushed.

And then the sky above them exploded in a storm of purple
clouds and silver lightning. The strange storm seemed to mesmer-
ize the ogre, freezing it in place, arms raised above its head as it
stared up at the sky.

Vaaler and Shalana scrambled to their feet and began to run,
not knowing or caring what was happening. The storm vanished
a few seconds later, and Vaaler heard the ogre unleash another terrible, gurgling roar. Glancing back over his shoulder, however, he
saw the beast wasn't following them. Instead, it had turned on the
Danaan soldiers that had rallied around it: massacring the men and
women who, only moments before, had been its allies.

Standing in the back ranks of the Danaan army with the still-
dominated Rianna at his side, Orath felt a sudden surge of power
as the Chaos storm materialized above them. It invigorated him;
restoring much of the power that had bled away since he'd crossed
the Legacy.

But he knew the ogre felt it, too. And while Orath was descended from countless generations of men and women mutated
and transformed by the terrible power of unchecked Chaos beyond the Legacy, the ogre's connection to magic was far greater.
The beast was Chaos Spawn, born from the most primal fires of

creation. It fed on the storm's fury, drinking deep and growing stronger—too strong for Orath to control.

With a roar that echoed across the entire battlefield, the ogre wrested its mind free, shattering the invisible chains the Minion had used to bind its will. Orath staggered from the shock as his connection to the beast was severed, a sharp pain shooting like a knife through the back of his skull.

Beside him, Rianna—still linked to him through magic—gasped and doubled over, clutching her head with her hands.

Orath ignored the Queen's suffering, his mind racing. The ogre was free, and though there was still a tenuous link between them, without another ritual he wasn't strong enough to dominate its mind again.

But the link is still there. The beast can sense you. It will seek revenge.

Orath hated to abandon his hunt for the Ring, but the mortal who carried the Talisman had not joined the battle. And now he knew where to find another Talisman.

The storm had come from the west, and though it had passed, there were still lingering traces of its power traced across the sky. Orath could follow them back to their source and resume his search for the Ring after he had claimed Daemron's Crown.

With a flick of his wrist he ripped away the magic binding the Queen to his will. She fell unconscious to the ground, her body limp as a marionette with its strings cut. Orath knew she might never wake, but her fate mattered little to him.

He could feel the ogre's brutal, bestial mind probing for him, seeking him out among the Danaan ranks, and he knew it was time to flee. Unlike Raven he did not have wings, but there were other ways to fly. The spell was difficult and taxing, and it required such intense concentration he could only sustain it for an hour or two at a time, but he was driven by the direness of his situation.

Calling on his renewed reserves of Chaos, he began a quick, rhythmic chant. The air around him began to swirl rapidly, lifting him off the ground. When he reached a height of twenty feet, the pitch of his words changed. In response, the spinning winds shifted direction, whisking him away from the battlefield, the ogre, and the Ring.

Andar was up at dawn, though in truth he hadn't slept the entire night. When the horns sounded the initial charge, he found a small hill from which to watch the battle at a distance, trying to gauge the ebb and flow. The barbarians fought with savage desperation, inflicting heavy damage. But the Danaan had too great an advantage in numbers, and it quickly became clear the outcome was inevitable . . . though not before many, many more would die on either side.

But though he mourned for those who would fall, most of his focus was not on the doomed soldiers but the ogre that towered over them. The beast had spent the early moments of the battle in a strange, almost trancelike state.

It feels Orath growing weaker. It's fighting him. Trying to break free.

But despite its struggles, the Minion finally imposed his will and drove the beast into the fray, further shifting the battle in the Danaan favor.

And what happens when the last barbarian falls, and we still have not found the Ring or the Destroyer of Worlds? Will Orath simply turn the ogre on us? Or will he find some other use for Rianna and her army?

His thoughts were cut off by pealing thunder, the clear blue sky disappearing behind a sudden formation of violet clouds. Andar immediately recognized the power in the storm as silver lightning flashed above him: Old Magic—the same power he had called on in the forests around Ferlhame.

A desperate, foolish plan formed in his head, and he opened himself to the Chaos. The storm lasted only a few seconds, but it

was long enough for the former High Sorcerer to gather a concentrated reservoir of power.

He ran down from his observation perch, racing recklessly
through the tents of the Danaan camp. The power inside him
bubbled and broiled, making his skin twitch and crawl as it tried
to break free.

This is madness, he thought. *You are no match for Orath. He will
destroy you!*

But if the Minion was distracted, focused on the ogre, there
might be one chance for Andar to unleash the stored Chaos
against him.

When he reached Rianna's tent, however, Orath was nowhere
to be found. Instead, the Queen lay unconscious, partially supported by Greznor's thick arms. Lormilar, the unofficial chief
medic of the Danaan army, was examining her closely, a troubled
look on his face. Hexiff and Pranya were there, too, standing anxiously off to the side.

"What's wrong?" Andar demanded, throwing himself to his
knees at Rianna's side. The Chaos pumping through his veins
turned his concerned question into a frantic shout.

"Orath has disappeared," Greznor answered. "When he left, the
Queen collapsed."

"We have to fall back!" Andar barked, the only one who understood the true implications of the general's words.

"The ogre!" he snapped, seeing the confusion on their faces. "It
will turn against us!"

A look of dawning horror spread to each member of the war
council.

"Leave the Queen with me!" Andar shouted, reaching and
roughly hauling the unconscious woman from Greznor's grasp.
"Go sound the retreat!"

Spurred on by his manic urgency, the others scattered in all directions. Taking a deep breath to try to calm himself despite the fiery Chaos coursing through his veins, he lay the Queen gently on the ground.

He wasn't sure exactly what Orath had done to the Queen, but he knew her mind was lost, drifting in the void. Clenching his teeth against the pain of the searing heat burning him up from the inside, Andar reached out and placed his hands on the Queen's temples.

Unlike the human mages, the Danaan didn't use complex rituals and incantations. Their magic was primal, instinctual. Andar didn't recite any arcane words or mystical chants, he simply focused his will and released the Chaos he had gathered through his hands.

Rianna's body bucked and heaved, thrashing about in a violent seizure. Somehow, Andar kept hold of her head as his palms began to smolder.

Come back to us, my Queen!

He poured everything he had into his spell, igniting a burning flame to guide his monarch safely back from the void. But in the brief storm, he'd only gathered a few seconds' worth of power, and in only a few seconds his strength was spent.

Exhausted and drained, he slumped forward, resting his weight on his hands and knees, panting heavily. In the distance he heard the horns calling the Danaan into a full retreat. As if in response, Rianna twitched and moaned. Then—to Andar's great relief—the Queen opened her eyes.

Chapter 39

HUDDLED IN A small corner of her own mind, Cassandra slowly felt her strength returning as Rexol redirected the terrible, awe-inspiring power of the Talisman away from her and into himself.

Her former Master had claimed her body as his own, using it as a gateway to return to the mortal world and steal the Crown. But he had also saved her life. Even if her will had been strong enough to withstand the crushing force of infinite knowledge and awareness, her body would have been destroyed.

Now, however, she was the one trapped inside the Crown; an unsettling noncorporeal quasi-existence in the netherworld between Chaos and reality. Even for one used to the Sight, her perception was weirdly doubled and reflected. She had a broad, all-encompassing awareness of everything around her, as if looking at it from high above. Yet she also saw everything from the perspective of her mortal body, looking out from the center at the world that surrounded her. The effect was confusing and unsettling, her mind twisting in on itself over and over as it tried to find some way to reconcile the impossible duality.

How many weeks was Rexol imprisoned here? How did he keep from going mad?

The answer, she realized as he unleashed a massive storm of pure Chaos up into the sky, was that he hadn't.

Her mind flickered and spun, the two views overlapping and

blurring together into a radically distorted semblance of reality. She saw that the Crawling Twins were still there; coming toward them. She felt Rexol drawing on the Crown, carefully summoning Chaos now that he had cast off the first irresistible rush of power.

She could feel the spell as it took shape in the mage's mind, and she realized he had used similar—though far weaker—magic when he had compelled the Crawling Twins to attack the Inquisitors instead of her. There were no other enemies this time, so Rexol simply turned the Twins against each other.

The twisted creatures fought briefly against him, but their minds were crushed by the Talisman, their free will snuffed out in an instant. They threw themselves at each other, ripping, tearing, and shredding. Equally matched in their suicidal fury, their battle didn't last long.

Even a Minion can die from its wounds, she realized, *if enough damage is done.*

The blue one fell first, the killing blow coming as the other finally sunk its teeth in and ripped out its throat. But as the victor turned its attention to the human in the cell it was already struggling to stand. Dark blood poured from a dozen deep wounds in its bright red flesh to form a sticky black lake on the floor, including a hole in the stomach so deep Cassandra could see its twisted, twitching intestines. It took a single step forward, then keeled over, dead as its Twin.

Rexol didn't even seem to notice. He continued to draw Chaos from the Crown, reveling in the power of Old Magic. The steady influx of power began to build, pulsing out through the floor beneath Cassandra's feet.

With her new awareness, Cassandra felt it rolling through the entire city. Everyone it touched was struck with a sudden, violent madness. Some turned on each other, some turned on themselves. But most simply poured out into the streets and quickly banded together in savage mobs: smashing and burning everything they could reach and attacking anyone else who crossed their path.

It's over, Cassandra said, projecting her thoughts at Rexol in an effort to manipulate him the way he had tried to control her. *The Twins are dead. Take off the Crown!*

He didn't respond, and she wasn't even sure he'd heard her. What was one small voice amid the millions that assailed him through the Crown?

Rexol continued to channel Chaos through him and out into the mortal world, oblivious of the consequences. Old Magic was the primal essence of creation—a force so great even the Gods had been wary of it. They had used it to shape and form the mortal world; now Rexol was unwittingly tearing it apart.

The ground began to shake, the tremor quickly escalating to a massive earthquake. Older buildings began to crack and crumble, great chunks of stone toppling into the street.

It's too much! Cassandra screamed. *You have to stop!*

But Rexol couldn't stop. In trying to control the Crown, he'd dared to touch the very depths of the Burning Sea, and now he was lost in the ecstasy of absolute power. And then Cassandra realized it wasn't just Callastan that he was destroying. The raw, undiluted power of Old Magic was beginning to tear away the very fabric of the Legacy itself!

Jerrod threw himself at Raven, pressing the action to keep the Minion from targeting Keegan again with another spell. He didn't know how badly the young man was hurt, but with his Sight, he could tell Keegan was still alive.

Daemron's Sword moved like it had a will of its own in his hand, almost as if he were the weapon and it the wielder. The Minion was quick and cunning, slashing at him with her beak and claws and battering him with her wings. But Jerrod was able to anticipate and counter every move, fighting the creature to a standstill.

"Scythe!" he called out, leaping back to avoid a hooked talon that threatened to slice open his biceps even as he countered with a quick cut that just narrowly missed Raven's thigh. "Keegan's hurt!"

The catatonic woman didn't move, and Jerrod was forced to turn all his attention to the Minion trying to eviscerate him.

When Scythe used the Sword against the Guardian, she defeated him easily.

But she was touched by Chaos; like Keegan, she was born under the Blood Moon. Jerrod, on the other hand, had spent his entire life learning to deny and internalize the power he'd been born with.

Raven leapt back, and Jerrod feared she might be trying to flee. Not wanting her to escape into the sky only to come after them another time, he directed his fury at one of her wings. The Sword made contact, slicing clean through and leaving the membrane torn and tattered.

Raven shrieked in surprise and pain and lashed out with another spell. A bone-chilling frost sprang from the ground and raced up Jerrod's legs, encasing them in ice. But as it reached his belt he was able to break free, shattering the spell before Raven had time to take advantage.

She hissed in anger, the sound closer to that of a serpent than a bird.

The Sword absorbs Chaos, he remembered, thinking back to how the Guardian had survived Keegan's efforts to destroy him with the Ring. *It blunts her magic. Protects me.*

As the combatants circled each other warily, Jerrod realized the sword was helping him in another way. Despite their exertions, he wasn't the least bit tired or fatigued. The same could not be said of his foe.

Raven was moving slower as fatigue took its tool. The change was virtually imperceptible, but in two evenly matched combatants it would be enough to shift the battle.

Jerrod moved in to finish her off with a series of quick thrusts and jabs, but she summoned enough strength to avoid his attacks, the Sword carving the air fractions of an inch from her flesh as she spun out of the way.

The monk was preparing another pass when the sky above them suddenly turned dark. Bizarre violet clouds blotted out the sun, and silver lightning flashed. Raven seemed to draw strength from the storm, and she came at him with renewed fury. But she still wasn't quick enough to catch him with her rending talons or stabbing beak, and as he darted out of the way Daemron's blade lashed out of its own accord and left a long, thin gash on the Minion's left arm.

They circled each other once more, probing and prodding for an opening. And then, suddenly, Raven's eyes glittered with malevolent cunning. Bracing himself for her next ploy, Jerrod felt the warmth of soft magic flowing over his body. But instead of harming him, her spell seemed intended to heal. The bruises, nicks, and cuts he'd suffered during their battle vanished. And then the milky white veil covering his eyes melted away, and for the first time in thirty years he could see.

His Sight gave him an awareness of his surroundings, but it was something very different from the sensations of ordinary vision. With his eyes suddenly functioning again, he was overloaded with stimuli; his mystical perceptions and his mundane sight warring with each other for dominance and control.

Disoriented and confused, the monk staggered back, slashing wildly with the Sword to ward off Raven's inevitable charge and praying the blade would somehow still protect him.

As a hooked claw ripped open his cheek, he realized even the Talisman had its limits.

− − − − −

Fleeing the ogre as it indiscriminately slaughtered anyone in reach, Vaaler only paused to look back when he heard the Danaan horns calling for a full retreat.

We've won! he thought, his pace slowing in stunned disbelief.

Shalana took several more steps before realizing she had left him behind.

"What are you doing?" she shouted back at him over her shoulder.

"The Danaan are falling back," he told her. "It's over."

"Not yet it isn't," she said, her eyes looking past him.

Turning around, Vaaler saw the ogre standing in the middle of the carnage, surrounded by great piles of Eastern and Danaan bodies. For a moment it seemed the creature would pursue the fleeing Danaan, but then it paused.

It seemed to sniff the air, its head snapping from side to side as if looking for a scent it had suddenly lost. It let out a howl of frustration and slammed its fists on the ground, its head scanning the fleeing mortals as it searched for victims to suffer the wrath of its disappointment.

The beast's eyes settled on Vaaler and Shalana, lighting up with a malevolent spark of recognition as it let out a wet, bellowing roar.

It remembers us. We escaped it once, but it won't happen again.

The beast came at them, moving so fast they didn't even have time to run. But instead of trampling them, it leapt over them. Vaaler turned his head to follow the beast as it soared twenty feet in the air to land behind them, coming face-to-face with a blue-skinned giant charging down from the Maw's peaks toward them.

Shalana's mouth gaped in amazement, and Vaaler could only stare dumbfounded and blink. The newcomer was a heavily muscled man, naked save for a loincloth and a pair of massive black boots. In his hand he clutched an enormous spear, which he thrust into the ogre's gut as he barreled into the beast at a full run.

The ogre knocked the giant flying with a backhand slap, then reached down and broke the shaft of the spear, leaving the tip embedded in its own belly. The giant was already back on his feet, and—armed with nothing but his bare hands—he threw himself at the ogre.

The two behemoths wrestled each other to the ground, rolling back and forth as the perplexed clan warriors screamed and yelled and scrambled out of the way.

Grappling together, their fight became a brutal struggle. The ogre bit and gnawed at the giant's shoulder, neck, ear, and face, ravaging the flesh. But the giant refused to let go, its long arms wrapped tightly around the ogre's chest and arms in a bear hug as he tried to squeeze the life from the monster.

The ogre took the giant's eye next, gashing it with one of its tusks as it chewed relentlessly at his face. But the giant never faltered, his massive muscles contracting tighter and tighter as he tightened his grip on his foe. The ogre began to wheeze, spitting up a putrid green liquid from its compressed lungs. The giant coughed and sputtered as the noxious fluid crawled down his throat, but he never relented.

The ogre began to whine like a whipped dog, thrashing around in a futile attempt to break the giant's hold. The blue-skinned titan threw his head back and let out a fierce scream, his muscles shaking with exertion. And then there was a loud crack, like a dozen enormous oaks snapping all at once. The ogre shuddered, then went limp, its spine broken.

The giant released his grip and rolled off the beast, his mutilated eye weeping fluid onto his mangled, blood-smeared face. Still on his knees, he reached down into the ogre's stomach and pulled out the tip of his spear. Then he raised it up with both hands and brought it down, piercing the monster's heart.

For many minutes none of the warriors dared to approach the wounded giant, who knelt with his head bowed beside the body of his vanquished foe. Finally, Vaaler inched forward, moving cautiously. He didn't need to look back to know that Shalana was right behind him.

The giant turned its head as they approached, looking at them with its one good eye.

"I am the Guardian," he said, his voice so deep it made Vaaler's teeth vibrate. "Norr sent me to help you."

Shalana gasped, but Keegan only nodded.

"Are they still alive?" he asked.

"I gave them Daemron's Sword," the Guardian answered, speaking slowly as if every word was an exertion. "But I made them promise to go help Cassandra."

"Cassandra?" Vaaler said, the name triggering a memory of someone his Master had mentioned many years ago. "Rexol's apprentice? The one he lost to the Order?"

"She has the Crown," the Guardian gasped. "She's fled to Callastan."

"You're hurt," Shalana said, stepping toward him. "Let us help you."

The Guardian shook his head, his movements so slow they looked surreal.

"Poison," he whispered. "From the ogre. There is nothing to be done."

He coughed once, then bowed his head, closed his eyes, and was forever still.

Jerrod lashed out with Daemron's Sword, swinging it toward the confusing collage of overlapping images assaulting his senses in the hopes of landing a single lucky blow. But he struck only air, his double-sighted blindness sending the blade well wide of its mark.

From the corner of one eye he thought he saw Raven flicker

into view beside him, and he spun wildly only to realize too late that she had come from the other side. She drove a claw deep into his side, twisting as she pulled it out. The pain made Jerrod arch his back, his arm held wide, and Raven slapped the blade from his hand, sending it skittering across the snow.

Jerrod sank to his knees, and the Minion clutched the sides of his head with her sharp fingers. The monk screamed as he felt her feeding on his thoughts, sucking the very memories from his mind. He tried to resist, and for a moment he held her at bay. But he was losing blood quickly, and Raven was too strong to fight for long.

And then suddenly the vicious psychic assault stopped and the claws clutching his head fell away. Still confused by the twin visions, he was just able to make out the woman's body lying on the snow beside him, but her avian head was several feet away, the red light in her eyes replaced by the blank stare of death.

Standing over her decapitated corpse, clutching Daemron's Sword, was Scythe.

The earthquake still rocked Callastan; the floor and walls of the single-story jail had developed massive, rapidly spreading cracks. Cassandra screamed over and over at the mad wizard to stop before he brought the entire city—and even the Legacy—crumbling down, but Rexol was completely oblivious.

He can't hear me, but there is still a link between us!

Rexol had put his mark on her when she was a child, binding her to him. He'd used that connection to make her free him from the Monastery prison. He'd used it to manipulate her into using the Crown. He'd even used it to claim her body as his own.

But the bond works both ways.

Rexol was the greatest Chaos mage to walk the Southlands since the Cataclysm. But she was the one who had carried the

Crown across the entire breadth of the mortal world, not him. She was the one who had borne that great burden, not him. And she was the one touched by Chaos, born in fire under the Burning Moon.

I'm stronger than he is!

Through the heightened awareness of the Crown, she felt the Legacy shudder and shake. She could sense the armies of the Slayer massing on the other side, eager and hungry to return. There was no time left to wait, no time to gather her strength. If she didn't act now, it would be too late. Everything she had devoted her life to, the only thing that ever mattered—the protection and preservation of the Legacy—would be lost.

Opening herself up, Cassandra called upon the power of the Crown as she seized hold of Rexol's mind. Even once removed, she could feel the incredible rush of Old Magic as he channeled the Talisman. If she wasn't careful, she could fall under its spell just as he had.

Rexol! she shouted, letting the Talisman's power flow through her. *The Crown is not meant for you!*

Fueled by the power of Old Magic, her thoughts drove themselves into the mage's consciousness like a nail through a block of wood. The head of her own body snapped back as if someone had slapped it, and she knew that this time he'd heard her.

The power of Old Magic is mine! he howled back at her. *I am a God!*

You are nothing! she shouted, wrapping herself around the wizard's consciousness, ripping it free from her body and hurling him back into the Crown.

In an instant, everything changed as her own mind snapped back into her suddenly vacant body. She was no longer looking at herself from the outside; she was no longer a helpless prisoner forced to watch another wearing her face and flesh.

But now she felt the full force of Chaos as it raged through her, threatening to sweep her away.

It's incredible. Glorious! Magnificent!

And then she snatched the Crown from her head, banishing the Chaos only seconds before the Legacy gave way. Swaying on her feet, Cassandra reached out with her Sight, seeking any breach or tear in the barrier.

Feeling nothing, she tried to walk toward the open door of her cell, only to collapse as her exhausted, traumatized body surrendered to the blackness.

Epilogue

THE DANAAN WERE gone, fleeing back the way they had come, retreating to their hidden cities in the North Forest. But as he helped the warriors sort out the bodies strewn about the battlefield it was hard for Vaaler to believe the clans had won.

There were too many dead to bury, so the bodies were being sorted into two massive funeral piles—one to honor the fallen Easterners, the other to cleanse away all trace of the invading Danaan.

He tried not to look at the faces of any Danaan he came across, but every so often he would see someone he recognized. He tried not to react—they had all lost friends and family in the war—but it was still shocking to see the faces of those he had served with on patrol.

"You still think of them as your people, don't you?" Shalana asked, noticing his reaction.

"In some ways," Vaaler admitted. "It's hard to forget what I spent my whole life believing.

"Ever since I was a child, they told me it was my destiny to be king," he said. "I was supposed to guide my people through times of trouble. I was supposed to protect them and keep them safe."

"Sounds like what you did for us," Shalana told him. "Maybe your destiny is still to be a king ... though among our people we prefer the title of chief."

"The thanes welcomed me as an adviser," Vaaler said with a shake of his head. "But it's you they followed."

"We're a package deal," Shalana said, wrapping her arms around him and pulling him close. "I think everyone understands that."

She kissed him, and Vaaler simply enjoyed the moment for as long as it lasted. But once it was done, he said, "So what happens now?"

"I don't know," she answered. "But the Guardian's arrival made everyone a believer in the legends you and Norr were following. Even my father can't deny them now.

"If your friend Keegan really is destined to save the world," she said, "maybe we should try to find some way to help him."

Keegan, Scythe, and Jerrod walked along in silence, trying to put as much distance between themselves and the unnaturally rapidly decaying corpse of Raven as possible before nightfall. The monk was in the lead, healed of his wounds by the Sword, just as Keegan had been. He was still struggling to reconcile his Sight with his restored vision, but he seemed to be adapting quickly: he was already able to walk without difficulty.

They were still heading southwest toward Callastan to find Cassandra and the Crown; despite everything that had happened, their mission had not changed. But now they were three instead of four, and instead of Jerrod carrying Daemron's Sword it was Scythe.

Even handicapped by the restoration of his eyes, Keegan had expected Jerrod to offer some objection purely on principle. Instead, the monk had surprised him.

"I finally understand the prophecy of the Children of Fire," the monk had explained before they set out. "I now realize why it was difficult for our prophets and seers to identify the savior.

"Your destiny is tied even more closely to Keegan's than I ever imagined," he'd told Scythe. "There is not one savior, but three; just as there are three Talismans. The Sword is meant for you, just as the Ring is meant for Keegan and the Crown is meant for Cassandra."

Instead of mocking him for revising and reinterpreting his prophecy yet again, or making some snide remark about not wanting to be a savior, Scythe simply nodded.

He could tell she was still suffering, but it was something more that held her tongue. She seemed different, as if she had somehow changed after using the Sword to kill Raven.

She's gone cold. Hardened her heart.

Could he really blame her? Norr gave his life for Jerrod's beliefs. Maybe Scythe had decided the best way to honor his memory was to embrace the prophecy and do everything in her power to destroy the Slayer.

Despite this change, however, he could see that she was hurting. Suffering. He wanted to go to her—just as a friend—but something held him back.

It feels like a betrayal. You still have feelings for her, but Norr was your friend.

Maybe Scythe was right to harden her heart; it made everything much simpler.

You should do the same. Ignore your feelings for Scythe and focus on finding Cassandra.

"A few more miles," Jerrod said, interrupting his thoughts. "Then we can rest."

The others didn't answer, and the three of them trudged on in grim silence, each knowing they had many weeks of travel ahead before they reached Callastan.

Once we get into the Southlands, the Order will be looking for us.

Glancing over at Scythe, Keegan had a feeling she'd be ready for them.

— — — — —

Cassandra's first thought when she woke was that she was in another prison; the room around her was very small, and there was only a single door and her legs had been tightly bound. But then she realized the bed she lay in was too soft and comfortable for any cell, and the walls of the room were filled with hundreds of vials, bottles, and jars. And her legs weren't bound; someone had splinted them.

Is this an apothecary's shop?

Her next thought was of the Crown, and her heart skipped a beat until she realized it was tucked safely away in its sack and resting on a small table beside her bed.

The door to the room creaked open and a tiny, scholarly man entered, carrying a small candle.

"I'm sorry," he said, seeing she was up. "Did I wake you?"

Cassandra shook her head.

"Are you hungry? Thirsty? Do you need anything?"

"No," she said, though her mouth was dry. "How did I get here?"

"I found you after the riots," he told her. "Some of the locals spotted the bodies of the . . . those things in the jail. They wanted me to come and look, to see if they were diseased."

"You are a doctor?"

"At times. And I spent many years sailing the Western Isles, so the locals all consider me an expert in the strange and unnatural."

"Those bodies should be burned," Cassandra told him. "Just to be safe."

"I thought the same," he said, nodding. "And they were.

"But in my examinations I also discovered you," he continued. "None of the others had actually dared to enter the building, of course."

"They were afraid. Why weren't you?"

"Oh, I was," he assured her. "Yet I reasoned that anything powerful enough to kill those monsters would already have ended my life if it was still a threat.

"Reason is a powerful tool to overcome our emotions," he noted, like a wise teacher instructing a student.

"Once inside, I spotted you curled up in a corner, clutching that headpiece so tightly I could barely pry your fingers loose. I thought it must be important, so I put it by your bed."

He nodded in the direction of the table.

"What happened to my legs?"

The man hesitated, then said, "Stress fractures. Very strange. As if you were standing at the center of an incredibly powerful burst of energy. Like the kind that could cause an earthquake."

Cassandra ignored the implied question. *He's clever. He knows more than he lets on.* But she also sensed something sincere and fundamentally decent about this bookish little man.

"Why did you bring me here?"

"To better treat your injuries," he said. Then after a moment of careful consideration, he added, "I feared what the people might do to you if they discovered you were one of the Order."

"I'm not," Cassandra said. "Not anymore."

The man shrugged. "As you will. In any case, you're safe for now. If someone is hunting you, they won't find you here. At least not until more of your kind—sorry, your former kind—arrive."

"The Order is coming here?"

"Callastan is in ruins. The city has been ravaged by powerful magic. Word will reach the Pontiff soon, if it hasn't already. In a few days our streets will be overrun with Inquisitors."

Of course. Yasmin will come for the Crown. And in the wake of the destruction, the officials and citizens who opposed her Purge might have a sudden change of heart.

"I don't know how to hide you from the Order if they're looking for you," the man warned her. "But I will do what I can for you until they get here."

"Why are you helping me?" Cassandra asked.

"You remind me of someone," he said. "A young woman I used to know. We ... grew apart some years ago."

"I look like her?"

He laughed softly. "No, not really. She was an Islander. But there's just something about you that made me think of her. I can't really explain it."

"I cannot thank you enough for all you have done for me," Cassandra said, realizing she hadn't shown any proper gratitude yet. "I owe you a great debt, sir."

"Please," the man said with a rueful smile. "Calling me sir makes me feel even more ancient than I am. My name is Methodis."

Daemron the Slayer stares out from atop the battlements of his castle, his gaze moving slowly over the cramped buildings of the mean and meager city that has grown up around it. Just beyond the last of the small, squat structures a field of large crosses has been erected. Mutilated corpses—the parents, siblings, and friends of the would-be assassins who dared to attack him—still hang there, slowly rotting.

They died in gruesome public executions: slow, agonizing deaths meant to serve as a visceral reminder to his subjects of the consequences of rebelling against their king and their God.

The loyalty of his followers had grown fickle. Their ancestors swore fealty to him and joined his war against the Old Gods. They had shared his sin; it was only fitting they share his punishment. But many of those he rules over now—twisted creatures malformed and mutated by the Chaos that poisons the land—feel they are unfairly condemned. Bitter and resentful of their lot, they follow him not out of loyalty but only out of fear and desperation.

The whispers of festering rebellion were growing ever stronger; the assassination attempt stark proof of how bold his enemies had become. Yet he knows that all the bitterness, resentment, and rebellion will be swept away in an instant if the Legacy falls. If the barrier keeping him and his followers trapped in their prison world crumbles, even the most ardent opponents will flock to his banner, eager to join the ranks of his armies as he marches upon the mortal world.

That time is drawing near. The Legacy has grown thinner than even he had realized. The Crown alone nearly brought it crashing down; he'd felt the pounding Chaos battering against it, causing it to bend and bow. But just when he had been certain it would shatter, the Talisman was silenced. Somehow, the Legacy still held.

His subjects had felt it, too. The echoes of Old Magic reverberated across his kingdom, loud enough that even the weakest of his followers could not help but hear it. And though the Legacy endures, his people now have renewed hope. Faith in their Immortal ruler has been restored.

Beyond the city and the crosses, the once-empty plains of his kingdom are dotted with thousands of small camps, his followers gathering in response to his call ... and the call of the Talismans. They have crawled forth from the caves and tunnels, assembling en masse at his command, eager to be unleashed upon the mortal world.

Among the gathering army walk his generals, weeding out those too weak to join in the great battle that is to come. Resources are scarce in this nether realm; food and weapons are in short supply, and those that cannot help bring him victory must be identified and cast out to fend for themselves.

So far, none of his subjects has been foolish enough to oppose the culling—not with the grim reminder of the price of disobedience still dangling on the nearby crosses.

He feels no remorse for the lives he has taken, or for those who will surely perish after being exiled from his army. He created this netherworld. All life that walks, flies, and crawls across the plains of ash belongs to him, to do with as he chooses. His subjects understand that now. Once again, they know him for what he truly is . . . as does he.

For a time he had forgotten himself. Centuries of exile had made him hesitant, afraid, uncertain. But the cowardice and self-doubt that plagued him is now gone. He remembers who and what he is.

I am Daemron the Slayer: wizard, warrior, prophet, and king! I am the last of the Immortals—a God! And when the Legacy falls, the world will tremble at my return!

Acknowledgments

The publication of *Children of Fire,* the first book in my Chaos Born trilogy, was the culmination of many years of work and preparation. I'd written and rewritten the manuscript countless times over the past decade, slowly polishing it until it gleamed. And though I had planned out the second book in the series in great detail, I didn't actually begin the writing process until very recently. And for the first time in my professional life, I was nervous about a project. Would I be able to create something in a single year that matched the quality of a book I'd spent almost a decade revising?

Fortunately, I didn't have to take on this daunting task alone. With the help of my editors, Tricia Narwani and Michael Rowley—and the support of my incredible agent, Ginger Clark—*The Scorched Earth* became a worthy follow-up to *Children of Fire.* And as I work on *Chaos Unleashed,* the final book in the series, I'm no longer nervous. The amazing feedback from readers who loved the first book has inspired me; your enthusiasm for the story and characters is the most rewarding thing any author could hope for. I can't wait for fans to see how the Chaos Born trilogy ends, and I hope you're all as excited as I am. Thank you for your support!

ABOUT THE TYPE

This book was set in Bembo, a typeface based on an old-style Roman face that was used for Cardinal Pietro Bembo's tract *De Aetna* in 1495. Bembo was cut by Francesco Griffo (1450–1518) in the early sixteenth century for Italian Renaissance printer and publisher Aldus Manutius (1449–1515). The Lanston Monotype Company of Philadelphia brought the well-proportioned letterforms of Bembo to the United States in the 1930s.